The Product of My Melancholy

Arashnoor Gill

ISBN: 979-8-234-00164-1

To the most precious souls,

Ash and Ashleen

The Product
of My
Melancholy

FLIGHT

I stand at the base of the mountain, for what feels like a moment of oblivion.

Petals and leaves flow past my body. The wind smoothly glides around me. The scent of honey rises up my cheeks and sinks into my skin. Working nerves recognize the nectar and remind me of memories of sickness. My feeble eyes overflow, leaving trails of tears strewn across my face. My ragged and patched face, adorned with a stubble of thorns, faces down in disbelief. And tears drip down onto the fallen blossoms. Saline seeps into the cracks of my lips, and in cleansing, I taste my shame. I am exorcized of humanity yet feel the fullness of living in this moment.

All matters of pretend and fiction are dead. My hands cannot stretch and hold the tools of artists and thieves, no more. The castles in the air are besieged, burned, and in ruins. The loud cries and cheers are now faint and dismissible, only apparent in my fading memory. No roars or jeering, just simple silence exists. The halls are eerily quiet. When I wander into them, I see that they are all dead. The companions, citizens, and creatures of these castles are no more. The sight of their absence startles me. I have never felt this alone before. Even when my hands failed to work and sew their fates, I could account for their presence. Now, they are simply dead. Their bodies lie scattered across the floor with knives stabbed into their hearts and blood obscuring their faces. I knew him once, I loved her too much, and I respected all of them. Now, I can't help but be in misery because I will never see them again.

My heart accelerates as its chambers contract and release. I lose my breath and begin to fade, but feel my heart contract and release, contract and release, and slowly fill my body with blood. My mind fires in response to the quickening pulse but is soon left empty and furrowed by the lack of messages to send. Everything is tumbling. The mental beams that support my lobes and these walls are collapsing and down goes everything with them. As the beams crash down to the dirt, I hear their screams and feel their pain. For a second, I see glimpses of them as ghosts. It all ends with a sharp breath. All sense of life and identity is fleeting. I am, as the world addresses me, nobody.

Now, I stand in this forest. With the brunt of the damage behind me, my muscles tense and resist any effect of the wind and what it whispers to me: its promises, its kisses, its sweet nothings. I watch it play with a lonesome feather in the air. I cannot take my eyes off it. It softly guides the feather. Taken by a hair, the feather dances in the wind. The trees obscure the light, but the feather is caught by illumination. Darkness surrounds it all, but the dance remains in the light. The feather falls and rises, teasing the blue and beautiful sky. It enjoys its temporary state, but it's inevitable where the feather will land and forever be. It is a castaway from the angel that it belonged to, and it is meant to rest in the dirt.

My feet are firmly planted in the dirt, where they will remain. The wind shoots past my ears and propels my hands forward. My head faces the sky, cast in another lonely source of light. My neck twitches and my legs quiver. A thought begins to form in my head.

I feel the wind beneath me, the way it holds me, its soft touch on my skin, and its promise. It moves all the leaves, flowers, petals, and debris around me, pushing and pulling. Gliding with the natural flow, nature surrenders all movement and control to the breeze. A soft breeze will only push gently, and the trees will dance freely, accepting their friend in merriment. Nature trusts the movement and places no resistance. It relishes in the freeing dance where all its movement is acted upon it, and none of it is foretold.

As the breeze fastens, I want to let myself be taken and float toward the firmament in the gentle hands of the wind. It will either carry me and take me to the sky, or it will push through me. Whether it is my lack of faith or substantial doubt, I assume my body would not lift off the ground. It would face the wind and all its might and be awoken or buried underground. Yet my heart yearns for the sky. The wind promises me the sky. Take me with you, where I may witness the beauty of a feather bending on a wing, seeds spreading their beauty all across, peach blossoms raining on laughing children, and castles forming in the sky. Ah, the most beautiful is the dance: the dance of one and his million unique parts—the dance with the wind. When the body relishes each movement and gesture, it learns to dance and fly.

All things fly past me. I stand on the ground and begin descending to my inevitable grave. At the heart of the forest, I lay facing the sky's light, melting into the earth with no movement in my hands, face, or body. My heart skips a beat as my mind cracks into pieces. It all ends with a lonely breath.

I will cherish your promise.
I will dream that you carry me with you.
I will watch on and witness the flight of the angels and the dance of the free.

THE SEA

I recall when I first opened my eyes to this world. I was maybe six or seven years old. Everything before then feels like a faint memory.

The waves rolled in at the beach. From afar, the waves were blue. As they approached the shore, they changed to white. Quickly, the tide raced back, sloshing back and forth, and became consumed by a larger wave. Then the waves washed back upon the shore, leaving small remnants of it trapped in the sand. So, the sand soaked in the sea in a perilous effort to offset its immortal enemy. The sea regrouped like nothing and attacked again, ferociously striking the shore with all its power. The splash subsided, and the wave reached out with its webbed hands, creeping further onto the shore and nipping at my toes. All the sea could do was have a mere taste before retreating, while I ran back myself. The sea brought wind and gray clouds with it. It seemed to be angry.

I planted my bucket in the dry sand by our blanket. Then I carefully flipped over the heavy bucket packed with wet sand and parts of the enemy. I tapped the bucket over and over like I'd been taught. Lifting the bucket revealed the ruins of a sandcastle I couldn't quite figure out. I shivered sitting there on a chilly day and dropped the bucket at my feet. Whatever stood of the sandcastle I destroyed with my hands, a giant had conquered the village. The castle was utterly destroyed, and I sat there with sandy and itchy bumps on my hands and legs.

I looked to the guardian of the castle and shouted, "Dad, I

can't do it!"

The wind accompanied his chuckle, "I'll be right there, Teddy!" Sadly, Dad listened and came out of the water. He took big and fast steps, throwing sand behind him, and ran up the tiny hill. He turned around to say to my brother, "Don't swim too far out, Ethan!"

Ethan complained and shouted something back. I didn't hear him. He was more than capable of swimming and handling himself, while I wasn't.

Dad dropped to his knees in front of me. I only had bits of wet sand on me, while my dad was covered. "What's up?"

"Dad, my sandcastle keeps breaking," I asked for help.

"Oh, really? Did you try the tapping trick I taught you?" Dad was always ready to help.

"I did, and it's not working. I can't do it," I was about ready to give up.

"You can do it. I believe in you!" My dad shouted over the loud waves.

"I don't know how."

"How about we go get some more wet sand? Show me where you got this from," Dad pointed to the ruins of the castle.

It took me a second, but I got up. I wasn't willing at first, but he stood there waiting for me and cheering me on. In one hand, I held my bucket. In the other, I wielded my shovel. We marched into enemy territory together.

Ethan was still out there swimming in the far reaches of the sea. Back then, I couldn't wait to learn to swim and feel free like he did.

Ethan shouted, "Hey!" He wanted Dad and me to join him, but the waves shouted like thunder over him.

Then I turned my head down, leading my dad to where the treasure we sought was. We scooped some wet sand together as I held the bucket, and he scooped with my shovel. He took some sand from here and some from there. We kept looking down when the waves surprised us. The water collided with our backs and washed over us. I yelped while Dad laughed with his mouth wide open. We were both faced toward the picnic blanket. In the distance, we saw Mom approaching, carrying her tote full of goodies from the car. She had gone to get all the treats, while the rest of us had begun to play.

The sea retreated again. The waves collided with each other as thunder struck again. It was winter, and I had annoyingly insisted that we go to the beach to celebrate my birthday. We saw Mom drop her tote and speed up toward us. She didn't run playfully.

She wore a panic and called loudly, "Ethan!"

Dad held me up in the unsteady sand as he tried to make out what she said and why she ran. I heard her clearly but stood half-buried in the sand as my useless self.

The tide ripped through the sky with a thunderous sound, once again. Mom tried to shout over it, but she couldn't. It was too late by the time Dad realized. He turned, and another wave splashed him in the face and forced me down. I was soaking wet and struggled to breathe through the suffocating and salty surprise. Dad left me and ran into the sea in pursuit of Ethan. There, the sea stood in front of me, my immortal enemy.

ALONE (FOR LUNCH)

I

I have felt alone, in some sort of way, all my life.

Cars suddenly whizzed by on the road ahead of me, breaking the afternoon trance I had been trapped in. I took off my backpack and placed it on the ground beside the bench where I was sitting. Afternoons at school were always characterized by this lull in energy and motivation—the so-called lunchtime stupor. My stomach growled and reminded me of how much time I had wasted during my lunch break already. Get on with it, I imagined it was saying to me. I slowly turned my head to my lunch tray. It sat right next to me. The tray contained a spicy chicken sandwich, two packets of mayo, a couple of baby carrots, a banana, and a half-pint of chocolate milk: what I considered to be the epitome of a delicious high school lunch. I lifted the tray onto my lap, excited to finally have food for the first time in the day.

Naturally, I skipped breakfast. Breakfast baffled me. The concept of breakfast seemed nice and so did many different breakfast food items. But what am I supposed to do if I don't have any cravings that early in the morning? I have heard it said many times that "breakfast is the most important meal of the day." I seriously doubt that's the case if it just makes my stomach ache. I hadn't quite figured out the whole breakfast thing yet. I would've gotten brunch, but they didn't have my favorite energy bar at the snack shop this morning. They hadn't carried the energy bar for a few weeks now, but that didn't stop me from checking again and again. The lunch—or in this case, brunch—ladies had apologized very sweetly and offered me a different flavor of energy bar, but I declined, choosing to save my two dollars instead of wasting it on a subpar brunch item. So now, I was starving, and that would only make this meal taste all the much better. I checked my watch to see how much time I had left: twenty minutes. Just enough time to really enjoy and savor this meal. I unwrapped the sandwich and took my first bite. There was nothing quite like the cafeteria's spicy chicken sandwich. Just as always, it hit the right spot.

I was sitting in the outer courtyard, isolated from the rest of the school, students, and life. I wasn't completely alone at the moment. A few other people were sitting out in the courtyard with me. Not with me, of course, but in the same area as me. As much as I tried, I couldn't ignore them completely. I wondered whether they were able to zone me out completely, or did I hold some sort of irrelevant place in their mind as well. Sometimes my wandering eyes would randomly meet another person's, resulting in a momentary state of mutual panic until we both diverted our gaze. I have no idea why, but this brief and completely coincidental eye contact felt nearly illegal. There seemed to be a presumption that if we held this eye contact for long enough, we would be ostracized from society or—worse—have to partake in conversation. The person whose gaze I would randomly stumble into would usually redirect their vision toward whomever they were with, while I would be stuck with nowhere purposeful to look, forcing me to quickly search for the nearest empty space to settle on. Moments like that reminded me that I was truly alone in the moment. My peers in the courtyard still had someone with them. I had no one; I was all by myself.

To explain who else was there in the courtyard with me but not with me: on one side, there were the girls whom I swear I had never heard utter a word in class. They weren't quiet due to their contempt or disinterest in school. They were smart, or at least they seemed smart. My running hypothesis was that maybe they were just shy or suffered from social anxiety. Perhaps they just felt as if they didn't fit in. What the heck did I know about social anxiety? Despite any of those possible conditions, now they were all chatting, laughing, and showing a whole new demeanor than what I would usually observe in class. It was nice seeing this side of them.

To my other side were couples who, for some reason—often PDA—had chosen to ditch the confining walls of the inner school. Here in this courtyard, there was rarely ever a teacher or custodian to enforce such rules. These couples usually sat out on the grass, far away, and kept to themselves. To provide some context, the previously mentioned quiet girls and I sat on the evenly spaced benches that lined a pathway going from one side of the campus to the other. Our seats faced the couples who usually framed themselves to be looking away from us and toward the city street. A large patch of grass—maybe 70 feet—along with a few stubby trees, divided the school from the few shops and suburban neighborhoods across the way. That was the glorious view I had become accustomed to while eating lunch.

Now, it may be expected that the street traffic would disrupt the peace that one would seek to inhabit while eating lunch, but the noise of cars driving by added to the perfect ambiance of the courtyard. The distance from the cars was just far enough to render the sound as background noise. After all, the road, shops, and homes were just the background for all the cringe smooching and nuzzling that ruined my view. While these couples may have chosen this courtyard for the privacy it gave them to express their affection, they also seemed to genuinely enjoy the courtyard's peace and quiet. Due to this, they were welcomed neighbors. However, maybe I was just defending them because part of me wanted to be like them. Part of me wanted to lie down in someone's lap and look at the sky and have a better view than the suburban dream across the way. The more I thought about it, the more I realized I shared in common with these two different groups in the courtyard with me. We weren't so different, after all. I wasn't a quiet girl, nor was I in a relationship, but we all craved some form of escape from school, or maybe I just thought this way to fill the isolation I felt. After all, I was completely alone. They weren't.

I took a bite of my spicy chicken sandwich. Luckily, it was still warm. My favorite part about the sandwich was that it actually somewhat lived up to its name. The spice didn't make me sweat or make my nose run, but it gave a necessary amount of flavor to a rather dull-looking sandwich. Sometimes the sandwich ran on the dry side, but usually a packet or two of mayo would be enough to fix that issue. I set aside my lunch tray and carefully tore open a packet of mayo and emptied it on top of the chicken patty. I did this again with my second packet of mayo. Simply because the more mayo, the better. I brought my tray back onto my lap and bit into my sandwich as it leaked mayo underneath me and onto the tray. That was the sign of a perfect mayo-to-sandwich ratio.

I looked out into the distance as I chewed. Cars continued to drive by. I wasn't looking so much at the cars or anything even behind them; my eyes settled for a soft focus in that general area. They searched for something to fill my interest. The buildings on the opposite street drew my attention to them as did the cars, but they were such ordinary sights by now that my eyes slowly glazed away from them and drifted back to nothing. The monotonous act of admiring and analyzing the same buildings had worn me out, and what I saw in front of me now felt like an indistinguishable cloud of nothing. My eyes failed to recognize any depth and drew an invisible barrier that enclosed me in the nothingness.

In a quick second, I became hypersensitive to what I was doing or what it appeared I was possibly doing. Obviously, I was staring out into the distance. How did it appear to my peers, though? Did it seem like I was doing this merely to look interesting, or did my eyes seem genuinely interested in exploring my environment? Was I the curious or observant type to them, or just a shallow person trying hard to appear deep? Or did they concur that I felt lost and lacked any way to fill my loneliness? With one last blink of goodbye to the view ahead of me, my eyes wandered back to my mayo-filled sandwich. I raised it to my mouth and took a bite.

Perhaps I thought about the loneliness so much because I still had friends and occasional moments of togetherness. A friend had even walked with me to get lunch from the cafeteria and then to this very courtyard. Just as I had set down my lunch tray, he had wished me goodbye and left, almost as if he had realized that this place was too far beneath him. I had several friends, but none to have lunch with. They usually hung out with others or were too busy to hang out. I was okay with that. It didn't bug me, not too much, at least. The loneliness didn't bother me so much as it fascinated me, I suppose.

I had only found this courtyard a few months ago, even though I had been at this school for three years now. This courtyard often went ignored by the majority of students, from what I saw. Many students would leave campus to get their lunch or find a spot under the covered benches. People would even flock to sit in the hallways of certain buildings to have their lunch. All of those places came before this courtyard. In my last two years of high school, I never quite found a fitting place to properly eat lunch. Leaving campus would often result in no time to eat your food, especially in a relaxed manner, meaning you would either have to stuff your face as you speed-walked back to campus or somehow get permission from your teacher to eat in class after lunch had ended. Neither one of those scenarios sounded ideal, and I would never think to ask Mr. Park such an insane thing.

Finding a comfortable and non-embarrassing spot to have lunch was crucial to leading a "normal" high school experience. As for sitting under the covered benches, there was rarely ever any space. Those benches would be so overcrowded that it would become socially awkward to even stop and look for a space there. Of course, sitting near a large group for lunch brought its own concerns and the possibility of crippling social judgment. The thought of other people's eyes being hyper-focused on you and criticizing your every move, forcing you to be hyper-conscious of your own identity and being, should be best avoided. I suddenly thought back to when I was looking out into the street and cringed. I definitely didn't have it the worst, but the effects of social pressure still lingered and would probably stay for the foreseeable future.

As for sitting in the hallways, I just never understood eating there, to be honest. Sure, you would be protected from whatever weather conditions were in store for that day, but you would be making these hallway spaces a living hell to walk through and infesting them with wrappers, food crumbs, and all sorts of trash. Not only did this make the school look like crap whenever lunch was over, but it made the custodian's job harder. Eating in the hallways just felt like such an inconsiderate thing to do. With that being said, I did try eating in the entrance hallway of the library for a while. Food wasn't allowed in the library past the entrance hall, and it was rather normal to see people quickly eating their lunch before proceeding into the library to do work. However, eating in the entrance hall got tremendously awkward. As previously mentioned, people would usually only eat in the entrance hall when they had work that needed to be done. I was never one of those people. Maybe sometimes I'd have homework that I could start early or find an assignment to waste my time on, but rarely did I ever proceed into the library intending to get work done. I just wanted a nice place to eat my lunch. I would always finish my homework at home. Plus, I preferred to work by myself. Even if I tried to work at the library, it would be way too noisy to focus and too busy to find an available seat. Another con of eating in the entrance hall was all the weird looks you would receive from people as they entered and exited the library. These people carried textbooks with them to study and complete homework, while I stood there eating my carrots and drinking my milk like a freaking reindeer on Christmas morning. Sometimes my fellow library lunch-goers would make small talk with me. Yes, the small talk would be awkward, but I appreciated their efforts to build rapport, until they would end our interaction by saying they'll see me later (inside the library). I would just smile and say the same thing back to them. Then I would wonder how disappointed they'd feel when I no-showed the actual library component of the library, wasting my entire lunch break in the hallway eating lunch. Yeah, the library entrance hall was definitely not the ideal place to have lunch.

Through my years of experience, I had determined that the outer courtyard definitely seemed to be the best spot to have lunch on campus. It was for its indescribable sense of tranquility: its lack of social hierarchy, its physical and mental separation from the internal structures of the school, and the respite it offered from the daily tasks. However, this was just the meaning that the location had for me. I'm sure that this place meant something completely different and held its own personal meaning to the people sharing the location with me. Instead of assuming whatever definition they would ascribe to this location, I stopped myself.

I looked at my watch and saw that five minutes remained for lunch. However much these people may have cherished this courtyard, I knew that I truly appreciated it. As I brought my meandering to a close, I smiled, feeling at peace and knowing that I could come to the courtyard and partake in my inner dialogue and have my lunch without (much) judgment. I took a baby carrot and aggressively bit down on it. My head nodded with the motion of my chewing. I followed the carrot with a sip of my chocolate milk. Ah, what a wonderfully awful lunch this is.

II

It was lunch (of course it was). Even more importantly, it was Monday, the only day in the week I was now free to have lunch in my favorite outer courtyard. It had been a year since I had found the courtyard, and I was still having lunch there, even if only once a week. I don't know how, but life in the last year of high school had really picked up. On the other days of the week, I was in meetings for various clubs with various teachers on various subjects, working on various projects and various ideas. Amidst that, I was taking more rigorous classes, prepping for more AP exams, and honestly struggling with the material. I don't know what intrinsic drive had kicked in for me to make this last year of high school so much more difficult for myself. It wasn't for the sake of building out my transcript or increasing my chances of getting accepted into my dream colleges. Many peers had told me that colleges really only pay the most attention to your sophomore and junior years of high school. I didn't know if that was correct, but I took this to mean that senior year was meant to be a relaxing one. Maybe in a way, I was making up for being—what I considered—a subpar student during those earlier years. However, I couldn't deny it; I felt a genuine interest in being more involved and engaged with so much at school. None of this meant that I was an excellent student passing all his classes with flying colors; in fact, I was doing horrendously in AP calculus. The extracurriculars and those external sources of engagement were what gave me fulfillment.

I moved my lunch tray from my lap onto the space next to me. I took a sigh of relief, decompressing and taking in my familiar surroundings. It was strange how similar but different this place felt. While the location seemed almost the same as before, I felt different inhabiting it, almost as if I was gazing upon it with a pair of fresh eyes. After all, I was only at the courtyard once a week. I made it my mission to savor lunch in the courtyard before I lost it all in the chaos of the week.

In the present moment, I felt—for the lack of a better word—present. I felt more conscious of my body and the space it took up in this sphere. I felt my mind come to a rest as oxygen slowly filled up the hollow space and outstretched itself to every corner of my body. The exhale brought relief and subtle contentment. My presence in that very moment made me ask the question: had I really not taken the time to be present here in the past? Sure, I hadn't paid the best attention to which specific quiet girls I found in the courtyard on a given day, but I felt energized in my body and starkly aware of myself and my surroundings. I must've felt present here before, but why had I never felt this same sense of contentment that I felt now? There were differences in me now versus the past, but nothing that felt too significant, especially within the span of just a year. I don't know what new philosophy I had unlocked to perceive this new sensation. This sense of peace and contentment was novel to me. I wanted to savor that as well, along with the lunch in the courtyard.

I took the apple from my lunch tray that had replaced my usual banana—since the cafeteria was out of bananas—and took a bite out of it, while watching the street ahead of me. After one bite, the apple skin immediately lodged itself between my front two teeth, reminding me of my justified hatred for apples. I began to try to fish out the pesky apple skin with my tongue, meanwhile reflecting on my newfound awareness and appreciation of the courtyard. In a way, so much time had truly passed and it felt unfair and impossible to judge my own presence in the past. Even if I had tried to be present in the past, there would be no appropriate and objective measurement for it. The present judgment of a past act would always be flawed, and retrospectively assess the past as passive before any semblance of presence could rise to the top. I knew I felt a sense of peace before, but the peace I felt now was different. Both feelings were in ways similar but different. Right now, however, peace was lost and could only be attained once I freed the apple skin from my teeth.

I resorted to using the nail of my pinky finger to try to push the apple skin down. I lowered my head to cover my shame. As I played with my teeth, I felt a person come and stand over me. Before she uttered a word, I recognized it was Chloe and looked up at her with my fingernail still in my teeth.

"What are you doing?" She asked, halfway concerned and grossed out.

Embarrassed and taking my finger out of my mouth, I answered, "I got a piece of my apple stuck in my teeth."

"Oh, that sucks," she responded, sitting beside me. "Sorry for being late. Aisha was telling us about the physics test."

"No worries. I was just chilling."

Chloe took off her backpack and put it down beside the bench, taking out her lunch box and hand sanitizer. She zipped open her bag and used the hand sanitizer to clean her hands. Before putting the sanitizer away, she offered me some.

"Thank you," I said, spreading the small dollop of sanitizer over my hands.

We exchanged a quick peck. A few months ago, Chloe and I started dating, and she began to join me for my Monday lunches at the courtyard. This was the one day a week when we also got to have lunch together. Our schedules conflicted with various prior commitments we had. I usually spent Fridays doing homework or having lunch in the entrance hallway of the library; I could never quit that place. Sometimes, though, Chloe would ditch her friends to hang out with me instead on Fridays, and those days would make me very happy.

Chloe opened up her lunch box and took out her neatly packed bento box, which she always prepared in the morning. Her meals were always different but followed a theme throughout the week. For example, today was leftover day, which meant Chloe's meal consisted of the leftover cauliflower tacos that her family had for dinner on Sunday night. Her meal also included an assortment of berries, orange slices, a side salad, and two homemade oatmeal raisin cookies. Needless to say, her bento box put my lunch tray to shame.

I became completely absorbed by Chloe's presence as she got situated, almost even forgetting about the apple skin stuck between my teeth. I leaped back into my mouth with the longer nail of my index finger, turning away from Chloe as I did so. I could feel what I thought was the apple skin but struggled to get it to move in any direction. This was the reason I hated apples and avoided them at all costs. I don't know how people ate apples normally without experiencing this crippling injury. If my family ever had apples at home, we ate them with their skins peeled off to enjoy the flavor of the apple better and lower any possible risks associated with them. I didn't inherently hate apples, but I didn't understand other people's interest in wanting to eat them wholly intact.

"Just leave it. It'll go away by itself," Chloe said to me.

"Wait, I think I got it," I said as I flicked a tiny piece of apple skin sticking out from between my teeth. It failed to move again. "Never mind. I'll stop."

I helplessly placed my hands on my lap. Chloe began to eat

lunch. I turned to my tray and unwrapped my spicy chicken sandwich and proceeded to fill it with my preferred amount of mayo.

"How's your day been so far?" I asked Chloe.

"It's been okay. Oh my God, drama was so bad though. Jeffrey and Dalton had to perform their scene today, and it was so hard to watch," Chloe shared and bit into her taco.

"Oh no, what did they do?" I asked with intrigue about their new antics.

"They were like running around the entire theatre and even the house, and at one point, Jeffrey fell on his knees on stage, and it was so loud. It sounded like it hurt so bad."

I cringed, "Hey, I love his commitment at least—"

"He got up, and his knees were literally bleeding. When we asked him if he was okay, he was acting all cool about it like, 'Nah, this is nothing, dude.' That boy needs to chill."

Chloe's impressions always put a smile on my face. "I so badly wish I had a class with him." I brought my lunch tray to my lap. "Literally nothing exciting ever happens in my classes. We had somewhat of a debate in AP Gov today. But like always, it just ended up in Mike saying something problematic and everyone getting quiet and not knowing what to say, until Mr. Collins just inevitably put on an episode of John Oliver and just stopped teaching for the day."

"I'm so glad I didn't take AP Gov."

"It's interesting. I think you would've enjoyed it," I finished, and started to bite into my chicken sandwich. Mayo immediately began to drip out of the sandwich and onto my tray.

"That's so gross," Chloe remarked on my excessive use of mayo.

"It's perfect." I savored it, as always. "How's your lunch?"

"It's good. My dad said he didn't season the cauliflower enough, but my mom and I thought it was fine."

"Yeah, those look really good." I watched her eat her superior lunch.

We sat in silence, eating our respective lunches. I watched the street while Chloe scrolled on her phone. We took pride in our ability to sit in silence together. Chloe chuckled at something on her phone. I munched down on my sandwich. Cars whizzed by. A quiet girl sitting a few seats away let out a cough. The small talk was over, and the silence grew emphatic.

"You seem kinda quiet today. Everything okay?" I finally broke.

"Huh?" Chloe set aside her phone. "Yeah, I'm fine, just kinda stressed about the physics test next period and then the calc test on Friday."

"We have a calc test this Friday?" My eyebrows shot up.

"Yeah, it's on the syllabus."

"But he hasn't even mentioned it yet. Maybe he'll move it?"

"I doubt it. We're caught up with everything, so it wouldn't make any sense to do that."

"But he could just push it back for the people who don't feel prepared, like me."

"You should start studying then," She knew my poor study habits. "You're caught up on the homework, right?"

"Yeah."

"Well, it'll be just like that."

"The homework is never anything like the tests," I pointed out correctly.

"Eh, it sorta is," Chloe defended sheepishly.

"Well, you're just smart," I was correct again.

"No, I'm not."

"You really are. You're doing great in his class. You always do great on his tests or any tests, and you're gonna do great on this one too," I let Chloe sit with that fact. "You're gonna have to help me with all that 'limit' stuff. I don't get any of that."

"Yeah, I can help. When do you wanna study?"

"Hmm… let's see," I mentally checked over my calendar. "Would lunch on Friday work for you?"

"Really? You wanna wait till the last day to study for it?" Chloe squinted and looked at me lowly.

"What's wrong with that?"

Chloe stammered and stopped herself from expressing her annoyance.

"So are you free that day?"

"I'll try to make time, but you should definitely start studying before then," Chloe insisted.

"Yeah, I'll try," I shrugged.

I know I said I was becoming a better student, but I was still far from an ideal student. The idea or act of studying just didn't work for me. I attempted to engage intently with the material presented, trying to learn it well by relating to it. I thought so hard about it in class that I felt no need to sit and reassess my memory to study it. Plus, I'd rather use that time I'd spend studying doing something better and more fun. I saw the errors of my ways, though, because Chloe was right. It was something I was very slowly working to fix.

Chloe was not at all like me in that way. She would study for every single test and quiz and complete every optional, bonus, and extra-credit assignment. She went above and beyond, always seeking to apply herself as much as possible. She was one of the smartest people I knew. I'm sure her transcripts reflected that too. Despite that, Chloe never failed to get extremely worried and anxious about every exam, assignment, or anything school related.

One time, Chloe's physics teacher accused her of cheating on a pop quiz. Chloe had gotten an email from her teacher stating that they needed to "have a talk" regarding her performance on the latest quiz. This email was accompanied by her teacher giving Chloe a zero for that quiz. I wasn't with Chloe for her initial reaction, nor did she tell me about her initial reaction to it, but I can only imagine the shock that zero must have given her. Eventually, she called me and told me about the email, and proceeded to run through a hundred hypotheticals about what had happened to cause her to fail the quiz. Maybe her teacher had confused Chloe's quiz with someone else's?

Maybe she had misread what Chloe had written? Maybe someone had framed Chloe, and maybe her teacher would be left with no other choice but to give Chloe an F for the entire school year? Maybe Chloe would be forced to repeat the class over the summer? Maybe this would cause Chloe not to get accepted to her dream college? Maybe her teacher would report it to the principal, and the principal would have to suspend or even expel Chloe for plagiarism and cheating? After all, that's the school policy, right? I listened and tried to calm her down at every question she raised, but her anxious streak continued. Chloe started to cry over the phone as I struggled to find the right words to comfort her. Then we sat there in silence for a good fifteen minutes before she told me she had to go. Later on, as I was drifting off to sleep around 2 AM to the sound of YouTube videos, I received a text from Chloe saying she couldn't go to sleep. She would typically go to sleep around 10 or—if she was feeling particularly enthused about a book or show—11 PM. I again tried to comfort Chloe, telling her that it was probably nothing serious. Her teacher had probably just misunderstood her quiz answers. After an hour or two of back and forth, Chloe finally texted me saying that she was going to try to sleep and prepare for the meeting tomorrow. I was glad she had chosen to go to sleep, but sad that I had seemingly been of no effect in making her feel better. Chloe still saw this meeting as some sort of catastrophic event, which in reality would never be the case. No matter the misunderstanding that had taken place, Chloe's good and studious nature spoke for itself. In the case it didn't, I would be there to support her.

I saw Chloe that morning and, if her deadpan and disparaged expression wasn't enough, she said she wasn't sure if she slept at all last night. I tried to hug her and told her that it'd be over soon. We stood plainly in front of each other with nothing else to say. The bell rang, and before I could offer additional comfort, Chloe said see ya and walked off to her first period.

I wouldn't see her until lunch. I couldn't imagine how she'd fare through the first half of the school day. I'd be in the middle of listening to a lecture and then drift off to imagine how anxious Chloe must be feeling at the moment. During my second period, I asked to go to the bathroom. I took the long way there so I could walk past Chloe's classroom and catch a glimpse of her. I couldn't. The door was closed.

I tapped my foot and watched the clock till lunch came around. It was a Thursday, and I had informed my peers that I wouldn't be able to attend the club meeting that day. I made my way immediately to the science wing. Noticing the door to the physics classroom was open, I stepped up to the door and saw that Chloe was inside talking to Mrs. Morozov. Chloe sat in one of the desks in the front row—probably her actual seat—on the verge of tears as Mrs. Morozov stood in front of her and leaned against her own desk. Mrs. Morozov had crossed her arms but wore a look of sympathy on her face.

I abruptly stepped in, "Hi, Mrs. Morozov. Hey, Chloe. I hope I'm not disturbing anything." I trailed off.

"Hi," Mrs. Morozov said in surprise. She looked to Chloe, "Is this your boyfriend?"

"Yeah," I said as Chloe nodded. I had Mrs. Morozov as a teacher last year, but I clearly had not been smart enough to leave an impact on her. "I had you last year, Mrs. Morozov. It's nice to see you—"

"You can wait outside. It won't take too long," Chloe looked at me.

"Oh, okay," I took a half step back. "Sorry."

I stepped outside. I stood against the wall, far enough to avoid being a disruption and close enough to try to listen in on their conversation. I couldn't hear much of what was being said. Both of them spoke in a hushed manner. Not that I wanted to eavesdrop, but I wanted to be available to clarify any misunderstanding and stand up for Chloe.

From her slow and deliberate tone, I could tell Chloe was trying to hold back her emotions and tears. This meant a tremendous amount to her, no doubt. She cared about her learning, far more than

I did, at least. Her reaction did seem somewhat overblown, but it made sense for who she was and what she valued. Her feelings were valid. She had the right to feel hurt, offended, scared, and however else she felt. She didn't seem to care too much about whether her feelings were valid or not; she just wanted to resolve them. By stifling her own crying, I could tell that a part of her was denying herself the validity of her full emotions and avoiding perhaps the discomfort of crying in front of others. Many times had she cried alongside me, into my shirt or sweater, and apologized. Never was the apology needed. To me, it was a privilege and responsibility to be trusted with that vulnerability. To be confided in and trusted was the greatest honor. I just wished I could respond to this tremendous honor with something more than a pat on the back and a "there, there." I wished I could do more for her.

My stomach grumbled as I recovered from zoning out. I didn't want to leave Chloe to get lunch. I would bring my lunch back here, of course, but what if her meeting had finished while I was gone? She would think I had abandoned her or—worse—she would feel alone in a moment of vulnerability. Plus, I had no idea how long I'd be gone. It was still relatively early in our lunch period, so the line to get lunch would surely be long and move slowly. After thinking for a long time, I slowly slid down the wall and let myself drop to the floor. I might as well sit if I wanted to wait for Chloe.

The outdoor science wing faced the gymnasium, undoubtedly the biggest building on campus. The enormous building, which had recently been renovated, took up my entire view. One giant ass building for sports, assemblies, events, and PE. It was only about 50 feet away from me. My unwillingness to further observe the building's design was because, to me, there wasn't much more to it than it being a giant ass building that blocked my view.

Of course, people walked across the pathway between the gym and the science wing, but I couldn't watch them due to obvious reasons. In my brief glimpses and through my periphery, I saw them carrying food with them, mostly fast food, soda, or milk tea. I wished that I could summon the courage to call over one of them and ask for a French fry. I tried to remember if I had packed a granola bar for myself this morning. I had started to bring my own energy bar to school after I had accepted that the school would never restock my favorite energy bars they sold. Who knows, maybe they were in stock? I had given up hope on the brunch cart and chosen to save my two dollars instead, putting it toward a better cause like a date. Plus, two dollars was way too expensive for one single energy bar. I started to search through my backpack's middle pocket for a snack. After finding nothing, I turned back to my view of the giant ass building.

The building didn't stimulate me much. I generally dreaded being in there. I hated walking into there for assemblies when literally everyone and their mother would be there. I hated looking for a seat among the cramped bleachers and rows of people. I hated it whenever the person hosting the assembly would ask us to cheer, imply they couldn't hear us, and then ask us to cheer again, but even louder. I wanted them to just get on with it and say whatever they needed to say and stop wasting our time. Oh, I hated it whenever the speaker would patronizingly wait for everyone to be quiet to say what they needed to say. I could hardly even hear the speaker properly with the awful microphone and speaker setup in the gym. I was sure that most assemblies would be better if they were just summarized and shared with students via email.

Just then, I saw people I recognized walk past the gym. Fight or flight engaged, and I dove into my backpack again to appear busy. This time, I searched my front pocket for the supposed snack. Lo and behold, I found a crushed granola bar. Even though I had found the said snack, I continued to look through my backpack, simply rustling through loose papers and useless crap. When I had looked for a purposeful amount of time, I quit the act and, with my granola bar in hand, turned to face the giant ass building. I gently tore open the granola bar as tiny crumbs of granola fell onto my pants. Having lunch like this felt oddly familiar. It was both a comforting and discomforting feeling. I slowly ate my granola bar and watched the useless building ahead of me. It was one of those moments where I took a breath, activated autopilot, and took my hands off the controller, slowly zoning out.

After an unclear amount of time, Chloe came out of the classroom and began to walk away from me, surely not having seen me.

"Chloe!" I called.

She stopped, turned in surprise, and headed back to me. "I thought you left," she said. Her slow and deliberate tone had been replaced by a loose and slippery one that communicated frustration.

"No, I wanted to wait for you," I said, having gotten up, holding my empty granola bar in hand. "So how'd it go?"

"I'll tell you later. Let's get out of here."

"Where do you wanna go?"

"The courtyard?" Chloe filled in with an almost default response.

"Let's go."

We sat there quietly. Chloe quickly unfurled her lunchbox. Even though we only had about fifteen minutes of lunch left, Chloe began eating her lunch as normal. I sat there playing with my granola bar wrapper, which I had forgotten to throw away. Chloe ate her salad slowly, concentrating on all the various ingredients making up her salad. She knew how to eat properly. Through her slow chewing, I made out a look of slight annoyance on her face. She seemed nowhere near as upset as before, however. No matter how well her talk with her teacher had gone, there was no way those feelings would have just vanished. I kept my eyes on the ground, unaware of what to say. I get that sometimes it's easier to put on a façade to make everything seem better. The truth, however, was that everything was not suddenly better and that the unwanted feelings could not be repressed perfectly nor forever. They would come out in one way or another.

"Is everything okay?" I turned to her. "You're really quiet. How are you feeling?"

Chloe finished chewing and said, "I'm fine. This salad just tastes weird." She let out a forced smile and resumed eating.

I nodded, "Okay. Well, if you want to talk about what happened, I'm here for you."

I turned away and looked out at the street, playing with my empty wrapper and feeling that sensation I had grown so accustomed to. I absorbed the loneliness until the bell rang and marked the end of lunch. Chloe put away her stuff and got up to leave. I slowly rose. Our next classes were in opposite directions, but we'd see each other for our last period.

"Well, see ya—" I said.

Chloe hugged me, and my heart calmed down a bit. She said, "Thank you."

"Of course, I'll be here—"

"Thanks. Thank you, really."

I squeezed tightly and savored the moment of togetherness, "Of course."

Chloe suddenly got up, "I'm gonna go throw this in the trash. Do you have anything you want me to throw away?"

I looked down at my relatively untouched tray, "I'm good." In the silent reflection on the past, I had lost my appetite.

Chloe walked away as I turned to my view of the street. I was alone for a moment, and I was dazed by the speed of the cars. So many thoughts and feelings came, but I stayed on the one that reminded me of how familiar this loneliness was. It was comforting and discomforting and gave rise to the smallest lump of anxiety within me. I urgently turned to look at Chloe, who had stepped away from me.

Chloe reached the trash can, threw away a napkin, and turned around to walk back. As she returned, I felt my heart letting go of the tension it had been holding. It relaxed and swelled, and my appetite began to return. She came back to me, and the bell rang, ending lunch.

"You barely had any of your lunch," Chloe said to me.

I nervously laughed, "I know. I wasn't feeling that hungry. I'll try to finish it on my way to class."

I folded my sandwich back up in its wrapper and pocketed the baby carrots. I packed the small carton of milk into the side pocket of my backpack. Chloe put away her lunchbox and put on her backpack as I quickly ran to the trash can to throw away my lunch tray. I ran back, put on my backpack, and faced Chloe. Her eyes suggested her impatience in wanting to get to class and in waiting for me. She always overestimated how long the walk from the courtyard to her class would take. She had her physics test next period, and I knew she'd ace it.

"Good luck on the test," I wished.

"Thanks," she smiled. "I'll see you in Calc."

We hugged and kissed. I said goodbye to her and went in the opposite direction. With my sandwich in hand, I walked through the now-empty courtyard. All the couples had surprisingly cleared, and the quiet girls surely wanted to be first to their fifth period. I watched the road to my side and took in the peaceful view before I couldn't see it anymore. A wall came in the way and marked the end of the courtyard.

III

I haven't been eating much recently. I haven't had much of an appetite, I guess. I've just sorta been lying around.

I wasn't sure of the time, but I saw some rays of sunlight slip in through the blinds. It was some time in the day, at least. I had woken up twice earlier and then just lay there before pulling the comforter up and around me and drifting off back to sleep. My phone was dead, my watch's battery needed to be replaced, and I refused to keep a clock in my room because it only amplified the futility of time and how I wasted it.

I have felt alone, in some sort of way, all my life. That much is certain. I thought I knew what being alone felt like, but I really had no idea. For most of my life, I have had the pleasure to keep the company of good friends and acquaintances. Even now, I live in an apartment with two other roommates. I attend class in large lecture halls every Tuesday and Thursday. I go grocery shopping every week or so, run into several strangers, and sit in traffic among hordes of people. I wasn't alone in those moments. I needed to just look to my side to see at least one other person and know that I was not alone. Yet, in those moments, I felt so trapped in a state of loneliness. There were just a couple of feet between me and any random person at the grocery store. There were just a few thin walls and square feet between one of my roommates and me. However, the emotional state of loneliness I felt so trapped in could never be traversed. Those few steps to the next person could never quite repair my loneliness.

All the time that I had been lying in bed, I learned to distinguish the differences between being alone and feeling lonely. The physical state of being alone or in solitude can be, in most scenarios, easily repaired. However, the feeling of loneliness can possess you anywhere. While being alone could certainly inspire loneliness, one does not need to be alone to feel lonely. This was when I realized that I was not just alone. I was lonely. This whole time, I was surrounded by people, but then there I was still in my head and lonely. The two constructs sure may be related, connected, and hated, but they are separate. All these years, I thought I was just alone, but I had also been lonely. I would fixate a lot on my mental state, and I thought I knew exactly how it felt to be alone, but I was so wrong. I had been wrong about so much—so much. I was not just alone. I was alone and lonely.

The comforter was wrapped up and around me, and a small cavernous hole allowed me to stare out into the rest of the world. I lay there on my left side, facing the wall. The distance to crawl out of the abyss seemed so far, and I just fell deeper and deeper into my fixation and broken state.

Over the last two years, I have felt myself contract. I have followed the downward trajectory of this trough and shriveled inward and devolved into the person I used to be and see myself as. My posture has grown lame. My handwriting has suffered. My head and body have ached. My eyes have stayed red. I lost my interests, energy, passion, discipline, motivation, and—many times—my will. I could not say why, besides the forsaken and lonely place I seemed to be sentenced to for life. It took away all meaning, all sense of logic, and the feeling reigned triumphantly over all else that used to matter to me. I felt like a shell of my former self. These thoughts echoed around me as I dug myself deeper into the cave.

I awoke later in the evening. It was dark. Loneliness just felt worse in the dark.

No matter how long I stared, I found that my eyes never quite adjusted to the dark. They remained clouded and just hovered over the shapes I saw ahead of me. At times, my head similarly felt clouded, and nothing came to it. Empty felt like the wrong word to describe it, but I had already verbalized the mistake. I didn't know what to say or do. When I tried to think, it was the same thoughts that came to mind, the same images, the same suffering, and it made everything feel so repetitive and meaningless.

I missed it. I missed it all. It all mattered so much, and yet seemed not to matter at all to others. Now, I felt alone, completely alone and lonely. I kept arriving back to that thought, that feeling, that state, that darkness, that cave, whatever it was.

It had been a while since I was at the courtyard. It was crazy to think of how confined I felt at the courtyard, when now I felt truly caved in. It had also been a while since I had talked to any of my friends. We had all started college at different places, and everyone seemed to have closed that former chapter of their life and moved on to writing the next one. My chapters did not seem to transition well. I had not understood the social rules and regulations that dictated that we were no longer meant to be in each other's lives. The people who had sworn to always be there, lend a hand, plan a trip, host me for the night, and other pleasantries had vanished. They had become the people who would not send a birthday message, not like a social media post, not initiate communication, and not even think of me. Some of them tried to hang on and preserve what we had, but they all ultimately lost interest.

Chloe left me about a year ago. We tried the whole long-distance thing, and it seemed to eat away at us both. I enjoyed the feeling of going back home to visit her. The visitations were what kept me going in my new life here. Yet, they were cut off eventually when Chloe told me she couldn't do it anymore. About a year had passed, and I was still not over her. That disgusted me, but I still found her to be one of the only remaining things in life that had given me comfort and relieved me of this loneliness. I enjoyed my time with her, even when I began to feel alone with her.

Every time I would visit, I would wait outside her door in anticipation of her to greet me. More and more time passed, and the less and less excitement our reunions seemed to carry. I would work up the courage to ring her doorbell, and, in the moment, panic and worry would ensue. What would her reaction be, and would this be the fateful day? I would reach for the bell, and then retract my hand, try to calm down, before trying to ring the doorbell again. I was paralyzed in that short moment before I greeted her. My heart would be beating so quickly and loudly. I would hear it in my ears, worrying about a certain thought, feeling, state, or whatever that single thought may be out of the 50 million possibilities that could take place. That one thought out of 50 million. That one idea. That singular belief out of so many possibilities loudly beating in my ears. Not numbers, not reason, only the thought from my worst days of my worst past and my worst future, loudly beating in my ears.

I would stop for a moment to look at the sky, listen to the traffic, and smell the cold, crisp air. Then I would look at the door I had waited behind so many times for a hug, a kiss, and enduring love from someone I adored. For a second, everything would feel fine. I comfortably thought that everything would be fine. The door would open. I would see her. As always, my heart would be filled with warmth and joy and cry as it saw her. My mind would slowly start to quiet. Hope and love would fill it, and loneliness would leave it. Then the jarring thing happened.

No matter what, no matter how much hope or love I held, I had no control over it, over her feelings, the future, or anything. No matter what, I had no control over life. Such was and is the nature of life. Life has never and will never wait behind someone's door to address them. Life will barge through.

You cried on your birthdays, letting out all the pain, and wondered, "Why me? Why now?" You exclaimed, "I don't understand," and questioned, "Why is this happening?" You sustained your temporary wounds, a sliver of love and hope, and whatever else you had. Yet, nothing quite protected you, and nothing ever will. No matter what you do, no matter who you are, no matter where you are, no matter why you are, no matter anything and everything about you, life will hit you.

And so, I have lain here and taken its beating over and over. I have confined myself to this dormant state because this is all I can take, and this is the only place of comfort I can find: a bed surrounded by four empty caving-in walls, a rigid door with hinges needing oiling, a dead phone, and a comforter to protect myself from all the risks of life. I felt the dampness of my comforter against my cheeks. Even though I was soaked in my own filth, part of me hoped that my phone would buzz with a message from one of my friends, a message filled with care and longing, and a request to be there beside me and nurse me from this sickness that had possessed me. Part of me desperately hoped. Part of me stayed to believe in the people who had abandoned me. Part of me still offered forgiveness and empathy. Part of me also died every time my hopes did not come to reality. It wasn't going to happen. It simply was not.

Languishing in loneliness was all I had left to do. This was it. This was the cycle. I would return to sleep, wake up, sleep, wake up, and continue being lonely.

IV

The reality of life is that you still have to get up, or you get swallowed by the deep spiral that seems to never end. How do you do so? Why does it even matter? I'm still working to answer those questions for myself.

All I know is that one day I sat up in bed and felt hungry. I felt like eating, nothing too heavy, and watermelon seemed to be the most appetizing. I started scrolling on my phone and found stupid YouTube videos to make me laugh and smile like an idiot as I lay in bed. I remember the day that lying in bed began to just feel disgusting. I enjoyed the way water trickled down my face when I stood directly underneath the shower. I began to crave the outside and the fine air that made me feel like I was alive. When I dreaded returning to my bed, I walked for ten minutes to the laundromat to wash my bed sheets with YouTube tutorials guiding me through the whole process. I don't know what guided me through the process of recovery, but all of a sudden, one day, I was standing and able to go on.

I was now starting my third year of college. It felt like I had slept two years of my life away. There was so much that I didn't remember about the last several years, but for some reason, the memories that came to my mind were the ones that took up these pages. This isn't really a diary, nor a memoir, but an amalgamation of what I consider to be ramblings on the moments in my life where I had felt the most present. I don't know what the hell "processing" is, but the internal monologues over these past five years rang through my ears and felt important to understanding my whole condition. What did I need to do to feel less alone in this world?

I had started seeing a therapist, which was—unbeknownst to me—a requirement for the psychology class I was taking. After having regained a basic level of functioning, this was a welcome addition to the help I could give myself. I didn't remember much of what we discussed over our prior sessions, but I remembered looking forward to each one. She would point out things here and there, distortions and all my faulty ways of thinking and overthinking. She suggested journaling to me, which I took with a grain of salt. Then again, this is not a journal. I took her suggestion to start writing and wrote what, I guess, would be considered a short story—because it was too short to be just a story. This is still the ramblings of my mind and the thoughtful pursuit of escaping my hellish overthought depression.

Writing enraptured me so much that I took a creative writing class as an elective. Writing, to me, wasn't even an escape; it was an endeavor. I struggled to commit things to paper, but the ideas that romped in my mind were just captivating. A shadow in the dark, a cat on the roof, a lost totem, a light blinking in the distance, a strange cawing, all of these mysteries captured my fantasy, and my mind would wander about them and their place in this world. What did they mean? Where did they come from? What if they... There were so many what-ifs, and that was the most exciting question to ponder.

A month and a half after we were done reading the textbook, we finally got to start writing. The first assignment included writing a page of pure observation, being an omniscient camera: going to a public place and purely observing. I rushed to finish the assignment till the last minute and skipped the actual watching people part and wrote just the observations part. I got a poor grade on the assignment—the worst I had ever done on a college assignment—and was told that I included too much of my own thoughts and opinions in the writing. At that moment, I thought, maybe this whole writing thing wasn't cut out for me.

I had applied for—and somehow gotten—a job at my college's psychology department office. I heard that the person previously filling my position had quit and that the office was desperate to hire someone. I needed to be able to pay for rent. My bank account had nearly been drained, and my shame kept me from telling my parents anything. I don't know if this was what I wanted or was cut out for, but it was certainly what I needed.

I walked to work every day. My apartment was just a twenty-minute walk away from work. In the morning, I sometimes got miserably stuck in bed for longer than expected and ended up leaving the apartment later than I wanted. I didn't eat anything in the morning, but I made sure to grab a disposable water bottle. Breakfast still eluded me.

I would usually get to work around ten minutes late. My tardiness, according to Google, was enough to get me fired within the first week. I would walk into the office and go straight to my desk. Each step I took toward my desk always felt so heavy with guilt. I hid myself behind my desk and computer so that no one would be aware of my tardiness or me. The brisk walk to work always left me exhausted, and I would guzzle down almost three-quarters of my water bottle immediately. It was good to hydrate early in the morning, but it left me dehydrated for the rest of the day. My coworker, Maraya, sat at the desk opposite mine, just all the way at the other end of the room. To our side was our supervisor's cubicle. I couldn't see into her workspace, but she was the one I tried my hardest to hide from. It was just one thin wall that stood between her and me.

I powered up my computer. Before the screen became blue, I saw my reflection on the desktop. I fixed my hair and wiped the sweat off my forehead. Sweat had lined the creases on my shirt, so I pulled on my shirt to let some air through and caught a whiff of my sweaty self. I recoiled in my seat, wanting to slide down and hide underneath my desk. Then I looked straight and sighed out a gust of air through my mouth.

Maraya was standing there, "Hey! Sorry to bug you. Nancy gave me these papers for us to sort into a spreadsheet. Do you want to take the H-N pile? I started on the A-G pile already."

"Yeah, sure!" I think I said.

"Thanks," Maraya smiled and gently placed the H-N pile on my desk. "Nancy said that if you have any questions, you can write them down on a sticky note and attach it to the file. She'll check them later."

"Got it, thanks."

Maraya nodded, smiled, and began walking back to her desk. She sat down and awkwardly looked back at me with a closed smile. She slowly turned her head to look back at her computer. Behind her overall generosity, I had the feeling that Maraya hated me and specifically hated looking at me.

I looked through the pile on my desk as Nancy's phone began to ring. It was a thick stack of files. I flipped through the pages and saw all sorts of names along with all sorts of private information about them. I signed into my computer. I didn't want to start. I logged into my email and found the Excel sheet. I opened it up and saw several color-coded columns lined with empty cells. I didn't know what the point of it was, but we needed to fill in row after row of information that these students certainly didn't want us seeing: high school GPAs, SAT/ACT scores, majors, addresses, phone numbers, emergency contacts, family income, financial aid status, and GE requirement status. These students would hate me, too.

One of the cells became highlighted with Maraya's name on the side. I watched Maraya, on the Excel sheet, fill in a random student's name. She went to the next column. I clicked on the same cell as Maraya. She quickly filled it in and moved on to the subsequent section. I followed her onto the next cell and watched her type away. I looked at her, in person, and saw her wearing earbuds and nodding to the beat of whatever song she was listening to as she worked. We had barely spoken to each other, in person or on Excel.

I sighed and looked back at my screen. I looked around the spreadsheet to find the H-N tab, clicked on it, and begrudgingly got started. Cell after cell. Column after column. What felt like an invasion of privacy after an invasion of privacy. And sigh after sigh. I would frequently look at the file and be dumb founded by the spelling or fragmented words I saw under some of the sections. For the ones I could not discern or understand, I'd take a sticky note and, in chicken scratch, write down "I can't understand." I followed my comment on the sticky note with some suggestions for what I thought the file meant to say, just so I didn't look totally incompetent.

People had the strangest names with the strangest spelling, which I made sure to get correct. They lived on streets I knew or ones that were relatively close to me. Judging by their GPA and SAT scores, I was surprised that most of them had done worse in high school than I did. My GPA in high school wasn't great, and it sucked in comparison to my peers back then. What sucked even more was my SAT score. What surprised me more was that somehow I had maintained a 4.0 GPA in college, even after two long and depressing years. That surprising feeling didn't last too long, though; all my classes had felt relatively easy. Plus, I was sure that my chemistry professor had taken pity on me and unfairly rounded my B+ up to an A. These students were all majoring in psychology, just like me. I don't know what called me to this field, besides whatever innate pull I felt toward studying other humans and their emotions and behaviors. I moved on.

At one point, the ridiculously high family incomes I inputted would've made me feel shocked and disgusted, but now I reacted with apathy. It was just digits on a long page of running code. Some numbers just happened to have additional zeroes than others. There were the people who got aid and those who didn't. Some people had met their GE requirements, and others hadn't. There were all sorts of emergency contacts, mainly family or significant others, but I wondered who would actually show up.

I kept typing until I felt my head starting to buzz and immediately pulled it from the screen. I grabbed my temples with my left hand and let my head hang. I looked down, feeling this familiar pain in my head. I would get it all the time when I was working or in class. I closed my eyes for a few seconds, hoping the pain would go away. It seemed the only time this pain didn't find me was when I was in bed, the lights were off, and I felt the comforter against my face.

"You okay?" Maraya had asked, standing in front of my desk again.

"Yeah, I'm good. I think I just need water." I picked up my water bottle and drank the remaining amount.

"Let me know if you need any pain meds," Maraya seemed to care. "Nancy asked me to go get her coffee. Do you want to come?"

"I'm sorry, I think I'll pass."

"Okay, see ya later," Maraya walked out.

Maybe I should've said yes. Maybe I should've made the best of the opportunity to get to know her and escape the office. Even though Maraya seemed relieved I didn't say yes, maybe I should've. She didn't need to invite me. She really didn't. Unless she was instructed to invite me, I doubt she would've asked. But she did ask. She asked me to come along and extended a handshake, and I turned it away. Why would I do that? I didn't want to be here, and some coffee, even water, or just a walk would have been so much better than this.

I got up and walked out of the office. Maybe I could catch her. I looked around the courtyard outside the office and didn't see her. There was the cafe in the library and the one across campus, and I didn't know which one she chose. I assumed she'd want to walk the shorter distance and started down the hallway facing toward the library. I reached the end of the hallway as it opened up into the rest of the campus. I didn't see her anywhere. It was too late, and I was stupid for pursuing her. I started back to the office, but took a detour to the restroom, just in case Nancy asked where I had gone.

I sat down and got back to the document, entering name after name. Nancy didn't say a word to me nor notice if I was there or not. Maraya came back twenty or so minutes later with coffee from a small local shop. She handed Nancy her order, took her own back to her desk, and got back to work.

I took an abnormal psychology class. The course covered various psychological disorders, their presenting symptoms, supposed origins, and treatments. The professor told us stories about seeing different patients who had the disorder of the week. Each story was captivating, not just in the nuances of the case being presented, but also in the sentimental interactions between the professor and his patients. How enriching the process seemed to be, being able to sit with people, helping someone who seemed to be at a low point, and reflecting to them their own strengths and resilience over the course of their nonlinear journey of growth. There was a raw gratification that existed in these stories. It's hard to explain it, but they were characteristic of life in the best possible ways. I saw myself in them. I was going through my own therapeutic process as a patient, but part of me saw myself joining the union of hurt and trying to help others. I imagined sitting and conversing with them the way my professor had, and the feeling that came along with it made me feel good.

I chose psychology as a major because it was a subject matter I was interested in learning more about, but this class made me see the potential this field offered. This was something worth exploring further, I made a note to myself.

"I'm telling you all, I know my stuff. Within five minutes, I bet I could figure out what to diagnose you with," the professor lectured. "If you're interested in being diagnosed, come talk to me after class."

The class laughed. I paused from notetaking and wondered what he meant. All of us have something, he suggested, and he could help me better understand what was going on with me. I sat through the rest of the lecture and flip-flopped between approaching him or not after class. I didn't know what to say or what he would say. I began to think.

Hi, Professor. I thought that was really interesting, what you talked about. You said you could tell us what you think we have. Could you tell me what you think I have?

Hi! I'm in your class, and I was wondering if you actually meant that—that you could tell us what's wrong with us?

This might be weird, but I'm really curious to hear what you think I have.

I really appreciate your teaching. It's made me very interested in therapy. Do you think I'd be able to do it?

Oh, sorry. I'm just walking through.

The professor ended class about fifteen minutes early. Everyone began to pack up and rush out of the lecture hall. I slowly put away my things and continued to mull over the professor's offer. I saw people approaching him after class. I couldn't hear what they were talking about, whether they were also getting diagnosed or just discussing their grades, but I didn't want to approach him until everyone else had left. I held onto my backpack straps while waiting in the side lane of the hall to talk to him. There were a couple of people waiting behind me. When it was my turn to talk to him, I saw him eagerly say bye to the girl he was just speaking with. I quickly turned around to let the girl behind me go first. She asked me if I was sure, and I eagerly said yes. She went ahead and talked to him for maybe thirty seconds and then left, thanking me again. There were still two people behind me. Before I could leave the room, the professor turned to me and recognized me.

"It's you! You know, you ask really good questions in class," he said to me.

"Do I? I can't even remember," I said.

"Yeah, keep it up. I can tell that you're really interested. Let me ask, what're you thinking about doing after college?"

"I have no idea," I quickly began to brainstorm for something. "Maybe school psychology. Schools are really important."

"Oh, that's really good. They get paid well. Nice, we need more of those."

"Thanks," I paused. "I wanted to ask you. You talked about being able to diagnose us by just talking to us for a few minutes. Did you actually mean that?"

"No, I was just joking," he chuckled. "Hell, if I did that, I'd have people lining up to see me." He laughed again.

"Gotcha. Sorry, I was just curious," I tried to chuckle. "Well, thank you. I appreciate you talking to me. I won't take up more of your time."

"You're good. Keep asking those great questions," he bid me a lively farewell.

I nodded and turned around to walk away, cringing to myself. I heard someone go up to him after me and ask about the specifics of an assignment. We had class only once a week, and I really hoped he wouldn't remember me when he saw me again.

Weekdays, I'd power through, willing myself onto the next class. On the weekends, I'd stay in bed until the afternoon. There was nothing really to get up for. I'd stay lying in bed, watching stuff on my phone, doom scrolling till my phone died. Then I'd finally think of my next move. I'd go back to sleep or, if I couldn't handle the congestion anymore, I'd get up and go to the bathroom.

On my way back from the bathroom, I looked down the hallway and, with pleasure, felt my stomach grumble and crave food. I looked through the fridge and found nothing of interest. I looked through the pantry and found everything to be too much work. I scanned the place and picked out a bag of bread. My go-to dish for breakfast, lunch, and dinner, when I was cooking for myself, had become grilled cheese. I threw the bag on the counter, untwisted the bag, pulled out the pan, placed it on the stove, turned on the heat, and waited for it to heat. I moved to the fridge, pulled out two slices of Swiss cheese, a bag of shredded mozzarella, and a block of cheddar. I also pulled out a jar of mayonnaise. All the things went on the counter, next to the bread. I opened the cutlery drawer and pulled out a butter knife and a cheese grater. Finally, I picked out a small plate from a cabinet. The plate went next to the bread and ingredients. I set the knife on the counter and placed the cheese grater on the plate. I poked the center of the pan to check the heat.

Could be hotter, I thought. I stood in the kitchen and looked around, placing my hands at my hips, waiting. I gently poked the pan again. I pulled my finger back, reeling from the heat. I turned down the heat, just slightly.

I began to assemble the sandwich. I had picked up a secret tip from a YouTube video on how to make the best grilled cheese: using mayo to toast the bread, which would result in a much finer crunch than using butter. I used the butter knife to apply mayo to the outside of the bread slices, just enough to cover the full surface. I placed the bottom slice on the pan to hear it sizzle. The sizzle was like music. Next went a slice of Swiss, followed by a generous handful of the mozzarella. I was careful not to let it fall off the slice and burn in the pan. Then I took the handheld grater and the block of sharp cheddar and grated the cheese onto the slice. The cheddar, in contrast to the mozzarella, went everywhere. My accuracy with the grater was never that good, but I only ever grated just a little bit of cheddar. Truthfully, I wasn't the biggest fan of cheddar and only preferred to have a subtle hint of cheddar in my grilled cheese sandwiches. The cheese had been grated, and the remaining block was placed back on the counter. After picking the cheese off the other side of the grater, I placed the grater in the sink. The cheese bits I had saved from the grater went onto the sandwich. The second and last slice of Swiss served as the last topping for the sandwich. The sandwich was then completed with the top mayo-buttered slice. I let the sandwich cook for a second.

I pulled out a spatula from the cutlery drawer and went to carefully flip the sandwich. I placed the spatula under the sandwich and gently held onto the top. This was the most stressful step. I counted down from 3 in my head.

3… 2… 1. Flip.

The sandwich landed in a disaster. The bottom, which was now the top, had partly slid off the sandwich, and a portion of the mozzarella and cheddar had fallen out of the sandwich and were burning away in the pan. My heart melted away with the cheese. The careful artistry of assembling a sandwich I absolutely loved had been flipped upside down with the stupid spatula I had and my damned, unsteady, and trembling hands.

UGH, I thought.

I did my best to salvage the situation and tried to put everything back together. Ultimately, the sandwich ended up somewhat burnt, and the cheese pull wasn't as satisfying. The pan was also adorned with scraps of burnt cheese that I needed to clean off. I left the pan on the stove for now. I'd wash it later, with everything else. I put the bread and all the cheese back, including the mayo. The knife, which I had used to expose the underwhelming cheese pull, went in the sink with its spatula friend. The sandwich sat on the plate, while I checked to make sure the heat was off.

I took my grilled cheese and a bottle of water back to my bed. I ate the sandwich—my signature dish—as I watched YouTube videos on my phone while it charged. I dropped some crumbs on the bed. I cleaned it all up later, but there I sat alone, eating and spending my life in this little corner.

There was something to be said about the isolating nature of college classes. Giant lecture rooms filled with fifty or more students who would show up one day, maybe not the other, leave early, or only show up to take the exams. I would typically sit in the back and near the sides, as I usually did during high school. It had all sorts of advantages: you got picked on less by the teacher, you were able to lean against the back or side wall, and you felt less crowded and more to yourself. Occasionally, I'd have to sit in the front whenever I was late to class, which was often. I didn't hate these seats, but I found there to be too much awkward eye contact exchanged between the professor and me.

Within the closing minutes of the class, you could hear most people beginning to zip open their backpacks, slam shut their laptops, and zip them all up in preparation to leave. Some would walk out immediately once they had performed their ritualistic disruption. Some would really rub it in your face by painfully dragging their chairs across the floor, even a slight amount, to produce an awful noise only comparable to nails on a chalkboard. To atone for my tardiness and also to show respect, I would patiently wait till the professor had stopped talking and excused the class to begin packing up. I put away my items one by one.

"Really great paper, by the way," my professor expressed to me.

"Really?" I suddenly looked up.

"Yeah, I left some comments on Canvas about it," she said.

"Thanks, I'll read them when I get the chance."

"I really appreciate the attention you give this class. It's so clear in your work and the questions you ask."

My other professor had said the same thing to me about my questions. Again, I didn't remember asking that many questions for these professors to be so impressed with.

"Thanks. I'm definitely interested," I said because I had nothing else to say.

"Have you thought about what you want to do once you graduate?" She asked.

"Not really," I answered and automatically thought of my next response, so I could alleviate her concern and show some level of competence. "I'm gonna be meeting with a career counselor soon, so hopefully that'll help."

"Good. You should definitely give it some thought. I could see you doing this."

I could hardly picture the next day, but somehow she could picture my calling.

I thanked her again, warmly, and walked out of the class. I wondered if I'd have a better sense of which way to go now, but I found myself unsure of how to even pass the time till my next class.

I was hungry, and so I did the usual. I went through a fast-food drive-thru, bought a really cheap meal, drove my car back to school, and sat in my car and ate while I watched my phone. Some people walked by as I ate. I tried not to pay them any mind, but eventually lowered myself and hid. There I sat, eating my cheap little burger and watching my phone as people walked by.

I was taking one more elective, which was American Sign Language. A class I chose purely because of how interesting learning another language seemed. My interests seemed to be building.

At first, the class was nerve-wracking. This was a very crowded and small classroom. I had to sit in the back-middle seat, feeling congested from every side. The whole class was filled with girls, except for another guy and me. A lot of my psych classes had a majority of girls in them too, but this was another level of discomfort with how closely they sat and how ugly I felt.

The professor, a charming old man who almost resembled Santa Claus, was the reason I stayed in the class and came to look forward to this class more than any other I had. Our professor was deaf and asked us all to refrain from speaking amongst each other in class as a sign of respect and, also, to properly understand everything he taught us. You had to be completely immersed in watching, listening, and minimizing any distractions. I didn't take any notes during class and kept my phone put away. I just watched him as he communicated with us using ASL.

I was engrossed as we learned and mastered the alphabet and basic numbers. I watched our professor, Steve, as he slowly signed each letter and mouthed the sound the letter made. He made his way through the whole alphabet, leaving us in bewilderment and stuck on the sixth one. He began the whole alphabet again, slowly making each sign with us and checking to see if everyone had it properly down. We moved on to the next letter and kept going. We would sometimes stop for Steve to motion at a student and correct them. Steve would just repeat the sign and have the student repeat it back to make sure they understood it properly. He smiled at them whenever they had it right. We completed one round through the alphabet, and Steve waved his hands to cheer for us. A lot of my peers did the same. He motioned for us to do the alphabet again, and so we did it slowly and carefully. He cheered for us again, smiling widely.

"Again," he signed.

We began at "A," thinking of ourselves as masters. We made our way through the first line, being led by our gentle professor. We reached "H," and Steve sped up with none of us to match his pace. He sang the whole alphabet with his hands.

"Ha ha," Steve signed and laughed. "I'm sorry," he signed to us from his heart. "Let's do it again."

We would always review the signs we had learned during our last lesson before moving on to new content. We were now learning family structure and size. We would sometimes get called up to the front of class to sign a sentence or have a mock conversation with our professor. One by one, Steve began calling us up to ask how big our family was and if we had any siblings. I was on top of it, after paying as close attention as I could to his lesson and practicing to myself over and over again. After all, my responses were easy: my family was small, and I had no siblings. I would help my peers figure out what each sign meant and practice their signs before they eventually got called up. The girl who sat across from me had finished her presentation to the class as Steve happily cheered for her and gave her a silent applause. She came and sat down. She looked around to thank her peers as they praised her. She and I happened to make eye contact. I gave her a thumbs up and mouthed, "Good job."

Next, Sebastian stepped up as a volunteer. He was shaking with energy as he stood next to Steve. Sebastian looked with complete concentration at Steve.

"Hi Sebastian! How big is your family?" Steve signed and raised his eyebrows.

Sebastian blanked. He asked Steve to sign the question again.

"How big is your family?"

Sebastian looked up and carefully thought about how to respond. He waved his hand at Steve to call for his attention and began to sign, "My family is big."

"Big?" Steve asked.

"Yes," Sebastian continued to sign.

"How many siblings do you have?" Steve asked.

"I have 3 brothers—no. I have 3 sisters and 2 brothers," Sebastian finished.

"Wow. Thanks, Sebastian," Steve signed.

"How many siblings do you have?" Sebastian flipped the script as all of us chuckled.

"Me?" Steve was humored. "I have 1 brother and 1 sister."

"Wow," Sebastian signed in response.

Steve patted Sebastian on the back and signed, "You're funny."

Sebastian signed, "Thank you."

As Sebastian returned to his seat, Steve signed something new.

I watched him earnestly and shot my hand into the air. He looked at me after a second and asked if I wanted to come up next. I said no and asked what that sign was by trying to replicate what he had signed.

Steve made an expression that replicated what I imagined was "Aha." He raised his hand to his chin and proceeded to sign what had made me curious. He took a dry-erase marker and wrote on the board, "Good job." He signed it for us, again, and smiled. He gave us a thumbs-up.

We continued with the presentations. Someone else went up next, while I sat by myself and quietly attempted to sign "good job" under my desk. I tried to pay attention to the presentations, but I became fixated on the movement that felt so satisfying to my wrists and curiosity. I kept signing to myself again and again. It began with the sign for "good." Then you quickly finger-spelled "j" into "b." There was another variation of it that he showed us. He told us they meant the same thing, and then he motioned to himself and said he preferred the former.

The class had come to a lull as we awaited our next presenter. Nobody was stepping up. Steve looked over the class with a smile, asking who was next.

I decided to finally step up. Steve saw me and cheered. He waited for me to stand next to him before asking me the same questions he'd asked everyone else.

He waved to get my attention. "How big is your family?"

I stood by him. "My... family is... small." I had practiced the signs and reviewed with the others, and when it came time to deliver them, I stuttered.

"How many siblings do you have?"

"None," I slowly raised my hands in two zeroes.

Steve cheered for me. He signed, "Good."

I watched him and slowly signed, "Good job." I held out a thumbs-up with raised eyebrows to ask for approval.

"Good job!" He signed back and smiled widely, nodding. "Good job."

He patted me on the back, and off I went to my seat with a

lump in my throat. My ears burned up, and I became very aware of the nervousness that I felt. I sat down and was congratulated by one of my peers. I dryly mouthed, "Thank you." I pulled on my shirt to alleviate the heat and sank into my chair, feeling the satisfaction of "good job."

I approached Sebastian after class. We had just filed out of the classroom into the crammed hallway. Everyone else had dispersed, while he seemed to linger and move slowly.

"Hey, good job in class today," I said to him and began to walk alongside him.

"Oh, thanks. You too!" Sebastian said back to me.

"You did awesome, though. Steve was so impressed."

"Oh my God, no. I was so nervous up there. You did a good job."

"Not at all. I went up there and choked, man. I thought I had it, but no…"

"I thought you did great."

"Isn't this such a fun class, though? I took it just as an elective and, man, I love it."

"Same! It's my favorite class, definitely, and Steve just makes it a hundred times better."

"Oh, totally. He's so sweet."

"Right? He's like a jolly old grandpa. I love Steve."

"Yeah, I can't imagine being taught in any other way than how Steve teaches us. He's just so good. I feel so immersed, you know? I'm like trying to pay attention to every little thing he tells us."

"For real. Ugh, Steve is just so good."

"If he's teaching the more advanced ASL classes, I would love to keep taking them. It's actually really interesting."

"Apparently, from what I've heard, ASL 2 and ASL 3 are set up like completely differently. Apparently, it's more like the history of ASL and stuff."

"Oh, interesting. I'll have to look into that."

"Same. If Steve is teaching it, I'd still totally be down."

"Do you have a class now, by the way?"

"No, I was just gonna go to the library to do some homework. How about you?"

"I don't either." I continued to get to know him. "What major are you, by the way?"

"Criminology, how about you?"

"Psychology."

"Oh, they're kinda related." Sebastian drew a connection.

"Yeah, totally."

"I don't know if you've learned anything about this in your classes, but we've been learning about psychopaths. Apparently, one in one hundred people in the world is a psychopath."

"One in one hundred, really?"

"Isn't that crazy?"

"That feels like too much. I don't get how… like that's wild to comprehend."

"Right? Like one in one hundred people we meet might be a psychopath."

"Dang…" I didn't know how else to respond.

"Me neither. Our professor pulled up the statistics and whatnot, and that's what it said."

"One in one hundred…"

"One in one hundred."

"That's crazy." I took in the fun fact.

"Imagine we know someone who is a psychopath."

"Wow. Could be, huh?" I chuckled and considered whether Sebastian was a psychopath.

"Do you think someone who's a psychopath would pretend to be normal to fit in, or would it be obvious that they were a psychopath?" Sebastian genuinely asked.

I considered it. "Well, I don't think they'd have the social skills to pretend to fit in. I think it'd be obvious, right? Like, I think if we actually knew someone who was a psychopath, it would probably be obvious."

Sebastian laughed. "I hope."

"I don't know, though."

"Who knows?" Sebastian was amused.

After taking the longer route, we were nearing the library.

"Are you a psychopath, Sebastian?" I asked

"No! I hope not. Are you?"

"No. I don't think so. I think we'd know if we weren't psychopaths, right?"

"I think so. I think you're right."

As we approached the entrance to the library, I looked at Sebastian. He walked a couple of paces ahead of me. What a singular conversation that was, and one that I'd love to have again.

"Here we are," I said.

"You wanna come inside with me?" Sebastian invited.

"No, it's okay. I'm gonna get something to eat." I felt that I had overstayed my welcome and didn't want to ruin a good thing.

"Okay. Well, thanks for walking with me."

"By the way, do you game at all?" I felt the courage to ask.

"Yeah, I do."

"We should game sometime," I smiled.

"Yeah, totally."

"Sweet. Well, I'll see you later then. Best of luck with your homework."

"Thanks, you too!"

Sebastian headed inside.

I walked away and headed toward the parking lot. I hadn't gamed in years, nor made sure Sebastian and I had the same console. However, he had said yes, and that was satisfying enough for now. I still wondered, though. Was Sebastian a psychopath? I wondered if he thought the same about me, and smiled.

On my way to the parking lot, I took a new route: a pathway that ran parallel to the main street our school sat on. As I walked past the shabby-looking buildings, I spotted a bench at the end of the lot.

It sat under a tree, off a beaten path, and right past the furthest building. The bench looked out at the street and the cars that whizzed by. It looked like a nice spot to sit for a while.

There was no one walking by, which made me feel more committed to the idea. The bench was far enough from the building that it gave the impression that it was isolated. The wood used for the bench was old and clearly showing signs of eventual ruin. I wasn't heavy, but I wondered if the bench was sturdy enough to even hold me.

Before I sat, I spotted some ants crawling on the sides of the bench. I cringed to myself and sat as far to the opposing side as I could. I took my phone and wallet out of my back pocket, so I could sit comfortably on my butt. I set my phone and wallet on my side. I slung my backpack off and put it by my feet.

I took a brief look into the distance: grass and the road. I didn't want to look.

I fidgeted through my backpack to take out a granola bar. This was my lunch for the day. I unwrapped it and held it in my right hand. I let my hand rest on my thigh.

This was a view that felt like home. It reminded me of high school, my friends, my family, and home. Cars whizzed by as the sun set in the background. The odd smell of car fumes and gasoline mixed with the fresh lawn clippings in front of me. I even smelled the chocolate flavor of my granola bar. I heard the occasional loud exhaust and the birds chirping beside my ears. I turned to check if ants were crawling over my belongings. I felt my items smooth to the touch and felt the wood coarse and rough. No splinters, though. I even double-checked my hands. I looked and looked and took a breath. I paid attention to my posture to make sure it didn't suck.

I brought my granola bar to my mouth and took a bite. The granola and chocolate combo was always good, but today it tasted even better.

I wondered if anyone driving by saw me and what they thought of me.

I went back to eating, though, strangely smiling to myself.

I saw a squirrel run in the distance. If he didn't have a seat, he could sit by me, and we could watch the sunset together. I chewed and watched, nodding to myself. Alone, and all to myself.

Promethean

When one can patiently sit and observe their view, they learn to see it all. I, however, see it again. I live it, day by day. Ahead of me, I witness all of the pain and sorrow, and suffer it again. I am chained to it.

I attempt to recant the tale, and this is how I see it. This is how I make sense of it.

~

The sun began to rise on the Caucasus Mountains. Two brothers slept by their extinguished flame. One began to stir awake. The other thought to wake.

Prometheus awoke first and laid his eyes on the dawn. His breath was taken from him by the fiery sky that awakened and became pulled over the tarp of night. He stood up and thanked the old Titan pulling the sun chariot for the beauty he was able to witness every day. Epimetheus kept stirring, tossing, and turning. When he finally awoke, he saw his brother standing with his mouth agape.

"What are you looking at?" Epimetheus asked.

"Helios, he's made his rise. You've missed it, brother," Prometheus smiled down at his seated companion.

"Have I? Damn me. I thought I'd wake in time," Epimetheus unsteadily rose, tripping on his robe. "The wine! It was the wine. My head is pulsing, and my body feels revolted. Why do I never learn?"

Prometheus grabbed his brother by the shoulders, steadying him and looking into his eyes with earnestness, "You do, brother. You just give in to temptation, from time to time."

"As do we all, don't we?"

"As we do."

Epimetheus laughed with contentment before his laugh became of concern. It had turned into a heavy cough as Epimetheus bent over, dry-heaved a few times, and expelled the vile sickness from his body. He spat at the soil afterward, almost to commemorate the completion of this wretched and ungodly act. All the while, Prometheus stood there at his brother's side, patting him on the back and groaning with his brother's poor health.

"I'll be alright," Epimetheus said in between spits.

Prometheus took that as his cue to step back and let his brother sit in his shame, just for a few moments. The only symptoms Prometheus felt were the coldness nipping at his cheeks and nose, turning them into a flushing red. He rather enjoyed the sharpness of the morning wind. It was one of those things that kept him grounded in his current state and reminded him of his well-earned merriment.

He, once again, turned his attention to the view. Helios was shining not just on his face, but down on the valley of the humans with their crowing roosters and domestic routines. Men and women rose with their young ones in full spirit, relishing still what felt like their first days on this land. Prometheus saw them from a distance; the women prepared the morning meals, the men quarreled amongst themselves, and the youth chased each other around the farmlands. Soon they would be at their stations, ready for the day, and working toward the flourishing of civilization. In a matter of what felt like days, they had progressed, even if just from sticks to stones. They had been born, living in fear within their caves, fighting to tame nature, and now forming societies and governments, controlling the flow of the river, and using power to become masters of their surroundings.

Prometheus could recall what it had felt like to mold them in his hands, to stretch out their limbs, and carefully place on their features. Hundreds of mounds of clay were discarded before Prometheus arrived at this current design. When he examined his failed creations, none of them seemed to invoke the essence of life and undeniable will as this race had. Prometheus had chosen to model the race of humans in the image of the newly crowned Gods. The ones who had defeated Prometheus and his brother's race of Titans, and the ones whom Prometheus had placed his faith and belief in during the time of war. The Gods possessed a rare new burning will for the world that had seemed to dwarf the Titans. The Titans were far more connected and amalgamated into the nature of the world that surrounded them. The Gods, in contrast, stood mighty—even if smaller in stature—due to the autonomy and independence in their being. They weren't reliant on the rest of the world, and they possessed the ambition to enact their will on the world. Some Titans had fallen victim to underestimating the Gods, clinging to what they'd seen as their world and their way of being. Fear had existed in the heart of the Titans, for this is why Prometheus inferred that Cronus had devoured his kin and the possibility of change in the future. Prometheus had been a Titan who had thought ahead and considered all such opportunities. He had envisioned the loss of the Titans and the burning will that would be enacted upon the world by the Gods, and Prometheus willed to share in this ambition. Epimetheus, headstrong and hasty, was eventually persuaded by his brother to step down from battle and kneel alongside him to their new king, Zeus. The brothers sought at the moment to self-preserve and became branded by the Titans as conniving and deceitful. As the defeated Titans fell to the dark depths of the underworld, Prometheus watched on and hoped to recover from his guilt.

Prometheus's forethought had helped the brothers earn favor with Zeus. Once the war was over and settled, the brothers were assigned by Zeus to fill the world with mortal creatures. So from mud came the various creatures that filled the world. Epimetheus crafted colorful and strange beings first with mighty abilities such as strength, speed, and flight. He, as his nature, fashioned them and placed them within the world without a second thought, and watched them tear each other apart limb to limb. These hasty creatures struggled to survive with the resources of any given region. Some laughed at him, but Epimetheus was no fool; he learned to reflect and become more aware of his wrongdoings. Viewing the life course of his creatures, in retrospect, he inspired the model for evolution. Each creature became modified and learned to acclimate to its surroundings as time took its course. Several generations of these creatures would pass before Prometheus would finally arrive at what he wanted to create. He created humankind, taking mild inspiration from his brother. Prometheus held a chunk of clay at the center and drew the arms long on each side, attaching opposable thumbs, and forming mankind into bipedal creatures with feet that would bear their weight. Atop the husk would be their head with small and delicate features that would allow for intimate communication and awareness of their surroundings. What took Prometheus the longest was fashioning the inner workings of mankind. The result of his labor was a complex system of interacting parts. This anatomy was unique in the way it fed information to the rest of the body and made the creatures not just a visual mimicry of the Gods. Prometheus had given them the ability to convey themselves, explore their sense of will, and act with intellect.

Epimetheus had wasted all the powers bestowed by the Gods on his creatures, so Prometheus was left with nothing to gift his creatures. Prometheus did beg Zeus for one gift that he thought might ignite the will of the humans and lay forward a path covered in light. Zeus had granted this request, that of fire.

Prometheus felt a twinge in his eye while he watched his creations stir. He adjusted his footing and moved closer to the edge of the mountain. With concern, he viewed the canals from a different angle and thought about how his children would survive when their nearest lakes ran dry, whether they would dig deeper into the ground or find ways to bring water from afar. When the water became contaminated from a creature's illness, how would they cure it and sustain themselves in thirst and disease? What justice would they enact when great cities would war amongst themselves with their own creeds and laws? He envisioned the kinds of creations his children would bear years from now. In decades, the heights their homes, temples, and offices would reach. In a matter of a century, the magic that they would possess at their fingertips as long as they continued to flourish. What took them days to do, Prometheus and his counterparts could fulfill in mere seconds. He saw an eerie beauty in their arduous labor. He crossed his arms as a proud and satisfied father, watching his children. Prometheus didn't relish in it for long; he thought ahead. That's what he always did.

The twinge turned to anxiety. One man had slept with another man's wife. One woman had robbed her neighbor. One man had sworn death upon a village elder. One woman had poisoned her husband's meal. One child had broken another child's leg. One family's bull had kicked in the head of a child. One child had been left stranded and slowly wandered into the land of the forest nymphs and satyrs. One babe had crawled and pissed upon the statue of Zeus.

Prometheus felt himself slip at the edge of the cliff as loose gravel and rock gave way under his heavy feet. He felt his weight drop, his stomach tighten, and felt himself beginning to lunge off the face of the cliff. With a sudden yank, Epimetheus pulled his brother back. They fell beside each other as Epimetheus began to curse his brother. Prometheus remained looking ahead, mouth agape.

He saw a sudden blur of motion rise past the edge of the cliff. He sat covered in sweat, hearing his heart beating through his ears. What he saw ahead of him became clear: a great eagle rising and flying toward the sky. It pierced through the wind, calling its mighty cry, and then began to glide and circle the peak of the mountain they were here to climb.

"What were you thinking?" Epimetheus yelled through the wind. "Answer me."

Prometheus stared at the great bird. He wondered if his brother had not pulled him back, would the bird have saved him or dug its talons into him? Would it have seen him as a child learning to fly or as prey? Even the suggestion of such a question would have caused great damage to a God or Titan's pride, but Prometheus thought through the pragmatics of it all. He knew he wasn't menacing. He knew that in size, he was dwarfed by the eagle. The power of immortality did not mean Prometheus or any God or Titan was safe from harm. Prometheus knew he could be picked apart in a matter of seconds at the hands of a powerful foe. Even if he may heal in time, any wounds or sorts of injuries would cause pain and deep scars. Scars that one could not see. Scars that healed over and over, testing the attrition of a godly body. Glances of violence had been enough to drive the fear of pain into Prometheus's mind. He had seen his fellow Titans butchered at the hands of the Gods. He had always struggled with the idea that he could have been one of them if he had not thought through the ordeal of war and done what he could to avoid that possible fate. He dreaded the thought of it. He worried incessantly about what could have been his fate, the imminent fate of immortal death and tarnation that could seize him at any point for his lowly act of betraying his family and thinking himself above the Titans and Gods. He saw himself as weaker than them all and therefore deserving of that fate, but no. No, no, no. To comprehend the idea of death and not existing anymore, the idea of his fire burning out and no remnant of it to be seen or felt again drove Prometheus to the edge of his state.

The sound of his heart grew and grew as he felt his breath pounce out of his chest, almost tears at his eyes as he attempted to comprehend the end of it all at the hands of some loose gravel. What would it all have been for, he thought. I don't want to go, not yet. He turned his body over onto all fours and dug his palms into the rocks beneath him. Hyperventilating, he thought that he must continue and think of the ways that he could continue to outsmart his foes. All the moments in which he must practice caution and doubt his surroundings so that he may not become the prey. And in this sudden slip, he may have become just that. And he can not let that happen again. This is too precious to let go. He clasped the tiny pebbles underneath him. Now, I have something that I want to continue on for and I will not have harm befall me for the sake of what I want to create, build, and stoke fire for; he challenged death. You will not take this from me, he thought.

He felt his brother tug on his arms. Epimetheus had been kneeling beside Prometheus, attempting to tug him back to calmness for some time, it seemed.

"Brother, brother, calm for me. You are fine, safe, and I am here," Epimetheus said.

Prometheus sat himself down and became more aware of his surroundings. He found himself holding onto his brother as tears streaked down his face.

"Slow your breathing. I'm here."

Prometheus captured his breathing and became soothed by his brother. In moments where such panic overtook Prometheus, Epimetheus was there to bring his brother into the impermanence of the moment.

"Thank you, brother," Prometheus continued to slow his breathing as relief filled him. He knew he had to slow himself. "Thank you."

"You must stop with these trances you fall into."

Prometheus patted his brother's arm to show he was secure enough now and that his brother may relieve himself of this caring task, and to also acknowledge his brother's advice. Moments like this reminded Prometheus that his brother possessed his own strengths and that Prometheus needed Epimetheus as much as Epimetheus seemed to need him. Yet, this was Prometheus's gift and curse. He knew that his forethought could often function as a mental trap, but he couldn't seem to just get rid of it. Besides, he needed to rely on it to protect himself and to withstand all the turmoil that was awaiting them. It had led the brothers to where they were now, and that wasn't a bad spot to be at all. And just how far it would continue to take them, Prometheus reassured himself and smiled at the sky ahead of him.

"So that was one of your birds?" Prometheus returned kindness to his brother and acknowledged another one of his marvelous feats.

Epimetheus stood now, looking at the sky. He stroked his chin and stated, "I think so."

Prometheus rested his hands on his knees. "You think so?" He squinted. "Well, it must be."

"I suppose," Epimetheus shrugged and turned back. He yawned and scratched his ass, treating the day like any other day. "I packed our things while you were off perverting over mankind."

"Perverted? You called me perverted?" Prometheus gagged in revolt, cocking his head.

Epimetheus lifted the magical sack that held all their belongings. "You don't see me talking to anyone else, right now."

Prometheus pushed himself up. "How dare you! I just almost walked off the mountain, and you have the dignity to stand there and insult me."

"I saw. I was the one who saved you."

"Have some compassion, would you?"

Epimetheus thought for a second and uttered, "I suppose."

Prometheus reminded himself to be patient with his brother's fast mouth and slow mind. After all, Epimetheus was the one who had talked his way into a drinking match moments before recruiting his brother on the grand hike of this mountain. The most beautiful sights you will see from the summit, he had yelled at Prometheus after pulling him away from matters more important. Epimetheus claimed that everyone had been speaking of this range, from Mount Olympus to the rats of the human village. He looked at his brother with those innocent eyes that Prometheus never saw a lie or deceitfulness in. Sure, Prometheus had said, laughing at his brother that night. He happened to be in a jolly mood that evening, which left him impressionable to Epimetheus's foolishness. Prometheus had gathered all the supplies they'd need, while Epimetheus had won multiple drinking matches. Then they had set off for their expedition.

"I'll carry the satchel then." Epimetheus then sheepishly whispered, "As a token of my apology."

"That's fair," Prometheus nodded, not giving a care to who wore the light sack on their belt.

Epimetheus waited for his brother to join him at the head of the trail. The trail had been marked by slightly more worn terrain than what surrounded it. The brothers journeyed forward, following this unsteady trail to the summit, where the eagle had flown and circled before disappearing out of their vision.

"I don't know about you, but I just love the way the morning cold bites at my face," Epimetheus said, swinging his arms and wandering a few steps ahead of his brother.

"As do I," Prometheus gave back to his habit of rolling his eyes at his brother. Even though his brother walked ahead of him, Prometheus scanned the path ahead and constantly watched for anything that might throw off his footing.

"You haven't told me, yet—"

"What haven't I told you?" Prometheus interjected.

"What were you doing last night that was so much more important than helping me finish those jars of wine? I had to finish the village's wine all by myself, you know," Epimetheus shortly turned his head back to attract his brother's sympathy.

Prometheus laughed, "First of all, I thought it must've crossed your mind not to drink so much, especially the night before setting forth on a journey up a mountain." Prometheus attempted to instill forethought into his brother.

"That doesn't answer my question. You keep avoiding it," Epimetheus was not pleased.

"I humored you enough by choosing to go on this fool's quest with you," Prometheus spoke plainly.

"You do avoid my question, and you must do so for a reason," Epimetheus won in his realization. "Attest to me, brother. You can tell me whatever you wish."

"Maybe in due time, but not now. The wind is too strong, and I'm afraid of just where it may take my words. We have committed enough treachery in our lives, so forgive me, brother, if I hold this one too close to my chest. It's just that important to me," Prometheus spoke to the backside of his brother's head, before looking downward at the path again.

"More important than fire?" Epimetheus turned his whole body around and began to saunter backwards up the trail.

"Brother, you must watch your step—"

"Answer me that. More important than what you risked everything for?"

Prometheus met his brother's gaze.

"It is, isn't it? Wow, you are mighty good at treachery, brother," Epimetheus chuckled and stood still.

"It is," Prometheus spoke through his teeth. "Now walk straight before you trip."

Epimetheus turned around and kept walking, "Just don't keep me in anticipation for too long."

Prometheus followed silently, thinking of the kinds of treachery that had unfolded throughout the prior week.

It would be remiss not to start with what Prometheus had identified as the moment that began the escalation of events. It was not immediately that Prometheus had arrived at fire as the gift he requested and needed for humankind to thrive. He had spent endless days throwing around lumps of clay in his and his brother's studio, trying to arrive at what he could construct that could give humans the spark to take on the wide and treacherous world. The world may have been safer were it not for Epimetheus's wild creatures, which seemed to rival and endanger Prometheus's creations at every turn.

"Would you mind withdrawing them so that the humans may survive for at least a few days?" Prometheus stood up from his seat to face his brother.

Epimetheus looked up from his magnifying lens, which was focused eagerly on the butt of the baboon, "Pardon?"

"They cannot seem to coexist, and I need you to exterminate your creatures so that the humans may at least have a chance to survive," Prometheus said with punctuation. He was out of ideas.

"I can't do that," Epimetheus returned to gently painting the baboon's ass.

Prometheus stepped away from the desk, placing his fist to his forehead. He, for the first time, felt bested by his brother at the game of thoughtfulness. What burned him the most was that his brother was simply more speedy and steadfast in his ideas than Prometheus was. The ideas were not of sense at times and mirrored some madman's attempt at producing whatever first arose in his mind, but his brother did produce much and often.

"Are you actually mad? How could I just go up to any one of my breeds and just simply wish them out of existence?" Epimetheus hardly ever reconsidered his deeds. "If you would accept my help, I could certainly help you design a skeleton that would be better suited for survival. How long have I been insisting that your humans need a tail, for example?"

"I don't want a tail! Do you have a tail? You certainly do not, for you would have learned of times to tuck it between your legs," Prometheus returned, inflamed.

It was not long before Prometheus had taken a mold of one of Epimetheus's creations and thrown it through the window of their room.

"That was my cow!" Epimetheus ran to the edge of the window.

"I thought it was just an empty lump of clay," Prometheus began to cower in guilt and sweat.

Epimetheus cursed repeatedly under his breath as he looked down the window at the great height of clouds his cow had fallen through. "You'd better hope there is a way to salvage this."

"I will find a way," Prometheus ran out of the room, still annoyed.

He later found and scooped the lump of cow off the flat land it had fallen onto, shielding it from the humans' eyes. Pushing animals off high places could've been a useful tactic for humans to learn, but it wouldn't have proven mighty helpful in the face of Epimetheus's deadly predators that roamed the land.

Prometheus had no clue what to do with the cow to save it from seeming utterly destroyed. If Epimetheus saw it like that, it could've ruined their brotherly bond for maybe forever. Prometheus, in his panic, thought of one entity he could turn to, someone who shared the brothers' interests for creativity and manufacturing, Hephaestus. The reason he referred to him as an entity was that sometimes it would slip one's mind that Hephaestus was a God after all. He would keep himself scrunched over and dirtied in his forge, working away in that chamber of steam and clangor. The burnt scruff on Hephaestus's face rendered him almost a cyclops, but naturally with two eyes instead of one. He possessed two of the best hands at his craft compared to any God or Titan. While Hephaestus and Prometheus were craftsmen in varying fields, they both shared a care for the nuances of their craft. Prometheus had often spent evenings in Hephaestus's forge, receiving feedback on his design for the human body. Hephaestus had been delighted to be consulted on the design of something so novel. It had taken him time to speak up, but he was shocked when he was actually treated with value when it came to his time and expertise on the matter of bending, shaping, heating, and cooling. Prometheus credited his friend for the way he learned to attune the human body to adjust its internal temperature. By forging humankind, something strange happened in the minds of intellectuals such as Prometheus, Hephaestus, and even Epimetheus; they learned more about how they themselves worked. Through Hephaestus's conjecture on heat, Prometheus learned the reason why the God and he sweat profusely in the hot forge and why their bodies needed to sweat to cool themselves. Since the master blacksmith had taught Prometheus so much, he thought of him often when he struggled or needed a second mind in exception to his brother.

Hephaestus turned the cow over and around, inspecting its tiny hooves and stubby legs. He blew air into the creature with his forge blower and saw inside its mouth, groveling at Epimetheus's decision to give the cow such an intricate stomach.

"It's a sturdy creature," Hephaestus bellowed. "It will graze on grass all day long and still not fill up. It should not be hard to replicate, I'm sure. The udders are low hanging, very low hanging."

"It's another one of my brother's oddities. Do you see any irreparable harm?" Prometheus asked, pacing back and forth.

"It should be just fine. Your brother has really given this creature everything: fat, bones, meat, hide, and this skin shall make just a fine material if I could see it through," Hephaestus had a glint in his eye.

Prometheus spotted that look and saw Hephaestus see promise in the cattle and see promise in Epimetheus. To Hephaestus, Prometheus pondered, he must have been just a distraction. Maybe Epimetheus had built a truly marvelous creature, but Prometheus wanted to find a way to tame it and bring it under his control. He knew he couldn't label the creation as his own. However, if he could lead it to humankind, then it may as well be his own. They could abuse it for all they could ever need. Yet, this couldn't be what humankind was missing. This was one way that he could take a step over his brother, but this was not the redeeming gift that would place humankind as the superior race in the land of the mortals and make them predators among Epimetheus's prey.

Prometheus looked past his friend and saw his forge and the fire burning within it. As Hephaestus wandered off to a workbench, Prometheus was left gazing into the flames that danced in the hearth. The fire crackled, and the cinders gave a persuasive glow, shifting their weight to support the flame that stood over them. The coal was not just fuel but the pillars upon which this heated monument stood. He had sat there and watched his friend many times in the past thrust his forceps into the pit with an item of his creation. His creation would return from the flames with a deceptively red hue that could burn a hole through Olympus itself and cast the world in flames. The tool would then be submerged in water, and a loud hiss would sound and fill the workshop with steam. Hephaestus possessed the hottest forge in all of existence. With it, he had forged the legendary weapons that had been wielded by the Gods and their allies during the Great War.

Prometheus tilted his head slightly with a devious thought. Would the Gods have succeeded in defeating the Titans without their arms? Was it merely these forged weapons that had granted the Gods the sharp edge over the Titans during the Great War? Prometheus knew the answer was no, but the question made him wonder what exactly the humans could achieve with weapons of such advancement by their side. Prometheus gathered that without his lightning bolt, even Zeus was far more susceptible to his foes. As Prometheus imagined the steam disappearing from his mind and leaving him in the open and exposed space, he left the forge with an idea that would continue to brew with him.

Up the stairs and into the grand hall of Olympus sat some fair Gods and Prometheus's simple-minded brother chatting over ever-flowing goblets of wine. A simple muse, the company delighted over a topic that mattered not to Prometheus. He stood there with urgency, while the likes of those fools sat there giggling and burping. Apollo would say a line, and Hermes would reply with a chortle, blowing bubbles into his wine. Epimetheus sat there with some semblance, at least, as he fidgeted with his goblet with one hand and with the other two clay figures, two long and skinny creatures. Through their gurgles and guffaws, Prometheus rolled his eyes and heard his brother lamenting the cow. Prometheus had come there to speak reason, to strategize, and gather wisdom on where weapons stood in his long-standing plan for creation.

"It has not been but one hour since we last spoke, and you are here drowned in wine," Prometheus lamented at his brother.

"Prometheus, you have finally joined us! Shame that you did not foresee this in your plans," Hermes raised his goblet with a smile.

"Yes, yes! Wise one, you abandoned us for too long. Perhaps a hymn could've caught your ear and brought you to frolic with us," Apollo sat spitting wine through his mouth. He then lifted his lyre from next to him onto his thigh and struck it with his graceless hand.

"Wow, wow, wow. How nice, brother," Hermes moved his head in rhythm.

"Come with me. I must talk to you," Prometheus leaned in toward Epimetheus.

"Why would I go with you?" Epimetheus leaned back with a scowl.

"Why would he return with you? Epimetheus informed us that you mutilated his cow." Hermes slung his arm over Epimetheus's shoulder. "I may not know what a cow is, but he will stay here with us. Plus, he says he shall fashion something just for us."

"Epimetheus, please. Hephaestus is examining the cow. He says it's remarkably sturdy and well-made, and it shall be fine. I have matters I must discuss with you," Prometheus placed both his fists on the table, looking toward his brother sitting below.

Apollo strung his lyre again and gathered into song, "*The brothers of fate...*"

"I seek your urgent and wise counsel," Prometheus attempted to appeal to his brother.

"*Tricked by their thought,*" Apollo sang.

"I am mad at you, brother. I know you—" Epimetheus spoke, dangerously pointing at his brother.

"*Knowing is my trait,*" Apollo struck a wrong chord.

"I know you think I'm not as smart as you, not as clever as you, not anything compared to you, but look at what I've made and look at what you have not," Epimetheus squinted.

"I sang that on the spot," Apollo exchanged a chuckle with Hermes.

"How dare you?" Prometheus furrowed his brow.

"How dare I, brother? How dare you think I am so incompetent and always beneath you?" Epimetheus rose from his seat and matched eyes with his brother.

"*One came before, the other came after. One took to soar, the other took to laughter. The brothers were united as a whole, until one was left as the sole,*" Apollo sang at the top of his lungs.

Prometheus banged the table between them, "I will not have you speak to me in this manner!"

Epimetheus returned the bang, "I will do as I desire!"

Prometheus hammered the table with anger, "You would be nothing without me!"

As Epimetheus went to copy, the clay figures flew out of his hand and flew at his brother. The long and skinny creatures both tangled around Prometheus's neck and, with a strong thrust, yanked him to the floor, leaving Prometheus gasping for breath and becoming slowly asphyxiated by his brother's creations.

Prometheus lay writhing on the floor, kicking the bench and table with his feet. Spit drooled out of his mouth as he attempted to pull these thick ropes off his neck. Their slimy and slippery skin left Prometheus with nothing to dig his fingers into. When he attempted to grab them whole and thrust them off, they squeezed tighter around Prometheus's throat and made him let out a yelp. He felt them pressing against his windpipe, slowly crushing it with their powerful force. Prometheus rolled left and right, attempting to use the movement to cast the creatures off. He pulled again and again, and nothing seemed to work. He had dug his hands into the skin against his neck in an attempt to create some space between him and the creatures atop him. As he lay on his back with the ropes squeezing the light out of his eyes, he made out an image of his brother standing at the table, frozen in the darkness. Epimetheus had always been quick to act, but here his inaction appeared to be a deliberate choice. With his sadness, Epimetheus had chosen to just watch on. Prometheus let go of the creatures and reached toward his brother.

Epimetheus then suddenly awakened, lunged beside his brother's red face, and attempted to pull off the ropey creatures. Both of them gave a strong and slow pull.

"I'm sorry. I'm sorry," Epimetheus cried beneath his breath as he tried to help his brother from death. "I'm sorry, brother. I never meant this."

No matter how strongly they pulled, they couldn't achieve it. They felt a gap of millimeters begin to form until the creatures came down harder against Prometheus's neck, squeezing and wrenching the remaining life from his eyes. With the sound of cracking bones, Epimetheus continued with his desperate whispers and pulls to yank his brother alive. He attempted to cast off these serpents, but he could not. Prometheus's bulging eyes began to lose sight and gave a lasting glassy look toward Epimetheus until they began to shut.

With a sound coming from behind Prometheus, Epimetheus looked up toward an opening door, in tears.

"What is this?" It was the voice of a woman. "Apollo, put down your lyre, and Hermes, help them!" She yelled, and so the Gods sprang into action.

Apollo gently set down his lyre and took up his bow and pointed two arrows at the serpents.

"No, don't!" Epimetheus yelled.

Apollo's shot did not miss. The shot did not pierce the serpents but ricocheted off them and weakened their grasp on Prometheus's neck. Prometheus's eyes came to, filled with water, as he gave a sharp and prevailing breath and began to pull the serpents off with his brother's aid. Next, Hermes threw his staff toward the desperate brothers. It was a thieving miracle; the serpents abandoned Prometheus's neck and crawled onto Hermes's staff. There the serpents remained, slithering over the staff and giving way to peace.

"Thank you, thank you," Epimetheus looked around him and uttered to everyone.

Prometheus fought his breathing and closed his eyes. He placed his hands over his neck, feeling his caved-in throat. As he breathed, he felt blood and spit come to the sides of his lips. Suddenly, his head was coursing with blood. He began to feel woozy and cold.

The footsteps of Hermes sounded next to Prometheus's head as he took up his newly decorated staff. Prometheus attempted to utter gratitude with the harsh dullness of his voice. Nothing came but more spittle and blood.

"You lot of dullards, come with me," the woman commanded and led the Gods away. She stopped after some steps and looked back at Epimetheus, "You must come too! You all must present yourself to

Zeus and tell him about your stupid mistake."

"Stupid mistake?" Hermes said with utter disagreement.

"Zeus?" Apollo suddenly began to sober himself.

"Please, grant me one second, Queen Hera," Epimetheus remained against his collapsed brother. He knelt further onto Prometheus and stroked his hair, "I love you, brother. I'm gravely sorry. I hope you can find it in your heart to forgive me." Epimetheus spoke under his breath, covering his mouth from further embarrassing himself in front of the Olympians.

"That is enough," Hera commanded. "Come."

Epimetheus rose, wiping the tears from his face, and trailed after the arguing Olympians who climbed the steps to where Zeus resided.

Prometheus gave himself further time to recapture his breath. He did not acknowledge or watch the departing party. With the gift of immortality, he felt the bones and muscles in his neck slowly begin to repair, but he remained impaired with the pain that lingered. Slowly, one layer after another, the muscles seemed to weave over each other and reassemble, filling Prometheus's hands where he had felt his neck dented. The solidifying of the bone gave no sound, but gave Prometheus the ability then to finally move his head and drop it back toward the floor. A wincing of pain escaped Prometheus from his breath. He dropped his arms to his side and touched the marble floor, feeling its coolness. The hard touch of the floor cradled the crown of his head. As the coldness of the floor entered him, Prometheus could not help but still feel the flight of blood through his head and body. For a moment, he felt almost no weight to his body. Then, slowly, as he began to tremble with the flooding of blood into its respective corners of his body, he felt the terrifying thought that had almost become his reality.

Tears stretched from the sides of his eyes, down his face, and onto the floor. Prometheus thought about death and how close it had once again come. He put his hand above his mouth and stifled his crying. A fearful fate that his brother had almost brought upon him,

Prometheus could still feel the tightness in his throat. His body bobbed up and down as he further choked on tears. With his eyes closed and overflowing with water, he couldn't help but imagine the slain Titans that lay on the battlefield. Helios was chained by his neck. Prometheus's younger, powerful, and raging brothers, Atlas and Menoetius, were held down by the might of Poseidon and Hades. His father, Iapetus, lay paralyzed and pierced by a spear, almost as if he were truly dead. The body of Cronus had been cut into small bits, and Gaia burned in the aftermath of the Great War. Prometheus had stood above them all, practically unscathed and having secured a seat among the generation of rule to come. All for what? He stood there in his lonely apparel. Even Epimetheus had been enchanted by the lust for war, but Prometheus stood there alone in his grief. During those moments, he came to understand that thought was his only solace. His thoughts would never abandon him.

As he lay alone on the floor, he returned his hands to the cold marble and further gave way to his senses to bring himself back to his reality. He smelled the stink of spilled wine. He tasted the blood on his lips. He heard what faintly sounded to be the crackle of fire among the large and empty fortress. The subtle whisper of a flame reached his ears. For a moment, Prometheus wondered, what was this delusion? In his time of near-death, he heard the fire that had just earlier teased him and enticed him to bring destruction into the hands of the humans. His ears felt hot at this thought. The loose hand of his brother had nearly brought death upon him, and Prometheus shuddered at the thought of what humans could become with fire to forge their weapons, just as the Gods had. Wherever Zeus struck with lightning, he left a flame burning to engulf its surroundings. Prometheus opened his eyes and saw the angular white ceiling above him. Still in his ears and mind burned the sound of fire. In the emptiness of the hall, the fire became more pronounced, and its allure almost echoed. Following the trail of fire with his ears, Prometheus further extended his head back and exposed his neck to the ceiling. Through the doors that had brought Hera, a small hearth stood against the back of a dark room.

Prometheus felt some relief at the confirmation that there was a hearth, but the longer he watched the flames burn upside down, the more lightheaded he became. Deep within the dark room, which had been closed off to the other guests in the hall, was the hearth and the fire within it. The fire seemed to almost shine.

Prometheus returned his head flat to the surface, mulling over whether to approach the hearth and whether anything could be gained of it this time. He had shaken his head clear of fire, but here it was shining at him through the dark. Turning to his side, he slowly brought his arms and legs underneath him and helped himself rise. For a moment, it felt as if he had forgotten how to walk, but he eventually approached the hearth and then again sat down beside it, thudding onto the floor.

This place was far different from Hephaestus's forge. Where the brutalism lacked, there was color and warmth that radiated from the interior of the room and the stone-lined hearth. While Hephaestus's fire was crude and served as the central focus of his unrelenting environment, this fire softly accentuated the tenderness of the small room. It diffused its hospitality along the walls and carpets. The shining light existed in a perfect harmony with its surroundings, giving it rich and mellow meaning that fed back into the silent serenity that Prometheus felt sitting by the singing flames. He held his hands toward the flames and felt them caressed with warmth. He brought his fire-kissed hands to his neck and cheeks and felt himself further healed by the heat, relieving himself with a humble sigh.

Just as Prometheus's mind began to simmer over the fire, in the flames he saw the face of the woman who sat behind him in this dark room. Her face seemed oddly familiar but obscured and protected from his gaze. There had been a subtle shift in the flames and how they carried their warmth through the room that made Prometheus recognize the soul that sat behind him and felt the fire like him, but also gave way to the fire.

Prometheus went to turn, "I'm so sorry. I believed I was secluded—"

"Do not turn!" The flames shot high in the face of Prometheus.

Prometheus paused and returned to his seat, facing the orders of the flame. "I will remain. I'm sorry," he uttered, feeling the hoarseness and itch in his throat that remained.

The fire sat with him. The woman's face appeared more clearly within it. "No one is allowed to be in my midst. However, I heard what happened to you, and I will allow you to sit and rest by my flame." Then, with some shyness, she followed, "Just for a moment, however. No longer."

"Thank you… May I ask how to refer to you properly?" Prometheus did not recognize this apparition, and yet he spoke to it with kindness.

"Hestia," the fire answered.

"I have heard of you, dear Goddess, but I believe I've never seen you at the council with the other Olympians," Prometheus had heard just whispers of her name before, as if she were a secret kept by the Gods.

"I requested King Zeus for eternal maidenhood. Therefore, here I remain bound under his command, unreachable from the hands of any man," Hestia shared.

Prometheus felt a slight twinge above his eye as he worried about what punishment he might endure if Zeus were to learn about this encounter. "Shall it be best if I were to leave, now?"

Hestia hesitated, "You may heal yourself before you go, if you would like."

Prometheus quickly moved his hands toward the hearth again as he sensed the fire burning stronger and felt the heat crawl up his wrists. "I must ask you, dear Goddess, do you maintain this flame?"

"I do. I am the Goddess of the hearth," Hestia humbly spoke.

"Your hearth is truly a gift. May I ask you, how do you fuel it?"

"Why do you seek to know?" Hestia spoke, mild-mannered.

"I have been granted the duty to create humankind by Zeus, and I have become lost in finding what gift to give humankind to ensure their survival. Most recently, I was exploring the possibility of fire. I believed that I understood fire from what I saw of it in the aftermath of the war and Hephaestus's forge, but this is completely different. The fire there felt tainted and almost designed for destruction, but your fire here is warm and nurturing."

Hestia held her tongue.

"I would not request this fire from you if you do not wish. Yet, I am simply curious. Why do your flames heal me so and make me feel the comfort almost of…" Prometheus trailed off, struggling to say.

"An embrace?" Hestia sang.

Prometheus's cheeks were filled with warmth as he nodded and thought of his brother caressing his head just moments earlier.

"Some do sit here, often seeking to find the same warm embrace of those close to them."

Prometheus thought of Hera, who had previously been in this room. Was she sitting by these flames thinking of Zeus, he thought. "Do you long for that as well?" Prometheus asked with curiosity.

The crackling of the fire filled the silence.

"I apologize for my insolence. I now recognize the tone with which my question may have come across. I did not intend for my message to—" Prometheus attempted to course correct.

"You are forgiven. You are curious and full of thought. Not always thoughtful, but certainly in thought," Hestia returned and then bit her tongue.

"Well, I'll certainly take that feedback—" Prometheus reacted with some offense.

"I'm sorry. Forgive me, I was just—"

"No, you have done nothing wrong. No need to apologize, dear Goddess. I asked my question only because I want to understand why your fire feels as it does. Is it because you seek that embrace as well, or are you so familiar with it that you can personify it here?" Prometheus returned to the crux of his interest.

"Before I became devoted to my solitary maidenhood, Apollo and Poseidon tried to vie for my hand. It was hard to live through their boisterous displays of affection and pride. It was also not what was meant to be for me." The fire stood still for a moment. "In truth, I don't know how to answer you. I'm sorry, you ask far too many perplexing questions of me. I am used to others thawing in front of my flames, but you are inflamed by them."

"I may be. When I stare deeply into you, I see the nurturance you hide inside. The way your flames cry and carry your warmth across their hands and onto their recipients," Prometheus reached closer to the hearth. "You spread your embrace onto them and offer them care and healing." He hovered in front of the dancing flames, watching them with a smile, as they slowly reached toward him now. Without an ounce of pain, the flames climbed onto Prometheus's hands and reached down his wrists and embraced his arms. "Your gentle embrace, you can share this with all of humankind." Prometheus looked down at his hands and thought, you can share this and, with it, give warmth, healing, courage, inspiration, and just something else that feels to be missing. Prometheus felt an absence of a singular thing as he felt the burning idea within his fingertips.

He looked up. This time, within the flames, he saw promise. He saw the towers and homes of humankind in the distant land of the future. Prometheus saw the torches of discovery running from one end of the world to the other. With fire, he saw the cauterizing of human flesh and the marking and cooking of cattle. And he also saw the brandishing of weapons, the sound of hammers, a trail of combustion, and he saw the humans launch burning rocks as high as Olympus. Explosions sounded in his faint dream as Prometheus began to, all of a sudden, feel his hands beginning to burn and smell the stink of singed hair. He went to drop the hot iron blade in his hands before realizing the fire was a part of him. The fire quickly grew further down his arms and began to consume his whole body. As if in wisps, the fire had latched onto his body from different parts and now crawled up his being, growing in size and strength. Fire grew in Prometheus's abdomen and chest, a heat far greater than any liquor. The fire stung so. When Prometheus went to yell in pain, he realized his mouth and voice became fire too. He screamed fire through the room as the fire engulfed his body, burning him away. Prometheus felt the heat off his own body as he fell back on the floor and writhed in his swollen state. What was pain became charred numbness, and Prometheus saw in his vision that he now lay hardened on the bloodied ground beside the dead Titans. The small bleeding pieces of Cronus lay in his vicinity, and above Prometheus stood Zeus with his lightning bolt. A flash of lightning accompanied the sound of Zeus's yell, and Prometheus sank into ashes, becoming smaller than what remained of any being.

"You are consumed by fire," Hestia whispered.

Prometheus suddenly awoke on the floor of the dark room. He frantically checked his body and saw he was clear of fire or burns, but lay breathing heavily and covered in sweat. His chest rose and fell as he saw Hestia's hearth grow with her voice.

"You seek fire to destroy!" Hestia had suddenly turned the dark room into light. "Just like the others, you see into it and envision doom."

"No!" Prometheus quickly shielded his face. "In the fire, I also see you. I see you spreading warmth and cheer into every home. Through every hearth and pit, you accompany them. You give them light in the darkness. You give them sustenance. You enrich their embrace, the lonely ones who suffer not just alone but in their minds and hearts. Some may inevitably seek to stoke your fires and use the burning coals for their gain, as one may do to survive. But others will let you breathe, they will watch you burn, sitting with their families and looking into all your beautiful colors. They will dance as your flames do until they are no more, but in the soul of the burnt coal and ashes."

Hestia's fire halted.

"You allowed me a seat, and so I ask you to offer one to the lonely child I see wandering through the dark woods," Prometheus finally realized that fire was meant to be the gift. "So that she, who is alone, may heal and not suffer alone without knowing the gift that is warmth and a gentle embrace in the coldest of nights."

"And what if they misuse me?" Hestia wavered.

"They may, but I have seen into the hearts of the humans, and they know no better than what we show them. I swear to you, dear Goddess, I will be their earnest father and teach them with a watchful and caring gaze. No more will I scrutinize their mistakes or lead with envy, but let them breathe and live as they would see fit. As I said earlier, I would not take from you without your permission. I will not betray you. I will protect you, and I will tend to you."

Hestia began to dim. In the dying of the flame, Prometheus made out tears in the hearth.

"In my confined pit, I sit. I give myself to you, Titan. In the hope that your creation and hope may save us all and release us from our bounds," Hestia stated and became a gentle blue flame, as small as a wick.

Prometheus felt the compulsion to nod, bow, and come to tears in his sweat-covered state. In gratitude, he approached the flame more gently this time as if he himself was the humble receiver of a gift. In his hands, he took the blue flame of Hestia, protected from the heat and filled with grace for its host. As he turned his back and went to leave the room, he felt the hearth ignite behind him and knew what he held in his hands was the heart of the fire.

On his knees, Prometheus presented this fire to Zeus. In tears and sweat, Prometheus conveyed to Zeus the promise of fire and the promise of humankind. With his head bowed, Prometheus shielded and protected the hidden form of Hestia. Prometheus looked up at the all-mighty Zeus, who smiled on his throne, and received the gift of fire to pass on to humankind.

The brothers looked toward the sky to hear the call of the same great eagle, suddenly apparent and urging the brothers to climb the mountain. Behind the eagle, Prometheus peered at darker clouds beginning to move toward them.

"So what do you think?" Epimetheus regained Prometheus's attention.

"What do you mean?" Prometheus wanderingly replied,

returning from his reverie.

"You're telling me that you didn't hear any of what I said," Epimetheus knew.

"No… what did you say?" Prometheus questioned.

"You are lost in your head again!" Epimetheus suddenly stopped and swung to smack Prometheus on the backside of his head.

"What was that for?" Prometheus stopped himself. "I'm sorry."

"Whatever," Epimetheus now carried forward on the trail beside his brother.

"What was it that you were actually talking about?" Prometheus tried to make it up to his brother.

"Just how Zeus is such a bitch."

"Watch your tongue!" Prometheus stopped and attempted to put his hand on Epimetheus's mouth. "What are you saying? You shouldn't be saying things like that."

"Why? He is. I will never forgive that bastard," Epimetheus had caught Prometheus's hand.

"Stop it. As I said earlier, the winds carry our words, and you must watch what you say." Prometheus covered Epimetheus's mouth with his other hand.

Epimetheus wrestled Prometheus's hand off his mouth, "What does it matter? Everyone has something foul to say about him. You forget about his wife? Hera is constantly nagging at him."

"That doesn't give us the right to join them. Also, you seem to forget that we are Titans. We do not have the privilege of the Gods or even the spirits. Our kind is marked in his eyes."

"We are marked and unfairly so," Epimetheus released Prometheus's hands. "Now that we have finished with the creation of the moral creatures, we must consider what is next for us."

Prometheus was shocked to hear Epimetheus wondering about the future. Epimetheus kept strolling forward.

"Why are you worrying about the future?" Prometheus followed with stress in his brow.

"As I said, we have fulfilled our purpose to him. As much as I enjoy delighting in drinking and the festivities, I recognize this gives us the agency and freedom to bring our attention to something else," Epimetheus spoke with sternness. "I still possess the unrivaled anger that I felt back then, from watching the injustice our father and brothers endured. The age of Gods will not last forever, and we must find a way to wrestle our kind free and find longevity in this world."

"Are you mad?" Prometheus felt the stress fill his body. He clenched his fists. "I share the same sentiments as you do about our kind, but we were smart enough to survive. We cannot risk what freedom we have earned for the slight hope of gaining the power we used to possess. We made the mortal world, and now we must tend to it."

"My creatures are free to run wild as they wish. Maybe you should grant the same trust to yours. Place your focus on something bigger." Epimetheus extended his hands. "Brother, you are a master of risk and cleverness. I need you by my side as we traverse through the rest of time and this age of rule."

Prometheus turned forward in frustration. Epimetheus kept looking at his brother, hoping that his brother would hear him. The summit of the mountain was still far, but Prometheus wanted to reach it already and return to the comfort of his usual worries, in his study and in the villages. He had worked hard at this thing to create, and now he was merely entering the next chapter of what humanity could achieve. Nothing within him wanted to change his aim. The humans had taken only their first steps and begun to walk. Prometheus would ensure that, one day, this mountain shall be their playground.

In the distance, Prometheus suddenly began to see two figures forming out of the haze and traversing down the path toward them. Typically, Prometheus's vision allowed him to see far, but here it was obscured by his worries and daydreams.

"As I said earlier, watch your tongue. We can discuss this later. For now, someone is approaching," Prometheus felt his heart beginning to race. He began to worry about who would cross their path.

"It's probably just some nymphs," Epimetheus shrugged.

Prometheus wasn't convinced, "Or it could be a pair of Olympians who heard you or were ordered here by Zeus, all because of your tongue."

"There's no way. Besides, we pose no danger, and we are well acquainted with the Olympians," Epimetheus smirked.

"You may think so." Prometheus felt his breath beginning to lunge ahead of him with adrenaline. "Be prepared for whatever it may be."

Prometheus's heart kept racing at the thought of who these mysterious figures could be and what unforeseen reason the brothers were crossing paths with them at this instance. Fate was hardly what Prometheus credited such events to, but careful and elaborate planning and execution. And just maybe, these two figures weren't alone, and what would appear around the brothers would be even more Olympians and foes, leading an ambush to make the brothers atone for their conspiracy, rebellion, and for the fact that they were Titans. There certainly had been some truth to what Epimetheus had said; they had eroded their purpose set forth by Olympus. Zeus had enacted vengeance against Prometheus once, and he would easily do so again. This time, the vengeance would perhaps be even more deadly, in the form of the looming storm above the peak. As the figures appeared closer, Prometheus made out that one figure was larger than the other, while the smaller figure wore something on his back, a round shield perhaps. His mind began to ruminate on all that he knew that might match this description.

"I see a shield on one of them," Prometheus whispered to his brother. "The smaller one may be Ares, but the other one I can't decipher."

"I see," Epimetheus began to smile. "And on the other, I see the torso of a man and the body of a horse. Chiron!" Epimetheus began to wave from afar.

Prometheus dropped his arms to his side and froze as the wind carried Epimetheus's echo to those ahead of them. Then, slowly as the sound approached them, the larger figure waved his hand above his head and greeted the two brothers.

"Why would you do that?" Prometheus began to rapidly reassemble himself. "Why would he send Chiron and whoever that is? It can't be Apollo beside him, surely. He wouldn't carry a shield. Hermes has never been one for Chiron's company. I doubt Ares could stand him either. Who is that? It can't be Him in a different form, can it?"

"Brother, shut it. You worry too much. It's simply Chiron and some man. You're right, he's wearing a shield, but it's wooden. He carries a rusty sword at his side, and he looks young, meek."

"It can't be just a human," Prometheus rubbed his eyes to try to regain his focus. He looked again and saw the figures appear closer. He saw the man, as per Epimetheus's description, by the great centaur's side.

The centaur began to race toward them, as did the man. Prometheus began to reach for the dagger at his belt, as Epimetheus further waved his arms above his head. In a blink, Chiron had arrived, slowing his trot just ten feet ahead of them. The man was still running toward them. By the time Prometheus saw Chiron in front of him, he had stuttered and completely failed to accurately reach for his dagger, missing it and then letting his arm dangle back awkwardly. Chiron made note of this.

"Master Titans, it is pleasant to see you both," Chiron bowed his head. It was rare to see centaurs bow their head.

"Chiron, it is nice to see you," Epimetheus said and properly shook his hand. "You must tell us what brings you here. What fate do we owe this random encounter to?"

Chiron and Epimetheus entered into an exchange as Prometheus felt beside himself for his poor and irrational judgment. How could I be so stupid? He grasped his head. This worry is unwieldy, he realized his mouth was agape, and his brow was covered in sweat. These sudden, untrustworthy moments had recently brought

Prometheus almost to a panic. Unlike his brother, Prometheus felt he truly did have some misdeed to hide, not just words but something he had carried out.

Chiron's eyes fell on Prometheus, "Are you okay, Master Prometheus?"

Prometheus slowly drifted his attention to Chiron, "Forgive me, Master Centaur. I cannot define what illness has taken me, but I share my brother's cheer in seeing you again." Prometheus approached Chiron and, with a limp hand, greeted the wise master who stood in front of him. "It's very nice to see you, sir. You must tell us of the adventures you have found. We haven't spoken with you since you broke from your herd."

Chiron was the first of his kind, but unlike the rest of his kind. The centaurs were known for being wild, stubborn, and quick to anger. They enjoyed their liquor and, even more so, partaking in the hunt and savagery that accompanied their raids on human villages or the homes of nymphs. Because of Chiron's unique nature and history, Prometheus shared a rather interesting bond with him. The man who had birthed Chiron was Cronus. Titan blood flowed through Chiron, and in many ways, Prometheus saw himself as similar to Chiron. They were unlike their kind, and both had taken on a thoughtfulness and care for their craft. However, Prometheus was sure that Chiron was by far a much better master of all crafts than he was. And while Prometheus had employed his thought to align with Zeus during the Great War, Chiron had remained neutral and watched from afar, still earning the reputation and favor he had from all—or most—beings in the world. The reputation that he held was one of respect, for being a master of integrity, kindness, humility, and unconditional regard for others. Those who had seemed not to care for Chiron included his herd, who had seen debauchery and storm clouds at their birth. Yet, even Chiron had known strife in his own right. He had been abandoned by his mother at birth for being a horrid and ugly creature, the first of his kind. Cronus did not accept him, for Chiron was born out of an affair. Cronus's wife, Rhea, opposed the existence of another child that the Titan of time would eat away. So Chiron became the immortal creature he was, sitting idly at his home on Mount Pelion. Chiron eventually found the company of the Goddess Artemis, who encountered him while on a hunt. Upon realizing Chiron's delicate nature, Artemis helped raise him alongside her brother, Apollo. As Chiron came of age, the pair of Olympians watched him cast off into the wilderness. Alongside further exploring himself, he sought society and community. When his herd abandoned him for his morally just ways, he searched the planes until he uncovered Prometheus's creations. Chiron became a teacher to them and, at times, a doctor, protector, and even a judge. For all these roles and attributes, the humans came to see Chiron with warmth and strength. Prometheus, in many ways, longed for that as he had continued to watch the humans from afar.

"I've been fortunate enough to help the humans with their everyday quandaries," Chiron provided gratitude to Prometheus.

"You've strayed far from your home. Why? Why do you not spend more time with us, or even the Gods?" Epimetheus scratched his head.

"Not that I don't enjoy what you speak of, Master Epimetheus, but humans have a great need for help everywhere, and I have been fortunate enough to earn their trust," Chiron raised his posture.

"I'm indebted to you," Prometheus looked up at Chiron.

"I am indebted to you, Master Prometheus. We all owe this gift to you and your ingenuity," Chiron humbly spoke.

"No," Prometheus felt he owed the credit to many others for the creation of humankind. "How has it been?"

"It has been well. They are making steady progress. You should be proud. We are all fortunate that fire has been gifted to us again," Chiron looked toward the man running now. "My friend, running there, can certainly share with you some of the horrors they faced without the fire."

"Who is that?" Epimetheus looked over at the running boy.

Chiron chuckled, "I'll allow him to make his own introduction.

He is well and capable of doing so, if you grant him patience."

Prometheus was caught in some shock by Chiron's statement. He wondered if Chiron knew the circumstances under which, after Prometheus had brought fire to humankind, Zeus had stripped it away. Prometheus had passed on the gift of Hestia to humankind. He had built her a temple, allowing her to pass on the knowledge of fire to humankind, and he had sat there admiring her burn in the temple's mantel. He had seen this gift bring prosperity to humankind and watched them thrive and dance around the fire. Prometheus had smiled most when seeing Hestia burn with joy, free from the captivity of her royal prison. However, Prometheus felt himself incapable of joining in the dance. All he had known was thought, and the act of creation had exhausted him. He came to struggle with a fear of the foreign experience, which he felt himself challenged to navigate. Whenever he tried to stand and dance, he felt himself paralyzed in place and distrusting of what this action would bring without giving it the calculated thought he had given everything.

The fires had brightly burned in this sunny valley, even at night, until Zeus felt himself recoil at humankind's cheer and came to Prometheus demanding sacrifice. He had acted as the all-mighty and powerful ruler over all and exacted a price for the burning gift he had permitted onto humankind. In Zeus's eyes, this was his kingdom, his rule, his creations, his gift, and his pleasure. Long gone were the days when Zeus had sought freedom for the world from the grasp of the Titans and Cronus's stomach. Zeus, now, walked Olympus with displeasure in his steps and a pain in his head. Some blamed Hera, who continued to row with his ear, but whenever Zeus spoke now, there came the sound of thunder. During a rather strange council with Prometheus, Zeus had looked down at him with lightning in his eyes and demanded that there be a sacrifice from humankind.

The running man slid to a stop in the beaten dirt path. He hunched over and held onto his knees while panting for breath, "My… my… apologies. That was… a long… distance."

"Brave job," Chiron stated, patting the man on his back.

"While you recover, let me introduce our guests."

"Normally, others do not bow to me, but yours is welcome. I am the Titan, Epimetheus, son of Iapetus and Clymene," Epimetheus put his hands at his hip.

"Wow, I've never met a Titan before. It's an honor, sir. Chiron has educated me on who you are," the man still recovered his breath and spoke with a pain in his abdomen. "Many of my kind don't know that we owe our lives to you, but I do. I'm indebted to you, sir."

Chiron cleared his throat, "I think you're mistaken—"

Epimetheus laughed, "I do like this treatment, but you've got the wrong man."

"I do?" The man looked confused.

"I am Prometheus," Prometheus spoke softly and looked at the tired man.

The man looked at him for a breath with what appeared to be hesitation. Then he dropped onto his knees and clasped his hands toward Prometheus, "Please forgive me, sir Titan! I humbly apologize. I understand if you wish to punish me for my foul deed."

Epimetheus laughed as Prometheus struggled to find what to say. Prometheus looked down at the man, then up at Chiron, and across to his bumbling brother. He outstretched his hands as if wanting to help the man up, but remained trapped in place, with his jaw open, and a frog in his throat.

Chiron looked to Prometheus for some signal. Upon seeing his continued disarray, Chiron gently tapped the man, "Get up. Master Prometheus is not one to take grave offense. Is that right?"

Prometheus croaked, "No. Yes, I am not offended."

Chiron helped the man up and dusted off his robes, "Mistakes are common. We have all made them, and it's ill befitting to cower with them. Stand and accept your fate."

The man slowly raised his red face, "You're right, Chiron. I embarrass you and your teachings and, for that, I apologize." The man locked eyes with Prometheus. "Master Prometheus, forgive me, for I am a mere mortal with limited knowledge of this world. We, humans, don't know much about the affairs of Olympus nor the Titans, but we're slowly learning. It's only with your will that we've succeeded thus far. And it's with your will that we will continue forth, putting our mistakes behind us and working to honor you and perfect human nature. I began by crawling until I learned to walk, tumbling many times. With steady steps underneath me, I learned to run. Now, I am scaling the Caucasus. Without your hands and—I must insist—Chiron's teachings, I wouldn't be standing where I am, where all I have been, and where all I hope to go. I am Hero, one of the many humans you created. I stand in your shadow, all your shadows, and I am honored to share that we all possess shadows. May we greet each other, in another attempt, with grace."

Epimetheus broke the silence, "Chiron, well, I must say, you've trained him rather well." Epimetheus patted Chiron on the back.

Chiron looked to Epimetheus, "Hero has certainly proven himself capable of learning, and showed all the marvelous traits that one hopes to find in a pupil."

"Where'd you find him?" Epimetheus asked Chiron, speaking not to Hero but of him.

"Epimetheus, you will find that we are not that much different from humans, you and I," Chiron moved toward Hero. "Come, Hero, we shall not disturb the Master Titans any longer. Let us carry on with your training."

Suddenly, Prometheus approached Hero, "It's an honor to meet you, Hero."

A smile took over Hero's face, and Hero grasped Prometheus in a hug. "This'll be the first of many meetings, Master Prometheus. I'm honored."

Epimetheus let out a breath from his mouth, attempting to disguise his laugh.

Prometheus didn't know how to receive this gesture, but let himself be taken by the hug. He grabbed Hero back, closing his eyes. In that moment, Prometheus felt discomfort, but he felt the same tether that he sensed when he stood on the edge of the hill observing and caring for humankind. In the hug, he sensed the same spark that he felt from across the bonfire at the dance.

When Prometheus released the hug, so did Hero. Prometheus looked at the man who mirrored him, "We both are scaling this mountain for the first time." Prometheus then looked to Chiron, "Shall we sit? Gray clouds approach us. Perhaps being covered with company shall make the storm easier to weather."

Chiron smiled back at the Prometheus he knew, who seemed to have finally taken control over his mind, "If you both see fit, we would be honored."

Epimetheus clapped his hands, "I suppose, why not? Tell us more about your adventures, Chiron."

"I shall lead the way. We passed a cave, just a bit up the path," Hero began to run back the way he had come.

Hero raced by himself at the head of the group. Chiron and Epimetheus followed him, exchanging pleasantries. Prometheus trailed, while his shadow once again trembled with worry. Underneath his smile and pleasant nature, Prometheus still lay in caution of the dark clouds approaching. The mysterious figures had shown their faces, but Prometheus felt the shaking dread that something terrible was afoot. Perhaps it was just the nerves he felt before a harsh rain, but he felt his head tense with the image of Zeus's demand for sacrifice. As he kept walking up the path, Prometheus itched the insides of his hands, feeling an emptiness where once he held the creativity for clay and passion for fire.

As Hero had said, he had done. He had led the party to a small cave off the path. Chiron had mindfully watched his way into the cave, which, given his stature, had presented a challenge. Once they had all gathered into the dimly lit space, Epimetheus had instinctively pulled a jar of wine from the satchel he wore.

Hero looked at this feat with fascination, "Wow. How is that possible?"

"What is?" Epimetheus followed after taking a sip. "Oh, we have Hephaestus to thank for this. He's the master blacksmith when it comes to weapons and wonderful contraptions such as this. My satchel can hold all the wine and treats I could want."

"That's fascinating," Hero's humble mind was stunned.

"Brother, may we have some fire?" Epimetheus gently looked at Prometheus.

Prometheus wanderingly gazed at Epimetheus. The emptiness in his hands felt heavier.

"I can make us a fire," Hero heralded.

"Hero, please! The request was not made of you," Chiron chided Hero.

"It's okay, Chiron," Prometheus still looked wanderingly into the disappearance of light. "Hero, proceed."

"Thank you, Master Prometheus," Hero whispered and maneuvered around the cave, fetching the old scraps left there by prior guests of the cave.

Epimetheus and Chiron became engaged in stories about all sorts of things related to Mount Pelion, Apollo, and Artemis, while Prometheus watched Hero engage in the intimate act of assembling the fire. Hero set some tinder down in the center of the cave. Prometheus held his breath from the sideline to examine with scrutiny Hero's handling of fire-making. As Hero spilled the dry grass from his hands, Prometheus imagined the sensation running through his own fingers. Prometheus's ears listened for the snapping and cracking of twigs stacked on the side. Hero built around the base a pyramid of kindling and wood, fixing the toppling wood pieces to stand in an arrangement together. While the scent of the dry wood was faint, Prometheus keenly focused on the pieces of wood in attempts to amplify the scent. Hero smiled, setting down the last of the firewood, feeling impressed with the structure he had built and excited for the striking nature of the next step. The sight of his smile disconcerted Prometheus; this wasn't meant to be a matter of enjoyment—it was meant to be serious. Hero held his flint with fierceness and with his other hand slowly aligned his steel fire striker. Prometheus watched the slight gap between the flint and steel and Hero behind it. Hero breathed in and struck the steel against the flint to spawn flying sparks. Prometheus sighed in relief at the sparks that flew away into the darkness. The clashing sound of flint and steel suddenly escaped from Hero's hands twice again in quick succession, catching Prometheus by surprise. Hero gritted his teeth at the annoying incompetence of his hands. Prometheus felt his ears become warm like the utensils Hero held in his hands. Hero slowly looked up and caught Prometheus's eyes and let out a quick breath, one that suggested a smile. Prometheus sat neatly with his hands in his lap and clenched his jaw, feeling fire emerge through his throat. Hero used his certainty to strike against the flint as whispering sparks invaded the tinder. He hunched even more over the tinder and blew into the dry weeds, casting a spell. Prometheus's lips lay slightly opened, hoping to cast the fire, but he was too late. Hero slowly closed his eyes and uttered a short prayer to the Goddess Hestia. Soon, the sparks took the fuel and began to erupt in height and weight, and a strong and lively fire stood at the center of the cave. Prometheus watched the spark that was born between Hestia and Hero: the gift Hestia had given Hero and their sweet exchange over the kindling of the flame. With this feat conquered, Hero slowly hobbled back away from the flame and took a seat, and enjoyed the gales of chatter with Epimetheus and Chiron.

The flame slowly began to blur in Prometheus's eyes as he began to picture Hestia sitting ahead of him and facing the fire. He saw the back of her head and her flowing auburn hair tied together. The bonfire cast a glow around her head, and Prometheus wanted to reach out and grab her. He hoped that she would slowly turn and that he would see the corner of her smile, inviting him toward her. She sat there almost lifeless, as he remembered. The more he thought of her, the more his head began to lighten and feel as if Prometheus's consciousness was slowly emerging out of his body, watching the back of his own head and Hestia sitting ahead of him. Almost as if a transparent cloud, he hovered above his thinning crown and felt himself beginning to detach and wander unknowingly. Away from the cave, out from within time, nowhere in specific, Prometheus wandered and dissociated.

Hero was warming his hands in the fire, "I hold high gratitude for these flames. Some say that you don't know the value of something until you've lost it, and these flames are something that I'll never take for granted again."

"Do you know why these flames were taken from you?" Epimetheus questioned.

"No." Hero turned to Chiron. "Why were they, Chiron?"

"I've failed to share this with you—" Chiron began to say.

"Zeus," Epimetheus said. "Just as with most torturous events, blame Zeus."

Hero's hands dropped, "Zeus, the mighty King of Olympus?"

"The one and only, he abandoned you," Epimetheus nodded at Hero.

"I assume it must've been some kind of test," Hero defended.

"No, he doesn't care about you. He doesn't care about humankind or anything mortal. He doesn't care about his own wife. He didn't care for his father. He doesn't care for anyone outside of himself," Epimetheus spoke in a low tone.

"How could you say that?" Hero raised his tone.

Epimetheus shrugged while taking a sip of wine.

"Chiron? Is this true?" Hero turned away from Epimetheus.

"Zeus banished almost all Titans. Understand that Master Epimetheus, here, may hold some resentment," Chiron crossed his arms.

"It's not some resentment, Chiron!" Epimetheus snapped and jerked forward his goblet, spilling wine beside himself. "You know all the kinds of beings he's forsaken. Zeus knows nothing but power and pleasure."

"Master Epimetheus, I would never speak out of turn with you. You are a Titan endowed with whatever you may wish to pass on to young Hero. But I must provide caution, Hero and the rest of humankind do not hold the same powers or protections you or I may possess, in the event of Zeus's wrath."

"I understand, Chiron," Epimetheus turned to Hero. "If it all comes to shit, I'll stand by humankind and the rest of the mortals. Just as Zeus began the Great War and took power from the Titans, there will be another war. There will be ruin. It's meant to be. If Zeus believes that Olympus will sit freely and unbothered, he is wrong. He's marked himself and his rule for ruin, and the ones with indignation will rise again and must do so together."

"How could you say such a thing?" Hero stood up. "He is our King. He freed us."

"Hero—" Chiron went to grab Hero.

"Freed us?" Epimetheus stood up, opposite Hero. "Tell me, by what means are you free? Or am I free?"

"I am free to—" Hero puffed out his chest.

"Hero—" Chiron lowered his voice.

"You are not free! We live under his rule. We do as he commands," Epimetheus pointed up. "You think I had a choice in the task he gave me? You think I could've objected and negotiated the terms of indentured servitude? You think you could've survived if it weren't for my cunning brother and me?"

Hero began to tremble.

"Zeus wanted to starve you. He wanted humankind to sacrifice all their game and resources to him and the Olympians. He wanted absolute fealty," Epimetheus pointed to Hero.

"Hero, sit," Chiron grabbed at Hero's robe and pulled him down.

"Zeus said he wanted humankind, but he soured quickly. He looked at you all with disgust and disdain. He wanted to see you snuffed out in a way that would cause pain, not just to you, but to me, my brother, Chiron, and all of us who have put our faith in you.

"He's insane! Think. A child abandoned in isolation, designed to be eaten, devoid of nurturance, with the jolt of lightning coursing through his veins, tore the world in half to find his kingdom. He didn't do so for the prosperity of the world. He wanted to wield power. He didn't expect to share his rule with his unruly siblings. So now he sits dismayed at the agency he sees others possess, the way he sees others take life into their own hands and believe they hold power too. Zeus believed that your race would have finally fulfilled his vision for power and fallen in line. That you would've given him the remembrance he so desires, but you all have defied him. Your very nature has refuted that which is his dream. You're born to marvel at the world around you and receive it with virgin eyes and gratitude. Your small stature has given you a greater sense of appreciation. While we Titans were born in accordance with the world, you have been offered it as a gift. We are one with it, and you are the humble recipients of it. The way you have raised societies, crafted weapons, and found your will sends a shiver down Zeus's spine. If you could be born with such mental faculties, then one day the occasion may come that you may rise above him and render no need for him.

"Therefore, he thought to punish you all. He thought to starve you and demand sacrifice of you, for you to pay tribute. If it weren't for my brother and me, that surely would've been your fate. Yet, we deceived him. We fooled him." Epimetheus laughed and took a sip of his wine. "We were the ones to deceive Zeus. We played his side during the war, and then we played him again to keep alive the subjects that will defeat him."

Hero watched Epimetheus, his eyes wide open.

Epimetheus bit his lip, "And you will defeat him. Won't you, Hero?"

Hero's mouth opened.

"You must. You will join us, won't you?" Epimetheus extended his goblet to Hero. "Because of us, you may feast on the best meat and wear a creature's hide, while Zeus chokes on the bones and drowns in fat, that big fat fool!"

Epimetheus turned his hand and mistakenly poured out the wine onto the fire that sat amongst the group. He reached to try to catch the wine, but he was too late. It trailed through his hands, and the fire sat snuffed. The remaining flames trembled before their knees collapsed, and they too fell into the pool of waste. Hero's pyramid fell by the beam as each log thudded onto the cave's floor. The room became submerged in darkness.

"For our deception, he took your flame," Prometheus stated, looking toward the extinguished flame. He had broken from his trance, "He punished you for our misdeed."

Hero's mind was whirring to grasp what the Titans had shared, "But the fire returned. Zeus returned it to us."

"I did," Prometheus confessed to his sin. "I stole the fire back and returned it to humankind."

Hero looked at Prometheus and heard a voice he recognized to be in dread, feeling almost as if a weight lay on his chest. Hero grabbed at his forehead and leaned forward, attempting to fathom what he understood of the fires and the skies. While he thought silently, his breathing began to accelerate.

"So what, brother?" Epimetheus broke the tension, looking at the dark silhouette of Prometheus. "We are Titans. We are now at the precipice of Zeus's downfall—"

"So what?" Prometheus looked up. "What we did was foolish and wrong."

"Foolish?" Epimetheus shifted his feet to face his brother. "What are you saying—"

"Yes, what we did was foolish and wrong!" Prometheus sat in silence while grasping his head.

Hero glanced up and saw, in the dark, a mirror cast Prometheus's silhouette onto him.

Prometheus brought his knees close to his chest and rose, "What I have done is something wrong. All my life, I have led with forethought, and every fatal choice I have arrived at with deceit. I attempted to carefully maneuver and try to guarantee the most ideal circumstances, but somewhere I have made a mistake. I don't know what else to justify the state of my mind. My head has been in pain, not often here, but to scrutinize every little detail and drive me into a cacophony of thought. I have thought so hard about everything. When I thought I was doing good and something of benefit, I am now clouded with guilt and dread. I've wronged you all. Perhaps if I were smarter, I could've prevented this, but I fear for us all. In every way I see this scenario, I see failure. And I'm so sorry I couldn't halt my ambitions. I wish I could've just sat with you all and warmed myself by the fire."

As Prometheus's words filled each small crack within the cave, the sound of thunder came from afar. Darkness cloaked them from the looming lightning that felt a distance away still, but they all sat aware of the storm approaching. They had gathered there to wait out the storm, and now they all sat in cover and silence.

Chiron sent his voice through the cave, "What is it you're saying, Master Prometheus?"

Prometheus turned to him, "Chiron, I can't shake this feeling." Out of Prometheus's mouth came a wail, "I don't know what's wrong with me. I fear ruin comes for us, that ruin sits afoot."

The storm was approaching, Hero thought. The storm, he thought, hearing Prometheus's cry. Hero drew his flint and steel and tried to viciously ignite the campfire again.

"What are you doing?" Epimetheus asked.

"If I can ignite this flame, then perhaps everything will be okay," Hero spoke with shallow breaths as tears began to break through. "If Zeus cannot be dissuaded, perhaps Master Prometheus can have his wish."

Hero continued to keep striking, giving piercing grunts with each strike. Sparks flew from his hands, insignificant but masked with pride. Hero persisted and displayed his resilience until the steel flew out of his hands and into the darkness. Hero, as well, fell to his knees and began to cry.

Chiron breathed heavily, "Tell me what you have seen, Prometheus."

Prometheus and Chiron's eyes began to adjust to the dark as they met each other's gaze. In the center of Prometheus's dark figure, Chiron saw the light within his eyes.

"Would you be kind enough to leave the two of us to speak?"

Chiron began to rise.

"Your wish is our command," Epimetheus dropped his arms to his side. He walked over to the weeping Hero. "Come, let's go."

Hero pushed himself up and went with Epimetheus. Approaching the opening to the cave, Epimetheus let go of the goblet hanging from his hand. The goblet clanged with the rock underneath and rolled toward the side wall. Watching Epimetheus drag his feet, Hero was unsure as to whether Epimetheus had dropped the goblet out of despair, loathing, or mere fatigue. Before he left, Hero looked over his shoulder and saw the silhouettes of the wise figures disappearing into the darkness of the cave.

The cold wind slammed into Hero's body upon stepping outside. Besides the sheer brightness of the gray sky, the wind forced Hero to squint and divert his gaze. Sediment flew at his eyes, and he felt a granular muck beginning to form on his face. The wind dragged at his loose hair and robes. Hero naturally looked down to see his cold feet and the shadow he cast behind himself. He turned and looked in the distance, against the force of the wind, and saw the clouds of concern. Prometheus had spoken correctly; a storm was approaching.

Hero quickly diverted his eyes again as the wind strengthened in almost a sense of retaliation. The wind howled in his ears, but Hero heard the laughter he remembered from his village and all the villages he had come across. The chatter and kindness of the folk who had received him with grace and a tight embrace. Hero crossed his arms, thinking of the folks and feeling the chill of the wind, his teeth beginning to chatter.

Hero had come to be himself after displaying great courage in the face of the ruthless herd of centaurs. He had earned the respect of Chiron by encompassing his courage, but also his humility and compassion. They had tended to the damaged parts of nature and lost woodland spirits on their journey. Each village they came across, Hero had made himself available to attend to their chores and needs, and assisted Chiron to the best of his abilities. Whenever a villager needed an extra pair of hands, Hero showed initiative. To fetch the stuck kitten, Hero was called. To wrestle the loose bull, Hero was called. To tame the wild stallion, Hero was called. To stand in honor of humanity, Hero was chosen as their champion. There was no formal decision made. Not even Chiron had placed such a title upon Hero, but this was a mantle Hero held up to himself. Perhaps this was his ambition: to be humankind's champion.

Where do I belong, Hero wondered as his hair flew across his face. He stroked his hair away while remembering the words of the Titans. Zeus wanted fealty, or he would demand sacrifice, death, and ruin. Hero had been taught to take pride in sacrifice, but now he reconsidered. Instead, he thought, how do I help those I cherish and how do I protect those I hold dear?

Epimetheus watched Hero from afar, leaning against the opposite end of the opening to the cave. He didn't think humankind was at all that interesting until Hero arrived. Now, he felt himself beginning to fancy them. Everything he had spoken inside the cave was now a matter for another day. All that stood in his mind now was his attraction.

Hooves began to stumble against the ground while making their way out of the cave. Chiron bent his large upper frame to mind his head as he joined Hero and Epimetheus in the wind. He fixed his satchel across his back and looked down the mountain and then at Hero. Next came Prometheus and, with him, he carried a fennel stalk burning with a glowing flame, something warm and tender at its core.

Prometheus stepped to Hero, "Protect this, Hero. I entrust you with this, if the darkness may ever come again. You may wield this fire and use it to light the hearth at Hestia's temple, giving birth to light once again, so you may never suffer in the dark."

Hero began to question Prometheus's decision in choosing him, until stepping forward and becoming the champion of Prometheus's gift and Hestia's flame. He took the torch into his hand, "Thank you for all that you have done, Master Prometheus. I will hold this with never-ending gratitude."

Prometheus and Hero shared a moment with their eyes and

hearts. Prometheus reached across and held Hero's arm, and felt the same tenderness of watching humankind from the cliffside and sitting by them at the bonfire.

"Now, Hero, we must make haste down this mountain. Are you capable of running?" Chiron stepped toward Hero with respect.

"I can run, Chiron," Hero looked up.

Prometheus watched the two begin to race down the mountain. Hero carried the blazing beacon that had cast away the dark silhouette on Prometheus's face, and Chiron trotted behind him as his attentive guardian.

"What was that about?" Epimetheus said, standing behind his brother.

Prometheus continued to watch his companions, "Chiron and I thought it would be best if humankind were entrusted with the eternal flame. I summoned the flame and gave it to Hero, for if their hearths ever go out again. I'm unsure exactly as to what Zeus's punishment shall be, but Chiron has reassured me. I have become a victim of my decisions, and I must now bear whatever ruin Zeus wishes onto me."

"So you're really set on this idea of impending ruin, huh?" Epimetheus said with a scoff.

"Have you seen the clouds, brother?" Prometheus turned around slowly with the sound of colliding clouds.

Epimetheus crossed his arms toward the sky, "I see it."

Prometheus stood with him, "Chiron and Hero have left to seek shelter. I leave your fate in your hands. Soon, the storm will reach us."

"My fate?" Epimetheus skeptically scanned the gray clouds. "What of yours?"

Watching the storm clouds, Prometheus saw a flash of lightning within them, "I must climb to the peak. We sought to do it together, but I will understand if you wish to leave with Chiron and Hero or wait for me here—"

"Why have you taken to this mountain all of a sudden?" Epimetheus suddenly turned to Prometheus.

"The eagle calls me," Prometheus turned to face the peak of the mountain and view the dark bird circling it. "I wish to watch humankind from above."

Epimetheus stared on, watching the back of Prometheus's head and the summit of the mountain just out of range and focus, "I suppose, I will join you. It's only proper. You are my brother."

Prometheus turned back to Epimetheus with a warm smile, "Thank you, brother."

Epimetheus turned to face the path ahead, waiting for his brother to join him. Prometheus felt hesitation in his first step. His mind immediately took to Chiron and what he had helped him see and the hope he had helped him feel. Over his shoulder, Prometheus saw the small figures, which he was once fearful of, become smaller and smaller and disappear into the terrain of the mountain. Prometheus then sent a signal down his leg as each corresponding part moved one by one ahead of him, moving him forward and toward his destination.

Lightning had shaken Olympus that day, when Zeus had pulled fire from the realm of the mortals and returned it to its confines on Mount Olympus. Anger took its form in the dark storm clouds that hovered around Olympus. Every so often, lightning would strike, sending a blinding light through the windows and halls of the grand palace. Zeus's rage resembled thunder as he took turns shouting and berating the subjects of his palace. He wanted all to perceive his power.

Prometheus ran down the stairs from Zeus's hall, watching his feet and shielding his eyes from the blinding light. He knew that this was the price of his deceit, clashing storms and eternal damnation for the mortals he and his brother had made. Prometheus could barely feel the tears streaking down his face until he saw droplets fall onto his feet and the steps underneath him. His tears clashed against the white of the marble and that of the lightning. He noticed that his tears even stood apart from everything that surrounded him.

Why am I still standing? Prometheus doubted himself. Why does he leave me here to watch them suffer? He turned to face up toward Zeus's throne. Why would he punish them and not me? He felt himself filled with anger. Now, Epimetheus was the one to receive Zeus's thunderous scolding. His punishments were cruel and cunning. Prometheus knew that Zeus was a tactical and winning general with a striking strategy for order. Why else was Atlas forced to carry the burden of the sky and not confined to Tartarus like the rest of his kin? What cruel punishment would he unfold for me, Prometheus wondered.

A bolt of lightning shone off the marble columns of Olympus as Prometheus looked upward. His eyes stung and instinctively clasped shut. Prometheus stepped backward, using his hands to further shield himself. The cold and wet marble gave a slip to his foot, and Prometheus felt himself lose his balance and collapse down the stairs. Flipping upside down and feeling the jagged edges of the stairs scrape his back, Prometheus landed at the base of the stairs on his back, thinking himself a fool. The Titan of forethought's weakness was often poor instinct.

Yet, while he lay, he turned his head to the side and saw the formidable doors he had seen once before: the doors to a place of warmth, a cell to the one he had freed, and a shelter away from the storm. He began crawling before rising to walk and then running to the doors of where he wanted to be. Prometheus had kept away from this hearth since Hestia had left, in fear of other Olympians, but also in fear of feeling his own lonely presence without her. He leaned against the dark doors and pushed them open eagerly.

On the stone floor, Prometheus saw the silhouette of Hestia. She lay facing the hearth he had visited in the past, which was her domain and existence. Now, he saw her in physical form, the real body of Hestia. Her cloaked figure did not indicate injury, but he saw her body slowly expanding and filling with air, relieving Prometheus of worry. He didn't know whether to approach, but his hand itched to reach out. Prometheus caught this strange instinct. He knew touching her physical form would be far more dangerous than touching the hearth as he had before. She was sacred, not just to him, and he did not want to defile and disrespect her. Prometheus had sought Hestia's wishes before, and he would do so again.

"Dear Goddess…" Prometheus felt all words escape him upon calling to her.

He continued to watch her for some sign or recognition. Prometheus watched her carefully and saw her continuing to breathe as he waited for an answer. Every so often, lightning would strike behind them and cast a grave shadow of Prometheus's head against the back wall of the room, covering the dimly lit hearth. This was the same hearth that had so enamored Prometheus when he had seen it before, but now it served as an afterthought. His attention remained on Hestia.

"Hestia?" Prometheus called, hanging onto the door.

Hestia moved, ever so slightly, almost struggling to breathe.

"I am here, dear Hestia. How can I help?" Prometheus pleaded.

Her body lay and began to rapidly gasp for air. Her head shook and slowly began to cave in toward her knees.

Prometheus watched and made out the sound of tears. He let go of the door and slowly approached her, "I'm sorry, dear Goddess. The price of my trickery ripped you out of your temple and out of the homes of humankind."

Hestia's fire seemed to slow, and what warmth Prometheus had felt from it before, he felt retracting and pulling away from him and the room. The chill from the storm invaded the room as Prometheus sensed a breeze stroke his back where he had fallen. A chill traveled down his legs, and he suddenly shifted his hips to shut the doors behind him.

He let go of the doors and turned to see still flames and hear nothing but the echo of his breath. A coldness lingered in the room. The room, which was once warm like an embrace, felt strange and fitting of a cell now and a shell of its former self. While Prometheus had been occupied trying to decipher Zeus's reckoning, he wondered if this was how humankind felt in the punishing darkness. Prometheus had previously only looked down at the mortals in the dark, before the advent of fire, as a problem to solve. Then he had seen them succeed with fire in their hearths, only after himself feeling the warmth and the touching embrace of fire. Now, he felt the fire dissipate, and he sensed the cold and creeping dread behind him. Most importantly, he sensed a loneliness and a longing for what he once held dear but never recognized the full value of.

Prometheus slowly came to his knees, "Dear Hestia, I cannot imagine how lonely you must've felt and how much you must've longed for that sense of togetherness." He slowly moved toward her. "You helped me understand how it felt to have that longing be fulfilled, to see yourself in another, and feel that comforting embrace. I'm sorry to have toyed with you and gambled with your heart. I ask myself why I did it, and I arrive at the foolish answer that it was for ambition, legacy, and achievement. All of which has led me to this lonesome place. If I can do anything to remedy it, I shall."

Prometheus placed his hands on his legs and gently bowed his head. He waited for himself to harden in the cold or be scorched by Hestia's flames, but nothing happened. Before rising, Prometheus thought of his history of regret and guilt. He thought of his betrayal during the Great War and how rapidly his mind had worried and felt in panic, wishing to reverse his damage. The way he felt toward Hestia did not make his mind race, but slow and dwell and make him sink into the gravity of his foolishness. He languished in her pain. He felt his inner fire beginning to extinguish. With the last of his will, Prometheus rose to grant the Goddess peace and recover hope that he might one day think of a way to redeem her.

Yet, Hestia called out, "You may rest by my flame."

Prometheus pulled his lips back, tensing and feeling himself undeserving. He slowly lowered himself to the floor, watching the slowly rising body of Hestia sitting in front of her flame. The sound of Prometheus's breath became overtaken by the crackling of the fire. He saw Hestia and her auburn hair highlighted by the glow of her warm hearth.

Prometheus squeezed his palms, "Are you sure?"

Hestia's hair flowed, "Yes, you may heal yourself, if you would like to stay."

Prometheus released his hands, "Why grant me this kindness?"

"I am the Goddess of the hearth and therefore each heart that comes to sit by my flames," Hestia spoke. "So you may warm yourself by my fire."

Prometheus stood again and approached the flame by Hestia. Hestia slightly turned her body so that Prometheus would not see her. The Titan came to his knees, longing for the warmth, and maintaining his focus on granting Hestia her peace and redemption.

He reached for the flames ahead of him. When he expected to feel the hot dancing fire, he felt the heat of a hand. Prometheus pulled his hand back. Seeing Hestia had formed in front of him in place of the fire, he shut his eyes suddenly. His eyes strained, worrying further about the prospect of punishment.

"Dear Goddess, perhaps it would be best if I were to leave—" Prometheus stressed.

Before realizing, Prometheus sensed that he had reached out toward Hestia out of instinct. Their hands met again, clasping each other's fingers. He felt the warmth in her hand and the heat trapped in the lines of her palm and fingertips. He moved his fingers over hers while keeping his eyes closed. His heart jumped out from dread and into deep longing. Often, Prometheus had dreamt of this comforting touch. Trusting only his instincts, Prometheus reached out with his other hand and found what was Hestia's back cloaked in a thick wool. Hestia reached toward Prometheus's chest and gently guided him to the floor. Upon a bed of cold stone, Prometheus lay with Hestia and their hands interlocked in trust. Hestia sensed Prometheus release his breath as she lay on his heart, passing warmth through herself and into him. Prometheus sensed the comforting weight of Hestia lying on his chest and felt his head lighten and all thoughts escape him.

Fire burned within them. Tinder ignited to flint, steel, and wind. Kindling carried the light toward the peak of the pyramid, and warmth became diffused throughout their entity. A spark connected one's mind with another's heart. All that existed, in that moment, was a fire burning in the hearth. All that mattered, for that moment, was that Hestia lay on Prometheus's chest, dispelling his need for forethought. He felt the rush of warmth through him and felt the depth of trust, courage, longing, and love. He needed to no longer understand and seek to find understanding; all he would do was feel the comfort of her embrace. Within chaos and ruin, he sensed the togetherness of love.

By what mechanism to go on and what to strive for, Prometheus thought to himself. He felt himself a rock, and Hestia a flower unfurled upon him. The weight of her head upon his chest felt light as a flower but like the comfort of a smooth rock in and of itself. He could lay there for an eternity. It could be his tomb. Throughout himself, he felt the still peace from forethought. He need not be a Titan any longer. No more did he hold the inclination for thought, but gave in to the present comfort of being with Hestia, the host of fire.

Then, into his heart, he heard Hestia utter the words. *Steal me, please, and take me away with you to humankind and the world that is remaining.*

Prometheus grabbed tightly onto her arm. Why, he thought, let us rest here and spend our lives as such, peacefully. He clutched her wrist, scared to let go. He did not want to give this moment away nor give her away.

They need me. He heard Hestia whisper through the flame.

I need you, he tensed his eyes. Stay, and we can avoid all of this, Prometheus wished.

Fire is not yours to wield nor yours to command. Hestia had spoken the truth. *You told me that you would adhere to my wishes, that you would tend to me, and protect me;* she reminded him. Hestia spoke into his ear. *Therefore, I request, Prometheus, steal me.*

He heard her chant and call for him to take her eternal form and steal her forever from the bounds of Olympus. He wished he could ignore her or shake her awake and tell her no. He wanted to keep her in the palms of his hands, forever.

If you seek to escape, fly and leave me, Prometheus cried in response to her.

He felt her hand gently caress his heart. *You must be the one. I place my trust in you.* Her lips felt right against his ear. *I've sensed the humility by which you once carried me, the care you held for me, and how longingly you watched me*, Hestia spoke. *If Zeus recognizes this as my treachery, I fear what he would do to extinguish me, unless you possess the bravery to protect me*, Hestia wished.

She pleaded with Prometheus to hide her inside him and to be the one who would fall for her. Just as he found what was a fitting rest, he was compelled to act on deception again.

Prometheus imagined the bloody fields of the Great War and himself lying amongst the defeated Titans. Atlas's blood and fate pooled onto him. If he had never betrayed his kin, where might he have lain, and what fate would have befallen him? He may be in Tartarus and free from his own mind in a different kind of suffering. Prometheus wondered if the fate he was granted was truly the one that was meant to be his or if perhaps he had made a fatal error along the way. Yet, he felt the caress of Hestia's hand on his heart, and he cherished the comfort it gave him. Was this moment truly what he had traded his kin and what he would trade his future for? He envisioned the future that would befall him if he became the one to steal the eternal flame of Hestia from Olympus. The ruin that would befall him and humankind, Prometheus pictured exactly what punishment Zeus would lay in store for him. He shook, recollecting his knowledge of Zeus and all the ways he may practice his power over the people and paths Prometheus helped pave. Yet, he envisioned the way Hestia might survive and the way humankind might outlast him. His mind knew how to make these connections. Forethought gave Prometheus the way to the best possible circumstances. While trembling in dreadful anticipation of his fate, he felt himself endowed to Hestia and all others who would perpetuate the prosperity of humankind. Prometheus's premonition would perhaps one day produce hope.

Prometheus agreed to Hestia's wishes, and breathed her into

himself and kept her near his heart. Then he raced down the stairs of Olympus and returned fire to the villages of humankind. However, the Titan of forethought felt scared. His dread and fear fought him, and he kept the heart of Hestia inside him until he found the right home for her and the strength to let her live without him.

He remembered that was the same night when he had cowered away from Epimetheus, who drank away with humankind celebrating the return of the shell of fire. Humankind believed in their minds that fire was restored, but Prometheus kept the core to himself, longing to hold on and never let go. Prometheus and Hestia had sat in her temple with him, watching her from behind. He watched her glowing brown hair outlined by the surface of the flame behind her. Prometheus wanted to, once again, reach out and hold her and savor the solace that he had found. Yet, he felt her anguish and suffering at feeling trapped, and he slowly began to loosen his grip and breathe again. Prometheus slowly learned to embrace selflessness and sacrifice.

While climbing up the mountain, Prometheus still felt that emptiness inside his hands, but felt a fire pushing him toward the peak. He led up the path proudly. Now and then, the eagle called, but Prometheus maintained his focus on the path and the pebbles he stepped over along the way. Occasionally, he turned and looked for his brother, who seemed to be trailing and reconsidering this expedition. However, Epimetheus followed begrudgingly.

There where the clouds wandered, Prometheus and Epimetheus felt themselves covered in a sweat and dew. Light of the bleeding sun trickled through the spaces between the large gray clouds. The thunder and lightning had subsided, for now, as Prometheus and Epimetheus reached closer to the summit.

Prometheus wondered if Epimetheus would see through his lie; there was no clear view of humankind from above. He realized that maybe it was finally time to be honest with his brother about his true intentions.

"So, brother, are you still curious about knowing where I was the night before?" Prometheus smiled.

"What? What are you talking about?" Epimetheus could hardly hold onto his thoughts. "Ah, yes, the night when I was drinking with the humans. Where were you? Once we are done with this, I would like to drink with the mortals again."

"I was with a woman," Prometheus projected his voice down the mountain. "A woman I admire very much."

Epimetheus laughed, "And you didn't invite me, you scoundrel!" Epimetheus began to jog up closer to Prometheus. "So, who is this woman?"

"That is the thing. I cannot reveal her identity to you, but I promise you that she's like no other woman."

Epimetheus, all of a sudden, felt more energized to keep climbing. "So what were you doing with this woman?"

"Not much. We sat, and I watched her."

Epimetheus's silence suggested his disappointment, "What do you mean you just sat?"

Prometheus turned around and began walking backwards, "We sat. I sat behind her. That's it. I felt content."

"What a limp tale."

"That's what I enjoy, I suppose," Prometheus shrugged. "There was one time when I held her, and that did feel nice."

Epimetheus picked up his pace and grabbed for Prometheus, "Wait for me. I must tell you this."

"What is it?"

Epimetheus leaned onto Prometheus's shoulder, "Now, brother, you know that I have been with many women, but I tell you this in confidence. I think I want to meet my 'the woman.'"

"'The woman…'" Prometheus playfully accentuated.

"Yes, 'the woman.'" Epimetheus cleared his throat. "And when I find my 'the woman,' the things I want to do with my 'the woman.'" Epimetheus closed his eyes.

"Oh, and what do you want to do with your 'the woman?'"

Epimetheus's eyes opened, adorned with crow's feet, "I want

to hold my 'the woman.' I want to kiss my 'the woman.' I want to dance with my 'the woman.' I want to take to bed my 'the woman.' And when we're in bed…" Epimetheus moved his lips closer to Prometheus's ear.

"You pervert!" Prometheus pushed Epimetheus away and laughed.

"What do you mean?" Epimetheus stood there with his hands raised. "That's what life is all about, brother. You're missing out with your simple 'we sat together.'"

"Oh, am I?" Prometheus faced his brother and tensed his jaw.

"Whoa, whoa. Yes, you are, but it's okay. You shall learn with time. You have a brother who is an expert in such matters, and I shall teach you all my knowledge," Epimetheus pointed up with a scholarly stance. "The joys of exploring the curiosities of 'the women.'"

"I suppose we shall see," Prometheus relaxed his arms and moved closer to his brother. "Maybe once we reach the bottom."

"Indeed!" Epimetheus sent his arm over Prometheus's shoulder. "There shall be no 'I suppose,' only 'we shall.'"

Arm in arm, the brothers continued traveling toward the peak. Epimetheus continued to jest with his brother about his immaturity and ignorance in discussing such things. Prometheus laughed, but soon grew tired of his brother's annoying persistence and obsession with such things.

"Let's just talk about something else," Prometheus said, looking toward his brother. "How about the mortals?"

"The mortals, again?" Epimetheus rolled his eyes.

"Why not?" Prometheus asked. "You know, I am so proud of you, Epimetheus. You have made a magnificent array of mortal creatures that shall color this world with their lively sounds and spirits."

Epimetheus shyly looked downward. It wasn't typical of him, but he wasn't used to being affirmed by his brother.

"I will never forget when we walked the valley together and heard the howling of the wolves, the cries of the cats, the calls of the roosters, the songs of the birds, and the 'moos' of the cows," Prometheus looked to his brother, and they both shared a laugh.

"The laughter of humankind," Epimetheus noted. "You have done a remarkable job, as I always knew you would."

"No, no. I've barely done a thing. Chiron and Hephaestus—"

"Shut it. Of course, they've helped. However, you are the one who created them," Epimetheus poked his brother in the chest. "You are the brilliant mind who designed them, advocated for them, and gave them the eternal gift of fire."

Prometheus's face suddenly turned pale. "Well, thank you." Prometheus sensed a static beginning to form in the air. "I'm grateful to have shared the gift of creation with you, Epimetheus."

"And I, you," Epimetheus looked ahead and took the final step to ascend to the summit of the Caucasus.

Clouds covered their entire view of the valley of the mortals. No eagle in sight, Zeus stood with his back toward the Titans at the edge of the cliff. Then, in that moment, Prometheus realized the clouds served another purpose besides for Zeus's rage. They provided cover and hid the brothers and their meeting with the King of Olympus.

Zeus's voice thundered, "Prometheus and Epimetheus, what a delight to run into the two of you. What a joyous occasion we share."

Zeus turned, opening his arms. Prometheus was locked in place. Epimetheus pulled his arm from his brother's shoulder and squeezed his fists.

"Will you not bow?" Zeus beckoned.

The brothers remained in place.

"I see," Zeus replied to their insolence. "The humans greet each other differently, don't they?"

Prometheus imagined how Hero might greet the King of Olympus.

"I'm sure you must know of it, Prometheus," Zeus mocked.

Prometheus remained quiet and staring.

"I see," Zeus shifted his attention slightly and turned to Epimetheus. "How about you, Epimetheus?"

"I'm not sure what you mean, King Zeus," Epimetheus spoke, tight-lipped.

"Come," Zeus motioned his arms inward. "I shall grant you a gift."

"Why?" Epimetheus spoke with a shrill.

"Why?" Zeus chuckled. "You have completed your duty to me in such a fantastic fashion. You have made me the eagle, and I greatly admire the creature. It suits me very well, indeed. Both of us soar above the sky and above everyone else."

"I'm honored."

"So come," Zeus called. "I have retrieved the most precious of Dionysus's wine. I have another gift in mind for you, as well, in addition to another duty, a most important one at that."

Epimetheus dropped his resistant stance and coyly turned to Prometheus, almost for permission. Prometheus wanderingly looked at his brother.

Then, Epimetheus gave in to what he heard and joined Zeus. They embraced each other in a modest hug, joining their dominant hands, and Epimetheus placed a kiss on Zeus's cheek.

"So what is this duty, King Zeus?" Epimetheus kissed the back of Zeus's hand.

"In due time. First, I must introduce you to the finest mortal woman. Hephaestus helped me find her, actually. Come, I will introduce you to her," Zeus shifted again and began to lead Epimetheus down the trail.

Epimetheus glanced at his brother, once again. This time, he looked in shock and excitement. His dreams were about to come true. He followed closely behind Zeus.

Zeus turned. "Prometheus, I have a gift for you, too. Please take a seat. I will be with you soon."

Zeus waved his hand, and the clouds began to disperse. An opening formed from which Prometheus could watch the valley of the humans. Epimetheus watched his brother and smiled before being led away by Zeus. The two figures soundlessly strolled down the path.

Prometheus moved his attention to the cliff. The signals from his mind slowly led his feet closer to the edge of the summit. A rock sat in front of him, and he wandered around to sit ahead of it. He sat and saw the small villages of the humans, painted in the scarlet of the setting sun. He smiled at the distant figures he knew were the villagers, who prepared their meals and steered their animals to shelter, preparing to eventually go to bed. Prometheus knew now that their hearths would never go out. They would stay burning brightly, as would Hestia's temple, thanks to the likes of Hero and Chiron. Prometheus imagined the humans who would traverse far and wide to pay respects to Hestia and take in her glowing grace and be comforted by her fire's warm embrace. He imagined the way she would hide and cover herself from the gaze of the strange men and the touching nurturance she would pass on to the young and lost children. Prometheus could rest now with the reassurance that all would be well.

Pain suddenly shot through Prometheus's abdomen. He slowly looked down from the valley of the humans to his torso and saw the sharp talons of the eagle piercing through him. The sharp claws squeezed into Prometheus's body, immobilizing him. Spit and blood collected around Prometheus's mouth as the eagle tore its digits out of him, and he felt himself weaken and begin to fall back on the rock he sat on. Prometheus felt torn between calling to his brother and throwing himself into the valley of the humans. His brain surged with pain as tears pooled around his eyes and he clutched the rock beneath him, hoping to make a sound and summon help. He looked up and saw the same great eagle standing above him, aimlessly looking down at its prey.

The eagle stepped onto Prometheus's right arm, trapping him on the rock. Prometheus tried to reach for the eagle with his left hand, but he remained too much in pain to reach or move his body. The blood from his body pooled into his robes and seeped into the rock, painting streaks of dark scarlet across the rock's exterior. The eagle's claws dug into Prometheus's arms as he let out a blood-curdling cry that echoed across the horizon. In his desperate measures to kick and free himself, Prometheus slipped off the rock with his arm trapped above. The rock at his back and the edge of the cliff ahead of him, Prometheus made incoherent cries while trying to free himself from his pain. He kicked and tried to grab at the feathers of the eagle's tail, all to no avail. The eagle cocked its head and looked down at Prometheus, almost confused and with no clear expression or hunger. As Prometheus glanced into its eyes, he saw a gentle soul.

Tears trailed down Prometheus's face. He closed his eyes and, in his mind, he heard his own cries accompanied by the cries of his kin. I will be with you soon, Prometheus thought. Facing his fear of pain had silenced Prometheus's forethought. He lay in suffering, which he knew and predicted all too well. The eagle extended its beak above Prometheus, slowly bowing its head down. As the eagle's cold beak grazed Prometheus's chest, he felt the flash of fire through him and saw Hestia sitting ahead of him, encompassed in the glow of the hearth.

The eagle ripped into Prometheus's body and ate his liver. Zeus commanded this punishment to be carried out day after day as Prometheus's immortality forced him to regenerate his liver and flesh. Indestructible chains with the mark of Hephaestus had been used to bind Prometheus to the rock, so that he would remain trapped and endure his punishment. Prometheus would awake in the mornings as Helios dashed across the sky in his chariot, ignoring him. No one was permitted to visit him or assist him, besides the eagle that Zeus sent to eat his liver and unleash pain and suffering onto Prometheus. At noon, the eagle would feast as Prometheus would watch and cry out to humankind in the valley ahead of him. As his cries of pain became softer and softer, Prometheus would slip away into a comatose state until his body would heal, and the cycle would begin again.

The solitude that he suffered, being alone and only being able to watch his kin from afar—those human, Titan, God, and spirit—cast a dark wound onto his mind. He languished as his thoughts and dreams lay poisoned. While before, he immersed himself in the scrutiny of watching humankind from above or across the bonfire, he now longed to just sit by them and enjoy their advancements with them. He would speculate about humankind and their actions, but he did so without the company of his brother, Chiron, Hero, and Hestia, those who served to return him to reality and share a laugh and moment of joy with him. Now, he only heard the laughter of humankind from afar.

Prometheus was left with just his forethought. Through his forethought, he saw the worst of the worst, colored by his dark and lonely state. Prometheus predicted the gift granted to Epimetheus by Zeus: a beautiful mortal woman by the name of Pandora. Epimetheus would be beholden to Zeus and his task to keep Pandora from exploring her curiosities and opening the chest possessing the darkest of matters. This was a task that Epimetheus and Pandora were meant to fail, given Pandora's mortal curiosity and Epimetheus's afterthought, casting onto the world all kinds of evil creatures and curses. The purpose of Zeus's impossible task was to further torment Prometheus and to submerge the mortals into further ruin. Sorrow, disease, famine, and death were unleashed upon the mortal world, but Epimetheus and Pandora had been fast enough to shut the chest and save within it a remaining piece of hope for humankind.

Soon after, armies would rise amongst the humans. With blame and villainy being cast onto their neighbors, wars would erupt and tear the land of the mortals away from the peaceful haven it once was. The Olympians would further embolden the warring humans and cast their lot to play games and find amusement. Hero would be amongst the warring humans, seeking to foster peace and protect those dear to him. He would endure battles and wounds beyond any other human's knowledge, but meet his end at the hands of Olympus. Zeus's lightning would set ablaze his corpse and the villages that heralded him as their champion. Hero would serve his duty by passing on the mantle of the eternal flame into the hands and tombs of his successors. Chiron would weep for Hero's death and so many others that he would foster, train, and see as his own. Despite his sorrow, Chiron would retain his values to aid others. Hephaestus, however, would not see very far beyond the walls of his workshop, working for the will of Zeus and being gifted Aphrodite, the most beautiful Olympian, for his loyalty. Hestia, what would become of Hestia? Prometheus would be too tortured to recall the memories of Hestia and predict her future. All that would come to mind when he would think of her would be the delight he felt sharing the best moments of his freedom with her. Prometheus would never regret the decision he made to sacrifice himself for Hestia. In her freedom, Hestia could live on forever, making herself small to hide from others and big to scare off danger. She was in the hands of the many. Yet, Prometheus wished he could still hold her in his hands. Then, his reverie would end as the eagle would arrive and tear him apart to begin his punishment again.

From above, Prometheus prophesied the fate of each human. Within their fates, he also predicted the downfall of Zeus and the usurping of Olympus. Prometheus had conceptualized the manner by which Zeus would cease to exist and who would bring about his ruin. Something had happened. Someone had heard Prometheus's taunts to the Olympians. In his eternal punishment, the Olympians were not what Prometheus feared any longer. He lay anxious about whether his prophecy would be fulfilled.

However, one day, an owl would visit Prometheus on the peak of the Caucasus. At first, Prometheus would interpret it as a playful jest until the owl would transform into Athena. The new Olympian declared that she had been born from a pain within Zeus's brain. She was a sign that all wisdom had left Zeus and taken shape. Athena would plead with Prometheus, promising him a day of freedom from his punishment, if he shared his prophecy for the world. Prometheus took her wisdom to be flawed. It was led by a Godly impulse and lacked the thoughtfulness, anxiety, and humility found in the minds of humans. Athena's pastime was war strategy and punishing humans, while Prometheus found true wisdom to be in the protections granted by Chiron and his kindness.

Prometheus would not tell Athena anything, being willing to bear his punishment for an eternity. Athena would inform Prometheus that Zeus was beginning to lose his mental fortitude due to Prometheus's claims of knowing his end. And that Zeus threatened to submerge the mortal world under water, killing all that Prometheus knew. Even this would not break Prometheus and his will to protect the future. Athena would leave, and Prometheus would be tormented again.

Prometheus began to sculpt with the rocks that lay beside him. He would create a way to bring humankind back again after Zeus would order the great deluge. As the water flowed beneath Prometheus, he kicked over his creations onto the boat that floated, granting the descendants of Epimetheus and Pandora the gift by which to plant humankind and restore their hope. Then Prometheus would be torn in half and have his liver devoured again.

Prometheus's suffering would repeat. It would be a never-ending cycle, but perhaps for the one day that he may be set free. Each day, he remained chained to the same worries about his prophecy and whether he would ever be free. He hoped for the day that he might walk through the valley with grass beneath his feet, clear skies above his head, and hold the warm embrace of fire in his hands. In his longing and suffering, Prometheus would sit, watching humanity.

Somewhere in Between

Someone once told me that there are three typical responses a person exhibits upon reaching the summit of the mountain. One, the traveler who arrives at the peak, rushes to take a picture and then turns back to beat the darkness. Two, the sightseer who unfurls a picnic blanket and relishes in their feat, slowly devouring it with time. Three, the wanderer who arrives at the summit and then looks ahead to find an even taller peak to climb next.

Standing in my dug-out grave, I ask: what of the one who arrives at the peak and wishes to take flight?

I must admit, some force has pushed me forward. When I thought I couldn't crawl, I found myself learning to walk, steadily step by step. Climbing up the mountain like this is no easy feat. One step forward, trip on a rock, and three feet back. And at times, the journey feels as if you are pushing up a rock. It's a Sisyphean task, trying to climb and achieve what you believe is yours to surmount. I'm unsure as to what my mountain even is. However, I am sure that many times, I have lost the path upward and been stuck somewhere in the middle, between the summit and the base. Somewhere in between.

I search for a promising path that may lead me where I want to be. Though, how can I decipher what is meant to be for me?

Once, I searched for endless poetics in sight. Another time, I lost myself to the art of thinking and feeling. I even considered the study of teaching. I dreamt of exploring the vastness of space. I found myself an entertainer, a listener, a quiet disgrace, but nothing that I could call myself and my own. So where did it lie, the secret path that was mine to take with pride?

Mountains are easy to interpret, in that almost all think the treasure lies at the top after the arduous climb. However, what if that is the trick? What if that is the lie?

When I dive into a cave and put my ear to the floor, I hear the rapids cry. What if deep inside this mountain lay many paths unique in their ride? I'm not skilled in rafting or swimming, but what if the rivers deep inside pool into different realities that may all be right? Crystalline water accompanied by a dragonfly glow, no gems to mine, but a secret deep inside to find?

I take my ear away from the floor and forget my fiction. Once the rain passes, I shall continue with this exhausting affliction.

Someone once said to me, are you truly prepared to ferry this path, willing to listen again and again to the tortured souls of time? I said yes. Somehow, I knew deep inside that this was what called me. Then he looked and told me to make it my own, to find my own way, to reinvent the system, and to find my own orientation. I smiled, grateful for his belief in me. I eventually learned that this someone died. His words still sit with me, alive and inspiring. I imagine him on his own island among the hidden sea.

Many paths diverge from the original basin, cascading down into their own streams of life. Once you've traveled down the respective waterfall, you cannot reverse the commitment and strife. So now, I linger in the basin, wondering which path to try. At least one portal surely leads to his life. All the souls that touched me, whether loved or tortured me, I carry within me and float in this reverie.

Someone once said to me, why do we do this and write poetry? I said something poetic, but something that spoke to my core and my care for those around me.

Someone close said to me, you are a failure. I didn't have a rebuttal and contributed more tears to their troubles. I hope I can learn to row or swim, whatever would appease. However, maybe I'll never swim to your visions for me.

I told someone, I want to impact this sea. If I couldn't swim and the deluge was imminent, I would make my changes to this sea permanent. This someone told me to wait, and that this wasn't the way.

Then someone told me to stay in my lane, row, and not stray.

Someone then reframed to me, yes, proudly row in your river. Don't let others deter you from your river, and all that your river encompasses: falling boulders, extending branches, ebbs and flows. Yet, this is me on my course. Learning to row, learning to swim, I never knew I could do this without embarrassment. The wish for flight does not die, but now I am occupied with swimming this tide. I am afraid to drown and be engulfed by my fears that I will never reach the summit or the other side.

The rhymes end, and I find myself sitting at the crossroads, staring up at the many lights and their forms.

The mountain of determination, the sea of possibility, it waits for me.

And where do I lie?

Somewhere in between.

THE DOOR

I arrived in the first week of November. It was my brother's home. Brother, not by blood, but by friendship. The house lay on the outskirts of the village of Inanis, surrounded by nothing but grassland. The town itself had no more than a few hundred folks: farmers, proprietors, craftsmen, and the late artist who had made it his home for the last couple of years. The house was now small and dark. It showed no remains of the massive talent and light that had once shone within its rooms and corridors. I had seen this home only once before, but I remember it glowing.

A small dead garden bordered the stygian path to the entrance of the homestead. A funeral procession was laid out with dead roses, lilies, and carnations. White rose petals had wilted and lost their innocence to the dirty pathway, painting them in a dull shade of gold. The distance from the street to the entrance must have been ten feet, but I remember standing there in the garden for twenty minutes or so and watching the door and waiting for it to open.

The wind pushed at my being, littering my clothes with dirt and impairing my vision with tiny particles of filth. The ticking of my watch became subdued in the background as I became trapped in the cacophony of wind. My body stood as a thin barrier in the void where the wind screeched in my ears and warned me to turn back. I wish I had. I just watched and wished for the door to open. I whispered and hoped it would listen to me, slowly creaking open and welcoming me inside. The door resisted and stood still with a looming presence. It was a dark hole at the center of a once-warm soul and body. As I felt the presence of night overtake me, my urgency to escape this grasp grew even more desperate. It wasn't so much the cold but the absence of light that made the matter so much more threatening. In my catatonic state, I shook viciously, attempting to break out of this trance. My eyes sharpened their focus and envisioned a powerful tug at the door that could rip open a hole through the darkness. My eyes rattled in their cages, gripped by the looming shadow in the distance. It called to me and extended its golden hand. The last moment I remember in the garden: sweat dripped down my forehead before I suddenly shut my eyes and stepped to the door, overtaking its grasp.

Once I opened the door, the essence of the home floored me. My legs shook, trembling from the wind and the very position I stood. The floorboards squeaked and felt dilapidated. I was afraid I would fall through the floor and into the pit that awaited me underneath. The wind shut the door behind me, taking away the only light in the room. The only thing left was the mental image the room had cast in my mind: torn wallpaper, dead flowers, a ripped open settee, and a rocking chair in the corner swaying back and forth. While my wind may have put the rocking chair in motion, it was beyond me to envision what soul sat and rocked in it now in the dark. It's not so much the darkness that scared me, but the things that could lurk within it.

In August, I received a letter from a shepherd who lived near my friend's estate. He notified me that my friend had passed away. He had informed several of the people my friend was in correspondence with about this unfortunate news. None had replied. I contemplated whether I should go or not, but I dared not disappoint the shepherd who confused me to be my friend's brother. I knew the responsibility resided with me: to reopen the premises and unleash the years of memories. I was the only one who had taken it into his own will to honor this man who, by all accounts, was my brother.

After that visit to his home, I developed a tactic to enter the home without becoming overwhelmed by that horrid door. I kept my eyes toward the ground, and when I came to face the door, I closed my eyes and felt for the handle. The cold metal of the handle stood apart from the splintering wood of the door. I arrived at the notion that the wear and tear to the house could not have occurred in the few months between my friend's passing and my visit. Either my friend had neglected to take care of his home for the number of years he resided there, or some form of a catastrophe, nature or man or both, had struck this place.

Inside the home were aged memories and accomplishments. I did not care for them much at the start, but in time, I began maintaining them. Every brush gave me a deeper appreciation of this man and the part I played in his life. I felt deep sorrow for the fact that the world would not get to meet and learn about this person, who possessed the greatest aptitude for the creative. He was quite talented. There was a poem of his published in our local paper about the beauty of winter; a poem that we had all criticized and insisted be about spring instead. There were paintings from his childhood that he had insisted defined his core self: landscapes that were flat, farmland, crooked trees, and fields of wheat. In my contrasting opinion, he was always meant for the spirited nature of the city. It would have done him better, I believe.

In his drawers were his essays and stories. There was a multitude of them that were hastily written and riddled with his unique errors. I read them each again and recalled the times we had spent analyzing the craft and contemplating our love for storytelling and the creative. He had always served as a great and agreeable listener to my passionate ravings. My friend was passionate too, but expressed his own love for the craft through different means. He didn't need to talk about the craft at all times to show his knowledge or mastery of the trade. There were times when his lack of outward expression seemed to diminish his identity as an artist, but I knew he was an artist deep down. Despite all the responsibilities that tore at his identity, his work spoke for him. I was critical of his work as I have always been with my own, but this was because of how much I cared about our individual and collective growth. See, I had introduced him to some components of the craft, and he had made me very conscious of the fact that he believed I was the reason he committed to the craft with passion and seriousness. Even though he constantly credited me for this role, I denied it and maintained the belief that he was born an artist. His work spoke with such meaning and conveyed beauty through every phrase and idea. Perhaps it was my own bias and attachment to him that predisposed me to think so highly of his work. Yet, that talent, to me, is seemingly impossible to develop and is only naturally gifted. After all these years, I could still recognize so much of that talent in these old essays and stories. However, all these tokens were from our youth. Ideas that he had seen through to completion, and I had been there to witness. None of them revealed his newer perspective or the growth that he should have accrued over the years.

I had spent our time apart working more keenly than I ever had before. We had made a pact to commit ourselves to the craft and never stray from growing and developing into better and more fully-fledged artists and humans. With that focus and work came a degree of stress and pressure that was overbearing, but I had to endure. He had written me letters over the years that shared his passion, growth, and excitement for his new artistic works. In part, those letters inspired and motivated me to work harder myself. Sometimes he would share snippets of his writing in his letters, and these excerpts would reinvigorate me. Over the years, it seemed that his confidence had grown, as evidenced by the fact that he would more openly write about his craft and discuss his passion in his letters. In an interesting turn of events, my expression of passion had drawn more inward. My letters were often shorter than his. I often shared less about my work. I took longer to write back, and at times I did not write back at all. I had withdrawn somewhat but this was because of how busy my life had become in the city. This didn't mean I neglected to think about my friend and his promising work. The opposite, in fact: my friend and his work lingered in the back of my mind, and I could not wait for the day I would get to experience his brilliant work again. Now, upon visiting him and searching through his belongings, I came upon nothing. I had turned the house over and examined his work over and over again for a sign of what he had developed into, but found nothing.

My journey to understand my friend and what his life had become had faltered due to the mysterious circumstances of his passing. There was nothing to confirm my friend's passing but the written word of the shepherd. There was no body, no records in the village, no accounts of suspicion. Nothing. The shepherd had not even disclosed what disease or entity had taken my friend's life. I'm unsure about whether the shepherd even knew the cause himself. My friend was a healthy individual, to my knowledge. He suffered from a sort of melancholy as a child, but so did many others. We didn't think much of it, and he seemed to handle it well when he was surrounded by his friends, including me. His letters to me read fine, as well. Despite not finding any new works or records of his, I was determined that there would be something that would turn up.

The thought of robbers having stolen these precious items and being the ones to cause harm to my friend had crossed my mind. However, why would they have only stolen his newer work and left behind his older work, or targeted an artist out of all people? There was a slim chance that this could have occurred, especially given the ruined condition of the home. My friend could have possibly developed a personal vendetta with the individual who murdered and robbed him. Perhaps this individual had perceived the newer work to be more precious and profitable. The thief could have even been the shepherd himself, I considered. He could have been attempting to cloak his guilt by writing to my dear friend's beloved. After all, how could the shepherd have even known who my friend was in correspondence with? The shepherd also had the advantage of living within proximity to my friend's home. His occupation would allow him to easily slip out into the middle of nowhere to hide any pieces of evidence or the body. From my deduction, the shepherd was one of the primary suspects, and I desired to acquire all knowledge he had about my friend, his passing, and what his life had been like. It would not be a surprise if he were the culprit himself. Worse things have been done by those who walked the same path of life as he. These were the scenarios that crossed my mind in regard to what could have occurred to my friend and his work. Whether the cause of these missing papers was that they were never created or that they were stolen, I was set on finding them. This kept me coming back to the house, day after day.

After a week or so of traveling between the city and the village, I realized it would have been more appropriate to relocate to the village for the time being. I figured that I could spend about a month, at most, away from the city devoted to this journey. About half of November remained. Life in the village did not suit me, but this course of action would be more efficient in all ways. It would also be a lot better to resolve this journey before the heavy snow began. When notifying my colleagues and peers, I kept the reason for my departure vague. They didn't need to know about this venture nor the maddening devotion I held for it. I simply told them I was leaving to visit an elderly relative who had fallen under some ill condition. I kept the details of said condition very standard. I did not want to worry them too much, nor for them to think that I would return to spread some contagious disease. As long as I was able to produce some meaningful artwork for them upon my return, they would have understood my journey to be purposeful.

I spent the remainder of the month mourning my dear friend and dragging myself about the village. I would try to spend as little time as possible at his estate, opting instead for the local inn. Although I had become acquainted with his house by now, I still preferred the comfort of the inn, where I was at a much lower risk of being ambushed by a random robber or killer or whatever lurked in the shadows. In the beginning, the village was quaint and peaceful in its own right. I approached it with an open mind and looked forward to experiencing its humble lifestyle, which I considered capable of inspiring some new work.

It wasn't completely a fault of the outdated architecture, but the village quickly became an eyesore. It stunk of a sort of sameness everywhere I went. Gray clouds and overcast weather, day after day, added to the dreary climate of the village. All it took was three days for me to meet disappointment. The village let me down, despite my attempts to find inspiration within it, sapping me of my creativity and passion. I found that the longer I stayed there, the more the village revealed its flaws. Emblematic of the village's ruin: at the center of the village was a decrepit chapel, charred and ignited by a rebellion. There were no signs of reassembly. It was a marker that the village had lost hope. The village itself was broken. It ran on its few functioning institutions, but there were ruins in every corner. They, as a collective, were holding onto their past or, worse, they lacked the will to clear it all and rebuild. The reason could be that they lacked the resources to undertake such an endeavor, but it was most likely laziness and a lack of care that had cemented itself as complacency.

When it came to interacting with the villagers themselves, I spoke to no one, and no one desired to bother me. I would slide my coin over the splintered counter to the barkeep, and he would serve me silently. Wherever I went, I heard no discourse or chatter. Now and then, I would catch a pair of eyes watching and observing me. While such an act would be considered disrespectful in most settings, I came to understand that it was commonplace amongst the less privileged. It is rather logical to be so fixated on wealth and that which is new. Not only were these people impoverished, but their rigidly complacent and traditional lifestyle lacked excitement, meaning, and the sort of fervor that defined a worthwhile life.

The only good thing in the village was their liquor. I'm no connoisseur, but anyone could tell that their collection was priceless. I would spend a lot of time, especially during evenings and nights, drinking at the pub underneath my inn. Their wine was so soft to the taste that before you knew it, you would have drunk through an entire barrel worth of it. The only time I needed to make a quick excursion to the city, during the second half of the month, was to collect more coin. I had been spending far too much on the wine, but I did not regret it. I even thought of arranging some deliveries to be made to my home in the city. Enjoying the spirit in better company would have far heightened the taste of the already delectable wine.

The cause behind most of my late nights at the pub was my pursuit of the artistic masterpiece that I had promised my peers upon my return. Evenings and nights were all I had available to work on such matters. It was doubtful whether my peers would even remember or expect me to produce such a piece of work for them, but I so desperately desired to have something to show for the time I had spent wasting away in the village. In general, I was also committed to the pursuit of excellence within my craft. Therefore, seeking to produce such a piece should not warrant an occasion or reason of the sort. I should always be devoted to creating my next masterpiece. At first, I tried my hand at writing poetry and then essays. I lacked the visual scenery to inspire a beautiful art piece, so I remained confined to the written words of prose or rhyme. Being gifted in multiple forms of art was both a privilege and a curse. While it allowed me to be dynamic and free-flowing when it came to creating art, I also felt forced to triangulate my artistic vision and choose the best medium for conveying my message. There was also the challenge of pushing oneself in all areas and seeking to reach an expert level of knowledge and craftsmanship in all areas. Yet, this was the vision of creativity that I had developed when I was younger and wanted to firmly establish myself within the world of artists and creators. When someone is born an artist or storyteller, they should be able to make expert use of any and all forms of art to express their message in its best form. My circle of colleagues and peers consisted of many different sorts of artists: painters, poets, essayists, playwrights, and musicians, some of whom had even tried their hand at other forms of art. The only individual I knew who matched my creative prowess and filled the same image of a Renaissance man was my deceased friend.

Even though I refused to spend the night at his home, he was still in my thoughts. He was at the root of my thoughts for the entire time I stayed in that village. All my ideas and thoughts were somehow related to him. Some overthought-out worst-case scenarios of what happened to him became potential plots for novellas. My emotions, caused by my friend's passing, provided the tone for several of my poems, as well as the themes and motifs behind what I would commit to paper. The worst of my anxiety included the lingering questions that could not be resolved by my curious mind. These questions ranged from how often my friend tended to his garden to what had been the cause of his death. A question that pained me every time it came back to me was whether my friend had forgiven me. I had not been the kindest friend to him. In fact, it was this same fear or guilt that had caused me not to visit him before. The furthest I had reached was the entrance to his homestead, before the sight of that door had trapped me, and I had realized that I could not bring myself to confront him truly in person.

Our friendship as children began as firm and warm. If it were not for the natural bond we had discovered, we would not have become brothers at a later age. We grew up together, developed, and inspired each other. My definition and pursuit of art were in part defined by my friend, whose natural talent at many times eclipsed mine. Childhood was an enthralling time. We relished in our similar love for art and formed a unitary identity to share. Feelings of jealousy and bitterness began to brew as we eventually became older and slowly separated artistically and from each other in our own personal pursuits. My friend began to venture into whatever it was he wanted to do in the outcast village. I knew the city would serve as a more efficient terminal than the town we grew up in. Our hometown was nice, but the city was where ideas were truly born and where they could actually thrive. I always knew I'd move to the city. When we were somewhat younger, I even tried to convince my friend to move with me, but he rejected the idea. Perhaps if we had still been as close as we were as children, he would have listened and heeded my advice. If all had gone well, perhaps I wouldn't be here now, and he wouldn't be dead.

My attempts at any sort of writing, in that godforsaken village, were not fruitful. I couldn't seem to even compile a half-coherent and intelligent line, let alone craft some eye-opening and wise piece of literature. As the days passed by, my frustrations grew, and I turned more and more to the company of liquor. It was the last time I gave way to excess, I swear. The liquor took two courses. One, it angered me. My friend had inspired me in the past, but he failed to do so at that moment. At that very moment, when he should have improved even more and crafted even more meaningful pieces of work, there was nothing to witness. The man who had eclipsed my talent in our youth had failed to cast any sort of lasting shadow on me or the world. This baffled me and angered me. He could not have wanted the world to remember him for his accomplishments as a child. He must have written or created new pieces of art. Yet, the questions remained. Where were they? Where was his art? Where was his life's work? What did all of his effort and passion amount to? Such were my incoherent ramblings. Two, I considered the effortless escape I could make to my home. I belonged to the city, and I did not have a place in the village. Rather than chasing the ghosts of the past, I could have continued living a life of leisure in Victoria and forgotten these matters with time. In a few months, these issues would have dissipated and lacked any sort of impact they had on my life. However, I was the one who had been foolish enough to give way to these matters and to seek some sort of antiquated resolution. Coming to the village, I had doubted my ability once again to reconcile with my friend, but I discovered that there were no answers there.

I could not accept defeat so easily. Even though I had run my head into wall after wall, I still could not accept defeat. With four days remaining in the month, I marched back to my friend's shack for one last search, and then I would be finished. This moment of inspiration came after an unknown and unreasonable number of drinks. Yet, I was conscious enough to recognize the promise I had made to myself and that I was setting out to the estate at night. This last search could not wait until the morning. Perhaps the shadow of the moon would reveal some hidden detail I had overlooked this entire time. Possibly only under the night sky would I be able to uncover the answers I was seeking. Or possibly my friend's life and my journey had been a failure.

I stepped into the garden and confronted my challenge. The looming door in the distance had lost its power over me. I carried with me a lantern; meanwhile, a small candle hung beside the door. My source of light overpowered the flicker of the door. We were the only two sources of light in the dark night. I saw the moon with its sharp crescent hide behind the murky clouds. I did not know if I would see the moon again that night or ever. Under the influence of liquid courage, I barged inside. I had already drunk a lot that night, and I was sad I had not brought another bottle with me. My memory of the night isn't clear, but I am recalling it now to the best of my abilities.

The floor squeaked as I hobbled to every shelf and case. I searched every nook and cranny with a thirst for fulfillment. In the darkness, vases and frames must have been flung to the floor, done so by my impaired condition. From his drawers, I took out the old poems and essays I had found earlier. I read them front and back, held against the light of the lantern, looking for any secrets between the lines. I scanned each page more than twice and then flung it somewhere into the room behind me. As the loose pages disappeared into the darkness, so did my regard for them and any memory I held dear about their creation. The poems were through, and so I moved on to his essays. False words of wisdom lay sprinkled all over the old parchment. A sense of pretension arose from my friend's attitude and thoughts on life. Here he was living a plain old life while writing grand statements on the status of the world and offering his uneducated opinions. His thoughts on the purpose of life conflicted with mine. His notion on how one should seek to serve themself and their community conflicted with mine. There had been a multitude of differences between us, and for a second, I sat there confused about whether this was even my friend or not. How had we even come to be friends, let alone brothers, I thought.

Out of the mountain of papers, I picked out the next one and read its title, "On the love for art." I quietly steadied my hand and held his essay against the lantern. "On the love for art," it said. On the love for art? I was disgusted by that title. He had deserted and embarrassed the premise of art by his lack of willingness and desire for greatness. I dove into the pompous essay. As I explored the paper, I read through the lines on self-expression, meaning, empathy, and passion. The words lingered with me. They invoked passion. The words took on another life. They spoke with passion. The ink shone through the paper as I read and saw the words of passion. I was immersed in the language and compelled by the calligraphy. Every word and letter expressed a notion of meaning and urgency, amounting to the ostentatious sense of passion. I saw the fire through the page. I remained on the words of passion. I examined them and studied them, for only a minute more of admiration would perhaps result in the passion I had been awaiting. I had longed for this passion, and maybe this was the moment of transmission. I was dying for it. I began to read the paper once again until I felt the burning on my hand and saw fire beginning to consume the paper. The flame of the lantern had kissed the essay. Seeing the fire ascend line by line and devour the text, I quickly threw the paper on the ground and began to stomp out the flame. After the flame had died, I examined the shreds left on the ground. It was lost. There were ashes where the passion had once been. The essay had gone out and burned away. That was the closest I had come to seizing the passion I sought, and it was lost. For a moment, everything stood still in the thick coldness of the night. I was now standing and facing the darkness as I realized what I had just done. The lantern sat beside me, feeding the darkness and burning out from my desire.

My mind went to the new firewood I had moved into the house earlier in the month when I had still planned on staying at the estate. The lantern was out, and despite my frustration, I needed to form a plan of action to produce light. I loaded the firewood into the hearth. This would not be enough, however. In searching for some sort of tinder, my feet slipped on the pages scattered across the dark floor. They were all I had. They would have to do. I grabbed a bundle of papers from the floor and hobbled to the fireplace. A few papers slipped out in escape, but my grasp was too strong. I reached the fireplace and flung the papers into the pit. This needed to be done. The former essay had burned for a reason and, in its demise, dictated the fate of all of the pages.

The fire was born. The words of burning passion had birthed the flames. The hearth burned more brightly than ever before. I took a seat in front of the fireplace and continued to scan his work once again. Once I finished a page, I discarded it into the flames. Winter poems fit the season and made for sufficient sustenance for the hearth. Eventually, all of the papers were gone, burned away, building a bigger flame than before. In my seat, I myself began to become consumed by the fire. My eyes stared into the flames and witnessed the burning. My friend and his history seemed to burn away so easily. How long would I fare in the flames? The fire ignited a hunger in me. All things in the flame and the darkness beyond spoke in mockery. They poked and prodded and singed my soul.

My search through the house took on a new hunger. I felt as if I were a wild wolf tearing through his furniture and walls in search of some meaning and nourishment. With the fire behind me, I could witness the destruction I was causing. My consciousness benefited from it. The guilt waned to the overwhelming dispersion of anger and frustration. The fire urged me on. I rummaged through the cabinets with the swiftness of a thief that lurked in the shadows. I opened and shut doors with such force that I pulled them off their hinges. I scratched the walls, ripping down paintings in search of some hidden valuables. Then I discovered a small hatch at the back of his armoire. The secrets were beginning to reveal themselves. I snickered with the fire. In the hidden compartment of the armoire, I found the saint's hidden liquor. He had sworn off the devil's poison, he had told me when we were younger, but he kept it hidden in the crevices of his home out of desperation or deception. I struggled to open the bottle of whiskey. I realized then that the house smelled tedious. I forced the cap open finally. I took one swig and relished in the warm heartiness of it. It made me burn and smile. I held the bottle in one hand, spilling liquor as I stumbled to the living room. Half of the bottle I drank wildly in the company of the fire, and the other half I used to give the house a more humane scent. Liquor drenched the cushions of the torn sofa and seeped down into the wooden boards of the house. Finally, the house smelled as if it were the domain of a ruined artist.

I fell, holding the bottle to my chest. I tipped the bottle to my mouth to catch the last few drops. An unexpected waterfall of whiskey drenched my face and chest. I choked and coughed until I lifted my head and launched a glob of spit toward the darkness. My palate was overwhelmed with bitterness that I could not diffuse in any way. I lay back down and turned my head to the side. The bottle of whiskey, nudged by my body, slowly rolled away toward the door. I felt the heat of the fire behind me. It attempted to provide some comfort and the much-needed touch of recognition and validation I sought. My body suddenly began to feel so tired and weak. I had already felt so sluggish, but now I could start to feel myself drift off and, in the distance, make out the sweet embrace of sleep. I tasted the remaining droplets of whiskey on my lips and face. It inspired one last bitter thought. I finally considered that perhaps he had lied in his letters to me. There were no expansive ideas that he had birthed. No prose. No plays. No paintings. He had achieved nothing, and he was nothing. All these years, I had spent my time chasing lies, aspiring to create ideas that rivaled the size of his mind. When in reality, he had accomplished nothing. He framed the past to inspire and remind him of who he once was, how envied he once was, and cast an image of something he could never again achieve. He was starved of this creativity by no one but himself. Yes, my friend was the one to blame for what had become of him. My friend had failed, and it was all due to his own faults and lack of determination. Why dream such dreams when you know you can't accomplish them? Not all of us are destined for the summit of the heavens.

Slowly, sleep began to take me, and I felt myself drift away into the darkness. I did not fear the cold and darkness anymore; I was fire-kissed and warm with victory. What did I dream of that night? I can't quite remember. Yet, I am still uncertain if it actually was a dream or not.

I awoke in the middle of the night, aching, numb, and trapped. The warmth was gone. All around me was the darkness. Only a sliver of light shone from underneath the door frame, still partially blocked by the bottle of whiskey. I attempted to force myself up, but my limbs did not comply, and so I remained on the cold wooden floor. The bottle of whiskey teased me with its presence as it lay beside the door. I craved more of it, but what I craved even more was to escape the estate. A gust of wind blew in from underneath the door frame, pushing the bottle away from the door until it inevitably rolled back and collided with the door once again. The wind was not satisfied with this. A moment of stillness passed before the wind retaliated and pushed even more harshly at the door. The bottle swiftly rolled, losing its straightaway course and finding a new destination down the hallway. It vanished into the darkness, but I continued to hear the glass rolling across the wooden floor. I listened, waiting for it to inevitably hit another wall down the hallway. The wind continued to blow in loud gusts. The door withheld the damage. In the shrieks of the wind, I seemed to lose the sound of the bottle.

More light had exposed itself underneath the door. The sliver of moonlight shone brightly. It was the gray moonlight peering underneath. It only reached so far. I couldn't make anything out of the slight opening. I imagined what could be in the distance: the morbid garden path, the stretch of empty grassland, the sleepless barkeep, the trudging of the train, the bright rooms, the chattering artists, my littered desk, the empty pages, and the lonely grave. The reaper sat above the grave, sharpening his scythe. From far away, the reaper appeared as a crooked dead tree, only given away by the gleaming crescent by his side. His hand reached out to take the life of the fallen.

My hand quivered. It continued to shake until I felt a paintbrush in its grasp. I was at the base of the ruined chapel I had found in the village. The ardent pursuit of my masterpiece had brought me here at night. An easel sat in front of me. The painting was positioned at the root of the village's evil. The streets were empty but for the lanterns and the moths they attracted. Not one soul was out in the darkness. I was here alone with my own lantern positioned to provide light for my easel. At night, all the colors on my palette lacked their vibrancy, but in this way fit the tone of the totem I had sought to capture. Dark strokes painted the abandoned timber on the scorched land. As I painted, I recalled that not one soul in the village had ever peeked over my shoulder and inquired about my work. They had passed by without ever even batting an eye as to what my intentions were in their town. I shook my mind away from the village folk and returned to the subject of my painting. My eye and brush were drawn to the statue of an angel that had broken off its pedestal and become buried in a thick layer of dirt. Its face was tarnished with scars and filthy patches of soil. This was the level of detail I sought to capture in my painting. After all, this was meant to be my masterpiece. If the villagers had been there, I bet they would have trudged through the city with futility in their eyes and a lack of attention to the fine details of the world. The entrance to the chapel no longer existed; there was no chance of redemption for the village folk. Their hanging heads, long faces, and empty vessels had no care for the world. They were wasting space. Somewhere amongst the piles of ruin was a splintered cross; I knew it to be so. There sat a ruined chapel destroyed, whether by nature or man, but certainly uncared for by man. In an ideal reality, the chapel would still be standing as a beacon of fairness, mercy, and God. Yet, did the village deserve such fairness? The villagers meaninglessly peered, ignorant of my condition and ignorant of the world. None of them knew who I was. This village had no expectations of me and, for all I know, they believed me to be some aimless traveler who had stopped by for a drink. They were crude hosts. These people had no appreciation for me and the gifts I possessed. Such ignorance could have surely driven a man to the point of death. Don't you think? To not be appreciated, understood, and known is to strip life of any meaning. Without such necessities, a man could not embrace his own self nor attain what his heart desires. Such a fate could have surely befallen my friend. I cried out into the darkness, cursing the villagers and the way they had ruined my friend and his promise of art. My shouting was filled with hatred for their souls. I sought to purge the village of this evil and, in the process, purge my friend and his life of the same. They were fools! All of them! Fools commanded by the devil himself. They would not be welcomed into my heaven, sit alongside me, know my God, and rest in my realm. They would perish! They would rot and be erased from existence, buried underneath the same filth as the remnants of the chapel. This is what I had drawn too: a body buried underneath the ruined chapel. I could make out the body and the face until the light of my lantern died.

The only light in the home came in from underneath the door frame. It was the gray of the night. I stayed trapped in my condition. The wind had halted, and the door could finally rest. Silence had become ever so peaceful. Slowly, I began to become conscious of my breath and the way my chest rose and fell. I felt the space between my fingers and became acutely aware of the tactile sensation of the clothes on my body. I had realized that by focusing on these sensations, perhaps I could break out of this spell and stand afoot prepared to leave the godforsaken place. The floor beneath me impressively carried the load of my body. With one aggravated step, I could foresee my leg going through the floorboard and exposing itself to the darkness underneath the home. Whether that amount of darkness would be enough to corrupt me or entrap me forever, I did not know. The effects of the liquor had begun to wear off, and so I pressured my body to rise and lift off the ground. All my attempts were to no avail. I had simply over-exhausted myself. My ear hugged the wooden floor and made out the sound of my own heartbeat. With this notion of failure, my eyes fell to the light once again.

The light that had once shone through the door had been covered by two feet. A man stood outside the door, wearing dark shoes. The light curved around him and seemed to illuminate with more focus. A sliver of light hit my face. Someone had approached the door. My mind ruminated about who it could be, largely in fear of what my fate would become if he were to reach me. My ear hugged the wooden paneling of the floor. Underneath me, I heard a rapid beat, the sound of a heart begging to leave its earthly being. The thief had returned, I knew. The golden handle began to shake. The door would not relent. The thief had come back to take the goods he had left behind. If he were to see I had destroyed the remaining riches, he would kill me. He would plunge a dagger into my heart, expressing his anger and pain for the fact that I had destroyed his chance at a fortune. I knew it. He would murder me and rob me of my possessions, too. If I could speak, I could perhaps talk my way out of it and promise him wealth, but I could not. A thief would not listen to reason, nor would he respond to my potential. The sound of the heart grew in volume and touched the soft side of my ear. The door handle continued to shake. I inaudibly shouted at the door, yelling for the thief to leave, expressing my pity and painting the false bravado I wished to encapsulate. A sudden force struck against the door. The thief was trying to barge in. The door must hold up. The thief pushed at the door, far stronger than the wind, attempting to barge in with his shoulder, his leg, his back, and all the strength he possessed. My ear vibrated against the floor. The heartbeat prevailed like the sound of a hammer striking an anvil, growing louder and louder. A passionate strike led my ear canal to flow with wet and thick blood. A strong thud struck the door. The thief halted. The silence was followed by whispers urging to allow the intruder inside. He banged the door over and over again and begged for entry. When denied by my silence, he began to push himself through the door. I hoped the voice would offer me forgiveness and mercy.

The man's form of entry was not sudden or loud except for one last cry for help. Blinded by the light, I saw a face begin to form in the door. There was silence. Pools of blood painted the door until they collected into the torn muscle and skin. Slivers of flesh, like shredded paper, had begun to appear through the center of the door, slowly growing intact and coming to form one face smeared with dirt and blood. The intruder had used his will to push himself through the portal. His eyes formed out of tiny beads of water as they watched ahead and landed on me. His hair was thick with dirt that rained down on top of his face and underneath him. The sound of his teeth came cutting through the door like a scythe. My heart languished at the sight of his face and the horrific deed he committed. The face had formed and watched on with its loose tongue at my limp body. From it, I heard a faint breath, extending its grasp onto my soul. His tenebrous shadow grew closer to me by the second until I felt the weight of it on my chest and began to feel my breath fade away. Dirt fell on me as the shadow stood atop my body. The light grew dim as the shadow buried me with its pressure. I saw his face, and I saw the ruined pillars of the chapel rising beside me into the sky. In a moment of God, light shone through the outline of the door. When the light vanished, the man had retreated, leaving his mark on the door and me. I had been saved. There isn't much I remember from that night after that.

That was it. I had fulfilled my purpose in the village and had purchased a train ticket home, set to leave soon after sunrise. Yet, I had not found my friend's missing work, nor had I created my masterpiece. I lived with these facts as I sat in silence. From the lone train station, I saw the flat plains similar to the ones my friend had painted. A crooked tree cried in the distance. Undiscernible from the muddy snow and gray clouds, sheep entered the fray and slowly scattered across the grassland. They were led by a cloaked shepherd and his son. The distance between us seemed immense, but I crossed the plain in a mere second. I asked the shepherd what he knew of my friend. I asked how my friend was and how he passed away.

He knew who I was. He knew what I had done. He shook his head and said, *I just guide the lost souls back.*

Spiral to Hell

The forces of nature collide.

Falling.
I'm falling.
I'm falling.
I'm falling.
Darkness underneath me,
I'm falling.
I'm falling
Furiously.
The pain of everything's falling with me,
Like a boulder crashing into the sea.
The invisible shield of wind lashes against my body,
And I am falling.
Down a cavernous pit,
I'm falling.
I don't see anything underneath me.
It's just darkness and coldness ready to consume me.
With hate, anger, and blood in my veins,
I am falling.

The Wind

Dark red walls like the inside of a beast's mouth,
I'm falling.

Tears strewn across my temples,
I'm falling.
The tears are floating above me,
I'm falling.
I am falling more furiously.
The wind forces away all fluids:
My eyes, nose, and mouth run dry and useless.
I'm falling.
It tears at the fabric on my chest and legs.
It strikes the hair on my face and scalp,
Combing the hair in unfounded directions.
I don't move my face and feel the full brunt of the force on my body.
My eyes and cheeks widen with the full force of the wind,
Attempting to gasp for a breath in the
Undistinguished source of suffering.
I see it.
I smell it.
I taste it.
Something foul, rotten, ruinous.
Where am I falling to?
What is the pain that's awaiting me?
This is the pain.

The Mountain

It wasn't a tomb I set foot into.
The ground vanished underneath me,
And I was forced into this dark fate.
I don't recall the hands that tried to grab me
And save me from this fate.
Are they the reason I'm falling?
They're the reason I couldn't stand afloat.
The reason I wished for ruin and death.
The reason I bore slashes across my arms and legs.

The reason my shoulders and back crumpled.
The reason my mind split in half and caved in on itself.

The Fire

I am still falling.
Alone in a bottomless pit.
No hands to save me.
Alone.
Alone,
With my own devices.
Alone,
With my own ruin.
Alone,
I am falling.
Falling
Alone.
The wind whispers to me.
It reminds me of the seething words of the vipers
Who spat venom onto my skin.
I remember what is inside of me.
I am not alone.
The toxic flame takes its time
and takes its toll on my body.
The immediate source of death reminds me of life.
I am clutching for survival,
Begging for life.
Don't let it take effect!
Don't let it invade my skin!
Don't let it harbor in my blood!
Don't let it spread!
Don't let it consume me!
I feel the venom
Sinking into me.

Take it out!
Take it out!
Suck it out of me!
It stings!
It stings at the end of my veins.
It diffuses into my blood and suffocates me from the inside.
Slash me in half and eradicate my body of the poison.
Spare me.
Spare me this fate.
Please,
I beg you.
I was not meant for this.
I was meant for life.
I was meant for meaning and purpose.
I was meant for fulfillment.
I was meant for a legacy.
In another dream, I was meant to be free.
Spare me, please.
Venom courses through my veins.
I watch it spread,
Spread all over
Into coldness and entropy.

The Sea

I am resigned to this fate,
To this condition,
To this hell.
This is hell,
Blasphemy underneath the covers of humanity.
Slim pickings from the garden,
So I was thrown into this unjust hell.
The world would rather burn
Before granting me the chance to fly.

This is the Hell.
This is the end.
Conscious of my fate,
I am falling,
Falling
To Hell.
Whispers transform into laughter.
I hear the cackling of harpies.
They're invisible and ugly.
Their sharp wings glide in the wind as they watch me fall to my Hell.
The pit erupts underneath me into a fire,
Ready to consume me.
I feel a sharp blade against the fiber of my being,
Right against my throat.
I am one incision from falling to my end,
A weightless pile of flesh and bones.
I see the end.
I see the three heads of death:
Three open flames.
I go spiraling down.
Emboldened by the flame,
I go with the rage and deeper into the pit.
In its mouth, I see the pitfalls of humanity, life,
All molecular activity.
I rush to it with my weight underneath me.
One snip away
From breathing,
Living,
And remembering.
I recall my last memories, my last thoughts, and my last feelings.
Mother,
Why did I resist when you went to dunk me in the River Styx?
Why was I so foolish?
You protected me.

Why could I not protect myself?
I must pay the punishment.
I am sentenced to my fate,
To the deepest pit of hell,
Tartarus
To exist in meaningless parts of what I once was.
You will not remember who I was.
Now,
I am falling.
I am falling for life.
Falling
Falling
Falling
Till the end of the world.

———

Skeletons

Waiting feels dreadful. Nothing feels quite as wasteful as the act of standing and enduring through time, waiting for your turn. That was my first encounter with death, I believe.

It was a Monday, as I recall, when I had taken my friend to the train station and wished him farewell. He had asked me to escort him and for help carrying his baggage, and I had kindly obliged. Oliver was my last friend or associate left in the city. He mentioned to me that he had received a letter from his mother. The letter spoke of how sick she was and how she was unsure how much time she had left in this world. She was fortunate enough to have reached an elderly age, and now she wished for her son to be by her side during what felt like her last days. In the same way that Oliver had escaped from his family to be in the city, he now escaped the city to join the comfort of his family. I could tell that, underneath his reason for leaving, he had been growing tired of the city. It had alluded him. He had come here with aspirations and talent to cultivate, but the city had sapped him dry. It was not a manageable beast for all, I understood.

Oliver had sat on the bench, balancing his portfolio on his shaky knees. When the bell had begun to ring and the whistle sounded on the train, he slowly rose and fixed his hat onto his head, careful not to ruin a single hair. He then smoothed out his coat and removed lingering pieces of lint, while I took his baggage and waited for him. He stood frozen in his tracks, worried about catching his train but waiting until the very last moment to board. Then he handed me his portfolio, after consideration, and asked me to keep it safe. I sensed, in his disposition, some fear of dragging his artistic pursuits to where he had once come from, and so I became the guardian of his works.

Bidding farewell to him was bittersweet, I would admit. Despite struggling to pass through the raucous crowd to the platform, he seemed to stand proudly and wave goodbye to me. Then he entered the passenger car with his two suitcases, and the train took him away. There went my last associate.

I sighed to myself and entered the queue to leave the station. There were only two exits, and the newly installed turnstiles made entering and exiting the building a troublesome business. One that made an individual deeply consider whether to embark on any visits to the train station whatsoever. Since there were only two exits and far more platforms, everyone packed into the tight hallway that led out of the building. Bodies and bags collided in the queue as more and more folk filed in, forcing others deeper in the line, even closer. In such tight spaces, I hate being so close to others, so close that I can smell the rank scent of the collected sweat and grime on their clothes. I could not stand to sit in one of those forsaken train seats, let alone stand in a damn queue to leave the cesspool amongst the sitters. A sudden shove came from behind, and I was thrust into the woman ahead of me. She looked at me so plainly that I felt myself wasted to have thought she would have been offended. I keep the habit of bending my elbows and raising my hands to my shoulders to avoid any accidents or accusations of where my hands may land in a flurry, such as this. As more folk piled in, however, and thrust forward, I reconsidered my generosity.

The queue can only be at a standstill for so long until you start to question the competency of those around you. How were those fools not moving, I remember thinking to myself with my hands held in front of me and the portfolio against my waist. I remember seeing the end of the hallway and just some light peaking in from the exit, but a rabble covered my line of sight, and I could hardly see more than 4 bodies ahead of me. I don't know how the others would not have seen him. But from the crowd, passing by the men ahead of me, a skeleton turned the corner. The pale and naked skeleton, devoid of any features and somehow animated, passed by the shoulders of the men attempting to push ahead and slowly marched toward me. No one knocked into him. No one turned to see if it truly was a living skeleton walking beside them. But I saw, and the skeleton seemed to see me. He walked with his loosely connected bones through the tight space and right up to me. The skeleton looked at me and went to point. His finger touched my chest, just as he stood two feet away. His finger felt sharp, and I think that's when I became marked for death.

I believe he walked past me eventually, and I eventually made my way out of the queue. Once I was out, I just walked my way back home. There was a silence to that walk. I can't even tell you what I walked past that day. I would usually wave to Gustave in his book shop on my way home, but I can't recall if I did. Neither could Gustave, I imagined, with the number of faces he sees in a day.

I just came home, shook my head, and took it to mean that I was truly beyond myself while huddled up in the queue. I did find myself to be considerably fatigued that day. Another contributor could have perhaps been the fleeting but still present sadness I felt of losing Oliver. Even if he could not crack it, he was still the last associate of mine from our coterie. After his departure, the circle was effectively dissolved. A band cannot be composed of just one artist. Our circle would sit at the back table in the Phoenix's Den, the saloon which boasted the rebirth of art and human creativity. Oliver's departure was my signal that this vision had now died. It was time for me to begin the independent pursuit of what were once our shared interests and goals. All throughout my life, I had attempted to devote myself to my craft, but that is when I rightfully became preoccupied by the pursuit.

Oliver had sheepishly left me his portfolio, and so I was obliged to peruse it. As expected, I had not found anything of note.

No shocking revelations or repressed jealousy came afoot; I was deflated at most. I did find an incomplete piece he had painted of me, and it amused me for a bit. He had used a cursed yellow to outline my face and pigmentation, but half my face in the painting had sat hollow of any color or flesh. At that moment, I understood that his talent had perhaps never manifested. So I turned to my writing desk and set forth in attempting to capture the sublime.

Weeks had passed since I attempted to write what I sought out. Finding the truth in poetry is easier said than felt. During that time, a sort of affliction had consumed me. When I would sit down and attempt to commit myself to writing, my creativity and cognitive functioning would be stunted, and I would eventually become immobilized. I attempted all sorts of means to break myself of this. I would read. I would pace about my room and occasionally outdoors. I would turn to my phonograph and play Johannes Brahms's Violin Concerto, in D major, Opus 77. Not the best-known of the German violin concertos, but an obscure piece that Brahms dedicated to his violinist friend. It carried through it the ghost of Beethoven. And I preferred this piece by Brahms over the works of his contemporaries—damnation to his critics. He may not have been the most widely regarded composer of our times, but he was a man committed to his craft.

I would continue pacing while listening to the strangely placed oboes at the introduction of the theme. In my dullness, I would typically drink a glass of whiskey as the timpani rolled in and the solo violinist began to play. Just as the violinist would assume his descent and abandon his arching arpeggio, I would enter into a stupor while turning out my window and looking beyond. Most often, I'd find the mountain in the distance to captivate me. Then the violinist would emerge through a winding and flowing line and arrive at his own theme. Leaping down before dropping out, the soloist would continue to tease his ascent before descending. Past the development, the piece enters into an improvised cadenza by Brahms's friend, until departing from it and transfiguring the original theme. The tones of the violin become countered by the wind until the horns signal the cascading arpeggio after the violin attempts to reach considerably high. The horns animatedly ascend the theme until the steady march leads to the sharp stammering and the final punctuating chord, followed by the roll of the drum. The first movement ends, and the adagio takes over with its descending tone, often carrying me to the base of the mountain that I wished to one day climb. As I would attempt to look upward at the height of the feat, the gypsy like spirit of the third movement would then muddy my mind and take me away from my analysis of the art to how insurmountable this challenge seemed. The gypsies would dance while I banged my head against my novels to clear my creative inhibition. For the last few weeks, it seemed that inspiration would not gift itself to me. I was not sure of what I had done to make this romantic gift withdraw from me. I had cherished it and assigned it primary importance in my life. As I attempted to produce meaningful poetry that pursued what was once considered the supernatural truth, it had been snuffed out by the cruel and harsh realism that infected the world and its art. I would always forget when the third movement would come to an end. The prolonged and soft notes of violin and cello would then suddenly be whisked away, ending the concerto, and leaving me stewing in silence. I would be sprawled onto my writing desk, with my pen in my hand and pieces of parchment crinkled underneath me. In those moments, when the cylinder in the phonograph had reached a scrawling end, I would dearly wish I had been born a musician in another life. Then sleep would commonly overtake me while lying there.

Around that time was when I began to hear the knocks. Just as I would be simply resting or going about my business in my apartment, the knocks would come at the door. I recall the first occasion; a heavy knock had come in three sudden notes upon my front door, followed by a beat of silence. I had raised my head for the next measure out of curiosity and concern but never committed myself to movement.

You see, it was very uncommon for me to receive a guest or any solicitor at my apartment. I have never been the most well-acquainted with my neighbors, and therefore, I did not suspect them. To the left of my unit lived an elderly couple who could hardly lift a finger, and I hardly considered ever socializing with them. They had become accustomed to the loud music that rang out of my phonograph daily, or at least I assumed, since I had never received a complaint. On the other end lived a single mother and her sickly child. They covered their mouths whenever they walked by, and I avoided them altogether. Across the way, there was a couple, and then a man whose wife had left him. I knew of the solitary man's condition not through conversation but by recollecting the cries of a woman cursing and running through the floor and down the stairs, as he had yelled at her to never return and slammed his door. When she had left, she had dragged her heavy luggage with her, ripping a few tears into the carpet that covered the slender hallway. And a few shawls of hers had been abandoned during the sudden departure that neither the man collected nor the woman returned for. The husband had attempted, on occasion, to knock on the door of the newly separated man, but to no avail. The husband had worked at the railroads before suffering an injury to his hand that left him incapable of handling heavy materials. I only knew this because once—no, twice—the husband and then his wife had come to my door begging me if I knew of any work opportunities. I had refused to offer any assistance, and that served as the last contact I had ever had with them. I knew they had found some work, however. I heard them leave and return to their home throughout their day, but both of them seemed miserable. I could tell because through those thin walls, I would hear them drag their feet.

Then the sudden knock came again. They would continue for days, at various times. Never when I expected.

Once, I had rushed to the door immediately upon hearing the intrusive noise. Blindly, I had lunged out of my room to see not a soul in the hallway. But as I continued to peek, I believed I saw what seemed to be the sole of a shoe disappearing to my left and toward the stairs. I took a few cautious steps in the direction of the disappearing figure, but halted myself to listen for their footsteps or breathing. Nothing came to my ears, and so I stomped a few steps toward the stairs to pose as a threatening presence and ward off any troublemakers. Then I turned and returned to my unit.

Once I returned and locked the bolts on my door, I made a deduction about the intruder. I recalled that I never heard even a snicker of laughter come from the man as he made his escape. Therefore, the solicitor was not intruding on me for the pursuit of laughter or an elaborate jest. There was something more to the knocks. They came two or three times a day, keeping me awake and alert. Even when I left my apartment and attempted to watch the entrance from afar, I wouldn't see any strange suspects appear. Then, just as I would return home, the knocks would return with me. It was almost as if the intruder had known that I was watching for them or had grown suspicious of his activity. I even considered taking the matter to the police or consulting with my landlord, but I did not have it within me to socialize with them. My energy faltered over those weeks, and the knocking continued to disturb my sleep. Even if I covered my ears with a pillow, the knock on the door would pervade through the thin walls.

Then I finally decided that I would sit there beside the door and wait for the intruder to come. I positioned myself right by the door that day and grabbed a novel to maintain my attention. Romantic literature has always captivated my interest, but during that time, I had become drawn to the Russian great, Tolstoy, and his return to writing. His latest publication included the inspiring piece, *The Death of Ivan Ilyich*, which I am sure will survive our time and implant itself into the literary canon of many aspiring writers, as I.

I can't recall how much time had passed since I had been seated by the door, reading and waiting. At some point in time, I know I had fallen asleep with my head lying on my knees and the book beside me. Upon awakening, I recall the revolting pressure I felt of my hard knees upon my forehead and the throbbing pain that seared through it. Amongst the blasting pain, I wanted to lie on the floor and be taken by rest, but I began to hear the floorboards squeak outside. Just a very subtle series of steps slowly approaching from the left end of the hallway toward my end of the floor. And so, despite my pain, I rushed up as quietly as I could to defend my property and sanity, almost falling over. I waited with my right hand hovering just above the handle and my left hand ready to unlock the latch. The footsteps continued to approach. These footsteps were slow and intentional and could hardly be heard anymore. The other sounds from the flat had consumed my attention again, and I felt myself losing the sound of footsteps in the medley around me. So I was left simply to my exasperated gut and intuition to perceive the rhythm of the knock and know when to confront my intruder.

In a flash, just as I heard the sound of someone's fist grazing the door, I pulled open the portal and grabbed the soul opposite me. I grabbed his wool coat and yanked him inside, placing him against the wall where I had sat. His hat flew off during the affair and fell right behind him in the hallway as I suddenly shut the door. Once I had him secured, I placed my forearm against the stranger's throat and heard him gasp. Then I laid eyes on him and saw the skeleton right ahead of me. My forearm was dug into his neck, and he wore a black coat over his bony body. I was enraged that this same phantom had followed me from the station to my home and now had dressed himself to mock me. He had bothered me endlessly for days. A terrifying mockery was what I took it as. Meanwhile, he just stood there, restrained and choking. His feet kicked some, and I raised him above me. I rather enjoyed the rattling of his bones as he struggled fruitlessly against me.

My eyes were keenly focused on him to finally unleash my anger, but within them, I still felt a tinge of concern. "What in the Hell are you? Why do you bang at my door at obscene times of the day? If you were not some vicious phantom of my mind, a curse born out of my inhibition, I would have drowned you in the sea. Smashing you with rocks, and throwing you down in a small fish cage to disappear forever."

The skeleton kept stammering through my raving, making empty sounds through his mouth.

"I saw you previously at the train station. Why are you following me, huh? Why is it that no one else saw you? Why is it that you haunt me?" I grabbed the skeleton's throat with both my hands.

The skeleton kicked at me harder, but his feet felt limp. All I could make of his stammering were his desperate attempts for air.

"Answer me! Give me a damn answer as to why you have invaded my mind," I gritted my teeth and squeezed harder around the skeleton's throat.

The skeleton then slowly raised his right forearm and all of a sudden stopped struggling. "*Your technique is off.*"

My eyes were agape, unbelieving of what I just heard and saw. The skeleton spoke to me. I began to squeeze harder.

The skeleton yelped, coughed, and then began to laugh. "*I was being kind and playing along, but let me down now,*" the skeleton hung in front of me with his loose limbs. "*You can't choke me. I'm made of bones!*" His tone carried with it a sarcastic and profane attitude that left me not just confused, but offended.

I still stared menacingly, but I admit, my grip began to loosen due to my lost morale.

"*Would you mind letting me down!*" The skeleton yelled at me through his clattering teeth.

I then suddenly dropped him. My mind was pacing, trying to discern what this heathen truly was. If he were a phantom of my mind, I realized I should be able to destroy him at my hands, whether by choking or slamming him against the wall. But I also considered what if he truly was some extraordinary supernatural being sent to me.

As he had finished adjusting his coat properly onto his shoulders, I turned up and met his empty and dark eye sockets. There was nothing within them, just like his mouth and the rest of his being, but I felt a strange presence watching me through that emptiness. He stared directly at me as I feigned the same confidence I possessed earlier, until he began to look past me. The skeleton shifted around me and walked further into my unit. I wanted to pull him back from further cursing my home, but I was unsure if any attack of mine could truly affect him. The skeleton looked like a comedic sketch in a newspaper from behind. He wore sleek black dress shoes, and only parts of his slender legs were visible between his tall coat and shoes. None of it made sense to me as to why the skeleton stood, walked, dressed, and talked in his frivolous and ironic manner. It was hard to take him with authority, but I could not deny that a living skeleton stood in front of me.

The skeleton sighed to himself and placed his hands at his hips, "*This is a shithole.*"

I wanted to protest, but I didn't know whether I should try my luck.

The skeleton then turned back to me, "*What's wrong with you? Are you not aware that it's rude to stare at others?*"

I was seriously taken aback by this creature's manners.

The skeleton then clapped his hands and began to feel his head, "*Oh, it seems like I've lost my hat. No wonder I felt a chill.*"

He somehow felt a chill, but did not feel his throat being constricted.

He began to walk to the door, "*Best to retrieve it before it's stolen.*"

To think that a skeleton would worry about having his hat stolen. I responded with casual confidence and opened the door to the hallway.

"Are you not afraid of others seeing you?" I spoke to the skeleton as he stepped out.

The skeleton lifted his hat and dusted it off, "*It's quite all right if they do. I am well known amongst the folk.*"

Yes, of course you are, I remember thinking to myself. Just as the skeleton placed on his hat and turned around, I slammed the door and locked it shut. I pressed my palms against the door to shield myself.

"Stay out, you heathen!" I yelled. "You are not welcome. Leave me bloody alone!"

"*Who's not welcome?*" I felt a whisper in my ear and a presence above my shoulder.

I turned and saw the skeleton standing in front of me wearing his large top hat.

"How? How did you do that?"

"*Do what?*" The skeleton tilted his head at me. "*Excuse my manners, however.*"

The skeleton took off his hat and carried it with him to my writing desk. He sat in the chair and referenced the materials sitting ahead of him.

"You have no right to be sitting there! That is my desk. This is my home. Leave! I don't know what sorcery you possess, but go and entertain some pathetic and lonesome soul. I have urgent matters I need to attend to, and you are seated at my desk—"

"*If I left, where else would I possibly find a pathetic and lonesome soul?*"

"How dare you!"

The skeleton began to flip through my old manuscripts.

"Unhand my work," I marched up to my desk and pulled my work from the skeleton's hands.

"*That's not very wise. Don't you want others to see your work?*" The skeleton calmly spoke.

"Well, you have seen it now, and that is more than enough. Since you have done me this honor, I pray, please take your leave."

The skeleton sighed, "*I suppose if you insist.*"

I quickly followed with a sigh of relief.

He had risen from my desk and was walking toward the door when I began to utter, "Yes, please leave. Leave and do not come back. The trick that you did, I don't know how… my mind must be playing tricks on me."

"*You think so?*" He turned to face me.

"Yes," I suddenly realized I was starting to breathe heavily. I grabbed hold of my knees as I began to lean forward. "I just wish to write in peace. Leave me to rest and be at peace."

The skeleton then appeared to think to himself before replying, "*Hmmm, what do you suspect I'm here to do?*"

"I don't know. I don't care," I tossed my manuscript papers beside me.

"*Are you aware of who I am?*"

"You are some phantom. I am not convinced you are real, but I ask that you leave me be."

"*And who are you?*"

"What do you mean, who am I? You're standing in my apartment and have been harassing me for the past few weeks, and you don't even know who I am?"

"*I know who you are, but do you?*"

I caught my tongue, "What do you mean? Yes, I know. I'm Peter. I'm a writer."

"*Well, thank you for confirming. I'm glad I've got the right man,*" The skeleton chuckled to himself. "*Peeter, I must inform you. You do not have long to live.*"

"What? What do you mean?"

"*Your end approaches.*"

"How would you know that?" I steadied my posture while attempting not to break down in a pool of sweat. "Are you the Grim Reaper? Have you come to take my soul?"

"*Heavens, no. I am not he, but I know precisely how and when you will perish, and I have come to be with you during this challenging time.*"

"No, no. You don't know me. You have the wrong man—"

"*I have always been there, pursuing you, knocking at the door, watching you at the beach, waiting along the cave. It is just now that you have decided to open the door and greet me.*"

"No, you don't know what you're talking about. You need to leave."

As I uttered those words, I saw the skeleton move his attention to outside my window. He glanced past the window. Then he approached it and stood beside it, and became quiet.

Seeing him come to rest by the window, I struggled to maintain a proper gait as I traveled to my rack of alcohol. I had felt a certain strength leave me that day, perhaps from the skeleton's touch or perhaps that death was truly approaching. However, I hoped that a glass of whiskey would inspire me with some courage and strength in that moment. I poured myself a glass and stood at a fair distance, watching the skeleton as if on patrol. As I turned my glass upward and felt the whiskey cascade down my throat, I felt the skeleton's limp presence remain where I last saw him. I swirled my glass and stared down at the brown whiskey swirling about as I recalled the remarkable high notes of Brahms's violin concerto. Just as the liquor sat still, I felt myself return to my dignity.

"Who in the Hell do you think you are?" I said to the skeleton.

The skeleton simply turned.

"How dare you just barge into my home and defile it with your cursed hands? Making all kinds of remarks about my mortality?" I placed my free hand into my pocket, assuming a stance of authority. "I will not stand for this insolence. As far as I am concerned, my mortality is a matter exclusive to me and my whiskey. I will not dare to hear a stranger remark on my life, and especially to say that 'ooo I herald your death.' Take your cursed foresight out of my home and away from my eyes."

The skeleton just stood there.

"I have dealt with many fools such as you who have wished me nothing but anguish. And I will not be deterred by you, phantom. You will not stop me from actualizing my legacy. Look at you. You are nothing but bones and a shaggy coat and scuffed shoes. Even if you are just a trick of my mind, I know that you are nothing compared to the flesh and muscle I stand as in front of you. I have evolved past you, and you are nothing but some shit remains—"

"You are going to die!" The skeleton yelled at me.

"You are a piece of shit!"

"You will die!"

"You are worthless. You know nothing!"

"It is time to take this seriously."

"My pursuits are serious."

"You will be dead!"

"Stop standing in my damn way then and leave!"

"I will never leave you, Peeter."

"If you won't leave, I will cast you out and break you apart."

"If you must play this game, I will dance on your grave happily and laugh at your pitiful existence," the skeleton laughed.

"You can't stop me!" I yelled and launched my glass of whiskey at the skeleton.

The glass collided with the window. In a loud clash, fragments of glass became scattered everywhere. The shrill and rapid whisper of the wind, where once was a small window, filled the room with a sudden cold. I started to shake, seeing my shattered window. I felt my body exhausted of its remaining strength and clutched onto the nearest counter to save myself.

The skeleton turned back to me from the shattered window, *"Lovely mountain in the distance, isn't it?"*

Then, in the cold, I felt myself slip from consciousness and collapse onto a bed of glass.

When I woke, it was just me, to my lonesome. I was lying in my bed, and as I looked ahead, I saw that the floor was clean of any glass. The room still felt chilly, and the window remained broken, confirming that I had indeed thrown my glass at it. There were no signs of the skeleton, and so I remained confused about whether he truly was a figment of my imagination or an agent of death. It may also be said that he could have been both.

I forced myself to sit up, still feeling a malaise dragging me down. However long I had slept, I did not feel rested. A pain still blasted through my temples. In honesty, my sleep had not been of the best quality for the last few weeks. Not just because of the disruptive knocks that came on the door, but I struggled to fall and stay asleep, waking up throughout the night in a cold sweat. I did not dream much either. It was just the faint noises of the flat I lived in or passers-by on the street outside my window that came to me when I closed my eyes and lay in bed. Then I would finally wake up and feel unrested and parched. Perhaps that was another reason why I drank, so that I could peacefully sleep.

That morning, I took myself to my lavatory to wipe myself clean from my nightly sweat. I ran the tap and splashed myself in the face with cold water that further made me shiver. I began to splash my face with vigor to cleanse myself and forget my fatigue and the skeleton. When I looked up at the stained mirror, I saw myself with dim eyes and a languid face. I kept splashing myself until I felt more energized. I found that only anger was what entered me. When I turned back up to see my appearance, I was rather heartbroken to see how sickly I truly looked. And I wondered, was this what the skeleton referenced, that death was approaching?

As a writer, death has been a common topic that I have perused, discussed, and read. It is a theme and concept that has enamored many and has always remained hard to understand. Despite my romantic inclination, death has been a thing in which beauty is hard to find, especially when it marks the end of an empty life that has yet to seize its potential. In truth, I found that I was scared of death. That is not a novel idea. But to me and the bravado I attempted to face the world with, it was a harsh burden to confront. That I would one day meet my end, and that the skeleton had perhaps indeed heralded my end. I did not believe in an afterlife. I did not believe in reincarnation. I struggled to even confront the question as to what lay ahead of me. Therefore, I redirected my focus and clutched onto my sink, thinking furiously about how to mitigate this disease.

I examined myself further in the mirror and saw a yellow hue come from my body. It stunned me, and I felt Oliver's painting of me come to life. The undertones of my skin had transformed yellow. Worse, the whites of my eyes had disappeared, and they lay yellow. Yellow, which I had always seen as a color of friendship, life, and warmth, was now transformed in my eyes. The yellow glow that came from my eyes reminded me of a greed that possesses one over their life and a severe indicator of the golden sky before a storm. The blood vessels in my eyes cut through the sky and created cracks of red with the signs of Hell coming through. I kept washing my face, attempting hard to rub off the yellow underneath my skin. I cupped my hands and held them up to my eyes to blink out that golden liquid. However, no matter how hard I tried, I remained in my exasperated fatigue. My shirt had been drenched in water as I continued to scrub. I eventually clawed off my shirt and threw it against the wall in anger. Not seeing any success, I ran my bath and stripped myself down. I had no time to heat my water and plunged into the cold and stabbing water, taking the washcloth hard against my skin. I scrubbed frantically into the yellow itch upon my skin. The friction tore into my skin and left red marks across my body. For a moment, it seemed the yellow seemed to disappear while I scratched at it. However, it returned and continued to persist. Scrubbing hard at my body stripped me of any remaining energy, and I felt my stomach churn inside out. I felt a humidity underneath my skin while I sat in a cold basin of filth. Before I could control myself, I turned over the side of my bathtub and vomited, truly feeling myself finished. I remember breathing hard, slowly embracing this cold and cruel fate. I then just wiped my face clean of any drool and took my sickly body out of the bath. I wiped up the vomit with the same washcloth and folded it neatly on the side of the tub. My desire for cleanliness and organization had ceased, and all I wanted to do was lie down and sleep.

Later, I had decided that I would visit a physician, for the second time in my adult life, to consult on my fate, for he would know far better than the skeleton or I. I hardly ever consulted with a physician when it came to matters concerning my health, but this occasion warranted a breaking of my stubbornness. This was the family physician I held throughout my entire life. An individual who was intimately familiar with my history and all medical knowledge, and would do his best to provide me with an objective and professional opinion on the matter.

When I had finally sat through hours of waiting and been allowed into the doctor's room, the gingerly old man sat down beside me and softly said, "Oh, Peter. It has been a while."

"It has, doctor," I nodded, and noticed the doctor had aged considerably since the last time I had seen him.

The doctor lifted his stethoscope to his ears. "What brings you in today?"

"Well, you see, I've taken on a rather strange illness. My body has felt fatigued," I braced as I felt the coldness of the stethoscope against my chest.

"Oh, has it?" The doctor silenced me through the subtext. "Take a deep breath for me."

I cooperated and breathed in, holding it until I began to feel myself tense, and released.

"Good, another one please," the doctor shifted the placement of his stethoscope.

I breathed in and out, "My eyes and skin have become yellow. I've been feeling rather ill, unable to sleep—"

"Yes, your skin does appear to be yellowing. One more deep breath, please," the doctor shifted his stethoscope again. Then the doctor moved behind me and held the stethoscope to my back. "Slow and deep breaths, please."

I held myself up by placing my hands on my thighs.

"So how is Sophie?" The doctor gently asked me.

I sat still, "I'm sure she's well."

"Good, good."

The doctor moved closer to me, "Alright, lie down for me, Peter. I need to check your liver."

I lay down on the examination table as the doctor placed his hand on my bare abdomen. He felt the right upper side of my abdomen, gently resting his hand atop my ribs. He extended his fingers and tapped them, moving further down my abdomen. The doctor ordered me to breathe, then pushed deeper into my abdomen and clawed into me with his fingers. His fingers did not cut deep, but caused a wincing of pain through my body. He released my liver and drew back and asked me to sit up at my own pace.

"There is some inflammation in your liver," the doctor stated to me. "Tell me, Peter, do you drink at all?"

"Not really," I lied.

"You are exhibiting signs of liver failure, but to narrow it down further—"

"Really?"

"Yes, I believe so. We should run additional tests, including a biopsy of your liver. There is research suggesting that the condition could be hereditary as well. I need you to lay off liquor while we treat this. Do you think you can do that?"

I didn't know much about liver failure, hepatitis, or jaundice, but the doctor helped educate me while I remained divided with my attention. He further examined my abdomen and told me to drink plenty of water, include a healthy portion of physical exercise into my routine, and remain circulated with him and his staff to schedule following treatment. That was the last I spoke to my physician.

After I visited the physician, I sauntered down the alleys back toward my apartment, reckoning with the news. My mind was a blur as I struggled to calculate my next move and return to normalcy. However, I found that normalcy as I knew it would never quite exist again. The more I pondered the news, the more inwardly anxious I grew. The greater I wanted to transport myself back in time to when I never knew or when I walked freely of my labored breathing and the dark fate swelling within me. Even when my attention seemed to waver away and onto what I saw on the streets, the dark cloud would drift back and bring with it the same pain. My eyes would swell, and I would feel myself choking on my thoughts and emotions. This was one matter that I did not need to argue was fact or fiction. It was confirmed to me, and quickly it had absorbed into my identity and longevity.

How does one forget such an important characteristic of them, when it very much so shepherds your remaining life span? I pray you never have to reckon with the unfortunate news of a chronic illness.

As I walked, I happened to pass by a cemetery, a burial ground that was new to the city. Amongst the tall buildings, there it was, a small and low-to-the-ground inlet. It descended from the industry and development surrounding it. A product of religious and cultural fervor that offered itself to humankind as a resting place. All Saints' Determination Cemetery, the gate indicated.

A cemetery is a rather peculiar place. Graves litter the field, headstones protrude from the ground, casting a rather drab and austere feel. The ground attempts at beauty through its walkable patches of grass and occasional bushes of flowers. However, frolicking isn't welcome in a cemetery. One must watch their steps.

I carefully circled the cemetery, looking at the many unfamiliar names and the etchings on their tombstones. The startlingly short life spans and the devoted epitaphs from loved ones drew me to question how impactful these individuals' lives really were or how fanciful the loved ones' views of the deceased were. By far, most tombstones dictated the relation the deceased held to the ones burying them: fathers, mothers, sons, daughters, husbands, wives, brothers, sisters, even uncles. It was rather painful to read the same meanderings on so many epitaphs. Did these individuals really leave no such creative impression upon their loved ones, leaving those same loved ones to remember a man only as a loving father? The only remarkable tombstones stood tall and, more so, wore the creativity and merit of the masons, not the mourners. I found a revolting disgrace that lay with me while observing the graves.

As one does, I naturally wondered what my grave would look like, where I would be laid to rest, and what my tombstone would read. I will seek to answer those questions for you by the end of my time.

I seated myself at a bench, observing the drooping oak tree in the east and pondering my mortality. The newly developed cemetery possessed much emptiness to host many of the city's occupants. While I was pondering the empty lots, my eyes fell on a widow in all black standing at the grave beside the drooping oak tree. From where I was seated, I heard her cries to the deceased one she stood above. She pleaded with Death and God to return her loved one and offered to bargain anything, a rather terrifying proposition. I wondered to what limits this woman would be willing to go, how much her loved one truly belonged to her, and what she remembered him for. She uttered "my love" repeatedly, but what else was this man besides her love? What else did he manage to claim, and what did others inscribe upon his tomb? Eventually, the woman left, and I took her place, assuming the role of a mourner. But I admit, I stood there not to mourn but to scrutinize and unveil.

Beneath me, I saw the neatly fashioned headstone of an "Ethan Playfair." The surname indicated to me an odd calling. I looked upon the headstone and saw the man's short lifespan, marking his death to be just a few weeks ago. Then underneath it was nothing.

"*Peculiar, isn't it?*" The skeleton appeared above my right shoulder.

I became startled and turned, "What are you doing here? I thought I was rid of you."

"*Please, Peeter. Let's not make a scene at a place of rest. We must keep our peace,*" The skeleton waved at me and then returned to holding his hands politely in front of him.

I turned around as well, observing the unfamiliar grave.

"*I will also add, you can't get rid of me,*" The skeleton whispered.

I resisted the urge to turn again and grasp the skeleton by his throat.

"Good, good. Resistance is key. And remember, the choking trick doesn't work on me."

"How did you—"

"You've got your fists balled up, man!" The skeleton yelped.

"What happened to stay quiet and keep our peace?"

"Trust me, I happen to know quite a bit about resting in peace," he laughed.

"What are you? What are you doing here?"

"You're rather sudden with your questions: how dare you this, how dare you that, blah blah blah. Let me ask you a question for a change."

I remained quiet, supposedly inviting his questioning.

"How was your visit to the doctor?"

"How do you know I visited the doctor?"

"How could I not? I told you, I'm always with you, tailing you, watching you, everywhere."

"Everywhere? Can't you even spare me a moment of privacy? That's awfully inconsiderate of you, I think."

"Let's chat about how inconsiderate it was of you to throw your whiskey glass at me, huh?"

I remained quiet and then slightly turned to the skeleton, "Would you kindly go to Hell?"

"I've been, my friend, and I didn't like it," he chuckled to himself.

"I'm not your friend."

"Okay, fine, my brother."

"Stop it! You know what you're doing."

"Do I?"

I avoided the skeleton's annoying remarks and maintained my attention on the grave. I tried to direct my attention to this "Ethan Playfair" and what his life may have been like. What must this man have done to receive no ceremonial epitaph upon his tomb? What would I want etched onto my tomb?

"What are you thinking?"

"Stop disturbing my peace."

"My apologies, good friend."

I turned back to the skeleton and glared at him. He did not respond to my glare and kept his focus upon the grave.

"Cemeteries are rather somber places, would you not agree?"

"They are."

"Death is certainly not fun. There is no beauty to it, and there is an indescribable amount of pain."

"Is there?" I caught my breath. "Did you die once?"

"No, but I imagine it must be painful," he said plainly.

Upon hearing his plain sarcasm, I felt myself begin to get hot. "I could bury you here, so you could experience it."

"No, it's quite all right. However, you will be buried here, it seems."

"How—"

"The doctor told you that you're ill, did he not?"

"He did."

"Ha—ha—ha. What did I tell you? Your end is near."

I felt the same rage toward the skeleton as I had before, but now I lacked the energy to act upon it. His soul had somehow hexed me and now proceeded to toy with me, while I felt my hands dangle lifelessly from how tightly I had gripped them earlier. I swallowed my coughs to impersonate strength and maintain as tall a posture as I could within the cemetery on a rather strange encounter shared amongst me, the skeleton, and the corpse of Ethan Playfair.

"I will grant you a strange mercy."

My impulse carried my rage, "How? By cutting off my head now, driving me mad?"

"No, but I shall share with you a bit about myself, if you're intrigued."

My silence again invited the skeleton to speak. I was curious about what secrets I could learn so that I may defeat him.

"It is not customary for my kind to share secrets about themselves, but I feel obliged, since we are meant to be neighbors one day."

"What—"

"It may interest you to allow me to finish my dialogue before interrupting."

"I don't care anymore—"

"As I was saying," the skeleton cleared his throat. *"We are meant to be neighbors, one day. I am the spirit of the corpse you shall lay beside when you're buried—"*

"What? You make no sense. I've about had it with your lunacy. How do you know where I'll be buried? What if I am cremated instead?" I turned to face him.

The skeleton tilted his head in defiance to my interruption.

"I might as well throw myself into a fire now, so I can avoid you."

"Now that's just harsh. I don't believe I'm such dreadful company."

"Trust me, you are—"

"Anyway," the skeleton declared. *"That is not how your end will come, so you mustn't throw yourself into a fire."*

"What if I threw you in?"

"Your little jabs bore me—"

"You bore me."

"Are you inept at socializing?"

"Are you—"

"Stop it!" The skeleton held his hands out in front of me. *"Just stop it, man. I wish to converse with you at a profound level, and you attend the discussion with such immaturity."*

"Have you thought about why? Why would I want to chat with a skeleton, especially one who seems to have cursed me?"

"How dare you? It was not me who cursed you," the skeleton pointed at me. *"It was you."*

"Me? I was living fine before I met you."

"Oh, were you?"

"Yes, I was."

"What is it you think will be written on your epitaph? Who will even pay for you to be buried? Who will finance your tomb?"

"I will."

The skeleton chuckled at me.

"I will make my own arrangements," I said, knowing that I didn't have such wealth to my name.

"*How deluded are you?*" The skeleton asked, crossing his arms. "*You have secluded yourself in your apartment for the past several years and drank away your sorrows, and you tell yourself you are content with that—*"

"I am content with that. For years, I have calculatedly poured my efforts into—"

"*Yet, you stand here observing and wondering what others will remember you for. If you are so content and self-actualized, why are you so possessed with renown? Have you ever taken a lover or shared in the merriment of others' company? When have you dined at the table with your family or juggled pins alongside street clowns? How far past your home have you traveled? Have you visited the place where the sewer meets the sea?*"

"I have not, and I have no need."

"*Yes, because you precisely understand what it is you need. You know, pharaohs used to be buried with their wealth and pets. You will be buried with nothing but the shaggy clothes on your back. At this rate, no one shall pay for your tomb. Who would stand there and visit your grave and read your epitaph? If you are so content, as you say you are, return to your sulking and pitiful existence, the life you've wasted away, and the remaining life that slips through the cracks in your being.*"

I recall looking around the cemetery in that moment and feeling the dread and loneliness of such a place. All the quiet graves that lay there with nothing but an occasional visitor or a cleaner to pass by and a crow perhaps to cry in their presence. The sight of it all seeped into me, and maybe I began to feel myself becoming a new occupant of the cemetery. There was a painful truth in the skeleton's words, I realized. However, I did not allow myself to believe it.

"I will execute what my destiny is, and you will not seize it from me or cut my life short. Neither you nor the delirium know quite what I have committed to my craft and the quest for transcendence, but I know where my path lies. I hope you take your path back to Hell," I said, grasping dignity.

"If Hell is where I am meant to go, then that is where we shall be neighbors," the skeleton smiled at me.

I turned and began to walk toward the exit, leaving behind the thought of my grave or who shall stand at my tomb. In that moment, I stood content that even if no one were to know I was dead or where I lay, that if I had completed my path and goal, I would rest in peace.

For the next several days, I committed myself back to my craft, pursuing it with an ardent and timely fervor. I would not move from my desk, but to scarcely eat and quickly wash myself. Moments came when I felt my nausea overcome me and needed to escape to the lavatory, but I kept working. For the most part, I neglected the doctor's orders and still indulged in liquor when the creativity seemed to wander away from me. However, what freedom and disinhibition I experienced as a result of the liquor warranted my continued overindulgence. In addition, liquor still cast on the shade of sleep I needed every night to not be swallowed by my fatigue. All I simply concentrated on was writing. Without serious caution for style and grammar, I simply wrote. It mattered not what I wrote, but I wrote.

I recalled the grandiose paintings of Friedrich and how small he would depict man amongst nature, and envisioned my parchment as the grand horizon upon which a lonesome pen hovered, waiting to explore all that stood ahead of it. There were bridges that obsessed me, rivers, mountains, forests, the skies, clouds, all kinds of domains in which one being could swing from a vine and land upon another. I imagined a fantastical opening to a land where all spirits could speak to one another. Simple stories where a man would sit in a meadow and reflect on his surroundings and find himself enchanted within a layer of spiritualism in his environment, just as my pen would become one with the parchment. As I wrote, I found the man sitting in the meadow, but lost him when I considered what actions he committed next or how the sublime came to encompass him. What would this man do? What emotions or thoughts would he lead by? What would his purpose be? What impression would he leave upon this fictional world? What would be his fatal flaw? Any person could identify a man sitting, but how would I spring him to life and make him embody the core principles I had come to believe and channel them through my writing? The man remained sitting, while I occasionally turned to pace. I played the same violin concerto by Brahms, and this time felt incapacitated with my pen. It merely lay still in my hand. A sort of phantom seemed to possess me as I struggled to jot down words and etchings describing my visions. I saw them within my closed eyes, and then an invisible force blocked me from it. I could not push the pen further onto the page without thinking about the weight of each word I etched and its place within the greater context, and if all married to create the coherent beauty I sought. As I scanned the introduction to certain pieces, I crossed out wide chunks of writing, rewriting, omitting, and rewriting again. When a page contained far more scratch marks than eligible words, I crumpled the paper and restarted entirely.

The man who sat in the meadow—no.

The man who got lost in the forest—no.

The man who approached the mountain—no.

The man who fell into the sea—no.

The man who traded his life to dance—no.

The man who stood in his own grave—no.

Empty and null ideas.

I asked myself, why had this path been cast for me? Why was writing made my vice? The craft of writing had been a torturous pursuit throughout the ages, and rarely had it yielded what felt to be moments of grandeur and transcendence.

When ink met paper and truth met poetry, there lay the sublime answer to my worries. Maybe it was a foolish thought I had come to believe as a child. There was one such occasion when I had asked Gustave, when he used to sit at our table, why we pursue the arts. He had looked at me and laughed, saying, "Because we wouldn't have shit else to do with our time." He seemed to comfortably run his book shop after that, reading for the rest of his life with no purpose in pursuing writing. It was hard for me not to look at the likes of him and Oliver with some dismay for the abandonment of their craft. Why did they not persevere and cement themselves into the artistic canon and transcend from our world? I still did not waver from that quest.

To me, writing has been a necessity for daily living. It has been fused into my bones. I don't know what compels me to do it, but at times I find myself thinking in poetry and prose and understanding the world better that way. To see the existence of folk in forms of dialogue and couplets gives it structure and allows me to bend such things within my hands and etch them according to my view. The fact that I have picked up a novel and have been moved by it and deeply compelled to fathom life according to it acts as my proof that writing is a credible endeavor to pursue. Yet, through time, there have been many styles and findings into the truthful form of art. There has been much rubbish to masquerade the truth and cloud one's path to the sublime. The romantics and transcendentalists offer this path to the sublime, where one may look past themselves and into the vastness and spirituality of nature and find the truth to be a form of peace and inherent beauty. Since then, the realists have urged us on to look at the world with unwashed and cruel eyes, seeing the grime and wrinkles, and kept us oppressed in our ordinary societies with no form of idyllic freedom. I have contested this harsh painting of the world and clung to my idealism for the goodness of the world by portraying a bearer of the torch that shall light the way in the dark. I seek to compel the world into the sublime, but also to find it myself through writing and finally feel at peace and perhaps rest atop the mountain. Scrawling onto papers all the ideas I had ever considered to desperately find the spark that would ignite transcendence, I eventually grew tired and pondered who would visit my tomb upon the mountain.

In my childhood, what had I done besides being playfully neglected by my parents and peers and taking the pen? In my novels, what did I find but the charismatic figures who entranced my days and captivated my attention? They were all I had. Those figures who had roamed the halls of that crammed house with me, where did they now sit? Now, when I wrote, none of them seemed to emerge onto paper and carry with them the inspiration I felt upon reading Emerson, Poe, Keats, Melville, Shelley, Hawthorne, Brontë, all the ones I admired. Perhaps it was a true sign of failure and creative abandonment.

Trust, in that moment, I truly sought to stand at the pulpit and either die or be signaled by God that my gift persists. Yet, I felt, in that moment, he doth abandon me. Therefore, I shall fall with gravity into my tomb.

There in my tomb I shall lay, deserted and alone.

Right before I crumpled the next page, I realized tears began to flow from my eyes onto the paper. Small dots, but by far the most emotion that graced those pages. What frustrated me was that the emotion did not come from my creativity but from my sulking. A vision of that damned skeleton ran through my mind, and just at that moment, I heard my door creak and swing open.

Gentle but solid steps guided the visitor in, who now bore a cane in hand. He grew richer as I grew more miserable. A scarf even hung down from his neck, adorned with fanciful colors. He pulled in a chair and sat behind me, above my left shoulder. This time, he did not approach too close and kept quiet.

"Why have you come here now? Have you come to torture me more, you foul beast?" I cursed him as spittle and snot rained down from me. "Have you not had your fill? You eat at my soul. I regret to inform you, there is not much more of me left."

He kept quiet.

"What has silenced you now? Seeing me in this pitiful state? You said you knew how horrible my existence was," I accentuated my words with emotion.

The skeleton remained silent, holding his cane between his legs. He gently lowered the cane and, with a soft clearing of his throat, said, "*Peeter…*"

"Why have you come!" I suddenly yelled in response to him. "I desire to be alone. Let me rest alone."

The skeleton pulled his staff closer toward himself.

"I am working. Let me work." I lifted my pen to the paper in front of me.

"*Aye, then I shall just sit here.*"

I avoided the skeleton and attempted to give him no mind, continuing to flutter along the page with my pen. It was rather odd that the moment I had been reminded of him, he had suddenly appeared. His coincidental appearance made me consider again whether he truly was a phantom of my mind or a corpse of my future neighbor, as he had said. Whatever he was, I still questioned what his purpose was in torturing me over these days. Even if he had always been tailing me, why did he choose this time in my life to appear and make himself felt? It truly felt as if he was toying with me. Was this the end that I had earned through my actions in life thus far? My mind had been scrambled already, and his cold presence sent me further into exhaustion. He sat behind me and watched aimlessly, it felt, while I continued on my quest.

Dusk quickly approached, and as I wrote through the night and into dawn, the skeleton remained sitting beside me. He stirred not a bit, but to crack his neck or knuckles or adjust the position of his cane. His bony hands made a tapping sound on the cane topper. There he sat with his empty gaze upon my back. I worked away, mumbling to myself as I wrote dialogue that I later spat away. Moving my head with the rhythm of speech, until I'd bite my tongue and slap my head with my palm. I raised and lowered my pen with the rhyme scheme of each poem I attempted, until the next rhyme seemed to just not arise. I scratched at my eyes, attempting to dig them hollow, but they only became more bloody, ensnared by the piss yellow of my eyes.

I had hardly slept over those days, and my affliction grew worse by the day. The coughs would come more chronically and deafeningly. I felt more pain in my abdomen, and whenever I tried to eat or drink, I found it hard to keep anything down. Whenever I left my desk to rush to the lavatory, I'd return to find him still sitting there. I was running low on parchment and ink, and all other necessities. I'd wipe my mouth clean with a handkerchief, continue to avoid the skeleton and the mountain that sat beside me, and attempt to resume my writing. I turned to the nearest folder of papers to find some stragglers I could use. What I turned to ended up being the portfolio that held Oliver's paintings. They were amateur sketches of folk he knew, including me, but I felt envious that he had still confidently committed them to paper, while I had yielded nothing. I saw the yellow and bony silhouette Oliver had cast of me, and over my shoulder, I sensed the skeleton perk up a bit.

"*You draw as well?*" He asked.

"No," I quietly uttered. "These belong to my former associate."

"*It's kind of him to paint you, I reckon,*" the skeleton scratched his head. "*Where is he now?*"

"Gone." I did not know why I was all of a sudden entertaining him. "He has left to care for his ill mother in her last days."

"*I see. What about his ill associate?*"

"It seems through his drawing that he saw my sickness before I did. Rather prophetic. He's better off with his mother." I shut the portfolio and set Oliver's parting gift aside.

"*What of your mother? Where does your family reside?*"

I wanted to tell him to shut up and question why he would ask me such a thing. I wanted to just ignore him, but I uttered, "They're dead. Most of them, at least, are gone." I rewarded his patience and company, I suppose. He had sat beside me at the table for so long without interrupting. Then I went to insert myself properly into the seat and resume my writing.

"*Most of them?*" He interrupted.

I dipped my pen in ink and lifted it to the parchment, paying him no mind.

"What do you mean, most of—"

"I'd rather you not interrupt me. I'm attempting to leave behind something that can outlast me once I pass." I took a breath. Then I lowered my head and began to write off intuition, whatever arose to my mind.

I let my hand guide me. With my pen's crooked slope, I placed faith in my instinct despite how much my hand cramped and stuttered. There appeared the curves in the possessive and followed by it, I found a favor for the fanciful in a large "F." Suddenly, I found myself writing, "My family is dead." I looked at the words I had written and agreed with them. My family no longer existed in my life. Mother and father lay dead, I don't know where. Father was a builder. Mother was a nurse. I was a coffin between them, growing up. A sickly child, a peerless child, an ambitionless child who received no harsh remarks but no distinction, alone in the tightly crammed house. I escaped from them when I became of age and left the family behind to find what the ones I pursued had found. They may have looked for me for a while, but I doubt their attention remained too fixed on me; they tended to my baby sister. She was young, far younger than me, and there she grew up in the same home. I saw them hold her, and I tried to do the same. She came to see me and follow me through the hallways, but I ran away and preserved my books and writings. That was something I guarded from her, despite her innocent persistence. I wish I could've conveyed that I maintained my guard so that I didn't lose literature nor lose myself. I sought to protect the one solace that gave me a place within the home and what seemed to be my life. So when she reached for my pages of fiction, I slapped her hand away. I yelled at her to step away. I thrust my arm away to keep my grip around what mattered so much to me. She would beg and cry, and mother or father would pick her up and take her elsewhere to a different part of the house. In that corner, I would remain carefully guarding my books. All the others would leave, and there I would stay alone with my books.

I thought of Sophie. I couldn't help but think of Sophie, my younger sister. In those moments when the novels seemed not to inspire and my inkwells ran dry, I thought of Sophie and her cries and attempts to grasp at me and reach into my world. I thought of her little fingers and how small they seemed across the spine of my novels. The way she so naturally clutched onto whatever pieces of parchment she had access to. How I would occasionally find a novel of mine missing and find it beside her as she played with her dolls. The way she enacted her dolls reading into those novels, which held such importance to me. Then, how I had barged into her room and stolen that moment from her. I remembered her telling me, I want to read and I want to write. In response, I would scowl at her. I stormed out of my parents' home and left behind a crying sister. Back when I made my escape, I didn't think she would miss me. I thought she might cry because she would have one less soul to torment, but she would calm down because she had wide access to all the novels I had left behind. That would surely occupy her for the rest of her time. I wondered if she had learned to stop crying and whether she had learned to stop slurring my name when she called for me.

I knew she remained. I had seen an article, years ago, documenting her marriage to a senator in the city. The senator remained in power, and she stayed in the same government-funded house he did, unless she didn't. I knew of its location. I knew the distance away it was. I had never gone, but my heart fluttered to see her and see her little hands grasp at the same novels I stole from her. Oh, I really hoped she was still there, living, breathing, healthy, and as I remembered her.

I gently rose from my seat with my remaining strength, "I have urgent business I need to attend to." The fatigue had been beaten into me. My muscles cramped and ached as I stood and walked away from the desk.

"*Where? I shall accompany you,*" the skeleton rose after me.

"There is no need. It is a private affair," I lifted my coat off the rack beside the door.

"By the Heavens, you are in no condition to travel on your own. I shall go with you—"

"Leave me be, please."

"Do you see your condition?" The skeleton placed his hands at his side in a patronizing manner.

I realized my breath had been escaping me. As I leaned with one arm against the door, I felt sweat drenching my forehead from the exertion that came with putting on my coat.

"I may be catching a fever," I said, looking away.

"Perhaps it may be best to stay—"

"No!" I exclaimed. "I must go. I must do this." I placed on my hat, lowering the brim, so most of my face would be covered. "You may come with me, if you wish."

I realized I did not have the energy to waste in a contest with the skeleton, so I gave in to his company. He had sat as a silent companion, and I assumed he would follow a silent one as well.

We left my apartment, as I locked my front door and stowed the keys in my pocket. We traversed down the road, heading east, and I mostly maintained my gaze on the floor, occasionally looking up for the guiding landmarks and street signs. There was a rather loud frenzy on the streets, and my eyes and ears avoided it to maintain whatever sanity and energy I had left. I was afraid that if I stayed too long to gaze at what took place on the side of the street and which strangers passed by, I would be stricken off my course forever and never see what I longed for in that moment. I feared falling and that portion of the sidewalk becoming my eternal resting ground. Whenever I seemed to misstep or needed to stop for a second to catch my breath, the skeleton approached and waited beside me. He watched the crowd around me and stood guard. He flared his cane by his side and stood tall. When we came into the smaller blocks, he even walked a few steps ahead of me, whistling and carrying himself with an amusing energy. I watched his feet that seemed never to stutter, and glided from the heel to the toe with each successive step. A skeleton, who was formerly dead and had returned from Hell to usher in his neighbor's death, was my guide to my destination. Every so often, he would turn to make sure I was following him at a steady pace and had not slipped or fallen. He would even call out to me with which street we were coming to cross and ask for directions. I would oblige, telling him to carry on forward or make a turn.

During our walk, he asked, "*Who are we going to see?*"

I dragged behind him, but answered, "My younger sister."

"*Oh,*" the skeleton turned to me and waited for me to catch up. "*Is she expecting you?*"

"No," I scoffed. "I'm sure you knew the answer to that."

"*Oh, well. I'm sure she will be delighted to see her stray brother return,*" the skeleton continued to swing his cane as we walked along the way.

Will she, I thought.

Soon, we wandered into the nicer part of town, which held the tall and impressive home of the state senator. I pointed out the home to my companion so that he may approach it with more caution. Around the time we arrived, the sun was beginning to set. The gas lamps were lit, and both the foreground and background dimly glowed. The home's blank white walls were accented with a royal yellow and adorned with Christmas decorations. A short steel fence blocked the small staircase that ascended to the large door of the home. This was by far a more impressive home than the one we had grown up in. My companion opened the gate for me, inviting me to lead. I watched my steps to the door. Before anything, I looked down at the skeleton as he waited for me by the gate, watching the distant horizon grow dimmer. I dusted off my coat and then reached for the door knocker.

I waited a moment. Hearing no answer, I struck the door again, thrice. No answer. I looked down toward the skeleton, who looked at me and tilted his head. I turned back to the door and knocked again with more force and waited. I held my hands politely in front of me, waiting and thinking that any moment the door would open and there would be my darling sister. I stood and received no answer. I knocked one last time with my bare knuckles and remembered that dreadful feeling of waiting.

Then the door opened. There stood an older lady wearing an apron, a maid from the looks of it, looking exasperatedly at me.

"What is it? What are you knocking on about?" She sharply spoke to me.

"I… I wanted to see…" I struggled.

"What do you mean you wanted to see? Have you no manners? Look at what time it is," she chided me.

"I came to see my sister, Sophie." I looked at her, clutching my hands together. "She does live here, doesn't she?"

"Your sister?" She looked at me sideways. "Madam Sophie has never mentioned a brother the likes of you."

"I am her brother. My name is Peter," I pointed to myself.

"Well, Peter, Madam Sophie and Mister Samuel are not home at the moment. They have taken the children on a visit out of the city. I'm sorry to disappoint you. It would do you better to wait for the madam's usual meeting hours. I'm sure she'd be happy to schedule a meeting… with you."

"Children? She has children?" I almost smiled.

"Yes," she squinted at me. "Some brother you must be. If you are who you say you are, you're welcome to return later. Please, thank you—"

"Wait! When will she return?" I reached closer to the door to stop it from shutting. "I must see her soon."

"They left a few weeks ago, and will not be back until after Christmas," she politely smiled at me, signaling our exchange was nearing an end.

"The matter is urgent. Can you—"

"I'm sorry," she dragged out the words.

"I just want to see her one last time."

She paused for a moment and then strengthened her grip around the door handle, "I'm really sorry. Please try after Christmas. Goodnight!"

Then the door shut.

I stood there, taking in my failed attempt. If she were gone out of the city, there was no way I'd be able to see her, before what felt like my approaching end. I resisted knocking again, reminding myself that it would not be worth it.

"*What'd she say, chap?*" He called to me from the gate.

I turned around this time, seeing the skeleton in greater darkness. His words felt mocking to me, just like the way he had knocked at my door and exposed me to this sickness. I imagined he must have overheard my awkward exchange with the maid and seen my gloomy appearance colored by the gas lamps. Like an impulse, the thought rushed through my head again that he was the one to blame for this imposed condition.

"She's not home," I declared down to him, standing still at the top of the stairs.

"*I'm sorry, my dear chap,*" the skeleton opened the gate for me.

Why should I walk down to you?

"*I truly am deeply sorry. I saw the look of longing across your face at the thought of your sister.*"

If he was prophetic enough to know my end, shouldn't he have known that Sophie wouldn't be here?

"*Come, I know where we can go.*"

Why would he lead me to this fate?

"*It may offer you a moment of cheer.*"

Why would he toy with me like this?

"*You've been there before. I promise you'll like it.*"

Why?

He looked up at me, and I silently placed my hands into my coat's pockets and approached him. I kept to myself during the walk, while he walked similarly as before in the direction of my apartment. He seemed to know his directions well as I pursued him with my eyes and remained fixed on him. His cloaked figure led the way in the darkness as the topper on his cane glinted against the light of the street lamps. The skeleton seemed to prefer to lead, leaping through the streets with a proud gait. He had done me the courtesy of allowing me to lead when we had approached the senator's home, while he had waited and aimlessly stared into the distance, seemingly with no need to pay attention to my interaction with the maid. Then he had quickly pivoted, almost with a set plan of where to guide me, and somehow I mindlessly followed him.

"Where are you taking me?" My voice felt raspy calling ahead to him.

"*You will find out soon enough,*" he turned and showed me his exposed teeth.

"I need to know where you're taking me," I retrieved my hands from my pockets to ready myself.

"*Why the haste?*" He playfully called back.

"You're aware of my condition. You know I can't waste precious time—"

"*Waste? You should spend your remaining time doing what you love.*"

"Yes, so tell me—"

The skeleton stopped and turned, "*Peeter, you don't have much time left.*"

I stopped in front of him, and we came dangerously close.

"*You need not wait any longer,*" he spoke seriously and reached out to me.

"What—"

He placed his hand on my shoulder, "*We have arrived.*"

The skeleton turned to the side and showed me the entrance to the Phoenix's Den. Finally, it hit me. I became aware of the sounds that filled the street and the loud and drunken chatter coming from the bar.

"Why have you brought me here?" I looked confused at him.

"*It's your favorite bar,*" he spoke candidly.

"How do you know?" I spoke softly.

The skeleton laughed, "*Come, my friend, let's enjoy a drink.*"

We entered the saloon, and I remembered it just as it was. The furnishing looked familiar, but the place was filled with new souls that I knew not. My eyes washed over the superficial details, almost unattracted to the bar because of the distant and changed aura it emanated. It was almost as if seeing a replica of the bar I used to visit, except it held none of the charm of the original. My mind seemed not to settle on the minute details of the place, feeling scarce for time.

"I believe you know your seat. I shall retrieve the drinks," the skeleton patted me on the back.

I tried to discourage him and tell him the drinks were not needed, but the skeleton walked away. There I was left in my old stomping grounds, where I had turned over many manuscripts in the company of my former associates. I did recall my seat; the back corner table was where the band met. The band that had saved me from a life on the streets and offered me a path to living in the city. I squeezed past the drunk strangers, not looking anyone in their eyes. And as I navigated the crowded front and middle, I saw the battered corner table in the end. The band and I were the ones who had turned it over and made it rugged, telling over it stories worth multiple lifetimes. One person sat behind the table. Gustave, the bookshop owner, sat and stared blindly into the room, drinking a glass of wine.

I stopped in my steps ahead of him, too surprised to call his name.

He blinked at me a couple of times. He had aged. He set his wine down. "Is that you, Peter?"

I was surprised, "It is. I thought you might not have recognized me."

He laughed from the belly, "I recognized you, alright. Your steps have a distinct sound to them." He smiled at me. "It may have just taken me a moment to see you."

Besides the long silver hair that covered his forehead, I caught sight of the cataracts in his eyes. His face scrunched underneath his eyes as he smiled at me.

"I didn't realize," I expressed my apologies. "How poor is your vision?"

"Dull as shit," he dusted off the chair beside him. "Come, join me."

I took my assigned seat, where I had sat plenty, debating with my associates about artistic style. Gustave, the way he usually had, abandoned tradition and sat in whichever spot he preferred.

"Did you get anything to drink?" Gustave turned to me with his overbearing stature and bulging stomach.

"No," I modestly replied.

"What? I must have you drink with me. What has it been? Two years?" Gustave turned toward the bar counter.

"Give or take," I turned to look at the counter and saw the skeleton dealing with the bartender. I didn't give it much thought at the time. Perhaps I had grown accustomed to the skeleton's presence around me, but I wasn't sure how the skeleton managed to interact with the barkeep, and yet he did. They seemed to exchange pleasantries.

Gustave raised his hand and called to the bartender a few times, while I hid my face and looked toward the wall. On the wall, I saw the little insignia Gustave had carved years ago during one of our meetings. There was a capital "P," representing the Phoenix. I had always seen it and read it as representing me, Peter.

"Ah, he seems like he's busy. We'll call him later," Gustave firmly planted his hand on the portion of the table ahead of me.

"Leave it. I don't need to drink."

"That's rather odd of you—"

"I just haven't been feeling the best."

"Why's that?"

"Nothing."

He remained staring forward. "How have you been? I haven't heard from you for a while. I wasn't sure if you still came by here, but I randomly thought to visit tonight."

"I haven't been in a while either."

"Funny that our paths just so happened to cross then, huh?"
He turned slightly in my direction and chuckled, making no eye
contact with me.

"I suppose so."

My chair was inched behind Gustave's, and I similarly tried to
avoid directing my gaze upon him. Not only did it present a challenge
from where I sat, but the big familiar presence sitting beside me felt
to be enough. I stared forward and watched the same haze of a
crowd that Gustave laid his eyes upon. Gustave continued to sip
from his glass.

"What of Oliver and the rest of the band?"

"Oliver left for his mother's recently. I'm unsure if he'll
return. The others also slowly filtered out, since your departure."

"Ah, I see," he drank again. "I do reckon you understand why
I left, right?"

"Sure."

"I considered if I should have notified you all, but I figured
this wasn't the place for me—"

"I understand."

"No, I mean, I really did feel bad for leaving without notice.
We all shared a good rapport—"

"We did."

"I just figured I dragged you and the lot behind. I couldn't
keep up with you all," Gustave feigned a chuckle. "And now, the
band is dissolved—"

"It's okay, Gustave," I sensed some sorrow in his voice. "You
have nothing to apologize for."

"I was always at the book shop for you to visit."

"I know."

"Why didn't you?"

"I don't know."

A moment of silence passed between us again. Gustave
continued to drink, and I sensed his presence slowly departing from
me again. I distracted myself by turning to watch the skeleton. He

had attracted other drinkers, and they all seemed to share a laugh over a pint, leaning on the counter. A man shoved the skeleton in the shoulder as they all cracked up, a friendly rapport seeming to form between them.

Gustave set his glass down. "I'm selling the shop."

I quickly moved my attention back to Gustave, "Are you?"

"Yes. I'm getting old," he sighed. "And my eyes don't make the job easy."

"Ah," I could tell my response felt deflated. "What will you do instead?"

"Oh, no clue," he fixed his jacket over himself. "Whatever it is, I'm sure it won't last me long."

"What makes you think that?"

"I've run that bookshop for around 40 years. I helped my father run it before running it myself. I haven't come to learn much else to do. Even writing with you blokes was so foreign and unnatural. The smell and habits of that bookshop are all I've known for most of my life."

I sensed Gustave wasn't done speaking, so I let him continue.

"You know what happens to folks when they quit whatever they've been doing for most of their life?"

I shook my head slightly, uninterested in whether Gustave saw it.

"They die."

I quietly let a laugh out through my nose.

"I've seen 'em all drop dead, just within a while of quitting whatever they devoted their lives to. I'd have retired folks come to my bookshop, telling me about their former careers. Then, within a few months or so, I'd read their obituaries in the paper."

"Does that really mean you will die?" I felt the need to contest Gustave. In addition, I was the one who was dying. "Perhaps they were just old. Perhaps you're just looking too much into it."

"Could be." Gustave swallowed his anxiety. "It's been on my mind for the past few years. And so part of me thought maybe I could come here and reignite another passion or calling. Somehow escape death."

I looked past Gustave and saw the skeleton smiling and tipping his hat at the others.

"So you're afraid of death," I said to Gustave, keeping my eyes on the skeleton.

He looked back at me and scoffed, "As if you're not."

I matched his gray eyes, "I think I'll have to leave soon—"

"You haven't even had a drink yet."

"There's some writing I need to attend to—"

"Sit for a while longer, it won't kill you."

I was prepared to leave, but stayed put. Trying to rise from my seat, a pain shot through my abdomen.

"Let's philosophize like we used to," Gustave gently banged the table.

"I can't. I don't have the energy for that," I secured myself with the pain emanating through me.

"You're acting older than I am." Gustave ignored me. "Listen then, I've been thinking a lot about death."

I stared past Gustave and watched the skeleton wrap his arms around others, feeling the need to call to him to guide me home.

"There once came this professor to my bookshop, an anthropologist perhaps. He had a special interest in skeletons. He asked me if I had any books on them, especially as it related to their place in death rituals. Besides tales on the Grim Reaper, I was shit out of luck. I offered him those fairy tales, and that old man laughed at me. He said, 'No, I'm talking about historical accounts of skeletons arising from death.' I told him I couldn't help him, and he'd better try a different shop. But he lingered and seemed enthused to share his knowledge that he could tell I didn't know shit about.

"He sat me down and told me that through his research, he's learned of some cultures where they've accounted for the living coming back to life. Not permanently, he mentioned, but shortly in the form of skeletons to remedy their incomplete business on Earth."

"A sort of ghost or phantom," I questioned.

"Perhaps," Gustave nodded back at me. "He told me that often what they return for is aligned with their purpose in the living. There have been accounts of soldiers returning from the dead to protect their comrades. Pastors returned to deliver a final sermon. Ferrymen rowing down the streams at night. So on, doctors, professors, musicians, artists, even gamblers and smokers who return just for another thrill."

My eyes dwelled upon my companion skeleton. He held a bottle of liquor in his hand. With two fools around him, he danced. They loudly slurred broken lines of a song I didn't recognize and waved their arms around, spilling from their glasses. The skeleton widely smiled, and his teeth came down and loudly shut as he swayed to their staggered melody. His feet stomped beside him as he held onto his drunken fellow's shoulder and proudly sang with them. His hat had fallen, and I wondered by what folly I was his chosen companion. If the ritual of death described by the professor was true, then what purpose did the skeleton come to deliver on with me? Through the crowded room and loud chatter, the skeleton's hollow eyes met mine, and he gestured for me to join him.

Gustave set his glass down again, emptied, "Well, this is the end for me. It's getting rather late, and I should escape home now. I need to make preparations for the sale tomorrow."

Gustave rose, while I sat. His back was still to me.

"I hope we see each other again, Peter," Gustave said as he fixed his coat properly onto his shoulders and buttoned it.

"Likewise."

"If we don't, maybe you will come visit me as I parade around my bookshop as a skeleton," Gustave laughed.

I watched his burly body part through the crowded room, imagining what he might appear like if he were a skeleton.

The skeleton and I soon made our departure from the Phoenix's Den. The sharp pain in my abdomen still persisted, atop my feet dragging even more slowly. The skeleton and I leaned on each other as we walked down the roads. He carried me for my fatigue, and I supported him through his drunken stupor.

"How is it that you can get drunk but not choke?" I sighed.

"My body is very withstanding," he snarled.

"I can't stand you," my lips dropped into a frown as I groaned, carrying the skeleton.

"Tell me, is your friend married?" The skeleton gleefully asked.

"Why?"

"I'm curious. I couldn't help but overhear your conversation."

"You overheard us?"

"Just parts."

"He is married. He's worried he's dying."

"Rubbish! He shall live for longer than he fears. He's got ample meat on his bones. That love has served to fatten him up. "

Strangely, the skeleton's comments provided comfort. However, not for long.

"How did those folk not see you, fear you?"

"Simple."

I waited for his answer, "Simple what?"

"Oh, I thought I answered."

"No, you didn't. How were they not frightened of you?"

"Oh, I get it now."

"Get what?"

"I understand your question. You're asking why they were so simple?"

"You're a curse, you understand?" I looked at him and gritted my teeth. "I don't know why I decided to help you. I should've left you."

"You're mistaken, Peeter. I'm the one helping you," he pointed at me.

"You've been nothing but a thorn in my side."

"I'm sorry. Is my rib poking you?"

"You're simple! You're stupid. You're a curse, a phantom."

"No, I'm a skeleton!"

"Why? Why did you choose me to punish?"

"You're silly. I didn't choose you. You chose me."

"I never would've chosen to accompany you in a century."

"What about the century after that?"

"You say we're meant to be neighbors. How is that meant to be? I don't believe you, nor a single thing you've said to me, besides for how you've ushered in my death. I should've been writing all that time. Yet, you wasted my time with the pursuit of my sister and a stupid visit to the saloon. What did we go to the saloon for? For you to get drunk, while I was tortured by the ghosts of my past? What good did you think it would be for me to revisit these cursed parts of my life?"

"Well, you're the one to blame. Why didn't you drink?"

"Maybe for the fact that I don't want to die."

"Oh, that makes sense."

"You're a dullard. You've no brain, no senses, not a single care."

"But what I do have is a spine," he cackled.

I turned left toward a dark alley, a shortcut I was familiar with from my multiple trips to and from my apartment. The gas lamps in this part of town were much further scattered, leaving long stretches of darkness between each lamp. Due to this, the alley seemed to disappear into pitch black, not revealing any sign of where the end was.

"Oh, where are we going?"

"To the apartment, it's a shortcut."

"We can't go this way."

"Are you telling me you're scared of the dark?"

"No!" The skeleton yelled in my ear. *"It's not sensible for a skeleton of my stature to be scared of the dark. However, I am scared of the creatures that roam in the dark."*

"The creatures?" I scoffed at the skeleton.

Scurrying about in the alley ahead of us, I heard it. There was a quiet chirping of rats. So quiet that I needed to hold my breath still,

but I heard it. A hiss and squeak came from a band of rats further
along the dark alley.

"They're just rats."

"*Just rats! Easy for you to say. I'm terrified of rats.*"

"How could you be terrified of rats?"

"*Don't beg the question. We must go another way.*"

"No, I am tired. I am doubly tired from carrying you. This is
the fastest way to my apartment. I must get there soon and write with
my remaining energy."

"*Peeter, you don't understand. I have a deadly fear of vermin.*"

"You can manage," I pushed forward as the skeleton clung
even more closely to me, dragging me down.

He seemed to be a child on that occasion, lifting his feet from
the floor and wearing a tawdry costume, holding onto me for dear
life. He whimpered, "*Please, Peeter.*"

I looked ahead, trying to manage a steady footing. In the
darkness of the alley, I saw six or so rats scurrying about. They were
small silhouettes hugging the floor closely, nothing but small tufts of
gray fur. I marched ahead, dragging the skeleton as he slipped down
and clung onto my leg.

"*Please, Peeter. Do not march forward,*" he pleaded.

I continued, pushing further into the darkness. I walked as
the skeleton clawed into my leg, crying to me. His deadly fear was
ironic, and it satisfied me to see him suffer. As we approached the
rats, I saw them gathered around in a circle. A subtle but foul stench
hit me. Not of rubbish, but the scent of decay and death. I saw
amongst the rats, in the dimness of the night, the half-eaten corpse of
a bird that had lost its wing. Spread across the small patch on the
floor, the rats bent over the bird and bit into its tiny body, not much
bigger than each of them. They crowded the poor creature, stepping
atop its feathers, and eating its innards to the bone. The rats had
tasted blood. The color of the bird was indiscernible from the gray
and black of the alley and blood when it becomes old and holds no
light. Famished these creatures must have felt, sucking the life out of

the poor creature descended from the skies. They were ripping it apart, no mind for the purity and innocence of the bird that was simply trying to fly. Whatever dark force that had cast this bird down stripped from life the innocence and idealism that, despite an injured wing, the possibility still existed for flight. There rained the death of the sublime.

The skeleton fell off my leg, still clutching onto my foot, but almost immobile from his drunkenness and fear. His cries had not ceased, and he continued to plead with me, slurring my name less and calling to me with desperate sincerity. I looked at him, below me, and saw the shine in his porcelain colored bones. Why was he able to retain light in even the darkest of alleys that he feared the most?

Entrusting my instinct to cast away the curse that he had given me, I stomped him in the face. As if crushing the vermin that scurried through the alley, I stomped him hard, cracking his skull. And I continued to stomp, filled with rage for the vile idiot he made me out to be. The wasteful runt he considered me. His scathing and sarcastic remarks that stung and toyed with me. The way he led me and played with my hopes for life. I stomped him out from underneath me. His grip loosened, and his body began to lose motion. His cries gave no sound, and the snicker of the rats overwhelmed the melody. Not long after, the rats abandoned the bird and came to examine the skeleton. I took this as a sign and stepped away from the horrid creature. I walked past the band of rats and the decaying bird and continued on my way to my apartment.

I limped out of the alley and eventually reached the straightaway to my apartment. Every thirteen feet stood a gas lamp, painting the night in a golden hue. The walk to the apartment still felt so long. It may have been my madness or fear, but I began to run. Feeling myself free from the skeleton's curse, I ran. I ran away from him, the terror of my act, and to my comforting corner in this world.

Gasping for air, I climbed the stairs to my floor. The company of the skeleton was a curse to begin with, and I had exorcised that demon from my life. Wherever he had risen, he was left to die again in that alley. With my steps, I prayed I had cast him into the depths of Hell, never to return and be broken into pieces. I scurried to find the key to my door, so that I may return to the most important matter. While my mind felt free of the skeleton, my body seemed to languish in the pain that persisted through it. Stopping me from unlocking my door, my abdomen seemed to turn inward. I felt a deep stabbing pain through me. My door caught me as I winced and cried aloud throughout the hallway. Not a soul seemed to emerge and come to my aid. My key slipped from my trembling fingers underneath me. I felt no strength in me to even bend and retrieve them from the floor, without toppling over and disgracing myself. I assured myself that now there were no phantoms to accompany me, and I had beaten out whatever disease or inhibition that had tormented me. It had all been a figment of my creative inhibition, and I could triumph over the pangs of my body. My dignity would not halt or abandon me at the door to my palace. What I painted to be a glorious act must have seemed humiliating as I crouched down to seize my key and rise again. I clutched at my own abdomen, whimpering and gasping for air with my mouth open and drool pooling underneath me. I pushed the key in and fell against my door, barging in.

When I entered, I felt the cold. At my writing desk, I saw the skeleton seated. My eyes were paralyzed at his sight, while I felt my heart beating through the hand on my abdomen. The skeleton faced me and sat upright. From the gateway where I stood, his hollow eyes appeared to be even more empty than Gustave's, whom I had stood beside. In the darkness below his feet lay what seemed to be his cane and a sturdy box. Behind him on my desk lay my remaining parchment and ink. I thought I had left him behind for the rats.

I stood too speechless and in pain to say a word. The skeleton's teeth chattered as he laughed at the sight of me.

I pulled the door closed behind me. "Please, let me rest."

The skeleton laughed, "*You thought you killed me, Peeter.*"

His laughter sounded different. He sounded so dissonant and harsh, inharmonious with the way he had previously seemed.

"You told me you were deathly afraid…"

"*I was lying, Peeter.*"

"Why would you trick me?" I groaned and slouched as pain filled me.

The skeleton laughed again, slowly.

"I'm in a lot of pain."

"*So you thought you would leave me for dead?*"

"Please—"

"*You fed me to the rats! You caved my head in!*"

"My insides—"

"*After the courtesy I showed you, you abandoned me! You are vile, vile, vile, vermin. You are scum. I am disappointed to be neighbors with you.*"

"You must understand—"

"*Save your cries. No soul is here to listen.*"

"I don't have much time—"

"*Peeter,*" the skeleton rose. "*I am Death, and I have come for you.*"

I stared at him, "How much time do I have left?"

The skeleton turned and watched out the window, staring at the highest point. "*What do you wish to do with your remaining time?*"

"Please, allow me to write, and sit by my side. You said you have always followed me. I will remain here for you, now."

"*You will not run?*"

"I will not. All I wish to do is—" I crumpled upon the pain, falling to my knees. Bile excreted from my mouth, and I tasted the dirty floor of my apartment.

The skeleton slowly came to my aid with his gentle steps. He helped me rise, taking me upon his shoulder as he had before, and led me to my bed. We hobbled together to my resting place, and he laid me down.

"*You are very ill,*" the skeleton stood above me.

"How much time do I have remaining?"

"*I'm not sure.*"

The man contradicted himself, and I simply lay there staring at him gratefully.

"Would you please pass me parchment and my pen?"

The skeleton did as I requested.

"Thank you."

He pulled his seat closer to me and sat at the foot of my bed, while I began to write. I occasionally glanced at him, trying to discern what strange company I had shared with him. I began to write the accounts of my meeting with the skeleton, from my first sighting of him at the station to now. With my ink slowly drying out, I lay here documenting the tales by which I was visited by this ritual of death.

I continued to write. When I seemed to stagger and began to faint, the skeleton shook my foot and awoke me. I thanked him again and continued to write about his disturbances in my life. As I seemed ready to sleep, he asked me what he could do to wake me. I looked to him and asked him to play music. He turned and retrieved from his small box a violin and bow. Harnessing the spirit of Beethoven, he placed the violin under his chin and began to strum Brahms's violin concerto.

"You play fair," I said to him.

He nodded, and through the strings, he swayed and cascaded.

"*In the richness of life, much like music, are the highs and lows,*" the skeleton said.

I absorbed the sounds.

"Will you just wait here?"

"*I will.*"

"How long?"

"*Until you join me.*"

I passed away in the cold of the night and arose again in the morning, made of porcelain. I entrust these pages to you, Sophie. I shall deliver them to you, enclosed in an envelope with the address of my apartment, in the hope that you may reach me through these pages. I never shared my writing with you. All I have left to do is bring you this parting gift. My dear, I am sorry for not spending more time with you. I love you. I wish you my deepest apologies and kindest regards, and hope you live a long and healthy life. To your husband and children, I wish nothing but well. You are my sister, and I will always hold you close to me.

Lastly, here are simple instructions upon my death to follow. Bury me at All Saints' Determination. Specifically, there is an empty lot near a drooping oak tree that faces east. In the distance, the lonely mountain sits, the same one I observe from my apartment. So that when I lay to rest, ahead of me would appear the mountain of my dreams. In my coffin, stow Oliver's drawings. So that if he one day were to rise again, he may visit me to retrieve his drawings. Let my tombstone hold nothing of importance but what you consider my legacy.

I lie here waiting for you, with love, my dear Sophie.

Your brother,
Peter

VISIONS OF TRANSCENDENCE

I sit in the meadow. Looking down, I see cracks shaded into the earth. A pastel sunset is hidden behind the bleary mountains. A tiny pink house sits at the base of a hill. I'm not alone. The wind flies past me, carrying articles of life. Rocks sit crudely stacked along the perimeter. I'm not to cross the barrier. I'm staring at a painting. That's what it feels like. That's the effect of a scenic view, especially at sunset. The existence of such a sight is eye-opening. It reveals the beauty of natural and imperfect patterns. The tiny home reminds me of solace away from all of life. I have dreams of a hermitage. I always do. I dream of being born without a social imagination; birthed by nature.

My eyes would watch the world from a place within the stars and witness existence without consciousness. That is the image of transcendence. I rival the size of the sun and withstand its heat. The sounds of Saturn suffuse my plane of existence, carrying no tempo or meaning. In time, I exist and do not. Equilibrium is only noticeable in the presence of light. In the darkness, there are collisions. All forms of matter are destroyed by magnetic phenomena. Rampant destruction is unparalleled by the aimless creation of new matter. A singular well-known existence is enveloped in a far-reaching supercluster. The edges of the world do meet an end, however. There stands a barrier protecting the world's content and laws from others. The bubble is indistinguishable in the dark sea, drifting for the purpose of nothing.

A spark is lit beneath my eyes. All subconscious branches of thought cease in my current condition. I'm fortunate to be here. My eyes feel soft and purposefully open. The light is on behind me with the time in bold underneath it. The time is insignificant. I want this moment to last forever. The light can stay on. Nothing could inspire me to willingly move and turn it off. It's not laziness. I'm in love. She's in my arms, and the world is just out of reach. Luminous buildings are behind a glass pane, in the shroud of night and bordered by two curtains. No sound. The city is sleeping. No movement. Everything is at rest. The world is waiting to be stirred, and I am ready to challenge it. No aches at all, I'm rested and proud. There's tranquility in the air and within me. I imagine the sight of the window from the outside; it's just us, glowing in the darkness. My eyes won't leave the picturesque window. As my eyes soften, even more, a smile fills my soul. I hug her tighter. I want to remember this painting for the rest of my life.

I see visions of transcendence.

THE DREAM TO
JOURNEY THE MOUNTAIN
OR
TOM FOOLERY

Within the pearly sea stood the lonely mountain. One of a kind, it was the only mountain. Above the mountain floated the sky, changing colors and shades with the day and night. Clouds drifted amongst the sky like little impressionable companions. Unless, of course, the sky desired to be flat and dull. Below the mountain was the sea—the everlasting cerulean sea. It joined the mountain via the beach. They enjoyed each other's company. So much affection existed between the two that the sea cut through the island upon which the mountain rested. The sea, however, longed so dearly for more and even attempted to flow right up and through the mountain, climbing its peak and cascading down past the cliff into a magical pool. The pool attracted all fantastical things and spirits of enrichment. Underneath the waterfall, life was born. All sorts of creatures came to be and filled the forests in the marriage of the mountain and the sea.

The sea flowed gently and cautiously, and the mountain stood tall and mighty. The mountain appeared seemingly invincible but routinely shed its loose debris. This stirred the sea to want to fully join with the mountain and bring it beneath. So waves began to crash against the mountain's base. However, the sea's efforts were still slow and futile as it swayed against the rocks, weathering them and attempting to lower the mountain to its level. Even the rocks that rolled off the mountain were not enough to satisfy the sea. The sea wanted more than just small kisses, but to embrace the mountain in a long and never-ending hold.

One day, the sea believed it had found the answer to its suffering. The sea found within it a man drifting aimlessly. In the man, the sea sensed the hope for uniting with its love. The man was lost but possessed the ambition to conquer all corners of the world, including the heights of the tallest mountains and the deepest seas. Therefore, the sea washed over the man and tried to consume him. For days, they both clashed. The man attempted to weather the storm, but the sea was far too treacherous. It overwhelmed him and conquered his will. Dawn broke after the storm, and the lonesome man washed up on the shore. He lost his ship, crew, supplies, memory, but not his aspirations. Where the man lacked meaning, the sea whispered to him to journey and conquer the mountain.

As he awoke, it was the only thing he recalled, "My dream is to journey the mountain."

1

"Who are you talking to?" A voice came from above the trees.

The man looked around, unable to spot the speaker. "Who are you?"

Then the owl emerged from the dense forest and clung to a nearby branch. He was a dark-brown owl with slanted ear tufts and orange eyes. He hovered above and watched down at the man. The owl hooted, "Who are you?"

"I don't know," the man answered.

"Okay," the owl squinted, unamused.

"Where am I?" The man continued to look around before peering at the owl for direction.

"Okay, so that's not how this works—"

"Am I dead?"

"Excuse me, I'm the one who asks the questions," the owl said, offended and pointing to himself with his right wing.

"Is this the afterlife?" The dim man asked.

"Okay, I'm starting to get annoyed now," the owl perked up. "I will answer only one question."

"Where am I? How is it that you speak? This must surely be the afterlife, and I must be dead. Is this Heaven? Or Purgatory? Or are we in Hell, and you've been sent to peck at my body? Please—"

"What is the problem with you, human? You ask all these questions and then attempt to just answer them yourself," the owl screeched.

"You're an owl. How can I understand you—"

"Shut up and listen!" The owl ordered. "You're not dead. You're on the Island, which is the home to the Mountain of Determination. Anything is possible on this island." The owl steadied himself and cleared his throat. "Now, as the master questioner, it is my turn to question you. Who are you?"

"I don't know."

The owl led the man through the forest. While the human followed and remained curious about each tree, bush, and flower, the owl quickly hopped from branch to branch, growing tired of the human. The owl was also annoyed and kept muttering curses and complaints under his breath about why today needed to be the day out of all days.

"What did you say?" The man raised his eyebrows.

"Nothing! I said nothing," the owl said nothing and waited ahead for the man, quietly pecking at his feathers in between. "Blah blah blah blah."

"So where are we going?" The man casually strolled.

"Every time you ask me a question, I feel like snapping my neck," the owl then rotated his head and looked backward at the man.

The man shrieked in horror.

"Ha-ha, gets them everything," the owl looked ahead and continued to glide from branch to branch. "I'm taking you to the catfish. They will know more about you and your origins."

"The catfish?" The man spoke in confusion.

"Watch your intonation, boy!" The owl croaked. "You've disrespected me enough today, and you better not continue to rain down on me with questions, especially in front of the catfish."

"I'm sorry," the man said, seeming rather remorseful. "How should I refer to you?"

"Ouch, that one hurt." The owl shook his body as a few feathers flew off. "Call me Sir Owl. Pay no attention to what others call me. You call me Sir Owl."

"Owley," the older-looking catfish called slowly. "What brings you in?"

Owley stifled his annoyance, "It's a human. He washed up on the beach. He says he doesn't know who he is. So, I thought I'd bring him to you."

The older-looking catfish puckered her lips and lay lazily against the bank of the river. She held a makeshift fishing pole in her hand. Several other younger catfish were gathered around the riverbank, all fishing for smaller fish in a weird chain of command. Occasionally, one of them would catch one and show it to the others before throwing it back into the river. Then the same loop continued as they simply lay there.

"Present yourself, human," the older-looking catfish called.

The human stepped ahead and stood parallel with Sir Owl. Sir Owl took a step forward, setting himself apart.

"Hello," the human waved.

"Who are you, human?" The catfish asked.

Sir Owl looked away and covered his ears.

"I really don't know..." the human shrugged.

"Hmmm..." the catfish stroked her whiskers.

"I found him on the west side of the mountain," the owl clarified. "Would any of your catfish have any intel—"

"You look like a Tom," the catfish said to the human.

"Tom?" The human, who looked like a Tom, asked.

"Tommm..." the catfish smiled.

The owl yelped at the slow pace of things, "Kat, please ask your fellow catfish if they saw a ship or crew or something."

"A ship? A crew?" Maybe Tom questioned.

"Ahh!" Owley yelled and covered his ears.

"Okay, be back pronto." Kat set down her pole and jumped into the river.

Sir Owl and the human waited for the catfish to return. The human squatted beside the riverbank until Sir Owl yelled at him to get back. Sir Owl kept a vigilant eye on the intruder and thwarted any escape attempts, even though the man swore he wasn't trying to escape but just looking into the water. The man just barely made out his reflection in the water. It felt as if he was looking at a stranger; he really didn't know his name or who he was. He kept staring at the water, waiting for an answer to appear, until he made out Kat and her crew swimming back hurriedly. Kat perched herself back up on the riverbank, still sulking in the shallow river.

"Owley, we may have a problem," Kat burped from the excess air she had swallowed while swimming fast. "One of my lads found the ruins of his ship. There isn't much left, but definitely no signs of any crew. They weren't able to save any of the supplies on board, and there is no insignia marking the ship's home or allegiance."

"Who was it that found the ship?" Sir Owl jumped urgently.

A smaller catfish peaking from the side raised his fin.

Sir Owl approached him, "Come out. Tell me. What exactly did you see? What supplies did the ship carry? What direction did it sail from? What was the make of the ship? Did it carry any canons or treasure—"

"Owley," Kat interrupted. "Stop scaring my Fry."

The smaller catfish, Fry apparently, had begun to cry. Owley's eyes dropped into a scowl. Kat approached Fry and comforted him, bringing him in for a hug under her fin. She also whispered sweet and reassuring statements to him.

"There, there. I know, he's insensitive," Kat continued. She then turned to Owley, "You must speak to them more gently. They must be carefully lured out."

Owley rolled his eyes.

"What do you wish to tell me?" Kat held her ear up to Fry.

Fry turned to her and began to whisper as Kat continuously nodded and said, "Oh." The young catfish appeared enthused to share what he had witnessed and learned, speaking endlessly for at least five minutes.

"Thank you, my small Fry," Kat patted Fry on the head, giving him permission to jump back into the river. Kat then stepped out of the water and stood in front of Owley, building anticipation. "He said he couldn't say."

"It took him that long to tell you that!" Owley flapped his wings in frustration.

"Yes, and he also said that he doesn't like your tone. He asked for you to stop coming by the riverbank," Kat clasped her hands/fins.

"What!" Owley exclaimed.

"Is that a question?" Kat asked slowly.

"Ugh, no… You're not actually going to listen to him, right?"

"Listen, it may be for the best if you don't visit for like a week, at least. It'll allow the knot to get loosened. Plus, my knot cannot help you anymore regarding the origins of this man. You may want to consider taking him to the Koi."

"Really? The Koi Masters? I wanted to avoid involving them," Owley groaned.

"I know, but it may be for the best. Best to deal with it soon before the conditions start to worsen," Kat spoke candidly. Then she turned to the human. "Human, do you truly not know who you are and from where you come?"

The human who had still been squatting, "I might be Tom."

"Good. You better not be lying about your identity," Kat the catfish pointed threateningly. She then turned to Owley for their parting words. "Take him there, Owley. You must."

"I will," Owley sighed. "I seriously can't come by for a week, though?"

2

The owl and the human, maybe Tom, continued to journey through the island. They sought to reach the Masters of the island, the Koi fish. These Masters resided deeper within the island, past much of the forest and terrain. They were ancient and were alleged to know all, and would surely hold the answers to the human's origins.

"When will we get there?" The human named maybe Tom asked.

"Stop," Sir Owl called from the sky.

"Where are we going exactly—"

"Stop."

"How will we know we're there—"

"Stop!"

"What are the Koi like?"

"Stahp!"

"What color are they?"

"Stoppp!"

"I want to climb the mountain."

"I said stop—oh wait, that wasn't a question. Never mind."

"Is this the way to the mountain?"

"Ughhh…"

As Owley predicted, the man continued to bother him on their travels. It was bad enough that Owley needed to tend to his duties; it was awful that he had a human to accompany. He would've just left the man to his own devices, and as long as the human had stayed at the shore, it would've been permissible. However, now considering that Kat, the old catfish, had suggested Owley take the man to the Koi, he had to take the man to the Koi. If he didn't, surely a demotion or banishment would follow or—worse—he could get eaten. If it had been anyone else besides Kat who gave the order, Owley may not have needed to follow it. Yet, Kat possessed a reputation as large as her whiskers. She also sat by the water, and the water carried her wishes and delivered them to the Koi and wherever else the water flowed. Therefore, Owley was stuck taking the man to the Koi Masters.

A sudden branch snapped behind them. Owley froze and scanned their path ahead with his enhanced senses.

"What's wrong?" Asked maybe Tom.

"Hush!" Owley silenced him.

The man, maybe named Tom, listened, trying to understand what the owl had heard. Then another snap came from behind them. They suddenly turned and saw nothing. All that stood there was a giant tree trunk, from the direction they had come. An ample tree trunk covered their path back, waving its many loose and dried leaves. The coast was clear, or so they thought.

Owley watched the tree from above. He realized that he noticed the leaves lying beside the roots moving and stirring. The breeze wasn't strong, not enough to just make the leaves cheerily spin. Owley gave it more thought and then shouted, "Snake! Run!"

The two began to dash through the forest and tall grass. Owley's vantage was clear, and he was far out of reach of the ground. Tom, perhaps, was not so lucky; he rushed through a bramble bush and found himself yelping aloud. It pricked and poked him, and he went, "Ow, ow, ow!" Owley tried to hush him, but kept hidden behind the branches. While running, the man tripped over a loose root of a tree and banged his knee. Now, he was covered in thorns, dirt, and fear. The slithering seemed to grow behind him, and he thought to alleviate his tension, so turned to see.

The snake exited the large bramble bush, largely unaffected. As the snake came within sight, the human noticed. The snake was ginormous, but only in the middle. Its head was small and so was its tail, but bulging in the middle was a giant meal. Owley peaked and saw that the shape of the meal was that of a cow, loud and whole. The snake opened his mouth and went to bite the man, but as he did and brandished his fangs, out came the sound, "Moo."

Slowly, the snake realized his mouth wouldn't open much. He had eaten too much and was still digesting. His tummy grumbled, either to signal more hunger or argue no more.

"I'm sssorry. Thisss isss ssso embarrasssing," the snake slithered, taking his jaw off the man's boot.

"It's okay!" The man awkwardly shouted and scanned around for Sir Owl and some guidance.

"Thisss isss a sssticky sssituation I've put you in," the snake nervously gulped.

"It's really okay," the man gulped even louder.

"Ssseriousssly, thisss isss weird," the snake said and stared around. He seemed to think. "I've never been in a sssituation like thisss. To erassse the awkwardnesss, I guesss I'll eat you."

"What? No, that's not needed. All is forgiven."

"I insssisssst. Otherwissse, thisss memory will torture me and you" the snake continued to think. "You may end up ssscared of usss sssnakesss. That'sss not fair."

"Pssschh, no way," the man, perhaps Tom, lied, inching back. "You're so cool. How could I be scared of you?"

Owley slapped himself in the face, hiding above.

"You're ssso kind, but pleassse let me eat you or elssse…" the snake squared up to the man. "Plusss, that would make me sssmile."

The man picked his feet up from underneath him and began to run.

Owley whispered to himself, "You fool."

Snake gave chase to the man through the forest. The man knew he didn't have much of a chance, but he took the opportunity to escape. Whenever the man ducked in between the trees and low branches, the snake would swing his body and bring down the tree. This was the power granted to him with the weight of the cow he had ingested. As the cow would stand up again in the snake's stomach, it would let out another call, "Moo!"

The man rolled and ducked and attempted to free himself. In one instance, the man stood on one side of a tree trunk and the snake on the other, while the man attempted to jump and juke away from the terror. The snake confronted the man, threatened to crush his bones, and once again launched his snack at the tree trunk. Bark, leaves, and dirt flew everywhere, clouding the man's vision and breath and giving Owley a scare.

The human kept running through mountains of crushed leaves. Sometimes his foot caved in to where, from appearance, it seemed sturdy. He kept sprinting and hyperventilating, feeling pain in his abdomen, until he realized the mound they stood on came to an end. Might be Tom turned around and faced the fate that came for him. The snake lunged and wrapped around Tom(?) as they both realized no floor stood beneath them, and so they tumbled.

They went rolling down the hill as Owley watched from above, eventually losing sight of them within the cloud of dust.

Owley slapped himself in the face and said, "Why today of all days?"

2.5

The man slowly came to consciousness. He looked around him and saw himself within a meadow of flowers: white, blue, pink, and violet. All the wildflowers colored this hidden gem within the forest. A weeping tree hovered over him as the white and pink leaves glided down, mesmerizing the man, maybe named Tom. One little leaf floated against the wind, obscuring the sun above—it must be—Tom and landed gently upon the tip of his nose. From the moment it touched him, (what's his name?) Tom felt himself liven up and inhale. His eyes began to water, and upon seeing the sun clearly, Tom (or Tommy) sneezed.

"Achoo!" And his head flew up.

He saw the dried-up leaves from where he had tumbled covering his body, but above it lay just a gentle splattering of the weeping cherries. The Tom guy thought that he had somehow fallen deeper into the forest. But where he was felt far less threatening than the place before. There was no sign of the owl, the snake, or the cow. Maybe Tom or Timothy tried to listen for the quiet slithering, as Sir Owl had before, but he heard nothing.

Where did they go, he thought to himself. Then his mind sparked, and he thought of a brilliant idea.

He shot up and shouted at the top of his lungs, "Who, what, when, where, how!" He figured it would capture Sir Owl's attention. Let's call him Tom looked up and waited.

"Who are you talking to?" A mysterious voice came from behind him.

"Owley!" Tom jumped around. His smile quickly vanished for who he saw was not Sir Owl but a lady. Worst of all, the lady carried the snake around her neck, the same snake who had sought to eat Tom. The snake's belly, however, was now empty. Tom thought that the snake must've digested the cow, and the snake must be famished now and ready to eat him and the lady.

"I think you have me mistaken. I'm not Sir Owl—" the lady gently spoke.

"Ma'am, you must be careful! The snake around your neck is dangerous. He just tried to eat me, and before that, he ate a whole cow." The man looked almost panicked, bending his knees and ready to dash.

The lady looked at the snake and held his head gently with her hand. "Did you really?"

"I did. I'm sssorry," the snake felt ashamed.

"Sly, you know better than that. I did find it awfully convenient that I found you wandering the woods with Moorgan. Friends are not meant for eating," she carefully caressed the snake's head.

"I know. I'm sssorry. I ssspat her out when I fell," Sly the snake hid in the lady's hair.

"I'm not the one you should be apologizing to," the lady tilted her head as Sly wriggled to her other shoulder. "You can apologize to Moorgan."

Just then, a "Moo" came from within the meadow. Moorgan appeared from the trees behind the human. A flock of flowers hung out of her mouth, and a flower crown adorned her head.

"What?" The man exchanged a confused glance with the lady and the cow.

"You seem confused," the lady said. "You're not from around here, are you?"

"No."

"They're native to the island. Meet Sly and Moorgan," the lady then gestured.

"Sssup," Sly the snake said to the man.

"Moo!" Said Moorgan.

"What's your name?" The lady kindly followed.

The human felt hesitant to share. Feeling wary of the strangers, he returned to his original plan. "Who, what, when, where, how!"

"What are you doing?" The lady somewhat rolled her eyes.

"Calling Sir Owl," the man continued. "Who, what, when, where, how! Why! What! Where! How! Help! When! When will you come? When!" He looked up to the sky. "Whennnnnn!" With his last yell, the man began to wobble. His head began to spin and, all of a sudden, he collapsed again into the pile of leaves and flowers.

In his dream, he saw the mountain and the vast sea beside it. There stood the mountain of wonders, and he wanted to run and climb it. However, when he began to take his first steps, he felt a deep sense of loneliness. He was there just by himself. The man waited for someone—anyone—to join him. Surely, someone would appear if he just waited long enough… Then he realized that he was all alone by himself.

Then the man awoke, suddenly sitting up. Sitting beside him was the lady on her knees. Next to her were the snake and the cow. Sly, who hung off Moorgan's neck, keenly watched the man, while Moorgan munched away at the nearby grass. Seeing the lady beside him, the man felt somewhat flustered, additionally for losing his composure.

"I'm sorry. I'm sorry. It's just been a really long and strange day," the man named maybe Tom huffed.

"It's okay. No need to apologize," she gently said.

He looked past his current condition and saw her rosy cheeks kissed by the sun. He saw her cat-like eyes, filled with many beautiful colors, and felt he had seen them somewhere before when staring at the night sky. On her nose was a cute little divot, and the crown around her face was her chestnut hair. She wore a pretty locket around her neck, and the neckline of her dress was adorned with periwinkle forget-me-nots. Her dress fanned out like a flower. Amongst the tall grass and the lupine, daisies, and queen of the prairie, sat the princess, whom Tom thought was a fairy. His heart fluttered as he saw her. Butterflies weren't just flying around the meadow, but within his belly. Then she grabbed his head as he leaned back and offered him a shell holding a shimmering liquid.

"Here, you should drink this," the lady offered her help.

The man felt his head comforted by a cloud and let the liquid flow through him.

"What is it?" He asked, gulping.

"Water," she smiled.

That's the best water I've ever tasted, the man, maybe Tom, thought to himself. Feeling so soothed, he slipped back to sleep.

When he awoke, he felt a punch in his gut. He yelped and saw Sir Owl standing on his chest. Having climbed up, Sir Owl placed his talons upon the man's chin.

"Don't you dare ever run away from me again," Sir Owl ordered.

"What?" The man mumbled, slowly returning to his surroundings.

"I've about had it with your questions. My mind's been spinning all day from hearing them," Sir Owl flew off.

"Sorry," the man sat up. He scanned the meadow and saw nothing but the cow and the weeping willow. "Where did she go?"

"She? Who, the cow?" Sir Owl searched the cow. "Check your vision. She is here, safe and sound. The snake seems to have escaped."

"No, I don't mean Moorgan," the man said, seeming confused and sad.

"How do you know her name—"

"I mean the lady. She may have been a fairy."

Sir Owl side-eyed the man, "I have no clue what you mean. I don't believe in weird mythical things." He turned back to look around. "But we must search for the snake. He must be apprehended."

"No, it's okay. Sly was just hungry and made a mistake," the man said.

3

The man, owl, and cow carried on. They fashioned a leash for the cattle from a sturdy vine so she wouldn't wander off again in search of more grass. Sir Owl acted as the brains, while the man, maybe named Tom, attempted to tie the secure knot before they proceeded, gently guiding Moorgan along the path.

Now and then, the man would stop and ask, "Are you okay, Moorgan?"

Moorgan would reply, "Moo."

Sir Owl would be bothered and complain every time, but would generally hold his tongue since they were in the company of another.

"Typically, they never wander out this far," Sir Owl explained about the cow.

As they walked, they explored Sir Owl's explanation. They saw that the flat lands near the center of the island were dead and not of much appeal. The deeper they went into the country, though, the more they found other cattle grazing about. Stragglers, here and there, but past the forest came a kine munching together. The kine mooed upon seeing Moorgan. Man released Moorgan's leash and grazed her head and bid her farewell. She walked by, greeting her old friends, saying bye to the new ones, and swatting her tail at Sir Owl. It brought Tom peace to see them all together. He waved goodbye.

Sir Owl, however, said, "Good riddance." Then he turned away from the cows.

Crossing into the town, the man and Sir Owl began to pass small patches of grass, and within them crickets that watched them. The river ran past them at times as Sir Owl and the man strolled past several banks of catfish and turtles lounging and smoking bubbles. The watchers would stop what they were doing and stare, whispering their personal beliefs to each other. Sir Owl took it as commonplace for the creatures of the island to be nosey, but did not, of course, appreciate the added attention from his unwanted companion. The guy, maybe named Tom, couldn't help but stare as well. He was still bewildered by the nature of this island that he was on. At times, the man couldn't even tell who the watchers were staring at: him, Sir Owl, or simply the sky. Some polite citizens would at least begin to whistle and try to mind their business. Sir Owl came just so close to losing his cool and mouthing off at the passersby.

Along the skinny road, there eventually came a pack of performers: two catfish and a cricket, who didn't look like the rest of their kind. Their clothes were colorful and their spirits lively as they waved their arms to sing and dance, spinning each other in circles. The cricket sat atop a rock and played all the instruments, bouncing from one end to another: banging the drums, clapping the cymbals, strumming the guitar, and performing his classic chirp. Both the fish froze as Sir Owl and the man approached. Then the young catfish began to make random sounds and movements. Their music was rhythmic, not the most coherent, but the man named Tom stood and clapped as Sir Owl rolled his eyes and kept moving forward.

The dancers, a boy and a girl, performed the wave as they interchangeably sang.

"*Hello,*" the boy hopped up.

"*Hello,*" the girl jumped.

"*Hello!*"

"*Hello!*"

"*Welcome!*"

"*Welcome!*"

"*To our island,*" they both joined in together. "*Hello, hello. Welcome, welcome. Welcome to our island… the Mountain of Determination!*"

The cricket chirped.

Then the performers stopped, joined their opposite feet/fins and raised their arms to signal the big finale. The man felt obliged to clap but genuinely enjoyed the clap. He was considerably amused by the young performers, and clearly, the performers were too. The band bowed and directed the man's attention to the large leaf lying ahead of them with small knick-knacks, like nuts and rocks, gathered in praise of their performance. The man was stirred and didn't know how to pay for the show, so he signaled for the group to wait one second while he ran to the nearest riverbank. Into the river, the man stuck his hand and pulled out the finest thing he could grab. He went and proudly placed a clam at the feet of the performers as they smiled, cheered, and jumped into the air.

The man then jogged up to Sir Owl, who apparently hadn't gone too far. Sir Owl denied waiting, but he surely seemed to enjoy the moment of isolation.

"Do you—oh wait," the man put his finger up to his lips and thought. He corrected himself, "You don't seem to like the others."

"What? No, I don't mind them," the owl certainly lied. "But wow, look at that. You're catching on. Just to inform you, despite your efforts, don't for a second think that we're going to get along. I'm taking you to the Koi, leaving you, and that's that."

"Okay, I guess if you insist," the man somewhat disappointedly said, just as he had begun to enjoy his adventure.

This reassurance fixed a smile on the owl's face.

They reached the so-called town, actually named the Pond. Nothing special appeared at first, just flat land until the path broke off and traveled down. Downward, the path erupted with small and dark trees and sank into a swamp. Left and right were slow-moving water and trees adorned and dripping with moss like the wax on a candle. Fireflies flew through the weeds as the sun began to set. In some inlets of land, there were small bogs of mud. Frogs balanced on lily pads or swam freely, croaking giant bubbles as they sat partly submerged in the mud. They put the turtles and catfish to shame with the size of their bubbles and stares. As big as their eyes were, their pupils seemed superficial and wandered. They enjoyed their leisure until one decided to hop up and approach the visitors.

"Ribbittt," the slimy fellow said. "Hey, you, I haven't seen you in these parts before."

"Don't entertain them—" Sir Owl began to whisper, while covering his mouth.

"Are you talking to me? The man plainly asked the frog.

Sir Owl's jaw dropped before he lifted it and gritted his teeth, "Why would you do that—"

"Yeah, you. Ribbittt," the froggy fellow said. "What business you got here?"

"Our business does not pertain to you—" Sir Owl turned to face the frog.

"We're here to see the Koi," the man stupidly blurted out.

What accompanied was a chorus of croaks from all across the bog.

"Why would you say that?" Sir Owl dragged his face down in disbelief. "I am done with your foolishness. You can't follow a single one of my commands."

"Oh, the Koi. Ribbittt," the fellow croaked. "I'm actually good buddies with them."

"Are you?" The man eagerly knelt to the frog as Sir Owl continued to hover over and berate him.

"Yeah, we go wayyy back. Ribbittt. We were one of their first neighbors."

"Really?"

"Argh, you're a fool—" Sir Owl continued to complain.

"Yes, yes. Ribbittt," the froggy fellow croaked again.

"Oh, wow. So are they really important or something?" The man asked with curiosity.

"Oh, yeah. They are by far the most important, or maybe the second-most-important beings on the island. Ribbittt."

"Wow!" The man wowed. He wanted to ask who was first, but he was cut off.

"Yeah, it's a really big deal to be meeting them. Ribbittt."

"Oh, wow, okay." The man began to feel nervous.

"In fact, I can give you some pointers for meeting them if you'd like. Ribbittt," the frog seemed to look toward his crowd. The croaking intensified as a crowd of frogs surrounded Sir Owl.

Sir Owl became occupied as various frogs took turns picking on him. The frogs croaked loudly to cloud his hearing, and some even jumped to cover his line of sight. The owl attempted to avoid them and grew mortified by the social interaction.

The man saw Sir Owl distracted and took it upon himself to lean into the frog salesman and say, "Yes, please help me."

"Perfect. Ribbittt! All you gotta do is pay me a hundred flies and the help is yours," the slimy fellow offered.

The man seemed lost. "I don't have a hundred flies."

"How many do you have? Ribbittt."

"I don't even have one."

"What the heck. What about crickets? Ribbittt."

The man thought back to the field of chirping crickets and the cheerful cricket performer himself. "No, none. That doesn't seem right."

"Ugh, fine. I'll offer this to you free of charge since it's your first time. Ribbittt."

"Yay, thank you so much!"

The froggy fellow stepped aside, "Jump in."

The man made a "Huh" sound and scratched his head.

"The Koi love it when you visit them wearing mud, especially when you drag mud into their clear waters. Plus, the mud is mighty good for your soul. Take it or leave it. Ribbittt."

The man listened, nodded several times, and smiled. He looked up at the pool ahead of him, stood up, and—SPLASH!

"Why don't you ever listen to me?" The owl cried while flying beside the wet man.

The man's boots made a squeaking noise as he slowly walked in shame, leaving a trail of muddy footprints behind him. He heard the many frogs guffaw, for they had swindled him. On his face, he wore a long and disappointed expression that could only be seen once he had wiped his face clean. His shirt, trousers, boots, and hair all weighed down and soaked and dripped. While sad, the man reconsidered whether he should've trusted the frogs. He compared them to the snake. That lady had suggested to the man that they were all just trying to get by. That frog was one of the first creatures to actually approach him, and that is what had duped the man into a false sense of security and excitement. So the man attempted to find the silver lining; even though wet and covered in mud, he now felt somewhat cooler.

Down the winding path and into the sunken garden, Sir Owl and Tom(?) entered. They approached the home of the ancient Koi fish. Surrounding the perimeter were neatly trimmed and circular bushes of yellow, orange, and golden flowers, all lined up in a proper order. The fireflies continued to fly about, approaching and illuminating the various flowers. Where the path ended, there began the round and shallow pool in which the Koi swam. At the base of the shallow pond was stone, parts of which were covered in moss that Sir Owl directed Tom(?) to walk. At the center of the pond was where the Koi resided. With the sun setting and casting an orange hue, the water felt a tad chilly, but the man walked in, primarily concerned with not dirtying the waters with muddy clothes. Dirt washed off his legs and trousers and filtered into the clear and pristine waters. His boots sat beside Sir Owl on the edge of the path. Sir Owl covered his face with his wings, only peaking out barely. The man cringed to himself but continued to tremble through the ripples. He approached what he found to be two koi fish, circling each other at a gentle pace. The pace seemed to quicken, taking on a wild and chasing force. The two fish seemed distinct at first. One was orange and white, and the other was orange and black. One seemed to appear with traces of silver upon his skin, and the other gold. As the two koi fish swam, they seemed to almost blend into a never-ending circle.

"Whoa," the human said.

"Hello," said one.

"Hi," said the other.

"Hello, Sirs Koi," the human nodded.

"I'm a sir," said the one.

"I'm a madam," said the one or the other.

"Ah, I'm sorry. It's hard to tell each of you apart," the human watched the two fish swim in circles, crossing his eyes and not knowing where one fish ended and the other began.

"I am Ko," said Ko.

"I am Oi," said Oi.

"Together, we are the Koi," said Ko and Oi, the golden and swirling circle.

"Ko-Oi. Koi," the human sounded out.

"And you are…" said Ko or Oi.

"Your name is…" said Oi or Ko.

"I am…" the man thought. "Tom."

"Tom…" the Koi whispered.

"Yeah, I think so," the human addressed himself.

"Might be Tom," Ko or Oi.

"Maybe Tom," Oi or Ko.

"Kat the catfish seemed to think so," Tom supported.

"She did," said Ko.

"We heard," said Oi.

"The waves—"

"Told us."

"Oh, okay," stuttered Tom.

"Owley found you—"

"Guided you—"

"Brought you—"

"To us."

"Tell us—"

"Who are you—"

"And what you remember—"

"Tell us."

Tom shared, "I woke up on the beach, which is where Sir Owl found me. He took me to the catfish for help in identifying myself. I have no recollection of my name, memories, or anything. Kat and her knot managed to find the ruins of my ship, supplies, and possibly my name. That's all they said, and then we set off for here.

On the way here, I was attacked by Sly the snake, who had eaten Moorgan the cow. We ended up taking a tumble off a cliff, and I was awoken and cared for by a fairy. She nursed me and showed me that Sly didn't mean any true harm. He was just really hungry, you see. While I was unconscious, I had a dream that involved me waiting. I don't quite know how to explain it, but I felt as if I was meant to find someone here. It felt as if we were meant to climb the mountain together—"

"Mountain," hummed Ko.

"Together," sang Oi.

"It was a strange feeling. You know, like an emptiness that you feel from someone's missing presence…" Tom waited for some kind of response. He received nothing, so he resumed. "Anyway, Sir Owl and I reunited, and we returned Moorgan to her pasture. We also passed by some entertaining performers. A catfish duo and a cricket, they're awesome. There was also a prankster frog near here. About that, I'm sorry for getting mud in your pool."

"Sorry," Ko summarized.

"Apology," Oi highlighted.

"Accepted," Ko provided.

"I guess," Oi relented.

"I'm sorry," Tom cringed.

"Thank you."

"For your sorry."

"And for returning—"

"Moorgan—"

"To her—"

"Pasture."

"Of course," Tom felt glad.

"What to do with you?" Asked Ko or Oi.

"Truly, what to do?" Questioned Oi or Ko.

"Owley—"

"Help."

Sir Owl flew toward the group and reluctantly joined them, standing far from Tom and his muddy water. "Masters, I am at your command."

"Tell us—"

"Owley—"

"Your—

"Perspective."

Owley testified with a concerned expression, "Yes, Masters. I approached the man upon his waking up on the beach and declaring that he would climb our mountain. I attempted to question him and received no valid answers. Therefore, I took him to Kat. All of which he has shared about meeting with the catfish is true. I cannot attest to anything else. We were attacked by Sly, and when I attempted to apprehend him, he was nowhere to be found. I suspect Sly may have escaped with aid from the man, or the human may have eaten him."

"I didn't eat Sly," Tom refuted. "At least, I have no memory of eating him."

"He is clearly a ditz and a klutz, a fool surely. Harmless, probably, but stupid. I rest my case," Owley bowed.

"A fool—" said one fish.

"Surely—" said the other fish.

"Harmless—"

"But stupid—"

"What brings you—"

"To us?"

Tom felt lost again, but tried to find a straight path through the circling, "I'm sorry. I don't know exactly. All I know is I woke up here with only one thought. My dream is to climb the mountain."

"Hmmm…" said Ko.

"Hmmm…" said Oi.

"Rather peculiar."

"Very strange."

The Masters joined together, "We don't receive many humans, if any at all. You see, we are struggling through hard times.

Our island suffers, and so do we. We are losing our precious and natural resources. It may not look it in some parts, but we are growing more low and famished, disingenuous and afraid, and worried and hopeless about what the future of our island holds. Therefore, we are guarded and wary."

"Is there any way I can help?" Tom asked.

The Koi stated together, "No. Everything within our island follows a set course. Our spirit of the silver lining is slowly leaving us. It is the spirit that powered us, cared for us, and allowed us to thrive. Now, it is vanishing. We're afraid you cannot help us. You must not disturb our island's natural rapport with the spirit, so we may use our hope to rebuild our connection with the spirit. However, you have helped us by guiding Moorgan home, and for that we are grateful. We believe you are not here to harm us, so to reciprocate your kindness, we will allow you to climb the mountain."

Tom cheered, "Thank you, Masters Ko and Oi. I'm incredibly grateful. Thank you!"

"However, you must vow that once you have climbed the mountain, you will depart from our island," The Koi Masters ordered.

"I promise. I will leave you all to prosper and will not bother any of you at all," Tom held out his hand and placed it onto his heart. "I vow."

"You flow with our waters, and we are grateful."

"Of course," Tom smiled, preparing himself for adventure.

"One more thing," Koi began.

"For this trip—" said one fish.

"Since, Owley—" said the other fish.

"Is the one—"

"Who found you—"

"He must accompany you on this expedition," the Koi Masters finished.

4.1

"No, no, no, no," Owley cried. "There must surely be some kind of misunderstanding. My mind will melt if I stay with you."

The man who was now officially recognized as Tom walked beside the exasperated owl. The owl kept hopping and fluttering, desperately trying to comprehend his fate and escape. Owley had not even held his tongue in front of the Koi and expressed his concerns at a rapid pace.

Throwing his wings about the pond, he had argued, "What about this? What about that?" He tried so hard to instill some sense.

Ko and Oi had quieted him and together summoned him, "We call upon you, Owley, to assume this role as a guide and guardian to the human, just for this trip. We trust you with this."

It was a great honor, Owley could admit, but the process and ordeal of it caused him great distress. "Why did I have to find you? Ugh, why me? Whyyyy?" Owley cried.

Tom didn't know what to think. He felt some kind of guilt for dragging Sir Owl into this quest. However, this seemed to be the only way Tom could complete his quest.

"There, there," Tom squatted down and patted Owley on the back.

"Keep your condolences to yourself," Sir Owl swatted Tom's hand away. "Maybe tomorrow morning, we can visit the Koi Masters and ask them to reconsider. Maybe I can propose to them that I am content in my current vocation and that this honor be granted to Kat or even a frog. Plus, yes, they could just swim up with you on the stream that goes all the way up the mountain. Yes! I've figured it out. That is what we shall do. Perfect!"

Sir Owl seemed to have regained some hope and strolled further away from Tom, already beginning to distance himself. Tom felt glad, he guessed, and followed after Sir Owl to find their lodgings for the night.

The village of the Pond was gracious enough. Sir Owl was allotted a well-kept branch upon which he slept, while Tom was provided a shabby dirt patch right underneath the branch. Sleep didn't come so easily and comfortably there, so Tom let himself aimlessly ponder while staring at the moon and night sky as Sir Owl snored and hooted away. The stars were shimmering upon the blanket of night. It was the first moment of rest they were granted during what seemed to be, so far, the most chaotic day of their lives. One dreamt of warm and cozy horizons, watching the tide sweep in, while the other dreamt of being chased around by dragons and questioned by sphinxes as frogs guffawed and catfish fished.

They awoke, one more refreshed than the other, and marched over to the sunken garden the first thing in the morning. When they arrived, their findings made Owley's jaw drop and Tom rub his eyes. What they saw and heard was true. The Koi had vanished. They were gone, and now nothing filled the pond, except for loose gravel and dirt. There was no one to contest with. Sir Owl flew over the pond, searching for the hidden Koi. A lonely feather of his flew off and landed gently in the pond.

"I don't know what's going on," Tom expressed.

"Me too," Sir Owl said. "We should wait for them."

They waited for a few hours until they realized the Koi had truly gone. The Koi had left no notice of when they'd return, but Sir Owl seemed sure they would return. Tom and Sir Owl were left staring at each other, understanding that their fate was set in stone. What the Koi had commanded would be their true fate. They must journey on together.

4.25

Sir Owl was still not content or fully accepting. However, now there was no escape. He could feed Tom to the snake if he could find Sly, but that would take too much work and probably get Sir Owl punished. So they must journey on together.

Tom was excited. Even though he was disliked by Sir Owl, he still found Sir Owl to be far more serious and—therefore—reliable as a travel companion. If a dragon or sphinx may appear, Sir Owl and Tom could rely on each other to decipher the riddle or run away together. So Tom excitedly gathered all the supplies they could need and set off on this journey with Sir Owl.

"We're on an adventure!" Tom cheered, pulling on the straps of his makeshift backpack.

"Okay," Sir Owl begrudgingly responded.

"I'm very excited to have you as my companion, Sir Owl."

"I am your guardian, don't forget. Not a companion."

"Ah, yes. You're my guardian. What a reputable title. What title would you consider for me?"

"A fool," Sir Owl said and flew ahead.

Upon their departure from the village, they came across the same performers: two catfish and a cricket. It was still early morning, but the band was in full spirits and sang and danced. The boy and girl joined arms and frolicked around as the cricket steadily banged the drums and blew the horns.

"*Off to an adventure!*" Sang the catfish boy.

"*Off to an adventure!*" Sang the catfish girl.

The two sang, together, "*They are off to an adventure,*

"*Sir Owl and Tom, off to an adventure,*

"*Sir Owl and Tom, partners in adventure,*

"*They are off to an adventure,*

"*Through the pond, through the bush,*

"*Up the mountain, down the cliff,*

"*By the beach, in the pits,*

"*Off to an adventure, with one good push,*

"*Off to an adventure,*

"*Off to an adventure*

"*They are off to an adventure*

"*Sir Owl and Tom, off to an adventure,*

"*Sir Owl and Tom, partners in adventure,*

"*They are off to an adventure!*"

Tom applauded, and Sir Owl's jaw dropped again.

"Woo!" Tom cheered. He was marveled by their growth and evolution as artists. Tom went and emptied his pockets of all the nuts and snacks he had gathered in preparation for the journey.

"You fool!" Sir Owl jumped for the tossed reward.

"Thank you, thank you," the boy and girl bowed, especially grateful.

The cricket also chirped, "Thank you."

Sir Owl began to pocket the nuts and snacks thrown by Tom. "You fool, these are our rations. You cannot be giving them all out like this."

"Oh, okay," Tom gulped, and turned to the performers. "I'm sorry. I promise I'll bring you a treat that is worthy of your song. An ultimate treasure!"

"Woohoo, thanks," simply cheered the performers.

"Yay!" Followed the hard-working cricket.

Tom high-fived the trio and carried on with Sir Owl.

The adventurers traveled away from the performers. The repeating chorus of the performers became distant, but was retained in the minds of the adventurers.

"You fool, you cannot be making false promises to others," Sir Owl yelled at Tom once they were in the clear.

"But that wasn't a false promise," Tom was confused.

"Where are you possibly going to find a treat for them all? As the Koi said, these are harsh times for our island," Sir Owl exposited again.

"I get it, but I meant it. I'll find them a treat. They deserve it," Tom said earnestly.

"They're stupid for hopping around and dancing, hoping that others will throw them a treat. They need to act smarter and conserve their energy and devote it to something worthwhile."

"They're hard-workers."

"Ha!" Sir Owl guffawed.

"Plus, their song is so catchy," Tom began to hum. "On an adventure! On an adventure!"

"Those aren't even the right words!"

Tom continued to hum and improvise the song while Sir Owl and he traveled down the path. So far, they still traveled through pastures. Apparently, a few more villages would come until their path became more rural and treacherous. Sir Owl had estimated a two-day journey to travel up the mountain and one day down, expediting the whole process to make it efficient and shave off any excess time. The plan was to travel for as long as they could, without any stops, and rest at nightfall in the safest nook. Tom just nodded blindly, unaware of the path and relying upon Sir Owl as his guide, but he also just distracted.

The grasses on the journey were varying colors. There was something indescribable in the air that was rotting the vegetation. However, to Tom, everything appeared new, and so it all took on a magical appearance. Tall fields and fast rivers, a strong gust of wind in the morning, and a quiet sun painted the backdrop of the first leg of the journey. Sir Owl felt impervious to the environment, but Tom's teeth chattered. Now and then, on the path, Tom and Sir Owl passed by herds of cows. Tom would rush to greet them, even from afar, and make a habit of asking if any of them knew of Moorgan. Sir Owl would yell at him, threaten to leave without him, and start to leave, until Tom would run and catch up to him.

"Stick to the plan! At this rate, it's gonna take us forever to reach the top of the mountain," Sir Owl complained.

Tom took on an expression of confusion and concern, squinting further on one side of his face. "I don't get it. Why the haste?"

"Stop with the questions," Sir Owl hollered and halted Tom's questioning.

"What's wrong with asking questions?"

"What did I just say!"

"So I can't ask anything?"

"Ugh, no!" Sir Owl practically slapped himself in the face.

"What if I really needed your help with something?"

"No."

"What if I just wanted to get to know you?"

"No," Sir Owl was stern. "Absolutely not."

"What if—"

"No! Shut it."

"Okay, okay. Well, I guess if we run into a sphinx, we're screwed," Tom let his hands fall by his side.

"A what?" Sir Owl squinted his eyes in an unserious manner.

"Nothing," Tom responded with what he figured Sir Owl wanted to hear.

In silence now, they both kept walking. Sir Owl would shoot Tom a stare if he ever even thought to ask a question about something in their surroundings. He would also begin to cough and clear his throat viciously if Tom ever broke out into a hum or song. And so Tom stayed shut. They kept strolling silently, like music to Sir Owl's ears.

Soon, along the dirt patch formed a stone fence, short and not taller than Tom, or maybe 3 Sir Owls stacked up tall. The pastures continued, and the whisper of wind filled the silence on the bright morning. The wind eventually died down, and in its place, Sir Owl began to hear a distant whimper and bleating. He immediately suspected Tom, but noticed Tom was oblivious; Sir Owl's hearing was, of course, heightened, and Tom had not even caught on to these mysterious sounds. Sir Owl hoped it would stay that way and avoided addressing the foreign noises and put them out of his mind, only for Tom to shout aloud in recognition of these sounds. Tom said he heard a hollering, which almost sounded like a bark coming in occasional intervals. Asking Sir Owl more about the sounds was not even a question. Tom decided he would avoid it and try to approach the matter at Sir Owl's speed, and wait for him to acknowledge the sounds or express his concern—

"Why won't those sounds shut up?" Sir Owl jumped onto the fence.

"I was just thinking about the sounds," Tom delightedly expressed.

Sir Owl did not seem to share in Tom's delight. "Sounds like a dog."

"Yeah, a dog. I hear it."

"But where?" Sir Owl scanned and then saw. "There he is—"

"Over there!" Tom eagerly pointed.

Indeed, in the distance, there stood a dog on all fours, barking at the ground. After a while, the dog would stop, turn, and run toward a herd of sheep, bark, and return to his original spot of barking at the ground.

"I was going to say that," Sir Owl passive-aggressively replied to Tom. "But yes, it looks like that's our culprit. Enough looking now, time to continue—"

"What is he barking at, you think? Tom leaned forward on the fence, holding his face in his palm.

"Ugh… his herd, probably, but it doesn't matter. Let's go."

Tom kept examining, "No, that doesn't seem right. What could he be barking at on the ground and so far away from the herd?"

"Stop it. It's time to go," Sir Owl objected. As Sir Owl turned around to march away, he heard Tom's footsteps crushing the grass and walking toward the dog. Sir Owl jumped back to face the insolent Tom, "What are you thinking? You're defying me, again?"

Tom kept walking, focused on the dog.

"This will take us further off course."

Tom continued forward.

"We have a plan and itinerary we need to follow."

Tom looked around while continuing forward.

"I was assigned as your guardian, so return here at this very moment!" Sir Owl stomped and puffed out his chest.

Tom finally stopped and turned around. He gave Sir Owl an irresistible smile, "Would you please come and guard me here?"

Sir Owl made a disapproving motion with his head and hummed. Tom stood there gleefully and motioned at Sir Owl again before continuing forward. As Tom neared the dog, he also heard Sir Owl's fluttering close behind him.

When they finally arrived, they saw the dog crying and the reason why: a stray baby lamb had fallen into a hole. Meanwhile, the rest of the herd seemed to mind their own business. The dog appeared to be most concerned about the lamb's stuckness. So the dog ran back and forth from the group and the solo one, divided and caught somewhere in between leaving or helping the little one. Tom squatted beside the shepherd dog and looked down at the trapped sheep in the hole. It was too steep to climb out of and too deep and narrow for the man to climb into. The lamb tried hard to kick herself up, but her poor and clean wool became covered in the dirt that fell around her. This seemed like an awfully poor place to be stuck.

"Oh, wow," Tom placed his finger under his chin to contemplate a potential escape plan for the lamb.

"Wow, what a sight," Sir Owl awkwardly stated, not meaning a single word. "Great, now it's time to go.

Shepherd, the dog, barked at Sir Owl, and even Tom felt somewhat distraught.

"What do you mean? The lamb's stuck down there," Tom insisted.

"Womp womp—" Sir Owl complained

"She must miss her family."

"Well, they're gone. We should make ourselves gone too."

"She's a child—"

"Okay, so? She doesn't need the rest of her herd, and they don't need her. She can do her own thing. They would just drag her down. Let nature take its course."

This idea frustrated Tom. The thought of sitting there and doing nothing or—worse—leaving, as a little lamb stayed stuck and defenseless. He couldn't stand it. There was something just within him that challenged it and could not sit content. So he began to search through his backpack. Sir Owl stood there confused but continued to use his typical tactic to prompt Tom into following him. Meanwhile, out of his sack, Tom produced a long and sturdy rope.

"If we tie this around her, we can pull her out," Tom said with determination.

"Ha! Have fun jumping down there to tie it around her," Sir Owl remarked. "Then you both can stay stuck down there."

"Sir Owl, please. As my guardian, you can help unite her with her family," Tom held out the rope toward Sir Owl. "In return, I vow I will not ask you any more questions."

This proposition intrigued Sir Owl: the thought of peace from the man's silly questions. What a reality that would be, Sir Owl thought to himself, feeling rather pleased. If he was going to help, that would be an apt reward. So he took the rope and flew down into the ditch. Using his smarts, beak, and talons, he fixed the rope around the lamb's body and then waited.

Tom and Shepherd grabbed the other end of the rope and tugged. Tom tugged hard at the forefront with Shepherd pulling behind him. Just as they felt some progress being won, Shepherd dropped the rope from his mouth and realized he needed to tend to his herd. Too much neglect, and they might just wander off. Looking at Tom with his busy hands, Shepherd turned and barked at Sir Owl.

"What is he barking at me for? He'd better be thanking me," Sir Owl groaned.

"Well, he is very thankful, I'm sure. I think he would like you to keep an eye on his herd while we pull," Tom looked at Shepherd, who was wagging his tail while looking and barking toward his herd. "He seems worried they'll get away. If you could fly over there and hover above them, that would be much appreciated."

Sir Owl sighed and then barked, "If I could just fly over there… You say it like it's so easy."

Tom carefully thought through his words to follow through on his promise, "You are saying… that it is hard… for you to fly." Tom just barely nailed the landing with his intonation.

"Well, no. It's easy for me to fly, but did you ever think that I don't want any part of this buffoonery?" Sir Owl made his statement.

"Oh, so it is easy for you to fly." Tom relaxed his hand somewhat on the rope while tending to the conversation.

"Yes, of course!" Sir Owl said with pride.

Shepherd barked again, and Tom translated, "Then Shepherd begs you, as do I, please watch his herd for just a few minutes."

Sir Owl sighed again and considered it. He figured that he would much rather watch the sheep lazily grazing than Tom and the dog's arduous yanking. "Fine, but consider yourself extremely lucky." Sir Owl then flew over to the herd and mumbled to himself, "You do just one thing, then all of a sudden they think they can just boss you around… ugh."

So, Sir Owl surveyed the sheep, and Tom and Shepherd heaved. Tom clutched the rope tightly with both hands and pulled. Shepherd planted his hind legs and grabbed the rope between his teeth, and yanked. Sir Owl looked at the massive cloud of sheep and lazily hovered above. Tom felt the fibers of the rope burning his hands as sweat covered his forehead and back. Shepherd's face tensed as he growled and panted between his attempts. Sir Owl tried to busy himself and count the sheep but found himself in a daze and yawned. The lamb simply cried, "Baaa."

Feeling a strong pull from above, the lamb aided in the efforts and jumped out of the ditch when it became just shallow enough. Tom and Shepherd dropped the rope and cried aloud, celebrating their concerted efforts. The pullers and the pulled all joined together and hugged on the floor. The little lamb bleated in relief, Shepherd woofed in excitement, and Tom gasped in joy. Sir Owl drifted off into a micro-nap.

"Go and join your family, little lamb," Tom hugged her fully and wished her well.

"Baaa," the little lamb bleated.

Shepherd licked the little lamb's face, expressing his affection, before she bolted away to the rest of her family. Sir Owl was jolted awake, hearing the harmonious bleating of the herd welcoming their little lamb back. The lamb squeezed her way into the herd and crammed herself between the fluffy coats of her mom and dad. Even Sir Owl couldn't help but sigh in sweet relief, watching the sight of a family reuniting and the ending of what he considered to be an aimless side quest. He quickly turned to retrieve Tom and set off on their predetermined path, and what he saw was Tom laughing as Shepherd tackled him and licked his face. Tom and Shepherd both pet each other, smiling as they shared a sweet embrace.

4.5

"From here on out, no more aimless side quests," Sir Owl instructed, leading Tom through the pastures and toward the forest.

"But what—" Tom caught himself. "If others seem to need help… maybe we should stop and help. The Koi did mention—"

"Don't tell me what the Koi mentioned," Sir Owl interrupted.

"These are hard times for the folk on the island," Tom carried on.

"The Koi Masters also mentioned that you should not help. Your help and interference are not needed."

"But how—" Tom corrected himself. "I don't understand how you can walk by and not help. It feels good to help."

"You need to grow a thick skin," Sir Owl simply kept walking. "Also, I don't remember your dream being to help. We will climb the mountain and climb down, that's it. The sooner that is done, the better."

Tom's scowl hung.

"Now, we're about to pass through another village. Have your wits about you. We will be in and out!"

The two carried on and entered the forest. The forest was not as thick or scary as the one from before. The trees hardly reached high, and everything felt to be on a flat plain; no tumbling down any hills. Some trees bore fruit, ripe and juicy, while at the base of others lay rotten and crushed fruit, not right for picking. Some of the fruit that hung off possessed an absolutely irresistible and polished shine. They seemed to be growing remarkably well. Sir Owl pointed out that this village was famously known for its great produce. It was called the Garden. As they passed by, they spotted several small gardens and growing within them were red ball-like tomatoes, yellow cylindrical corn, green rock-shaped cabbage, orange cone-like carrots, and all around were crocheted flowers.

"Wow, they look… very interesting," Tom observed.

"They look fake," Sir Owl said blatantly.

"Oh," Tom scratched his head. "I thought you said this town was famous for its fresh produce—"

"I know. Just shut up," Sir Owl sighed.

They began to emerge into the populated parts of the village. Tom noticed the astonishing architecture. The homes and buildings appeared to be out of a fairy tale: giant mushroom-like homes, burrows in the ground, cozy cottages, well-painted murals on the side of the streets, and a lively town center. All the folks cheered as Tom and Sir Owl entered. Very welcoming, the travelers thought, until they saw that everyone's backs were to them. They all seemed to be watching for something in the other direction and paid Tom and Sir Owl no mind. Slowly, it seemed that they didn't even notice that the pair was there.

"What do you—" Tom caught himself again. "Sir Owl, I would really like to hear your thoughts on what you think's going on."

"Rather absurd that they'd leave their whole town unattended, attending to whatever that is. Anyway, we shall part the crowd and make our way through this village," Sir Owl provided his perspective.

They reached the crowd as Sir Owl attempted to clear his throat and gather their attention. He thought he could part them, but no one turned. Sir Owl looked at Tom, then flapped his wings and emerged above the crowd, crossing it via the air. Meanwhile, Tom was left having to navigate his own way through the crowd. Tom squeezed past the eager rabbits, worried tortoises, and sticky snails. In the crowd, there were the passionate porcupines, whose backs everyone avoided, and surprised squirrels, who squirmed around to catch the best view. Tom tried his best to carefully cross the crowd, but he couldn't help but accidentally bump into a few strange skunks who raised their tails and threatened to spray him. He quickly backed up and ran into an overwhelmed opossum, who couldn't handle the social pressure and fainted into the crowd. Tom apologized profusely, but she seemed to avoid him, blinking occasionally, and remained unresponsive. The cool coyotes pulled Tom up and pushed him ahead, quickly bringing their attention back to whatever was behind the wall of guests. Tom finally pushed through the crowd, and there was the deflating answer: an arch of balloons and a ribbon held in between. On one side of the ribbon stood a porcupine, and on the other side stood a pink swine.

"I don't get it," Tom said to Sir Owl, who slowly floated down beside him.

"Looks like they're waiting for something to happen," Sir Owl gave it a second and stared. "Alright, whatever. Let's go."

Tom and Sir Owl began to walk ahead, passing through the arch, when the crowd began to holler "Booo" at them. Tom stopped and turned around, concerned about whether they should continue. Sir Owl didn't look back and pranced ahead.

Then the swine turned and saw, "Wait. What are you doing? You can't go this way." His flared snout made him look extra concerned.

"Everyone is looking at us," Tom whispered to Sir Owl.

"I see," Sir Owl declared, and then simply continued walking.

"Halt!" The porcupine beside the ribbon shouted. He and the swine quickly spun to properly face the visitors. "You're not allowed to go through here."

Sir Owl sighed and then said, "We are here on a duty assigned to us by the Koi Masters. That human and I, as his guardian, must be allowed to pass. Move aside, now!"

A few in the crowd went "Oooo" and "Aaaa," but most predominantly jeered.

"We can't let you. We're in the middle of our town elections. You must wait for the function to end before you may proceed," the swine stated, and the crowd agreed.

"Ah, I see," Sir Owl replied. "Well, you're mistaken, we will pass through now. Thank you for your understanding—"

The crowd was filled with scorn, and then the porcupine screamed, "You shall not pass! Or else—"

"This is an ancient tradition sacred to our village. We can't let you ruin our age-old practice and stomp on our spirit," the swine said, assuming some authority.

"Tradition? Spirit? Are you serious?" Sir Owl squinted. "Alright, that's enough. Move aside, now."

"Never!" The porcupine shouted like nails on a chalkboard.

"Yes, every 8 years, give or take, we crown a new mayor. A race is held between the top two candidates. They race to the town center from the far end of the village. We're here waiting for a winner to be determined, who will cross the ribbon and crown themself mayor," the swine shared, earning Tom's respect for his well-spoken demeanor. "Today, we are holding the 49th mayoral election as the haughty and unhesitating Harry, the hare who also happens to be the heir of the last mayor who was also a hare—I know it's a little confusing, but let me know if you get lost—battles the very tame but thoughtful Curtis, the tortoise."

The crowd cheered for their chosen champions. Even Tom joined in and rooted for both of the candidates. Tom received a loud "Booo" from the crowd for being undecided.

"I stopped listening a while ago," Sir Owl was staring down the road. "Now, move aside. We're carrying on whether you like it or not."

The crowd berated Sir Owl and Tom.

"Listen, just because you have a stupid election doesn't mean the whole world revolves around you. Now, move!" Sir Owl bashed the town's tradition.

The crowd bashed Sir Owl in return. Through the chaos, the swine found some sense. "Whoa, whoa, whoa. Fine, if you say you're on official business from the Koi Masters, then we'll allow you to pass. But please go around the arch and ribbon. We beg you not to interfere with our election race."

Sir Owl and Tom exchanged a stare as the crowd sat silent in anticipation. The two gave each other a shrug and a slight nod.

"Fine, we'll go around your stupid arch and ribbon," Sir Owl groaned and flew over the ribbon, eager to get away.

"Thank you!" Tom pranced to catch up with Sir Owl down the path. He turned and held a thumbs-up to the crowd. "Best of luck with your election!"

"Thanks!" The porcupine screamed, and the crowd joined in for a cheer. "Who's ready to skewer the loser of the race on my spikes?"

The crowd raised their claws, fangs, and spikes, growling and cheering, "Skewer! Skewer! Skewer! Skewer!"

The travelers stopped and turned to each other. They made sure they were far enough away to discuss what they had just heard.

Tom said, startled, "So… I am curious to hear… your thoughts on the matter." Tom then thought to himself. "Wow, I managed to avoid asking another question."

"Shut up," Sir Owl said and waved off Tom. They continued for a bit on the path until Sir Owl stopped and confessed, "It's rather barbaric."

"Very," Tom frankly said. "So… on this occasion… your actions may influence the—"

"We have to stop them," Sir Owl interrupted with his intentions.

"Yes! Sir Owl and Tom, back in action, on another quest," Tom gleefully narrated.

"Shut up. We can't allow them to skewer their own kind. The Koi Masters would be mortified to hear about this." Sir Owl seemed to actually want to help.

"Awesome, let's do it. Let's start heading back," Tom turned around and began stepping.

Sir Owl pulled Tom back by his backpack strap, "Are you a fool? We can't go back there. There's no way we could manage to overturn or convince a whole crowd to change their anarchist views. Mob mentality, ever heard of it?"

"No…" Tom felt like a fool.

"If we go back there and try to reason with them or delay their gratification, then we may be the ones who end up getting skewered instead."

The two adventurers stood silently and contemplated their hypothetical fate.

Tom shivered out of it and said, "Then our next action should be…"

"Find the two candidates and convince them to do away with the skewering punishment. Or even better, convince the one who will win," Sir Owl strategized.

"Oh, wow! Yeah, that's brilliant. I didn't even think of that. That's a great idea! But how do we know who's going to win?" Tom suddenly clasped his hands over his mouth. His eyes appeared startled, and his voice became muffled. "I'm… so… sorry."

Sir Owl may have rolled his eyes somewhat, but this time he wasn't so bothered, "That's a foolish question. Of course, the hare will win."

"I think the tortoise might win," Tom suggested.

"Ha! You are indeed a fool. The hare is faster. He will hurry to the finish line before the tortoise is even halfway through," Sir Owl argued.

"But the tortoise seems more careful and perceptive. The hare may be faster, but a thoughtful leader seems a lot better," Tom tried to convince.

"No, the winner will be the hare."

"It could be the tortoise."

"The hare is faster!"

"The tortoise is more thoughtful!"

The two felt some tension beginning to brew.

"I will find the hare," Sir Owl declared.

"And I will find the tortoise," Tom cast his vote.

And so they split.

Sir Owl set to the sky to spot his prized winner. He traced the winding path from above as it became encircled by the forest. Not too far from the forest were the continuing pastures with little small sheep parting them. Sir Owl hadn't flown so high in a while. The wind grazed his face, and he could feel the heat of the sun and the thrill of flying freely again. Sir Owl felt a sense of calm wash over him as he realized he was finally free from Tom for a moment. The foolishness of that boy had been getting to him. Even the catfish or frogs weren't as annoying as him. To think that this foolish human had caused Sir Owl to be banned from the camp of the catfish! That was a thought Sir Owl had almost forgotten. However, now that he was free, he could finally reflect and feel the deep regret of approaching the man on the beach that morning.

"Maybe I'm the real fool here," Sir Owl mumbled to himself against the power of the breeze.

"Ha-ha! Ho-ho! Hop-hop!" A distant voice suddenly came from below within the forest.

Sir Owl scanned down and saw the hare travelling through the windy path, leaping with one foot in front of the other in a synchronized manner. That must be him, Sir Owl thought, and flew down.

"Ha-ha! Ho-ho! Hop-hop!" The hare's strange noises correlated with his hops, planting and pushing him forward. He carried on with his focus ahead until he suddenly halted when Sir Owl glided down in front of him and ruined his rhythm. "Hey! I'm hopping here! What's your problem?"

Sir Owl maintained his composure, "Hare, I am here—"

"First of all, my name is Harry. Get it right. Second, get out of my way, gramps," Harry the hare tried to skirt by, but was stopped by Sir Owl's widely extended wings. "Whoa, whoa. What the heck is all this?"

"I am here with a message—"

"A message? You gotta be kidding me! Are you kidding me? Are you pulling my leg?" The hare was unhesitating. "Also, why are your wings so big? I've never seen an owl with wings this big. You got a workout routine for them or something? What's your diet?"

"Halt! I'm here to present you with a formal message—"

"Oh, it's formal now, huh? You didn't say it was formal the first time."

"A formal message to remind you of the Law of the Island. No one—"

"The Law of the Island? What the heck is the Law of the Island? I mean, I know what that is, but when was the last time they edited that thing? It's so outdated—"

"Hush!" Sir Owl screeched. "No creature of the island shall intentionally harm another creature of the island."

"Okay, thanks for the history lesson, gramps. Now, beat it!" The hare continued hopping.

Sir Owl, somewhat stumped, sped up to match him, "Wait! I'm here to issue you a formal message on behalf of the Koi Masters." Sir Owl was overwhelmed in the face of a fast hopper. "Are you not scared?"

"Scared? Why would I be scared of those two fish?" Harry harassed from afar. "All they do is swim in circles. I have a race to win so I can be the best mayor on this island. Ha-ha! Ho-ho! Hop-hop!"

"Halt!" Sir Owl swooped in front of him. "How dare you disrespect the Koi Masters in such a manner?"

"I am a future mayor. And eventually, I will be mayor of this whole island. You all will bow down to me," Harry stomped.

This is going to take much more work than I anticipated, Sir Owl thought to himself.

Tom, who had seen Sir Owl take the advantage, decided to cut through the woods in the direction of Sir Owl. These woods were far easier to navigate than the forest Tom had tumbled through before. Surely somewhere on the path, Tom hoped he would find the wise tortoise. He slowly strolled through the woods with his hands in his pockets, humming his favorite tune. Off to an adventure, Sir Owl and Tom, except now it was just Tom. Tom had been apart from Sir Owl before, but he had never been alone. The closest he had come was when he had collapsed upon tumbling down the hill. Even then, he had awoken to find a fairy dressed in flowers. While she looked like him and moved like him, Tom was unsure if she really even was a human. She seemed to be one with nature and graceful in a way that made Tom believe she was like one of the magical creatures of the island. Sir Owl hadn't believed Tom's account of her. However, Tom couldn't deny the details that made his memory of her true. Tom wondered if she would appear now that he was alone.

He stopped along the path. Tom removed his hands from his pockets and looked around, setting his intentions on summoning her. He thought hard to himself about her and her delicate features. Tom closed his eyes and kept them shut, wishing for her to appear. He wished, please, come to see me. Tom remembered her chestnut-colored hair and her pink cheeks and how lively those features colored her face. He recalled her hazel eyes, which he had seen from afar, and wished to sit near her to observe the complex colors within them. Tom thought of the softness of her hand upon his head and how, in that moment, he felt so rested and cared for by her gentle spirit. He felt his eyelids soften in a sweet daze and then quietly opened them. She was not there. The girl whose name he didn't know hadn't appeared.

The foolish boy kicked some dirt and felt defeated. What did he expect? Despite how magical this island appeared, he didn't understand it, not fully, not yet. There was no such thing as sorcery or magic on this island, Tom just now realized. He was just a foolish boy taken away by the luster of how grand and new this all seemed to him. Before he left, Tom looked down at his feet. There lay something on the floor to cure his defeat and instill some hope in magic, a periwinkle forget-me-not, just like the one he had seen the girl wearing. He certainly felt the flower had not been there before. Therefore, Tom took it as a sign. The flower was a silver lining to Tom, who felt defeated and walked with his head hung low. He leaned into it, felt the instinct to smell it, and smile.

Ah, the pleasures of traveling slowly through the woods, Tom thought.

Sir Owl felt flabbergasted in the face of the hare's disrespect. It brought Harry contentment to unleash his radical views in his pre-declaration to victory. Searching through his mind, Sir Owl understood that it would take an impassioned debate to contest the hare's headstrong views.

"Well, tell me then, what even is your end goal with acquiring absolute dominion over the island?" Sir Owl led into the debate, standing behind his invisible podium.

"Fulfillment! Self-actualization, not just for myself, but as a society. Our people are starving, to the point that they struggle to have hope that we may survive on this island. We are done waiting for the Koi or any magical force to cure us, so we will take matters into our own hands. I will do my best to fill the plate of each creature on this island with food and hope, and uncover the resources available past our most immediate station. We are done being passive.

The law must be rewritten and reinvigorated, and we must rise and take what is needed," Harry, the mayoral candidate, said.

"You don't understand. Your scope of this issue is limited. With my bird's eye view, I can tell you that there aren't many resources available to us all—"

"I will not have you minimize our experience—"

"I'm not minimizing, but shedding light on a collective struggle we all face. We suffer together. This is no time for division—"

"I will not abandon my village—"

"Nor am I asking you to. We must not act with violence. Seek reason—"

"Reason? There's no reason for us to wait when we are suffering. We cannot let the Koi lead us on like this. We must take initiative and demand what we need and hold the Koi accountable—"

"Accountable? What does that even mean?"

"We will restore our access to the food supply, rather than wait for our allotted rations to arrive. And if the opposition does not comply, we'll hold them accountable at the end of a skewer stick!"

Tom continued to saunter through the woods, stepping out of the forest and onto the path, and then right back into the woods. The tortoise was described as tame and thoughtful. Considering that, Tom thought, where must he be in this neck of the woods?

Sir Owl began to shake in frustration, "Do not jump to such extremes, hare!"

"We have stood still for too long. Fast action is needed," Harry clapped with his bushy foot.

"You will endanger us all!"

"Everyone will have a choice. They can come with us or suffer the same fate on the skewer." Harry tried to move past Sir Owl.

"Halt, hare! Halt!" Sir Owl expanded his wings once again. "The skewers shall have their names on them."

Tom happened to cross another path. The woods carried on. The fruits seemed worse on this end of the woods. Where would a tame tortoise sit?

"There are other possible solutions! We are not meant to harm one another," Sir Owl grew more worried and big.

Harry stepped back and said, "Step aside, owl. I must make my folk full and happy, and win!" The hare then dashed forward and hopped over Sir Owl, continuing with the race.

Tom crossed another path and returned to the woods. He observed the fake painted fruit dangling off the tree. The fruit appeared to grow more and more lame as he progressed further. The paint jobs here left much to be desired. The apples looked more like tomatoes. The oranges were massive and malformed. The bananas were far too straight and neon yellow. The lemons were, for some reason, blue. And the cherries were just gray pebbles tied together. Inspecting them, however, Tom found his way to the tortoise. With his massive shell hanging behind him, the scaly fellow stood at the base of a tree with no painted fruit, but only old and rotten pears.

"It seems like you guys missed a tree," Tom attempted to break the ice.

"Ah…," the tortoise yelped and slowly said. While still in the slow process of turning, he said, "The rather strange… art… of fruit painting… my people consider it… one of their specialties."

"Oh, really?" Tom now looked straight at the tortoise, smiling.

The tortoise cast his eyes on the human. His eyes slowly began to expand and widen, and then he began to slowly descend and retreat into his shell.

"Oh, sorry. I'm sorry. Please, wait. Please, come back. I mean no harm. I'm here under the permission of the Koi Masters and under the protection of Sir Owl. He's gone to find Sir Hare, while I've been attempting to find you, Sir Tortoise," Tom waved his hands to catch the tortoise's attention, before realizing how threatening his waving may have appeared. Tom placed his hands calmly by his sides.

The tortoise stayed partly withdrawn. "You are a human."

"Yes, I am," Tom replied. "My name's Tom. It's nice to meet you, Sir Tortoise."

Sir Tortoise began to slowly rise, "Ah… I've never… been called… sir before."

"Really? But you're running for mayor."

"I indeed am… and I intend to…" Sir Tortoise now stood completely up. "… win."

"Fantastic! I wanted to bring something up to you, sir. Something that Sir Owl and I were really concerned about."

"Hmm… okay… what is it?'

"On our way to the mountain, we passed through your village and learned of this race. As we were leaving your village, we heard the crowd begin to chant that they would skewer the loser of this race." Tom kept his lips tight while sharing. He didn't want to speak the words into fruition.

"Ah… yes… I wonder who… led the chant." Sir Tortoise began to think and turned his head upward.

"Well, Sir Owl and I were worried, and we wanted to convince you and Sir Hare, whoever wins, to get rid of the punishment," Tom tried to make sure Sir Tortoise heard him.

Sir Tortoise kept his head up, "It couldn't… have… been… Susan… not George… couldn't be… Roald… not Raul…"

"Huh, excuse me?" Tom chimed in during the silence.

Sir Tortoise seemed not to hear, "Hmm… what about… Oscar… no, not him… maybe Paul…"

"I'm confused," Tom tried to capture his attention.

"I don't see it… Pedro… not poor Pedro…"

"Sir?"

"Hmm… I'll have to… think about it…" Sir Tortoise turned to Tom then. "Yes?"

"So… would you tell your folk to stop the skewering? It just doesn't seem to be the friendliest thing."

"Why… yes… of course… I do not… support… this act of… barbarianism… However, I wonder… if my folk… would listen… to me… Many tend to… fall asleep… during my… speeches and rallies."

Tom snapped himself awake, "You must try, sir. Please!"

"I suppose… I could… I'm sure… Trent… would listen… Tiana, too… even Samantha… maybe Estevan… Diego… may be difficult… Harleen as well… the people… who would disagree… absolutely… would… include… Josh… Benathew… Heraldo… Alsephanie… Cryptoliver… Jermiathan… Jessicard… Gregatalie…"

"Is that all?" Tom remained mindful not to interrupt and calmly sat down, leaning against a rock.

"Those were… all the… squirrels," the tortoise continued to think. "Moving onto the… raccoon family… there would be… Jeb… Teg… Laura… Seth… Pristin… Leothario… Veg… Crest… Test… Lest… Dust… Grrest… Tim-othy… Seebest… and Jeb."

"I thought you said Jeb already," Tom leaned on the palm of his hand. He tried to present himself as attentive and caring to boost Sir Tortoise's confidence.

"Ah… we have… two Jebs," the tortoise proudly tapped on his belly. "Moving onto… the opossums… Blairathena… Herockalyte… Sanemes… Tompollo… Heraphina… Hiseidon… Wheuz… Laydes… Mayres… Dafrodite… and Sara."

"Oh, wow!" Tom tried to respond with enthusiasm to keep himself awake. He was perplexed by these strange names.

"Then… we have the… pigs… Dig… Cig… Cedric… Rig… Big Mama—"

Suddenly, Sir Owl swooped down beside Tom, startling Tom and sending his face falling into the rock.

"What's going on?" Sir Owl asked, steadying himself.

"Sir Owl, please tell me the matter has been resolved." Tom picked himself up.

"No, it's worse than we could've imagined," Sir Owl sighed and seemed almost out of breath.

"Tell me about it," Tom let himself slouch.

"We must have a word, privately," Sir Owl gestured for Tom to step aside with him, watching the tortoise drone on.

"Okay. Sir Tortoise, please continue. I'll be right back," Tom crawled away and sat adjacent to Sir Owl.

The tortoise went on, "Hmm… what was… her name…"

"Is that the tortoise? How goes your progress with him?" Sir Owl whispered, covering his beak from the tortoise's sight with his wing.

"I just ran into him. He seems to share our cause, but he's been talking my ear off," Tom tried to keep quiet. "Did you have any luck with Sir Hare?"

"No—"

"Oh, I'm sorry," Tom covered his mouth in regret of asking a question. Just a little bit of time apart, and Tom had somehow forgotten.

Sir Owl just sighed. "I'll ignore it. However, no… Hare is very harsh and headstrong in his views. He wants to see those against him skewered. He's rather passionate about it."

"Really, why—" Tom failed to catch himself again. "Sorry. Please, tell me more."

"He said his folk are suffering, and he will not let others stand between his folk and their food. So he'll go to any limits to help them and hold the opposition accountable—"

"Oh no."

"He's willing to skewer the whole island for his folk."

Tom took this in and replied, "He sounds like he really cares for his folk—"

"Cares?"

"Yeah, he's so passionate about caring for them. But at the same time, he sounds really upset and scared for his folk, and whether they'll have enough food to live."

Sir Owl scowled at the idea. "He does not care. He's a ruffian. He told me he promised his voter base that he'd throw them a large feast upon his victory and give them free access to all their food and rations, in the name of self-governance. And any that oppose him will be skewered on the backs of the porcupines. He has no care and sees no reason." Sir Owl rested his case. "Now, tell me, how does it go with the tortoise?"

After a moment of consideration, Tom spoke, "Well, he agrees with us, at least. But I don't have the highest hopes. He says he wants to win, but he seems more focused on recalling all the villagers' names than actually on the race."

"What do you mean?" Sir Owl didn't understand what he meant by recalling the name.

"He just monologues about unnecessary details, names, and things that don't matter right now—"

"Names are not unnecessary!" Sir Owl seemed compelled. "It's a sign that he knows his villagers well. However, he does need to lift his butt and get on with it. If he goes on for too long, tell him to shut up and attend to the more urgent matters."

"I agree, but—"

"I'll keep trying to slow down the hare with reason, since he's ahead. You'd better speed up the tortoise and get him to the finish line, just in case."

"Okay, I'll try," Tom unconfidently said.

"Get to it, then!" Sir Owl shouted and spread his wings, flying away from Tom, yet again.

Tom turned around and saw Sir Tortoise sitting on a rock, still thinking to himself and calmly muttering the names of those villagers who wanted to skewer him.

Meanwhile, the crowd continued to chant in the spirit of violence. Sir Owl could hear it from where he flew in the air. The villagers drained their energy chanting, while their stomachs grumbled. Cedric, the swine, attempted to corral the crowd, but had no success. Even Prisitin, the raccoon, tried to help, but the crowd was just too passionate. Heraphina, the opossum, couldn't help but shriek and faint. Some said she passed out due to fear, and others claimed out of hunger. Prick, the porcupine, raised the pitchforks on his back and yelled the demands of the village, awaiting their victor to make their dreams real.

Sir Tortoise began, "Now… onto the… porcupines—"

Tom stood up, "Sir Tortoise, please, continue with the race with me. Your folk are—"

"Oh… human… all good things… take time… so let us… take our… time."

Tom ate his words and stood there, waiting. After all, he agreed with Sir Tortoise.

"I… have… not… finished… regaling… you… with… the… names… of… my… lovely… neighbors—"

"Sir, your neighbors seek to skewer you," Tom said in defiance.

"Samantha… and… Estevan… don't."

"But the rest do," Tom raised his voice somewhat.

"Not… all."

"Yes, not all. But you see, your people are starving while they wait for you."

"Starving? Why… they… couldn't… be… They received… their… weekly… rations… Sure, it may not… be much… but they do… receive them."

"They are, sir." Tom could not keep the truth any longer. "These are hard times for all folk on the island. Your fruit trees are proof. You can't paint over the truth. Your neighbors are starving, and they'll skewer you if you do not move."

"Well… I will… have… to sit… and ponder… this," Sir Tortoise looked up again.

"Sir, please shut up, stop thinking, and come with me," Tom spoke with urgency.

The hare had passed the last turn and was about to reach the last straightaway to the village. Victory was within his grasp, and he could taste it. Then again, like the curse Harry considered him, Sir Owl swooped down and stopped Harry in his hop-steps. The reach of Sir Owl's wings covered the width of the whole path. Sir Owl seemed to be almost shaking while keeping his wings extended this far: a new personal record, he thought to himself.

"It's you, again," the hare seemed to furiously stomp his foot.

"Stop… stop… hold on for a second," Sir Owl tried to catch his breath. "Hold on. I have to tell you something."

"What is it?" The hare questioned.

"Hold on… just give me… a minute, and don't ask questions… that doesn't make it easier," Sir Owl bent over and slowed his breathing. Once energized, he spread his wings and put up the wall again. "That is better. So I have to tell you to stop. Stop and reconsider."

"That's your big statement? That's it?" The hare rolled his eyes in disbelief. "Okay, now move aside. We've already been over this."

"Hold on!" Sir Owl stretched himself tall before reaching his limit and shriveling down. He tried desperately to find what to say. "I get it, hare. I know you care immensely for your folk."

"I do! Them above all."

"And I know you're upset with the way things have been dealt with so far."

"I'm enraged. Our current system has failed us."

The words were working, so far. "I know you must be scared for your folk—"

"Scared? I'm not scared—"

"It's okay to be. I understand. I'm scared as well. Our island faces the harshest season yet. Trust me, I'm frustrated and tired, and all I want to do is rest. However, I'm here trying to help. We must be here for each other—"

"Exactly, together against the empire! Ushering in a new age—"

"No!" Sir Owl furiously shook his head. "Yes, it's scary. Yes, we must take action. There are so many factors, however, that are out of our control, and we cannot act with haste or rush to recover the reins. There are times when we must pause or slow down, and take it all in." Sir Owl realized he was not speaking his own words.

The hare seemed to retain. He gave Sir Owl's words some thought while rapidly tapping his bushy foot. Then he looked up and said, "Nah, we must act now—"

"Wait!" Sir Owl thought on the fly. "Fine. I want to show you something then. An array of tasty snacks that will surely satisfy your folks."

"Hmm… you have my attention."

"I'm sorry for speaking to you the way I did," Tom apologized to Sir Tortoise. "This is just a matter of serious urgency."

The two trekked toward the village, following the winding path. Despite his newfound motivation, Sir Tortoise still walked slowly, "It's quite… alright… you are forgiven."

"Thank you, sir."

"As nice as it… sounds… no need to… call me… sir… Curtis is… fine," Curtis the tortoise strolled alongside the human. "I don't believe… I caught… your name."

"My name is Tom," said the human who had declared himself Tom. Then he quietly added, "I believe."

"Tom… we don't have a… Tom… on this island," Curtis thought while looking up and walking. "Nice to make your acquaintance… Tom."

"Nice to meet you, too, Sir Curtis," Tom smiled.

"Do you have a… surname?"

"No… I'm not sure if I do," Tom admitted. Even if he did, he certainly didn't know of it.

"Oh, okay… pardon my questioning… typically, humans have a first name… and a surname… I find names… deeply intriguing."

"Do the folk on this island not have a first name and a surname?"

"Not exactly… some have multiple names… one, they were born with… one, they choose to go by."

"I see. Two names…" Tom thought about his own name, but also Sir Owl, and maybe the fairy. What was her name, Tom thought to himself.

Sir Curtis the tortoise looked down and kept walking, "Tom… I'm grateful… to you. Without you… I wouldn't have realized… the real perils of my folk… You've helped me… understand and consider… our traditions and policies."

Tom couldn't help but feel shy, being acknowledged like that, "It's been an honor, sir. At each step, I assure you I never meant to offend, only to raise awareness."

"Yes… the awareness is felt," Sir Curtis considered. "We must modify… our ration size… according to… each of the creature's needs… And just like Harry promised… we will throw a feast… not too excessive… nor with everything… just what we can afford… to tend to our folks' needs… I hope we all may continue… working together… Harry… You… Sir Owl… Cedric… Pristin… Heraphina… Prick…" And so, Sir Curtis, the tortoise, went on as he accompanied Tom. The two of them slowly walked through the forest, somewhat faster than before.

Sir Owl sat with Harry at the edge of the woods, staring out at the pasture. They both seemed frustrated for their own reasons.

"So why have you brought me here?" Harry finally stopped in his tracks. "What are we meant to see from here?"

Sir Owl looked out toward the pasture and saw it, "Aha. There it is… a herd of sheep." And he waited for the hare to look.

Harry, the hare, caught sight of them as they lazily grazed on what was the forest's front lawn.

"That's what I wanted to show you," Sir Owl watched for Harry's reaction. "They are fresh for the picking. All young and juicy. I've met with them, and I assure you they are defenseless."

"Hmm… I see. They do look tasty," Harry giggled to himself, salivating.

"A troop of your finest soldiers, led by you, could easily take them down. However, it's best to pause and do reconnaissance."

"Aha, now I understand what you mean," Harry formed hand binoculars and looked out. "This may just be one of those moments where it benefits us to pause and slow down."

"Yes, exactly," Sir Owl continued to lead him astray, but still somehow in a thematic way. "It's only proper to take a head count of the enemy. You wouldn't want to be overwhelmed, and plus you can relay to your folk how large this haul would be."

"You're right…" Harry continued to stare. "You're absolutely right. Thank you, comrade Owl."

Sir Owl proudly nodded and offered to take notes, and then he waited for the inevitable.

Harry, the hare, began counting, "Let us begin with the reconnaissance… one… two… three… four… five… six…"

Sir Owl then quietly snickered to himself. Counting sheep had put Harry to sleep. He felt overjoyed to see his trick work. And for some reason, Sir Owl felt excited to tell Tom all about it.

Sir Curtis, the tortoise, and Tom reached the final stretch of the race. They approached the same turn where Sir Owl had hijacked Harry, right before the last straightaway. Tom looked around but saw no sighting of Sir Owl or the hare, and the group of villagers appeared so small in the distance. The crowd was impatient for their feast, cheering underneath their balloon and banners.

"Looks like we're almost there," Sir Tortoise said cheerfully.

"Yes, almost," Tom said to his walking buddy. "However, I must leave you here. This is your race to win, sir."

"Ah, I understand… that is awfully kind of you." Sir Tortoise and Tom exchanged a respectful handshake. "You will have a place in our village… whenever you return… If I can ever be of assistance to you… please do not hesitate."

"Thank you, sir."

Tom stepped back and watched Sir Tortoise continue. The old tortoise walked slowly, but Tom continued stepping back to visually add distance and soothe his worries. Surely, he'll win, Tom thought still feeling somewhat anxious. Only when Sir Owl joined Tom's side, they could both lean back and sigh in relief. Crisis was averted as they regaled each other about their respective stories. The two shared a laugh, surprisingly, and stared on as Harry slept and Curtis crossed the finish line. They lingered for a while longer to confirm everything did indeed go well. Sir Owl tuned in with his super hearing and relayed the post-victory speech to Tom. The crowd had accepted their new mayor, a feast was planned for later in the day, Harry had returned and been made second in command, the duo set new food regulations, everyone seemed somewhat content, and no one was skewered.

4.75

Sir Owl and Tom had left the village of the Garden and carried on. Along their journey, they found many others in need of help. Despite their initial plans, Tom led the two into each and every side quest. Sir Owl groaned, each and every time, but found himself wanting to fill the role of guardian and to get each side quest over with as soon as possible.

They helped a lizard track down her broken tail, only to realize she had begun to grow a new one where the old one had fallen off. The two stepped in to settle a dispute between two squirrels regarding the possession of an acorn. Tom had simply gifted an acorn from his rations to the other squirrel, so they could both eat and feel settled. Right before the pastures ended, Shepherd found the two and asked for their help to rescue the lamb again. This time, the lamb had gotten stuck in a tree, and so Sir Owl and Tom did their best to climb up and carefully lure the girl down. Eventually, she had hopped down herself. Sir Owl had given Shepherd a piece of his mind before quieting himself and remembering he had offered the herd of sheep to the hare as a joke.

They carried on and found another tortoise, one who had been flipped over onto his back. This tortoise cried that they had fallen and couldn't get up, but refused any help. So Sir Owl and Tom simply stood there and cheered, watching the tortoise rock and sway. Unbeknownst to two-thirds of them, Sir Owl had used his wings to cast a powerful gust of wind that had helped the tortoise stand up. The tortoise's lack of gratitude stung Sir Owl, but he kept his beak shut just so they could move on.

Along the path, they found a skunk who was traumatized and stunk, and the travelers helped her find a bath. And bathed themselves afterward due to her scent being so strong. Right after their stinky encounter, they found a mole-rat in the desperate pursuit to carve the most ideal tunnel. Tom volunteered himself and Sir Owl to pick up some human shovels and start digging in the dirt and helping the underground fellow. The mole-rat was very content and even offered to let the travelers crash at his place for a night and day. However, the travelers refused. They couldn't help but feel uncomfortable in the tight tunnels and surrounded by dirt. Continuing on their travels, next, they came upon a groundhog, who frequently hopped out of his tunnel to check the temperature. It wasn't a big issue. But Tom, with his newfound knowledge on the architectural design of underground tunnels, offered to help and set up a thermostat system. So the travelers remained covered in dirt.

They kept pushing on, battling against the sun. It was slowly starting to get dark. Within the heart of the forest that finally ascended the mountain, there came a loud cry. It was a frightening yelp that sent shivers up Tom and Sir Owl's spine. They approached, slowly and carefully, watching their steps. It was a giant moose, one that stood tall as the tallest tree and dwarfed the travelers. The moose's antlers had gotten lodged between two tree trunks. Sir Owl tried to convince Tom to flee from this dangerous encounter, but Tom persisted. The two overcame their fear and strategized to use sap and syrup to free the giant and humble moose from his own fears. The moose was grateful, but still reeling from feeling so stuck. He would've offered the travelers a ride to their destination, but he mentioned that his head still hurt. Tom denied the offer anyway, stating that the two preferred to walk. Sir Owl sighed, and Tom led this time, upon the final leg before they called it a night.

There was one last encounter they had before it came time to retire. From far away, Tom saw a rat scavenging through a creature's poop. Sir Owl couldn't be bothered, but Tom tried to intervene, finding the custom weird. However, the rat yelled at Tom to bugger off, and so he did. A rather strange encounter to close out their first full day of adventure.

They were supposed to have climbed at least three-quarters of the mountain, but now they ended their day at its base as night devoured their time and stamina. Sir Owl keeled over right as they neared what seemed to be a flat and open campground, seemingly safe from foreign trees and potential intruders. Tom sat down beside Sir Owl, admittedly also tired.

"Never again… never, again," Sir Owl mumbled, half asleep.

"It's been a long day," Tom took off and searched his backpack. "Before we doze off, let's have a late-night snack."

"No, shut up… and go to sleep."

"Please…"

Sir Owl responded with his snores.

"Okay," Tom disappointedly said.

The boy who had come to know himself as Tom lay down and looked up at the night sky, resting his head upon his make-shift backpack. His tummy grumbled, but he took his mind off it and tried to distract himself by staring up. Within the dark night, there lay the twinkling stars that stared right back. The stars seemed so far away, but they provided Tom with lively and shimmering company. In the past, the mountain had seemed so far, and now Tom lay right beneath it. Within another day or two, he would be standing atop the mountain. Tom wondered if, from the top of the mountain, he could reach the stars. He smiled while he thought about them. Upon the stars was another world of wild and fantastical creatures, crudely formed by imaginary lines connecting the stars.

And while Tom lay, slowly dozing off, he was interrupted by a quiet cry coming from afar. It did not resemble that cry of the moose, not loud or bellowing. This was a high-pitched squeak and stammering, coming from within the shrubbery. Tom couldn't help but sit up and pause. He heard the very faint squealing come again, barely audible and hardly energetic. Surely this cry belonged to a poor and defenseless creature, Tom thought. Perhaps this was the last side quest for the night.

Tom whispered, "Sir Owl." He moved closer to him, upon no response, and whispered just a little louder. "Sir Owl…" Tom then softly poked him and called, "Sir Owl."

"Ahh! What is it?" Sir Owl was shocked awake from his sweet dreams.

"I'm hearing something. Will you—"

"Shhhh," Sir Owl quieted Tom.

Tom thought Sir Owl was listening for the strange noise. However, Sir Owl returned to snoring soon after.

"Sir Owl!" Tom awoke him again.

Sir Owl turned over, "Shut up and go to sleep!"

"But I'm hearing something. It sounds like a cry."

"You've gone mad. Stop disturbing my sleep." He turned back over, away from Tom.

"Sir Owl, please. I need your help." Tom sat on one knee, ready to pounce in the direction of the cry and adventure.

"You're on your own for this one," and this time, for good, Sir Owl returned to his sleep.

Tom tried to wake Sir Owl two more times, but then gave up. He quietly rose, assuming the side quest for himself, and studied the sound. The same silent shout came again from the south. Tom began to slowly approach it. On his tippy toes, he turned one last time to seek Sir Owl's guidance. He had hoped Sir Owl would be awake and by his side, but Sir Owl was sound asleep. So Tom was forced to continue on his tippy toes into the darkness of the forest, approaching the crying sound and wanting not to startle it.

Tom pushed past a couple of bushes and made the discovery. There lay a gray cat turned to the side, while her baby feline cried and pawed at her back. The initial sight of it made Tom's heart sink. His heart was exhausted by investing itself in so many others' lives. And it was so late, but he fought hard to keep his eyes open and carry on ahead. The gray matter in the dark of the night cast a haze over his senses. However, Tom was sure the mother was alive, just occupied, occasionally meowing back at the kitten, but keeping her focus toward her front. Tom saw the kitten's size and felt sure he could fit her in the palm of his hand. She was just as small as a furball. The kitten was left largely unattended as she squealed up at her mother. Tom crouched and approached cautiously so as not to scare the feline family. The kitten kept crying, but her mom saw Tom and nudged the kitten toward him.

In the darkness, it wasn't clear when the kitten turned around and began to squeal toward Tom. She gently approached him, and he found her in the dark. Tom confirmed that she was indeed the squeaky little thing he had heard. He took her into his hand, looked at her, and carefully brushed her fuzzy coat, smiling while showing her affection and hoping she felt cared for. Tom wondered why the kitten may have been so incessantly crying. Then, as his hand grazed her, he felt her protruding ribs through the thin mass that covered her skeleton. She extended her tiny paw toward the center of Tom's comparatively large hand. The poor baby seemed scared at first, but

Tom tapped her toe beans and looked at her with warm eyes, and her crying seemed to slightly subside. Continuing to hold her, Tom understood just how malnourished this kitty was. These were hard times for those on the island, but this poor kitten seemed to be barely hanging on. She was so small and sickly, but her cute little eyes glowed even brighter than the stars in the night sky.

The more Tom caressed her, the more concerned he grew for her. His heart accelerated, and he worried. What do I do? What should I do? Do I take her to Sir Owl or the village? What do I do? Why is she so frail? What can I do? I have to help. Tom's mind raced.

Tom carefully moved to face the mother. At her front, he noticed a litter of kittens all lying by her and suckling from their mother's teats. There they were drinking milk in the shadow of their mother, while their smaller sibling suffered in Tom's hands. Tom squatted down, still holding the little one, and tried to see how he could maybe help. Maybe he could find a place to insert the kitten, so that she would finally be acknowledged and fed. However, he didn't want just to pry off one of the kittens, who also seemed to be hungry. They all deserved to eat, Tom thought. Then he spotted a long and skinny tail emerge from within the cluster of fur. It was something unbelonging to a kitten or any feline, for that matter. How strange, Tom thought. Some of the kittens shifted, and Tom saw what it was. The long and skinny tail belonged to a rodent, sucking milk from the mother cat's teat.

"What? You're not a cat," Tom said loudly.

None of the cats reacted, and neither did the rat.

Tom watched and felt his frustration grow with the lack of response. Maybe it was his exhaustion that contributed to his lack of patience. With what decency he could still manage, Tom set down the furry squeaker by her siblings. Then, with two hands, he prepared to yank the rat away. Tom lunged and pulled. The rat stayed latched on until Tom gave a hearty tug and pulled the rat off.

"Nooooo! Give me the milk!" The rat still tried to reach for the mother cat. He tried hard to grab for her, but his little hands were nowhere close to her. The rat then turned to Tom, "What is the meaning of this? Unhand me!" He spoke rather raspy and grouchy.

"You're that rat!" Tom recalled his tone.

"What do you mean?" The rat ignored Tom and kept reaching for the mom.

"You're the same rat I saw going through the poop—"

"No! How dare you say such a thing?" The rat's attention had been captured. "You must have me mistaken. That must've been my twin, Ralphtoni. I am, however, Rattoni. Known in some parts as the rat burglar. Now that you have interrogated me and we have cleared up the confusion, unhand me!" Rattoni banged against Tom's hand.

"Rattoni the rat burglar?" Tom raised his eyebrow. "I think you're definitely that rat I saw."

"Do not dare besmirch my name! Slander! This is slander. I will take you to court," Rattoni confidently said, forgetting his storied past as a burglar. "Besides, what is it to you? Just forget about me. I was never here, nor there. Now, let me go. We can all just forget about this."

"What're you doing?" Tom was utterly confused, and with his exhaustion, his understanding was also slowed.

"What does it look like I'm doing? I'm trying to eat. Now, let me go drink some milk," Rattoni continued to pine for the milk.

"That milk isn't meant for you," Tom made his tone more serious.

"What are you? The milk police?" Rattoni was repulsed. "That milk is mine. I found it."

"You stole it! You took the place of that poor kitten," Tom gestured to the small furball. "She's malnourished cause of you."

"Me? No, she's malnourished cause she's the runt. She was slow to get there, and so it's her fault she missed the nipple. Plus, I swooped in there while it was unattended. Finders keepers."

"No, that's not how it works." Tom's lack of sleep and excess of frustration made his head begin to hurt.

"Maybe it's for the best that she didn't get fed. Social Darwinism, baby! Survival of the fittest and down with the rest!" Rattoni flexed. "Now, I'm gonna tell you one last time, ugly. Unhand me or else!"

"No!" Tom yelled.

Then Rattoni sank his teeth into Tom's hand.

Tom yelped and dropped the rat, clutching his bitten hand. Rattoni rushed past the kitten, stiff-arming her in the face, and dove into the cluster of kittens munching away on dinner. Tom's face told the tale. His eyes glared and his nostrils flared, and whatever frustration he felt from his sleepiness doubled after being bitten. He used his non-dominant hand to yank Rattoni back by the scruff of his neck.

Rattoni attempted to kick, punch, and wrestle his way free. "No! You awful human, unhand me! Let me go!"

Tom held Rattoni in front of his face and stared at him, dangerously. "You, stop it! Stop what you're doing. You'd better behave and learn to share."

"Never! Finders are keepers—"

"You didn't find anything. They're mother and daughter. You burgled!"

"That's what I do! They don't call me the rat burglar for nothing," Rattoni caught sight of the little runt approaching the free teat. "No! You'd better not. Don't you dare. That's mine!"

"Hush," Tom whispered and covered Rattoni's mouth with his bitten hand, only to have it bitten again. "Ouch!" Tom just felt stupid this time.

"Leave that teat alone! Don't do it. Noooo!" Rattoni pointed threateningly and kicked to try to free himself.

The little kitten stood in front of the nipple and attempted to attach herself, but kept falling off. Tom moved closer to her and tried to guide her and lift her just enough, but the kitten still seemed to struggle. He even gently pried open her mouth and placed her on the teat, and nothing. She struggled to take it into her mouth and stay attached, still trying but slipping off every time. The baby would try to feed, but no matter how hard she tried, she didn't receive any milk.

"Come on, kitty," Tom kept trying with her.

The kitten still did not latch.

"Drink, kitty. Please," Tom grew more impatient and sad with each attempt, grabbing hold of the kitten's bony body. "Please, you have to."

She still didn't take it. She mouthed her mother's teat, but she couldn't keep the nipple in her grasp and failed again and again to suckle the milk. Tom began to frantically worry about what to do. Despite their combined efforts, the little kitten couldn't do it.

Rattoni's laughter broke through Tom's sadness and concern. "Hahaha! Victory is mine. It's too late, loser. She can't do it. She will stay the runt." Rattoni kept laughing, relaxed in his efforts to escape, but still shaking from his laughter. "She was born during the new generation of the island. Just like her mother, she cannot talk like us, and she cannot survive on her own on this decaying island. Hahaha! Some things are not meant to be. Let her die." Rattoni's laughter rang through Tom's ears and echoed throughout the night.

No, no, no, no, no, Tom cried to himself; I will not let her die. But how? How could he help? How could he possibly help in a defeating situation like this? How?

Tom dropped Rattoni, who scurried back to the mother's free teat and stole it once again. The kitten returned to her quiet and weak crying as Tom sat there feeling helpless. All he could think to do was hold her close to him and seek to comfort her and himself.

4.8

As the night continued, Tom just sat there, holding the kitten. The night was silent, except for the continued and weakening cries of the kitten. The brightness of the moon and stars had seemed to cower as well. There was nothing left to do, and hunger and sadness were triumphant in preventing sleep.

Tom realized he had been stuck staring at the floor when, from a nearby bush, he began to hear a rustling noise. He finally looked up to acknowledge this and hoped to see his guardian, who would surely have all the answers. What actually emerged was a fuzzy fox. It was a creature Tom had never seen before on the island. The fox was painted white, like a specter or the moon, while her nose and eyes were dark and steady as the night. She looked almost like a dog, except she was smaller and her features were sharper. Where Shepherd would have tackled Tom, the fox stood at a distance and watched him. Her ghostly presence gave off a glow, and she tilted her head at Tom, filled with curiosity. Although bright, Tom's eyes rested on her as her brightness dimmed to soothe his eyesight. Tom pulled the kitten away from his wet eyes as he watched the fox also with curiosity. The fox saw the tiny kitten and seemed to almost immediately stir, like she recognized her. She moved just a few steps toward the kitten, seeming more energetic and lively, but still a mystery. Then the fox turned and, with a gentle look, called for Tom to follow and went back toward the bush. Tom, still holding the kitten, couldn't help but spring into action and follow and chase the mystery into the darkness.

The glowing fox leaped through the dark forest. Whatever the moon couldn't illuminate, the fox lit. She acted as a guiding lantern to lead Tom through the darkness. If Tom were ever to lose his way or doubt where to step, she would appear again as a glowing halo and retrieve him, showing him the way. It was clear to Tom that she wanted him to follow. The night felt much brighter chasing the fox through the forest. They traveled further south, avoiding thickets and low branches. The fox seemed to be a natural adventurer with the way she leaped between gaps and seemed to know exactly where to go. And the longer the chase went on, the more Tom grew concerned about where and how far this side quest would lead him. Where, Tom thought, holding the kitty close, and why chase the fox? Tom continued to chase, even through gaps he didn't fit and places where he didn't belong. Yet, he persisted through the exhausting and sleepless trail. When he arrived, he found what was at the end of the chase. Ahead of him stood the beach and sea.

The beach lay covered in white sand and stone, and cast an iridescent glow. Not a glow that rivaled the fox, however, nor the moon or a specter. The sea, which normally appeared so dark at night, retained a deep blue and silver tone. Scenes like these must have been customary to the island, but blew Tom's mind. Within the center of the sand stood the pale fox. The glow around the fox seemed to shimmer as an apparition formed and showed itself, from behind the fox. It was the fairy. The lady's back was to Tom, but he saw the fox gently trot up to her and lie in her lap. The fairy or lady began to caress the sweet creature.

Tom hesitated to call out and seemed nervous to interrupt their peace. He wondered if he did call out, whether his voice would even travel over the sound of the waves washing up on the beach. However, his questions were answered when he saw the fairy briefly turn and, with a gentle nod, invite him toward her. Tom, indeed, joined her on the beach, holding the sweet kitten who purred and cozied up to him. While Tom was excited to see the fairy, his mind was occupied with those harsh words he had heard earlier, his fatigue, and the chill of the beach at night.

"Hello," Tom's voice cracked in the cold.

"Hi," the fairy greeted, ever-gracious.

Her legs were extended to her side. The dress she wore seemed to be darker than the color of the sand and the dress from before. Her pastels were replaced by warmer tones on this cold evening, and she seemed to be the gentle bridge between the dark sky and the bright sands of the beach. She seemed to be immersed in watching the sea as the waves fled back, collided, and rolled in ahead of their seats.

"It's calming," she serenely said.

"It is," Tom still felt cold and anxious.

They listened to the ocean waves together. Tiny water particles collected and produced sound that rivaled thunder or boulders crashing. However, the rhythm is what made it so enchanting. It wasn't always calamity. There were moments where the waves rested and became absorbed into the earth that provided comfort and relief. There was something about the waves becoming one with us, and not withstanding as a foreign force capable of much danger, that provided peace to Tom and the girl. The simple sloshing of the shallow water closer to the two felt far more friendly than the deep sea that lay out there. Despite the sounds of the sea, though, Tom still paid attention to the kitten's frail purr against his chest.

"Have you figured out your name yet?" She asked. "You never answered me."

"My name's Tom. I don't know my surname, but my name is Tom," Tom said, feeling the cool breeze and mist in the distance. "What's your name?"

The girl looked out to the sea. From the corner of Tom's eye, he saw a sense of peace leave her. She grabbed the locket about her neck, seeming to fidget with it in her hand.

"I don't know. I can't remember," the girl answered.

Tom felt a deep empathy. He could recall the moment when he didn't remember his name either. Besides for understanding her, Tom felt a desire to help her, just like how he desired to help the kitten. "Really?"

"Yeah, I've never had an inkling as to what my name could be. How do you know your name is Tom?"

Tom thought carefully about this. How did he know that his name was Tom? Whatever the real reason was, Tom answered, "I don't know. It's what Kat called me, and I believed her. I guess it stuck."

"What if she was wrong?" She turned toward Tom.

"I guess, I've never thought about that."

"So?"

"I don't know," Tom shrugged.

"Oh… so you don't know your name after all?"

"Maybe I do, maybe I don't. But I do like to call myself Tom," the human, who had dubbed himself Tom, looked down at the kitten napping. "What's more important is that I know what my dream is. My dream is to climb the mountain."

"Really? Why?"

"I don't know, but that's what I know for sure. That's what I remember from when I washed up on the shore." Tom looked toward the girl, not the shore, wearing an expression of passion.

She looked anxious. "I washed up on the beach, too… But I don't remember anything from when I awoke. This locket is all I had when I woke up."

"You washed up here?"

"Yeah, I did."

"From where?"

"I don't know."

"Did you have a boat?"

"I said I don't know."

"Oh, yeah. Sorry," Tom looked fascinated. "I thought you were some kind of a fairy when I first met you. But you're saying you're not from here. You're a human."

"I'm not from here. Some of the creatures on the island see me as a spirit of sorts."

"I thought the same. You just seem so…"

The girl squinted her eyes at him.

Tom saw her reaction and was caught by surprise. "Nothing bad. I didn't mean anything bad."

"Oh, gosh. Please tell me you don't think I look like one of the creatures."

"You don't! I was gonna say you look enchanting."

"No thanks. I'm just a plain human."

"Well, no. I'm sure I'm far more plain than you are. My hair's black and yours is like—I don't know—chestnut brown. And your eyes are so… colorful."

The girl cringed away, "Okay… no. Let's move on."

The boy cowered from his embarrassment. "I'm sorry. So what happened after?"

"After what?" The girl looked out toward the sea again.

"After you washed up here." Tom kept his focus on her.

"I tried to survive. Eventually, I found the creatures that fill this island. Silver was the first one I met," the girl looked down at the resting fox and graced her fur. "They were really sweet, all of them. They also struggled to survive. And so together, we helped each other survive. They all have such kindness in their hearts. I've looked after them, and they've looked after me. I've really gotten to know them. They're so sweet." She seemed to smile sweetly again.

Tom watched the fox slowly waving her tail in happiness. He didn't fully believe in the genuine kindness of all the creatures that the girl spoke of, recalling his run-in with the snake, frog, and rat. However, he felt the cheerfulness and genuine kindness in the girl's voice. "How long have you been here?"

"I don't know. An eternity?"

"Wow, that's a long time," Tom quipped. "So you've really helped them a lot throughout the years."

"I guess so," the girl continued to pet the fox. "Helping them makes me feel good. It's given me a purpose." She quickly scratched her nose and then returned to scratching the fox's ears.

"I get you." Tom smiled at her.

"They're just such innocent creatures, you know, deserving of all the good." Now, she played with the fox's paws.

"I agree." Tom kept his focus on her as she looked down at her companion fox, both of them smiling. The fox snickered with the belly rubs and scratches, and the girl snickered through her nose, watching her jolly companion. Tom observed that, slowly, the girl's smile began to fade. What took its place was an emptiness. The color of her face changed, and the smile in her eyes faded as her gaze grew blank. She looked as if she were now petting the fox out of habit, not joy. "Is everything okay?"

She slightly fixed her blank expression, "Yeah." Then, as the play continued, her expression and movements slowed again.

"I don't know about that."

"I'm fine."

"You can talk to me. What's there to lose with talking?"

"It's nothing," she avoided. "I'm just feeling cold."

"Me too."

The two sat there in the cold. Tom felt cold with her.

It was more than nothing. She shared, "I've been here for such a long time, and sometimes I just can't help but feel stuck. The sea brought me here, and I'm grateful for that. But sometimes I wonder where else the sea can lead me. What all is out there, you know?"

Tom felt sad for her, watching the emptiness she endured. She longed for more, he could tell. "It looks so vast."

"It does, right?" She looked out at the sea. "There's probably so much to see, and it would feel so nice to explore and travel the world." The girl sighed and then let her head hang. "But oh well."

Tom stared out at the sea, imagining all the places the girl must've dreamed of. All the dragons and sphinxes the world must hold. In her words, he sensed the inklings of a dream. "So do it. Go and explore the world. Be free."

"That's silly. I can't do that." She shook her head and refused to look up.

"No, seriously. Do it. Let's build you a ship and cast you into the sea, so you can explore the world," Tom looked at her with joy in his eyes. "That's what your dream is, right?"

"I don't know what you're talking about."

"Follow your dream!" Tom smiled at her, remembering his own dream and how passionately he wanted to conquer it.

She continued to shake her head, making herself smaller and holding the fox up to her cheeks. All she responded with was shaking her head as Tom sat there, holding his free hand out and his chest held up high. With Silver by her side, the girl watched the sea as it invaded her eyes. Her eyes pooled with tears, slowly trailing down, unacknowledged by the girl or Silver.

Tom responded hurriedly, "I'm sorry. Did I say something wrong?"

She continued to cry. Through her tears, she said, "But… if I leave… what will happen… to them?" She squeezed the fox even closer to her.

Tom wanted to comfort her, but felt too nervous to move and disturb the kitten. He slowly nodded with the girl, and all he could manage was, "Yeah…" Tom was reminded of how precious the sleepy kitten was to him and how precious the fox must be to the girl, and he was also reminded of how much the girl must have devoted to them. "Have you ever stared at the stars?"

"Yeah," the girl sniffled.

"I love the way that certain stars are always there and visible. The north star, but especially the constellations. They may be in different places across the sky, but the stars always appear together. The way a constellation is formed reminds me of you and this island. You will always be connected to them. You've poured so much of yourself into them, but you deserve to see different places across the sky. And if you ever travel, the stars will always be there to guide you back here." Tom hugged the kitten closer with both hands. "I'm here, too. I may not have the same connection you have with the creatures of this island, but I'm here to help them, too. You can go follow your dream, and I can stay here and care for them. I promise."

The girl began to weep, audibly, and held on dearly to her fox. The guy and the girl cried together as their tears welled up and washed down the shore of their faces. Around them, the sea swam, the stars sparkled; and the mountain stood above.

"They mean a lot to you, I can tell," Tom noticed.

She continued crying, "They do… I don't wanna lose them…"

Tom didn't know what else to do but comfort this fairy girl with whom he shared this special moment. He gently reached over and patted her on the back. "There, there." He was worried about how she'd react, but she seemed to lean into him and he into her.

They continued to sit together in the cold and underneath the stars, now leaning into each other's hearts. She cried dark polka dots onto her dress, while he sat there and felt sad at the thought of losing her. The two nobodies, who really didn't know their names, sat together and turned their sense of direction to the sea.

Eventually, the small furball began to squeal. The kitten had awoken, stood up, looking as tall as she could, and screamed for her milk. The fox even raised her head in concern. Tom refocused his attention on the small defenseless creature. Meanwhile, the lady calmly wiped her face and tucked her wavy hair.

"We should feed her. It's long past her dinner time," the fairy said.

"How?" Tom returned to his helplessness. "I was trying to, but the rat—"

"Ugh, don't get me started on Rattoni," the girl continued to clean the tears from her face, placing her fingers into the corner of her eyes. "Here, I can take her."

"It's okay. I can feed her if you just show me how," Tom tried to help and save the girl from more anguish, just as he promised.

"Okay, fine." The girl reached into a bag hidden beneath the fox. She retrieved from it a baby bottle with a toy nipple.

"Whoa, where'd you get that?"

"I made it. It wasn't hard. It was just a pain making the correct milk replacement."

The boy was too stunned to speak. This lady truly must've been a fairy, he thought.

"Except she hasn't learned to latch onto the nipple yet," the girl held the bottle over her free hand, slowly dripping some milk from the bottle onto her finger. "However, she'll drink the milk if I feed her like this."

The fairy extended her finger to the kitten's mouth. Her finger, Tom observed, was dry and torn. It looked almost mangled. Tom found out why very soon as he saw the kitten slowly reach up and extend her claws and latch onto the girl's finger. The kitten remarkably sucked the milk dripping off the girl's finger. For balance, the kitten clawed into the girl's finger, wrapping onto it tightly and not wanting to let go, especially when the finger ran dry of milk. The girl continued to drip-feed more milk to her.

The girl winced in pain, but said, "Aww… look at the cute little baby. You must've been so hungry… poor girl."

Some milk dripped off onto Tom's palm. The girl apologized, while Tom stared on, grateful for the sight he was witnessing. He considered himself lucky to firsthand witness the fairy work her magic on the island and its creatures. Nothing compared to the few drops on Tom's hand, the kitten's face lay smothered in milk. She, the girl or fairy, made it look so easy and sacrificed herself to care for these creatures. Tom couldn't help but watch on, observing every little detail from the fur on the kitten's head to the slashes and ripped skin hanging off the girl's finger and to the many beautiful colors that swam within the girl's eyes.

As Tom watched the girl bite her lip and squint her eyes in pain, he broke his silence, "Is there really no other way?"

"Hmmm… what?" The girl swiftly scratched her nose.

"Is there no other way to feed her, without your finger getting torn up like that?"

"No, I've tried. Nothing else works, at least not right now. It's fine though, she'll learn… hopefully."

Tom was reminded of the sea as a quick breeze rolled in and caressed his face. He was reminded that the girl sought to explore the world, but her focus here seemed so small when feeding the kitten. Without thinking, he extended, "Here, use my finger. Let me feed her."

"What? It's okay. I can do it."

"No, please. Let me feed her. I really want to," Tom insisted. He wanted to take this burden from the girl so she could stare at the sea instead. Yet, he also felt the urge to share this experience with her.

"Okay, fine," she obliged and dripped some lukewarm milk onto Tom's finger.

The kitten bit in, occasionally licking with her rough tongue. She was too young for her teeth to be fully formed and hurt, but Tom almost regretted his decision when the claws came into the picture. She plunged her nails around his finger as Tom whimpered and clenched his teeth.

"Are you okay?" The girl stifled a laugh and chuckled.

"Yeah... I'm good," Tom said, straining.

"You don't have to do this. I can do it—"

"No, no. It's okay. I got it," Tom braced himself.

The girl laughed with her eyes and continued dripping the milk, while Tom helped too. They both hovered over the kitten, sharing in the special act. The little kitten continued to lick and claw, always playfully desperate for more milk. She kept feeding until her belly began to swell up and become firm.

"Does she have a name?" Tom randomly thought to ask.

"No, I don't think so," the girl answered.

"You should name her."

"No, I can't do that."

"Why not? You're the one who practically invented a new method of feeding for her, so you should name her."

"No, I'm too indecisive."

"You're not indecisive when it comes to helping her."

"Well, that's different—"

"So help her by naming her."

The girl considered and stared at the kitten's little starry eyes. She booped the kitten's nose and said, "Fine. I'll call you Nastya." She placed a kiss on Nastya's head.

Tom smiled. "That's a pretty name. I've never heard it before, but it's worlds better than Tom."

They both shared a chuckle.

"Tom's not… bad," the girl tried to feign niceness.

"It's okay. It's grown on me," the guy took ownership of his name.

Nastya reached toward the girl, who accepted her into her arms. They cuddled over Silver, the fox. Nastya nuzzled the girl and her soft face before climbing onto her shoulder. A few red scratch marks marked the trail the kitten climbed up the girl's bare neck. The fox suddenly stirred awake and jumped out of the girl's lap and onto the shore. Tom watched the fox, a ball of shimmering light, cast away the darkness and obscure the ocean.

"She likes to be chased," the girl watched the fox trot in circles and occasionally steal glances at the humans. "I think she wants you to chase her."

"Me?" Tom questioned. "I'm not much of a runner."

"She doesn't wanna be left out."

"Okay, I guess, I can try," Tom rose. "Let's go, Silver!" He sauntered to the fox, who jumped and kicked her feet in the air.

Tom chased the fox up and down the beach as the girl sat and watched with Nastya on her shoulder. There were a few times where Tom almost caught Silver, but she continued to slip by, elusive and sly. As gentle and wise as the fox looked, Silver was a playful bundle of joy who yearned for an ideal chase partner. Tom was sure she wanted to keep running and escaping, almost always just for the thrill and never to actually be caught. The girl knew all too well Silver's tricks: the way she'd juke the very last second, scurry between someone's legs, and even hop over the pursuer and alter her direction. Watching from the sideline, the girl couldn't help but cuddle Nastya and laugh, throwing the occasional cheer and tease for Tom and Silver. Tom slowed down and eventually tagged the girl in. He was winded, still sleepless, and cried in defeat for a breath. All the girl did was giggle and get up, quietly tagging Tom back and continuing with the chase herself.

"No, not again," Tom cried, clutching his sides. But he swiftly turned and returned to their game of tag.

Tom chased the girl, who chased the fox, who chased fun, while the kitten hung on for dear life in the girl's arms. They all ran around each other in circles, skipping through the water and gleefully cheering when not caught. The boy and girl acted like kids, teasing and making menacing threats about catching each other. He splashed water at her, and she giggled and returned the favor. Silver hopped around the water, shaking herself and flinging water everywhere. Nastya meowed, ever so quietly. They frolicked around for the rest of the night, underneath the sparkling stars. He caught her for a moment, and the world seemed to stand still.

5.00

Tom awoke lying on the beach with the sun shining at his face from the east. The tiny kitten squealed at him, standing on all fours on his chest. In Tom's periphery, a figure appeared and blocked the sun from his eyes.

"What are you doing?" Sir Owl screeched. At least, he didn't jump on Tom's gut this time.

"Sir Owl!" Tom pushed himself up. "I'm sorry. Did I fall asleep?" He began to wipe his eyes.

"Yes, but look at where you are," Sir Owl looked around for dramatic effect. "You're at the beach. What are you doing here? You never returned to camp. Do you know how dangerous that is?"

Tom cradled the kitten as he sat up properly, "Were you worried about me, Sir Owl?"

"Stop it with your stupid questions. You look like a mess and are properly indisposed. What's wrong with you?"

The kitten squealed.

"And what is that kitten doing with you?" Sir Owl motioned to the munchkin against Tom's chest.

"Oh, that's a long story," Tom sighed.

"Why are you such a fool?" Sir Owl screeched and walked away. "I'm going back to camp."

"Okay, I'll meet you there soon," Tom replied.

The kitten hungrily continued to cry. Her little mouth and eyes opened wide as she stared at Tom and squeaked. Tom gently petted her and wondered. Where had the girl gone? Had she vanished like a dream again? Was she even real or had he imagined her? Was she a fairy or really a human with whom he had shared a laugh and a cry?

The ocean waves continued to wash in. This time, sounding melancholic. They were melodic and synchronized for nothing, it seemed. Last night, they existed for the girl, and maybe for him. However, today, Tom felt empty watching them without her. He closed his eyes, squeezed them hard, and wished for her to appear again. He opened his eyes, and there was nothing different he saw. It was still day and it was still just Tom and the squealing kitten. However, he did recall that the kitten was dubbed Nastya. The memory of the girl withstood.

Tom reached toward his feet and, upon looking down, found a gift. He realized that by his leg lay the same baby bottle he remembered the girl using the night before. A sturdy cap covered the nipple. Around the bottle itself was a pink ribbon fashioned into a bow. This was how he could continue to feed her and take care of her. The bottle lay filled with milk and lay steady against the pebbles on the sandy beach. Right beside the bottle, Tom spotted a hidden thing. Something had dropped within the white rocks. Moving closer, Tome realized there lay the necklace that the girl had worn. It was the same silver locket, fallen off her neck, with several lived-in knots across the chain and a small heart that opened out. This was the necklace she had motioned to and said belonged to her before she arrived at the island. Tom clutched the necklace and took it upon himself to keep it safe. He would surely find a way to return this precious item to her. Worried about it falling out of his pocket, he put the necklace around his own neck. A tight fit, but he felt it was a secure place and a constant reminder of his promise to the girl. Tom looked at his gifts and realized that he had indeed shared last night with the girl, and maybe all the moments during that night had, in fact, been real. Grabbing the bottle in his hand, he rose to his feet, looked toward the ocean, and thought again of the girl and her pleasant giggle. Tom was set on seeing her again sometime. Using the ocean water to rinse his face and hair, Tom turned back around and set out to climb up.

Tom traversed up the path he had traveled down the night before. Loud meows reached him as he enthusiastically stepped through the bushes. Sir Owl had gathered around the camp of the mother cat. Amongst the meows, he heard the ravings of a little rat. The cats seemed worried sick, while the rat sounded severely annoyed. Tom entered Sir Owl's conference with the cats and the rat.

"So is this all related to the kitten somehow?" Sir Owl sighed, looking over to Tom.

"Yeah… will you help me feed her?" Tom asked, holding out the baby bottle.

"Huh, what do you mean?" Sir Owl pulled his wings back and asked.

"So, here's the thing… she won't eat from her mother's teat. She's gotten very malnourished, and I learned of the only way to feed her," Tom said, attempting to recruit Sir Owl.

"What the heck are you talking about?"

"Just play along, please."

Sir Owl held the baby bottle in his hand and dripped the milk onto Tom's finger. Tom tried to recreate it as best as he could remember, the way he saw the girl do it. Nastya's squeaks eventually subsided as she occupied herself drinking milk and latching onto Tom's fingers. Tom, once again, groaned with the slicing and stinging pain. Sir Owl rolled his eyes at Tom.

"Thanks," Tom hissed, attempting to smile through the pain. "Her name is Nastya."

Sir Owl nodded awkwardly, "Hello, Nastya."

Tom then pointed to Rattoni, "And that is the problem. He stole the kitten's place and stopped her from drinking her mother's milk."

"Heyyy… I think we've got some kind of misunderstanding here. You never… umm… told me you were gonna bring an owl with you." Rattoni seemed a lot more nervous and well-mannered today.

"Hmm?" Tom was confused. "This is Sir Owl. Sir Owl, this is Rattoni."

"Hey, big guy, listen, I don't want any problems here," Rattoni held his hands up in front of Sir Owl.

Sir Owl's eyes widened with surprise as he looked down at Rattoni, "What are you talking about?"

"Listen, I know I'm in your turf, and I'm sorry about that. But seriously, just let me go. I won't be a thorn in your side." Rattoni casually implored Sir Owl.

"He's acting really strange," Tom whispered to Sir Owl. "He was being a lot more rude last night."

"Was he?" Sir Owl exchanged with Tom.

Rattoni awkwardly laughed and scratched at the back of his neck. He seemed sheepish in the presence of Sir Owl. "So you're gonna let me go, right?" Rattoni waved his hands about.

"I know how to deal with the likes of him," Sir Owl whispered back to Tom. Sir Owl outstretched his neck and, like a swooping lance, came down right atop the rat.

The rat yelped aloud and crawled into a ball, covering himself. "Ahhh! No! Please, don't eat me!"

Sir Owl turned to Tom, then back to Rattoni. Tom stood in bewilderment. Sir Owl's beak hovered right above the rat. However, obviously, he wasn't going to eat him.

"You stole the kitten's milk! You committed a crime. For that, you should be punished!" Sir Owl cast his shadow over the little rat.

"No, please! I was just hungry. I was starving, you have no idea how bad. I'll leave and never come back. Please, spare me!" Rattoni cried.

Tom gulped and tried to divert his attention from the harsh scene. He turned toward the kittens, who were surrounding their mother and calmly suckling away. Tom thought that maybe now Nastya would finally be able to latch, so he tried again. However, Nastya did not latch, and he could not easily forget the rat's actions. So he rose and returned to watching Sir Owl threatening the rat.

"What makes you think I'd spare you?" Sir Owl screeched.

"Cause I'm just a little rat. Please…" Rattoni's voice broke.

"Isn't that true? You're just a puny rat!" Sir Owl lunged closer.

"It's too late. What's done is done." Tom quietly broke the tension.

"What?" Sir Owl suddenly jutted his head out at Tom. "You said he's the suspect. Therefore, justice must be delivered." Sir Owl turned his attention back to the rat. "I am a guardian appointed by the Koi Masters!"

The rat yelled.

"No!" Tom interrupted as Sir Owl raised his talons, ready to claw Rattoni. "Leave him alone, please. Nastya won't latch onto her mother anymore. There's no point in this… Plus, he was just hungry."

Rattoni looked out from fetal position, smiling but still scared. The threat had not yet left.

"Just because he's hungry does not give him the right to steal," Sir Owl's claws landed over the rat, implanting around the culprit.

Rattoni hid and screamed again.

"It also doesn't give us the right to be so unkind," Tom thought of the girl and what she would say. "Yes, the rat is a handful and a headache, but we are not justified in hurting him. And the mother won't produce milk forever, anyway. It would be best for her milk to have some purpose and not be wasted. So let him go. Let him have it."

"How could you defend him?" Sir Owl screeched at Tom.

"It's for the best."

"Him! You defend the rat?"

"I'll defend any and all the creatures."

"You choose him over my orders!"

"I have to help them!" Tom defied Sir Owl. "So let him go! Please, I demand it. I order it." Tom raised his chin slightly, facing Sir Owl.

Rattoni peeked out from between Sir Owl's talons, his imprisonment. Now, the rat was smiling and salivating. Sir Owl looked at Tom, narrowing his eyes and raising his tufts. The owl's dignity was crushed. However, Sir Owl lifted his talons and released Rattoni. Tom couldn't help but gulp his worries away. The boy had done as he had promised the girl; he would help all the creatures of the island he could. The rat leaped in freedom and onto the mother in delight, and began suckling amongst his step-siblings.

Sir Owl brought his wings together and floated to a nearby branch, setting himself apart from the others on the ground. He turned his back on Tom. When Tom attempted to approach him, Sir Owl said, "Leave the kitten. It's not safe where we're going for her."

Tom felt a punch to his gut. He thought that surely he couldn't leave Nastya alone. Someone needed to feed her. Otherwise, she would remain malnourished and… "Sir Owl, please."

"No. You gave me an order, and I complied. Now, I'm giving you a necessary order. Do what is good for her and for your foolish endeavor," Sir Owl commanded.

Tom cried to him, "She will die—"

"Then perhaps you shouldn't have taken on that burden, which is her life. You cannot save or help everyone. You may try, but you may also fail. Learn to live with the consequences."

Tom watched Sir Owl from behind and saw the brooding silhouette he formed. He knew Sir Owl had never wanted to come on this adventure, but this coldness was a surprise.

"You have helped enough. You have wasted enough of my time. From here on, we will journey up the mountain and down. No distractions, and then I will be done with you. If you have any qualms, you may return to the Koi Masters and beg them for a new guide. By the powers granted to me by the Koi, I am your guardian and guide, not a companion or underling. We will complete this journey on my terms, and have no foolishness about. Ready yourself." Sir Owl assumed his guardian status.

Unbelieving, Tom's heart broke. His companion—no, guardian—had broken his heart. At that time, Tom thought to himself: how can I tell you then, Sir Owl, that I'm unsure if my dream still remains to climb the mountain? After last night, Tom had thought increasingly about his journey and the memories he had made along the way. Part of him wished to perhaps linger longer now to help others and explore all the vast possibilities around him. Tom found himself wanting to exist, not above the mountain or below, but somewhere in between with all of them.

"Hey, loser," Rattoni tugged at Tom's trousers. "Leave her here. I'll take care of her and protect her."

Tom was unbelieving, in a different manner, "Are you sure? Wait, how can I even trust you?" He knelt.

"You can't. But come on, it's not like you have many other options. Besides, I'm not completely heartless," Rattoni casually shrugged, giving it not much further thought. "I've kept 'em safe so far. Also, I can't deny it. I owe ya."

Tom wanted to cry and cradle Rattoni, the rat burglar. He reached out toward him, almost weeping, "Thank you so much, Sir Rattoni—"

Rattoni dodged the attack, "Whoa, whoa, whoa. Cut out the sentimental stuff. I said I was gonna do it, alright. Don't make me reconsider."

"Okay, sorry," Tom sat back and wiped his nose, respecting Rattoni's boundaries. Tom placed the kitten down, provided the bottle to Rattoni, and gave him the instructions on how to feed her.

"Oh, sheesh! This seems like a lot of work," Rattoni slicked back his tiny hairs.

"You'll still do it though, right?" Tom eagerly asked.

"Yeah, yeah… I guess." Rattoni then unfurled the bow from the bottle, saying, "This ain't my style."

Then Tom and Rattoni discovered that on the inside of the bow was written the recipe and ingredients for making more milk replacement.

"Whoa, that's some real nerdy stuff," Rattoni felt repulsed.

Tom took in the smarts of the girl, smiling to himself at her ingenuity and kindness. "This is amazing. You can use this to make more if you run out. I can absolutely take her back when I return."

"You want me to cook and brew potions out here?" Rattoni chuckled to himself.

"Yes," Tom plainly said. He took the bow and, as a parting gift, tied it around Nastya's paw. "This is for you, my cute little scratcher."

Tom wiped his eyes, kissed Nastya, and bade the camp adieu. Then he joined Sir Owl, his guardian, to lead him on the journey up the mountain.

5.6

The two traveled in silence. Up the hill and to the summit, they traversed. At times, the trail was steep, and there was not a moment when Sir Owl looked back and offered wise guidance or even a hand when Tom was slipping. So in those times, Tom fell and then helped himself up, helping Sir Owl along by remaining silent.

Tom did not lollygag or wander, but remained on the invisible leash led by Sir Owl. Whenever he thought of exploring or checking the cliffside for a goat's bleating, he redirected his attention to continue helping Sir Owl. Whatever small creatures that appeared out of the trees to watch or greet the travelers were quickly shooed away by Sir Owl's menacing glare. It was too late for Tom to chase them and apologize on Sir Owl's behalf. In addition, Tom's greatest responsibility now became to help Sir Owl finish his chore and return him to his everyday life, despite whatever impulse or wish Tom personally felt. The silence gave Tom time for immense self-reflection, and he figured he must have seriously offended Sir Owl and now suffered his punishment: the loss of his companion and maybe friend.

The sun was moving into midday behind them. Yet, the hike had felt long and strenuous; surely some credit lay with Sir Owl's regime of taking no breaks and not having even a single moment of rest. Even when Tom would trip and fall on his butt, no breaks were allotted. Sir Owl would continue to march up ahead, and Tom was expected to catch up. And so this pattern of silence continued, upon each step and mile up the mountain.

It was a nasty fall that Tom took. He scraped his hands, banged up his knee again, and even his ankle bent the wrong way and seemed to swell. He sat there in the dirt, watching Sir Owl climb up the path and become smaller and smaller in the distance. Tom was exhausted, sleep-deprived, and exasperated. Despite how much Sir Owl loathed Tom, he was still the first one to find him. Tom had been away from Sir Owl, but this was a distance he had never felt before: the hurt of having your first friend turn their back on you. Sir Owl continued to move away, and Tom so desperately wanted him to stay.

He looked up at Sir Owl and suddenly shouted, "What's wrong? Why are you doing this?"

Sir Owl stopped in his tracks, but did not turn.

"Please, just talk to me. This is getting insufferable. The silence, the climb, passing creatures by, for what? Why? What is it? What's wrong? What happened?" Tom was standing and shaking as he attempted to grasp onto Sir Owl from far away. "I don't understand."

Sir Owl paid Tom no mind.

Then an idea sparked in Tom's mind. "Who, what, when, where, how! Who, what, when, where, how! Who, what, when, where, how! Answer me!" Tom cried. "Who, what, when, where, how! Who! What! When! Where! How! Why! Why! Why!"

"Shut up!" Sir Owl snapped, grasping onto his head. He had turned around and extended his wings, looking down at Tom. "Shut up! You are such a fool. So foolish. Why do you never shut up!"

"Why! Tell me why!" The distance between them felt so long.

"Shut up, shut up, shut up!"

"Why, Sir Owl? Why? Please tell me."

"Shut up!" Sir Owl's eyes glared down at Tom. "The only reason we are here is because of you. This is insufferable and awful because of you. Because you are a fool! You are so foolish that you want to climb this idiotic mountain. You say this is your dream! How foolish is that?"

"Is it?" Tom quickly came to his dream's defense, the one thing he held with him from when he awakened. "Is it foolish? Is it so foolish to have a dream? What is your dream?"

"Stop with your questions. It is foolish, and you are a complete fool." Sir Owl seemed to wince at Tom's repeated questioning. "Don't you dare ask me any more questions."

"Why? Why are you so averse to others' questions?" Tom questioned. "Why is it that you may ask questions, but others may not? Why am I so painful for you to endure? We have journeyed together, visited the oddest places together, met the strangest folk, and now you just turn your back on me?"

"You mean nothing to me, human," the owl spoke.

Tom felt Sir Owl's strike from afar. The arrow struck him right in the heart. "What do you mean? How can you say that? You are Sir Owl, and I am Tom. We are partners in adventure! How do you just forget that?"

"You're just a human. I don't care who you are."

Tom, the human, considered who he was and who he was looking at. "Okay, Owley. If that's how you see me, let it be that."

Owley felt stabbed by Tom's disrespect. It was as if a spear struck him in his wing. "How dare you!"

"Why is it that everyone calls you Owley, but I must call you Sir Owl? Why? Why is it?" Tom continued to battle, unclear what he even battled for.

"Stop it! Stop it with your questions! Stop it with the disrespect! Stop with your foolishness!" Sir Owl screeched and ascended higher, ever so slightly brandishing his talons. "Stop! The questions are mine to ask, not yours. Now, you stop! Keep your voice down, and stop."

"Keep your wings down, Owley!" Tom raised his tone.

"Stop, you fool! Stop calling me that!"

"You stop, Owley!"

"Fool! You're a fool! You're just a foolish human."

"Owley. Owley! You are Owley!"

"Fool! Fool!" Sir Owl stuttered out of utter dismay. "Foolery!"

"Owley—" Then Tom suddenly felt himself get yanked down. His head hit the floor, and he began to fade. In the fading darkness, he reached out to Sir Owl, who screeched as well and thudded to the ground.

Tom awoke with a sweltering pain in his forehead, feeling sore and weighed down. It was all dark, and he seemed not to be able to move at all. When he attempted to move, he realized he was constricted all around. He was sitting up with his legs pointed out, tied together using a thick vine. His legs reached the perimeter of a tall canopy that had been constructed around him using large leaves. Tom's torso was even tied and, behind him, he felt something soft and feathery tickling his neck. From listening to his breathing and occasional snores, Tom realized it was Sir Owl who was tied behind him. They were both bound together by some strange assailant. Outside the canopy, Tom could make out a glow and crackling, which seemed to radiate from a fire within the darkness. The day had disappeared, and their predicament had gotten gravely darker.

Sir Owl began to regain consciousness, "What… what's going on? What is this?" Sir Owl turned his head to examine his surroundings. Once he was fully awake, he began to struggle furiously to free himself. His feathers shuffled against Tom's head. Sir Owl tried to expand his wings and set himself free, but the knot had been fastened tight and kept him imprisoned.

"I don't think that's gonna work," Tom commented.

Sir Owl stopped struggling, "I don't care what you have to say." Then he resumed his fight against the restraints.

"Please, please, please," Tom repeated, while Sir Owl tried every possible move he could. "I understand that you're mad at me. I don't know what's going on either, but we have better odds of escaping if we work together—"

"I am done working with you! The only reason we are here is because of you," Sir Owl seemed to retain his resentment.

Tom considered what possible way to defend himself and cast the blame back onto Sir Owl. If it hadn't been for Sir Owl's unruliness and stonewalling, this whole situation would've been avoided, surely. Tom went to retaliate, but felt his breath squeezed out by the restraints. He stammered and went to try again, but felt so much frustration that he couldn't manage it. So Tom shut his mouth, as Sir Owl had requested many times before, and realized there was no point in retaliation. Therefore, he dropped his head and allowed himself to feel the comfort of Sir Owl's feathers on the back of his neck.

"I'm sorry. I'm truly sorry, Sir Owl. I don't know what took over me. I made a mistake in disrespecting you, and I'm sorry." This felt far more appropriate to Tom and took far less energy as well. He looked toward the end of the canopy and realized his energy was far better spent elsewhere. "So please, work with me. We can free ourselves if we work together."

Sir Owl's erratic movements had stopped. He had expanded his chest and raised his head, pulling the vines against Tom. However, now he relaxed and let Tom breathe more. "Your apology is useless to me. Working together does seem practical, however. We shall form a temporary alliance to free ourselves. And afterward, we shall be done."

"I understand," Tom swallowed his sadness and set to it. "Let's figure out a plan to get out of this."

Sir Owl nodded and resumed his jostling about.

"I can barely move at all. Can you see or hear anything outside of here?" Tom attempted to collaborate.

"I'll check. But I'll remind you, no more questions," Sir Owl instructed. Sir Owl scanned and loudly blinked. He turned his head almost 360 degrees, save for into the back of Tom's neck. "There's a large fire. We're on the forest floor somewhere two-thirds up the mountain. The air is thinner here. Tall redwoods hang around us. Besides that, I can't make out much. I can't hear any other creatures. They're either not around or doing well at concealing themselves."

"Maybe it's the hare or porcupine, trying to skewer us," Tom suggested.

"No, I doubt it. Their footsteps are haphazard and loud. They couldn't have snuck up on us. Meanwhile, whoever is out there has watchful and sneaky eyes."

"Maybe it's a snake?"

"Snakes hardly come into this territory. There are two groups that are to be wary of in this part of the island: bears—"

"Bears?" Tom gulped aloud and began to worry. "Surely, it can't be bears. They're loud and burly. We would've noticed them."

"They're also fast and vicious. Especially during this time of year, they are desperate." Sir Owl scanned, once more. "Or it could be…"

The tall leaves covering them began to shake, creating a slithering and rattling sound as the thin edges of the leaves brushed against each other. Tom and Sir Owl hardened themselves for what would be the grand reveal. The canopy opened up, and a song began to play. From within the tall trees, a drilling and drumming sound came, followed by the monotonous plucking of strings on a board. Vocals followed in the form of high-pitched tweeting, encircling the whole fire and echoing through the forest. Past the fire lay a tall crooked tree, a redwood that seemed to have fallen off but spliced into another, creating a bend in the tall tree that rose into the dark sky. Glowing eyes watched down at the captives, reaching almost as high as the trees. The creatures appeared tall and skinny, Tom judged from the distance between them, and their bodies lay cloaked in darkness. The culprit was identified as a collective. If each of them only had two eyes, they would have far outnumbered the crowd at the Garden, who seemed to eventually become sound. The cloaked creatures sang a hymn in minor key, spooking Tom utterly.

They were awfully too tall to be bears, Tom thought. His fear began to somewhat loosen as he realized the identity of his captors. Instead of looking up, Tom needed to look down to catch sight of the little creatures illuminated by the fire's light. Little sparrows clutched the tall leaves, which had formed the canopy, within their beaks and paraded their plumed tails in a well-timed dance and series of steps around the fire. As the beat began to quicken, the sparrows moved faster and acclimated their dance to the rhythm. The dance they performed seemed to hold a significant cultural value, as other birds, Tom presumed, cheered and rooted from above. The sparrows, one by one, performed a spin, landing with one talon in front of the other, and their beak and the leaf held within it pointed toward the fire. A rapid drumming signaled the sparrows to shake and wave their leaves and tails, creating a natural rattling noise, like the one Tom had heard before. Then, with one resounding thud on the drum, the sparrows extended their necks upward, curled their wings behind their ears, threw the leaves into the fire, and bowed their heads. The fire bloomed as the leaves provided it fuel, lighting the whole venue in a warm hue.

Tom was feeling somewhat relieved after watching the performance and trying to tap along to the beat. However, he noticed that Sir Owl was shivering. It was a chilly night, but the fire warmed them. Besides, Sir Owl was typically impervious to the cold, and Tom was barely feeling the chill himself. Tom tried to call out to Sir Owl, but didn't receive a response. It seemed as if he was frozen, a state Tom had never seen him in.

The wild birds broke out into a new song. A timpani signaled the entrance of a grand figure. All the glowing eyes turned up. Then a profound crash came from the tip of the crooked redwood, shaking the tree in its roots and sending a tremor through the ground to where Tom and Sir Owl sat. Leaves and bark flew off the tree as whatever it was landed above it. The grand figure impressed the audience, for their beaks lay agape and wide open. The musicians almost forgot their cue as the grand figure signaled through a screech for them to begin their low hum in the background.

The authoritative voice thundered, "Welcome! Welcome, my flock. Bow down, and bear witness, with your keen eyes, my greatness. I, the mighty eagle, have arrived."

The flock was allowed to cheer. They stuttered at first, out of fear, and then gave a royal welcome to their fearless leader.

"Silence!" The great eagle demanded. "We are not here to dance and fool around. We are gathered here today to celebrate the latest victory of our proud troupe led by the red-tailed hawk, Haki."

The crowd cheered more freely now and even squawked. The aforementioned hawk descended from a nearby tree, not as tall as the eagle's tree, and made an impressive landing at the base of the crooked tree. He had twisted in a spiral formation, making himself narrow as an arrow, and then outstretched his wings and brandished his talons, flying near and dear to Tom's head and yanking a hair. In a split second, the hawk made himself a dart again and shot through a gap in the fire at the center of the camp, spinning and swiveling off the trunk of the crooked tree and landing gently. Upon his landing, he expanded himself and raised his wings, celebrating who he was, Haki. Eventually, the hawk closed his wings and let them hang by his side, only once the crowd's cheers had started to die. So Haki was the one responsible for this, Tom had thought. Other sparrow hawks, forming Haki's squadron, began to rain down together in a dance not as impressive as their leader's. The squadron slashed across the sky, barely noticeable like shadows in the night. As they approached the fire at neck-breaking speed, they screeched and suddenly swerved to save themselves and land proudly by Haki's side. There, the troupe showed off their skills and talents, the brilliant ones who had taken down Tom and Sir Owl.

"These are your champions," the mighty eagle declared, and the crowd cheered again. The formalities continued. "They have seized and brought to us a bountiful meal, consisting of a human…"

The crowd went "ooo" as Tom cringed to himself.

"And they have also brought one of our own kind," the mighty eagle built anticipation.

The crowd responded, in unison, "Who? Who? Who?"

The mighty eagle cackled, "For long have we waited for his return. He deserted us, fled from our flock, thinking himself too mighty compared to us. Now, he is served to us as prey and merely just an appetizer to our human entrée. The runaway has come back… Owley!" The mighty voice laughed again as the darkness carried his echo.

Just then Tom began to worry. He and Sir Owl had encountered many troubling scenarios, but this was the first instance where they were at the receiving end of all the torture. He had worried hard when it came to other creatures possibly being skewered, but now he was at the receiving end of a fire pit. Tom felt pressured out of his worries about getting eaten when he sensed Sir

Owl's body become limp behind him and fall against his back. All of
a sudden, Tom felt he was carrying the weight of himself and Sir
Owl, who now seemed to be unconscious.

Tom swiveled his head to check on his fellow captive, "Sir
Owl, you've passed out. Sir Owl, please respond. Sir Owl!" Tom tried
to avoid questions. "Sir Owl, please wake up! Sir Owl!"

It was not noticed by Tom, but the whole rest of the camp
had quieted to his cries of help. Some birds were flabbergasted by
Tom's interruption of the ceremony, while others were almost fearful
of the loud and babbling creature that Tom was. The mighty eagle,
however, did not stand for it.

"Silence! You, foolish boy! How dare you interrupt our
festivities?" The mighty eagle commanded attention.

Tom just continued, "Sir Owl, please wake up. Sir Owl, we
have to get out of here." It was almost as if, in that moment, the rest
of the crowd did not exist for Tom. "Sir Owl—"

"I demand your attention, foolish boy!" The redwood tree
shook with reverberations of the eagle's voice. "Do not dare
interrupt me and show me disrespect!"

"I'm sorry," Tom looked to the side and toward the redwood
as Sir Owl's weight crushed him and pushed him down. "I didn't
mean to disrespect you. It's just that Sir Owl has passed out. Can you
please check on him? He needs urgent attention."

Some of the smaller birds chuckled, and then the mighty
eagle followed and silenced everyone, "Your excuses are merely
that… excuses. What is this 'Sir Owl' nonsense? You are speaking of
a traitor who abandoned us!" The mighty eagle then sweetened his
voice. "That is our sweet little Owley, finally come back home." Then
the mighty eagle raised his voice and assumed an ironic stance. "Why
would we help him when we're meant to redeem justice and eat
him?"

The crowd cheered until Tom interrupted them, "No, you
can't eat us. Please! Sir Owl has told me that it is against the Law of

the Island. No one shall intentionally harm another, especially for the purposes of eating."

"Hahaha!" The mighty eagle laughed, and his cronies joined in. "We do not care about your Law of the Island. Here, on the mountain, we observe no law. We take control into our own talons—"

"But, sir—" Tom interrupted.

"Silence!" The mighty eagle quickly regained control. "You have interrupted me enough. You are in no place to argue or make a case for yourself. The only place you are destined to be tonight is roasting on our fire, within our bellies, and pooped out in our pellets. Your fate is sealed, foolish boy! You dare not challenge it nor challenge me. Otherwise, a greater power shall descend on you and tear you from your place in this world and all of time. I, the mighty eagle, usher in our feast for tonight!"

The flock roared, and the rampage of the drums returned. Sir Owl seemed to stir to the sound, mumbling small and incoherent things as Tom remained preoccupied with the anarchy of the crowd. The wild birds flew more freely now, changing branches, gathering closer, and having their short-lived fame, flashing their feathers and dances from the stands.

"Who…" Sir Owl mumbled.

"Sir Owl! You're waking up, yes," Tom said aloud between the two of them. "I'm here. I'm here for you. Please, let me help." There was no way Tom could help Sir Owl in that moment, but he kept trying to carry his weight.

"Who…" Sir Owl mumbled again.

The mighty eagle ordered, "Now, untie the human and owl, and prepare them to burn."

The sparrows followed suit and carried out the orders. Sir Owl and Tom were made to kneel by the fire, sitting next to each other as the sparrows prepared long and thick wooden roasting stakes to tie the captives onto. The vines were still tied on so strongly and skillfully that no matter how hard Tom tried to budge, they remained tightened just like new. Following through with the ceremonial proceedings, Sir Owl and Tom were tied to the stakes, which hung between two branches, slowly roasting on the fire beneath them. Meanwhile, the birds continued their barbaric dance, making the night hysterical with their vivid colors. The birds flew eagerly, awaiting their feast, while Tom struggled with his own flight of ideas. He juggled various scenarios on how to escape and called on Sir Owl for his calculated mind. Sir Owl did not offer much help, remaining passive and languidly staring up at the stars in the night sky. So Tom desperately thought on his own about routes of escape, but nothing seemed to loosen his restraints. The heat of the fire underneath made them sweat profusely. This fire would heat up soon, however, and begin to burn their backs and cook them alive.

The mighty eagle announced the next step of the ceremony: a competition amongst the birds to dance and sing, flaunt their talents, and prove themself worthy of carving the feast. So one by one, performers began to line up. A new performer would step up, perform their jig, wave their feathers, and the crowd would respond with cheers or jeers. Then another performer would take the stage and continue the competition, performing a new song and dance. From Tom's angle, most of the ceremony was missed. If he tried, he could pay attention to the chirps, but he remained focused on pulling himself and Sir Owl out of their predicament.

"Sir Owl, please help," Tom whispered to Sir Owl over the song and dance. "I need your help.

Sir Owl remained lifeless. Not even a feather of his seemed to lift.

"Sir Owl, please. Help me. Help!" Tom called.

Sir Owl kept his blank stare up ahead.

"Sir Owl! Help me!" Tom shook his whole body with all his might.

Small pieces of bark fell off the stake and into the fire as the fire reached out to swallow the pieces up. The fire gleefully smiled at Tom's backside, while the crowd celebrated Tom and Sir Owl's inevitable demise. The only ones who were miserable seemed to be Tom, Sir Owl, and the performer whose dance seemed to be overshadowed. Tom's roasting stake seemed to shift and bend slightly toward the fire where he hanged.

The roar of the fire seemed louder, so Tom shouted from somewhat underneath Sir Owl, "Wake up, Sir Owl!"

Then Tom saw it. Sir Owl wasn't looking up at the stars. High up in the branches lurked other owls. The parliament of owls had gathered and gazed down at the runaway, Sir Owl. They sat up in the rafters with their rigid postures, smooth silhouettes, their horned ear tufts, and shining yellow eyes. And for some reason, they were excluded. Barred from near the fire and made to watch as one of their own was roasted. However, Tom didn't understand whether the owls were excluded by orders of the eagle or excluded themselves because they seemed gravely uninterested in matters taking place underneath them. They wore the same sort of expression that Tom had often seen on Sir Owl's face: discontent and the inklings of a sigh or yawn. Yet, Tom abandoned their perspective and turned his attention to Sir Owl, who lay despondent. The only thing differing from Sir Owl and the stuck lamb was that one was bleating, while the other seemed hopeless.

"Sir Owl…" Tom whispered. "Sir Owl, please respond. Sir Owl. Sir Owl! Sir Owl—"

"Do not call me that. I'm not Sir Owl," the owl who lay tied beside Tom responded.

"Yes, you are," Tom instinctively replied.

"No, I'm not. That was a stupid name I gave myself. I am Sir Owl, no more." The owl resigned.

"Sir Owl, I will not let you give up!" Tom wanted to reach out and grab Sir Owl. "We need to escape from here, and we can only do so together. We've only been able to travel this far because we've been gifted with your guidance. You are my guardian. The Koi Masters appointed you as my guardian, and I'll always see you as that

No one can tear that away from you. I don't care what your real name is. You're my guardian. You're Sir Owl!"

Sir Owl lay still and watched what was above. If you looked at the sky for long enough, the stars may seem almost grabbable, so close, and within your reach, like everything you have ever wanted. Sir Owl imagined that peace. Then he slowly turned his head to see Tom.

"Tom Foolery, you're quite something," Sir Owl said to Tom.

Tom smiled and returned the favor, "It's nice to see you. Let's get out of here."

"Let us," Sir Owl blinked his orange eyes earnestly.

"Those owls above us. Do you—" Tom cut himself off to adjust the question.

"I know them. They won't help us."

Tom felt stuck again, but urged, "If you tried to compel them, then maybe—"

"They would not answer."

"But they're your flock, your family…"

"My family's gone." Sir Owl turned toward the sky again.

"Sir Owl—" Tom thought he had lost Sir Owl again.

"Those owls don't care for me. They're disgusted by me. I fled from them long ago. And now, upon my return, I can see the look of shame in their eyes."

"Just because you left them doesn't mean they don't care about you. They're still your family," Tom attempted to comfort Sir Owl. "You may not be like the lamb we rescued, hurrying back to your herd, but your herd will still call for you and welcome you back."

"Tom…" Sir Owl spoke with sorrow. "Those birds are not my family. I don't know where my family is. I'm not from here, you see." There was a slowness to the way Sir Owl spoke. A way that Tom nor any creature had ever heard him. "I only landed on this island due to a failed migration. My family continued to fly and never returned for me. And so here, I remained."

Tom thought of how to respond and comfort Sir Owl, but thought back to the moment of listening to the girl by the water. Tom listened.

"This was long ago. The parliament of owls lurking above is who found me as an owlet. They nursed me, for which I am grateful. Eventually, they realized that the owl they saw was similar to them but in many ways not." Sir Owl cleared his throat as the yellow-eyed owls watched the captives below. "My tufts do not extend like theirs. My eyes are not yellow like theirs. Our build and temperament varied greatly, and they saw me as I grew as something that was not one of them. Once I could fly, I attempted to give flight and hunt with them. At every instance, I was brought crashing to the ground. They spread their wings and pointed their talons at me, questioning, 'Who?' No matter what I did or where I went, I would hear the echo, 'Who?' They stood there questioning who I was. At every attempt to answer the question and make myself one with my found family, I heard the question ring through my mind. Who was I really? Who am I, now? 'Who?' They called me Owley because I was somewhat similar, but not really. Everything about my existence was questioned by this flock. 'Who?' What was I doing there? When did I get even there? Where did I come from? How? Why? Why did I exist? I have been ridiculed by these questions for all my life, Tom. Questions and never seeming to find the right answer."

The murmur of the flock continued as Tom and Sir Owl existed in mere isolation and hanging in the balance. They were not on the ground, nor in the sky, but somewhere in between.

Tom's heart felt warm, from the heat but also from what Sir Owl had trusted him with. "Thank you. You will forever be Sir Owl to me. I forever promise that I will never ask you a—"

"Shut up, Tom," Sir Owl shook his head. "That's not what this is about. I don't even know why I'm telling you all this. I suppose I have partly accepted our fate tonight."

Tom steadied himself the way Sir Owl had and said, "If this is where we meet our end, I will be honored to be by your side, Sir Owl."

Then, Tom and Sir Owl allowed themselves to drift off and stare into the night sky on a rather hot night. Tom wasn't sure if Sir Owl looked at the stars or the owls lurking above. However, Tom's attention was taken up by the small slice of the clear night sky that was visible to him and not covered by trees or smoke. The sky seemed a cool shade of black, and the bright stars floated above in neat formations of great creatures.

Reaching the final few performers of the night, the flock became even more festive and hungry for their prize. Sir Owl and Tom were turned over on the roasting pit by a large swarm of birds, who struggled to roll the stakes. Now, the fire met them face-first, taking away their view of the night sky.

Haki was the final performer of the night. His dance was enjoyed by all, even the mighty eagle, who laughed and savored Haki's every kick and thrust. All the while, Sir Owl and Tom roasted and cried to each other. Tom's tears dripped into the fire and vanished into thin air. Tom wished that his tears would stay longer on his face before dripping off, feeling frightened at losing himself to such a sudden matter change. There was a fascination that made it hard for Tom to close his eyes upon looking at the mouth of the fiery beast awaiting him. The fire and smoke stung his eyes, but somewhere within the flames, Tom was curious to find a saving grace. Yet, whatever silver lining he could imagine did not appear down there but hung around his neck. The locket of the girl hung from Tom's neck and dangled above the flames. It tugged at Tom's heart, reminding him of all that the journey had encompassed, all the promises he had made, and how he was not ready to give it up yet. His dream… the dream, whatever it was, Tom was not ready to give it up and let it become an evaporated tear, nowhere to be seen and felt. He would follow his dream even into the pits of the fire, hoping to somehow traverse past the flame, through the island, into the sea, and wherever his dream would take him. It was an impossible idea, but his passion made him shake and feel the strength to embrace the fire and somehow let it be him.

The last performer finished. The crowd cheered. The mighty eagle's thundering voice began to announce the winner as Tom cried with defiance and passion. Just in that moment, a bear came dashing through the woods and crashed the celebration of the birds. The bear let out a guttural roar, shocking all the wild birds into flight. In that moment, the bear appeared to shine brighter than the fire. Some small sparrows left trails of white streaks and droppings as they attempted to confront their fear. The big and burly bear dropped his front claws, landing on a now quiet stadium within the forest floor. Sir Owl had fainted from heat stroke. Tom saw all this and smiled in relief at the universe conspiring to save them, and faded.

The cave appeared very dim. Some water dripped in the back corner of the crammed space. Tom lay on the cave floor with his face hugging the dirt on the cold rock slab. He was drooling underneath himself. While he was heavily breathing and lying outstretched, a bigger creature took up most of the space, snoring and his body heaving with every breath. Tom had been abducted again, but this time not restrained or bound. Sir Owl also lay collapsed beside him. At first, Tom was startled by Sir Owl's position. The bear kept one paw over the wise owl.

Tom rushed to check up on Sir Owl and quietly poked him, whispering, "Sir Owl."

Sir Owl opened his eyes and quickly revealed his act. He had been awake, but pretending to be unconscious under the bear. "Shut up…" Sir Owl whispered, almost considerately.

"I'll help," Tom whispered as quietly as he could.

Sir Owl, who kept a look of total concern on his face, mouthed, You are a fool.

Tom gently guided the bear's arm off. As gently as he tried, the bear seemed to stir but quickly returned to bed. Tom felt the soft but matted fur of the bear, a creature that he, too, was afraid to see, but had saved Sir Owl and him. Sir Owl carefully made his escape from underneath the bear's clutches, tiptoeing up and toward the exit of the cave. Tom planned to follow, of course, but stayed to thank the fellow bear.

As Tom petted him, the bear began to mumble in his sleep, "Those dumb birds disturbing my sleep…" The bear grizzled to himself. "Food can't walk. Please don't leave. Last hibernation, maybe. I gotta stock up."

The bear placed his front paw over his face and returned fully to sleep. Tom stood and wished the bear his gratitude, hoping to meet him again one day.

6

The sun was breaking dawn as Sir Owl and Tom climbed up. Morning dew covered the grass and trees as Tom's cheeks grew flushed from the breeze. Tom clutched the locket around his neck. After that unfortunate encounter with the wild birds, the locket had truly become a symbol of hope and protection to him. Last night, when all things seemed sour and Sir Owl and Tom stared down the fire, expecting their end, some fragment of hope had come crashing through the woods and rescued them. Now, Tom was glad he got to share another day with Sir Owl and continue to remember the memories he held dear.

Sir Owl had still been strangely quiet since last night, but even he couldn't deny that he enjoyed the freedom from his tight restraints. Despite the detour that had made them reconsider their fates, Sir Owl still led onward and walked in his characteristic shuffle. He surely wouldn't have changed his whole outlook on life after that incident, but a subtle change did occur at least. Sir Owl walked, feeling somewhat less rushed.

"Tom," Sir Owl called from ahead, waiting for Tom to catch up. "About yesterday…"

Tom figured the awkward moment would come. "You don't have to say anything, Sir Owl." And Tom just kept walking alongside his guide. "Thank you. Thank you for trusting me, Sir Owl. I'm grateful for your help and very glad you found me. I think that you're the best guardian ever."

Sir Owl cleared his throat, "Now, you don't have to say all that—"

"I know," Tom looked at his companion. "I just wanted to."

"Well, don't expect any pleasantries in return!" Sir Owl returned to his typical squawks.

They continued alongside each other, up the mountain. From where they were, the summit didn't seem so far. Where Tom had been distracted before climbing up the initial chunk, here he maintained his focus on the path he was on. Beneath his feet, he watched the dirt trail, small pebbles, and occasionally a rock that would slip and roll away from him. It all came underneath him as he flattened the path and traversed ahead. There would be that occasional rock that Tom would be tempted to trip on, but he watched his footing and avoided any unfortunate falls. The dirt became darker the further they traveled up, and the rocks grew in size, too. However, nothing matched the massive structure that was the mountain they stood on.

"We're not far," Sir Owl said.

Then there existed the silence of feeling they were approaching something great, something monumental, and something mighty that would surely change their fate. This was what it was all building up to: the pinnacle of their adventure, the peak of the mountain, and the summit of determination.

Tom shakingly filled the silence, "Sir Owl, I've been thinking about things."

"Okay... and?" Sir Owl fished for more.

"I was wondering..." Tom hesitated. He looked up, all of a sudden, in thought. "Sir Owl, would you... I mean, please tell me about your dream."

Sir Owl began to think to himself. He had surely shared enough about himself to warrant a break: "You're really on a kick to get to know more about me, huh?"

"No. Well, I mean, yes, of course. But I'm asking—or talking—about this for my own sake. It would really help me to know more about your dream." Tom held his hands together nervously.

"Fine!" Sir Owl ran his wing underneath his chin. "Hmm… I suppose my dream was to nap as much as I could. Unfortunately, someone decided to throw a wrench into that dream."

"I'm sorry," Tom chattered through his teeth. "So you're saying… that you… you…"

"Spit it out, already," Sir Owl raised his tone, but not as much as before.

"Sorry! I'm just trying to figure out how to word it so it's not a question—"

"Just go and say it. Let's get this over with," Sir Owl sighed, preparing himself.

"No, I must honor my promise," Tom insisted. "You said that was your dream… Please tell me about any other dreams you have."

"What is all this about?" Sir Owl raised his wings.

"Please, Sir Owl."

"Fine!" Sir Owl put his wings behind his back and thought. "I mean, I guess I dreamed of finding my family and learning more about myself, but I let that go a while back. I realized I wouldn't even know where to start, and then I just got settled here and forgot about them."

"I'm sorry—"

"It's whatever."

"So what I'm hearing you say is that… you have had multiple dreams in your life," Tom reflected Sir Owl's statement.

"Yes," Sir Owl confirmed the obvious.

Then Tom thought he finally stumbled upon the right prompt. "Surely, you must have had an ultimate dream, though! Tell me about that."

"Umm… no." Sir Owl avoided staring at Tom due to his pointless statements. "Listen, what are you trying to get at?"

"Tell me about your ultimate dream, please!"

"I don't know!" Sir Owl squawked. "I don't have one."

"Oh." Tom stopped in his tracks.

Sir Owl hurried him, "What is it?"

"I'm torn." Tom wore a look of concern.

Sir Owl felt himself torn between carrying forward and waiting with Tom, and chose to say, "Tell me more."

"I'm sorry." Tom sat down on the dirt. "I came here thinking that my dream was to climb the mountain, but now I'm finding myself dreading it. I'm moving more slowly, tripping over so many things. I keep getting distracted by everything else on the trail. I feel my stomach turning and wanting to go back and play with the kitten and chase the fox. Now, I'm trying to course correct and keep my focus on the trail, but I don't know what's happening."

Sir Owl raised his head. "Are you scared?"

Tom looked up from feeling down, "Scared…"

"Scared of reaching your dream?"

"I don't know."

"That you won't know what to do next?"

"I don't know."

"Or that maybe you found yourself chasing the wrong thing?"

"I don't know!" Tom felt crushed. "This dream is all I've had since I woke up. But now, I find myself filled with more. I have things in my pocket, supplies on my back, memories in my head, and—most importantly—you by my side. I promised the Koi Masters that I would leave after climbing this mountain, but I also promised someone else that I would stay and help. And so, now, I'm torn. I don't know what to do. I'm also scared, Sir Owl, of screwing this all up, ruining things for you, letting down the fairy, and whatever it means to throw things out of balance. In all honesty, I don't wanna leave, and I also don't wanna abandon this dream of climbing the mountain."

Sir Owl just watched Tom. Despite his wisdom, he still didn't quite know how to respond. "I don't know, Tom. That sounds pretty complicated. Honestly, some parts of that make no sense to me, like the fox, fairy, or even that locket that you're wearing…" Sir Owl made a whoosh sound, signaling all those things flew right over his head. "I'll tell you what. You've come all this way. Put in all this work. And for that, I think you should see the summit. You've earned it. Maybe after seeing it, you may think differently. I've seen it myself before, and it's not too shabby. What do I know, though? I promise you, Tom, that if you don't feel resolved, we can talk about all this once we've climbed down."

Tom felt softened by Sir Owl's wisdom, so he looked up at him and smiled. Utterly grateful, he said, "Thank you. Okay, let's do that."

Sir Owl helped Tom up. As they stood together on the trail again, he said, "As your guide and guardian, my help applies to matters of all kinds."

The two, therefore, continued traveling. They chatted about more trivial things like Haki and his lame band of poopy warriors. They reviewed Rattoni and his renewed morality and stance toward parenthood. Sir Owl and Tom debated whether skewers or stakes were worse, and considered how all the silly creatures they had run into were faring. Where was Shepherd even taking the sheep? Sir Owl certainly didn't know. How morally and ethically weird it was to see the catfish fishing, and how Sir Owl just liked to hang around them and lounge. How were the tortoise and the hare getting along and working together? They also talked about somewhat more serious things, like how many more winters the bear would get to slumber. Within those final steps, Tom remembered the tune that was sung by those performers. This time, Sir Owl joined in, too.

They both sang, *"Off to an adventure!"*

Sir Owl and Tom had set off on an adventure. Sir Owl and Tom, partners in adventure, arrived at the peak of their adventure. There they stood at the summit of the mountain. Alongside them, a river poured out over the cliffside, sending a cloud of mist into the air that colored the sky with sparkles and a rainbow. The view was breathtaking. From that height, they could feel the grandness of the mountain, standing so mighty and high above all the rest. It was such a distance from the rest of the world that it all appeared to be a fantasy, and none of it felt real. Everything far took on a mirage-like appearance and felt like a two-dimensional painting cast on by their disbelief. Tom thought that they had done it. He exhaled with a smile and was glad he had persevered to pursue this dream by Sir Owl's side. Breathing in the fresh air and wanting to shout louder than the waterfall off the side of the mountain, Tom held his arms out and looked at what stood ahead of him. From there up above, he could see the remainder of the island. Ample forests and continuous pastures that were now suffering from a disease, unlike the typical cruelty of winter. Grasslands lay darkened, and the trees had shed all that they had left. It was as if a dark shadow had been cast on the parts of the island that stood ahead of the mountain. Tom wondered how the creatures in those parts had fared. The only thing miraculous was the unstained sea that circled the island and shimmered, appearing beautiful and endless.

That was the same sea that defied gravity and climbed up the mountain with the human, longing to unite with its desired. The loud gushing of the river beside the travelers gave no fright, but suddenly the ground began to rumble and groan as if to awaken. Tom and Sir Owl were shocked to see the ground shaking in a violent thrust to tear everything apart. Then with their eyes, they saw the earth split open. Part of the mountain began to crack and crumble, slipping away and driving a crater into the base of the island. The whole island was torn apart as the tectonic plates that held up the world shifted. Sir Owl and Tom fell with the looming quake into the shallow river beside them. The current was not strong, but they were doused in the waters of the oppressive sea that had now conquered the mountain through the will of Tom. Unbeknownst to Tom, he had lost his contest with the sea.

Tom lay ignorant of symbolic battles and worried about Sir Owl and how one misstep would've emptied them out. However, Tom risked it and moved closer to the edge of the mountain. Before he could see it, he felt the heat radiate from where the island had split open. Tom and Sir Owl rapidly cried to each other, trying to make sense of the monstrosity and chaos they witnessed. Where the island had cracked, magma began to pool and float up. Tom fell to his knees within the river, questioning what had occurred. His heart had leaped out from within him. When he looked up and away from the chaos, he saw the dark shadow descend toward him, blocking the sun.

The mighty eagle joined the fray and swooped down. The large eagle, who had shaken the crooked redwood tree, targeted Tom, baring his talons and prepared to cut him open. At the last second, Sir Owl dived and intercepted the attacker. Sir Owl struck the eagle away from his original path, and the two birds collided with each other and rolled off the edge of the mountain. Tom hurried to the edge and saw Sir Owl recover and take flight upward, while the mighty eagle pursued him.

The mighty eagle, the elder bird, targeted the runaway Sir Owl. From afar, Tom could make out the eagle's wider wingspan as Sir Owl seemed to fly away like a dart. Sir Owl was taken over by panic, flapping his wings desperately to escape his predatory king. He may have run away once when he was young, but he had never quite learned to fend for himself. He could intimidate small foes who he knew were afraid of birds of prey, but he didn't stand a chance to swoop down and catch something even as assertive as a snake. So he thought that his prospects of facing the eagle were little to none. Escape was the only possible route. He desperately flew as fast as he

could, swirling, spinning, and pulling any maneuver he could, while
the mighty eagle tailed him.

During his arduous effort to escape, Sir Owl's scope
narrowed as if plunging through a tunnel and hoping to make it out.
Not many places to go or wander, but stare down the road and speed
up. Sir Owl had entered the tunnel, being a lazy and grumpy owl. He
used to pass the time by napping and lounging around the catfish,
but his fate had been forever changed once he had found the human.
To thwart away the fear, Sir Owl closed his eyes as he barreled ahead.
Dashing forward, all he could think of was the island shattering.
However, over the mountain tumbling down and lava spitting out of
the waters, Sir Owl could hear the voice of the distant Tom calling
out. Behind him, he also heard the mighty eagle challenging the wind
with his aerodynamic force.

The eagle screeched a shrill call to his prey, but Sir Owl
would not stop now. Sir Owl flapped his wings furiously, attempting
to leave the ferocious flock's leader behind. The wind whispered
loudly in Sir Owl's ear. While the waters carried the wishes and words
of the fish, the wind carried the echoes of the birds. The whoosh of
the wind reminded Sir Owl of the distant but pressing memory of his
flock staring down at him and begging the question, "Who... WHO
are you?" Owley had escaped from the question before, but it found
him again. It chased him, just as the eagle did.

Sir Owl denied it. He thought of better times. The first thing
he recalled was running away as an owlet, stumbling upon the
villagers of the Pond. He learned to be wary of the frogs and was
guided by the Koi Masters, who admonished him for escaping from
his flock and cast him to the far edges of the island. There, Owley
grew up and lived with Kat and her knot, learning the secrets of
fishing. It was a tame life until Owley one day decided to survey the
beach and found him. Tom had washed up on the beach. At first,
Owley was wary, but then he heard the man declare his dream with
stupidity. During that moment, he saw the human alone and felt
compelled to approach him with the key question. Owley did not ask,

"Who are you?" But explored, "Who are you talking to?" He extended his wing to discover a connection. They were both fools who had landed on the island with no clue as to who they were. Together, they had begun to uncover the mystery and take on the challenge. Tom had called him Sir Owl, and Sir Owl had called him Tom. That's who they became to each other.

Tom watched on from miles away, feeling utterly helpless and scared for Sir Owl. From that distance, he saw Sir Owl turn and fly high toward the sun. The mighty eagle pursued Sir Owl into the rays of sunlight that blinded Tom. All Tom could make out was two small figures colliding into each other in the shadow of the sun. Each bird had their wings extended and somehow rivaled each other. It was too bright to witness—the glory of one bird and the downfall of the other. The champion retracted his talons, while the defeated fell from the sky and collapsed into the sea. The champion floated for a gentle second and then redirected his focus to the mountain. While the sun was magnificent and large, this bird seemed to rival it and, for a moment, produced a radiant shine. Then it came crashing down on Tom. Slowly growing in size and clarity as the bird came closer, Tom saw that the bird possessed the orange eyes of Sir Owl and flew as bravely as an eagle-owl. Sir Owl flew toward Tom, and from afar, Tom could see Sir Owl's eyes growing empty as he limped in the air with an injured wing. Tom realized that Sir Owl began to drop faster, losing his original trajectory and sending him in for a crash landing. But Tom realized that if Sir Owl continued on his current course, he would miss the summit of the mountain. In a frenzy, Tom ran to Sir Owl and reached, catching him out of midair. They fell together off the edge of the summit and into the world that split open.

7

Drifting in the pool underneath the mountain, there were the two friends who had scaled the mountain, saved each other, and cascaded down it. The force of the fall left Tom's back and most of his body numb. Sir Owl was protected within Tom's arms, but his blood trailed from him and began to color the pool red. Tom and Sir Owl faded into darkness. Into that darkness where mysterious things occurred.

As Tom slipped in and out of consciousness, he recalled several broken memories, not understanding if they were false or real.

In his heart, he sensed the loneliness and ghostly apparition he felt was meant to be waiting for him on the island, perhaps a friend.

He thought of the dream that had possessed him. Something that he couldn't quite define or rationalize, but felt to be an intrinsic drive.

He remembered the sound of Kat recognizing him. Tom, a name that had just stuck.

Tom felt the dizziness of watching the Koi fish and their hypnotic chase. They ordered him not to help, but he had disobeyed them.

Out of all the other villagers, Tom remembered Sir Tortoise first, who seemed to know and remember all the others' names.

Names… the fairy didn't know her name. Yet, she had found it within her to name the little kitten.

Nastya had felt so soft and comforting against Tom's chest.

Sir Owl, who was a grump once, had even warmed his heart to her. Sir Owl had fulfilled his duty to Tom as his guardian.

From the joys of friendship and companionship, Tom remembered the laughter he had shared with the mysterious girl.

Within the fragmented memories, Tom saw the girl again, swimming and pulling him out of the water. He felt the pressure of the water pushing him down, but he didn't let go of Sir Owl or the girl's hand. Then he felt the ripples become a powerful current around him as the Koi fish furiously swam in a blur of colors. Through his limited senses, Tom heard the girl's cries as the Koi spoke their fragmented speech in unison. Then he felt his body go cool and numb. Lastly, he heard the squeaking cry of a little furball licking his chin.

Tom startled awake.

"What's going on?" Tom asked before his eyes settled. He saw Nastya on his chest, and surrounding him were Rattoni and Nastya's mother and siblings. They were all in a round room, a cave of sorts, underground, and cool.

"Whoa, whoa, easy there! Be careful. You're still healing," Rattoni exclaimed

"What happened? Where are we? Where's Sir Owl? Why are you guys here?" Tom frantically tried to understand.

"Cool it, buddy. We're in a hospital. You're being treated by a frog doctor—"

"Where? Who?"

"A frog doctor. We're in the Pond."

"The Pond… are the Koi here?"

"Yeah, they kinda live here, bud."

"I saw them. What happened, Rattoni?" Tom tried desperately to gather what information he didn't know. With one hand, he held onto Nastya, and the other he used to push away the blanket that covered him.

"Slow your roll, buddy! You really shouldn't be getting up." Rattoni blocked Tom's path out.

"I gotta find out what happened and if everyone's okay." Underneath the blanket, Tom saw that his legs and torso were covered in thick mud.

"I'll tell you all I know, but you gotta rest and let the mud work its magic," Rattoni threw the blanket back onto Tom and Nastya.

Tom felt exhausted from even pushing off the blanket. He saw Nastya crawl up his chest, underneath the covers, and decided to remain settled. "Fine, please tell me what happened."

"Yes, yes. Just let me speak," Rattoni came up to the side of Tom's face. "So you suffered a great fall from the top of the mountain. It gave you some gnarly bruises and tore some tissue, so luckily not too bad. The frog doctor has been treating you here. While you've been asleep, the island has kinda gone to ruin."

"Ruin?" Tom thought maybe it had all been a nightmare.

"Yeah, ruin. Part of the mountain fell off. New ravines have popped up, filled with giant pools of lava. Whole forests were destroyed. Most creatures have been in a panic." Rattoni gave Tom a second to soak it all in. "Honestly, in my opinion, it's really not that bad. These creatures need to take a walk in my shoes for a couple of days. That'll show them Hell."

Tom swallowed in his disbelief. "I'm really glad you guys are okay. How'd you find me? What are you guys doing here?"

"What? We can't come visit our loser friend?" Rattoni chuckled and looked at the other unamused cats licking themselves. "Well, we actually came here soon after you left our camp. We ran out of milk. You wouldn't believe how much that little one drinks. And while we had the so-called formula, the whole bunch of us couldn't read it because we're illiterate. So we came here and found this smarty-pants frog doctor who could read it. Soon after, they drag you in, all banged up and unconscious. We had to come check up on you."

"Well, thank you. That's really sweet of you guys," Tom said, looking out of the bed at his visitors.

"Oh, shut it. Cut it with the sentimentalities, or else I'll take you to the top of the mountain and throw you off myself." Rattoni chuckled and tried to break the tension.

"I'm sorry."

"Whatever," Rattoni realized his humor didn't help. "Alright, we'll let you rest. Plus, it's the kitten's lunch time."

"Wait, Rattoni!" Tom called as Rattoni turned. "Where's Sir Owl?"

Rattoni turned and seemed to take on a grave look. He prepared Tom, "Now, listen, he's not in the best shape, but the frog doctor is trying his best—"

"Where is he?" Tom looked dead serious.

Despite his aching bones, Tom rushed up and went to see Sir Owl. The dirt-packed corridor led him to a similar room, but wider in size. There lay Sir Owl, asleep, with his wings spread open and covering the length of the room. Across Sir Owl's chest and right wing were four deep slashes that tore deep into his bones. Tom kept calling Sir Owl, but he remained unresponsive.

"Please, wake up. Wake up, Sir Owl," Tom leaned over him. "Wake up. I must thank you properly for your help. Please wake up. Sir Owl, please."

Rattoni pulled on Tom's trousers. "Hey, go a little easy on him and yourself. The doc said he's in a coma."

Tom looked at how still Sir Owl's eyelids were. Despite his slanted ear tufts, his expression appeared so plain and lifeless. "I need him to wake up. I can't lose him."

Tom's pleading to Sir Owl had worked before, and so he would keep trying. Tom sat in Sir Owl's room and waited for him to awaken. Rattoni informed Tom that it had taken four days for Tom to awaken, and Tom was willing to wait another four or however long for Sir Owl to heal and march out of the hospital with him. Sir Owl had said that the two of them would sit and solve Tom's dilemma, but now the only problem that Tom struggled with was wanting Sir Owl to awaken and sit by him. Many times throughout the day, Tom would lean over and cry for Sir Owl to awaken. Tom would sit by his straw bed and gently graze his feathers, and think of how hard Sir Owl had flown that day when they were atop the mountain. Tom couldn't help but feel guilt and shame for dragging Sir Owl to this fate, where he lay unconscious.

"If I could trade my fate for yours, I would, Sir Owl. I wish I had gotten slashed instead, and you were the one to awaken first. You flew so high that day, so high. You stretched your wings so wide." Tom cried over Sir Owl's bed.

The frog doctor tried to introduce himself and instruct Tom to go back to his bed, but Tom persisted. The doctor assured Tom that he was doing his best to tend to Sir Owl's injuries with specific mud-based ointments and medications. Tom was eager for each check-up performed by the doctor, but none of them yielded any significant results. The man of medicine confirmed the seriousness of Sir Owl's injuries.

As the frog doctor turned to leave, he seemed to hover and hesitate to say something. Then he croaked it out, "Tom… the Koi Masters desire to speak with you." Then, the frog doctor scurried out.

Tom was compelled to understand how the Koi Masters played into the story, but remained seated by Sir Owl's side. Although the doctor did not ask for a response and had rushingly left, Tom answered to himself by declaring that he would wait for Sir Owl to recover first.

So Tom remained waiting in the same room. Upon his next visit, the doctor was almost stunned to see Tom still there and not by the Koi's pond. However, the doctor did not repeat his message or bother Tom again, but kept his distance from the human.

Days passed by as the two companions remained underground. Any sense of time felt arbitrary with no sunlight or clock. Tom's energy and Rattoni's notices were the only indicators that suggested how much time had passed. As Tom's energy would fade, he would slip off to sleep beside the unconscious Sir Owl. In his dreams, he would see the same fragmented memories and feel the weight of the sea crushing him. Falling or drowning would be the common causes of Tom's demise in his dreams, and what would wake him up. No more dragons or sphinxes. And when he woke up, there he would be in the same room, watching Sir Owl lie still and his chest slowly expanding with air.

As more time passed, they would be visited by others. No water or wind, somehow the word had spread. First was Shepherd, who licked Tom's face again and whimpered at Sir Owl's feet. Sir Tortoise and Sir Hare came next to pay their respects, proving their teamwork to be quite complementary. Rattoni, Nastya, and the rest of the cats were regulars, but ran into the political leaders of the Garden and caused a ruckus. Sir Hare swore he recognized Rattoni from his wanted posters, but Rattoni denied and said that was his identical twin brother, Ralphtoni. Whether Ralphtoni was real or not, he had accrued himself a notorious reputation. Sir Tortoise was quite gentle with Nastya and fascinated by her name. It reminded him of someone else, but he couldn't quite put his finger on it. Rattoni always approached Sir Owl with caution, remembering back to their run-in and the fateful day he changed his way of living. Nastya's presence and cuddles always comforted Tom. He enjoyed holding her close to him. It almost made him feel like everything was okay for a minute.

On one occasion, Rattoni told Tom that a moose had arrived in town. The moose tried to make his way to see Sir Owl and Tom but wasn't permitted into the minuscule hospital tunnels because he wouldn't fit. After the news, however, Tom could swear he heard distant calls from the moose and even moos from the cows every so often. Those Tom wouldn't have even expected somehow made the trek to see Sir Owl. The groundhog somehow dug his way into the room, while the mole-rat took a while to blindly stumble into the right room. Even the lizard and squirrels they hardly knew came to visit and showed their support. The hospital staff had stopped a stinky skunk from entering, who brought news of another tortoise that was trying to attend but had tripped and fallen. Truly, what surprised Tom was seeing a troupe of sparrow hawks line the corridor and welcome Haki, the hawk. Tom was prepared to defend himself and Sir Owl, but Haki bent the knee and begged forgiveness for the actions of their former tyrannical leader. Haki proved himself honorable and offered that Sir Owl visit with him after he wakes up to explore a possible position on their court.

Sly, the snake, didn't really know Sir Owl, but still visited anyway and scared the whole town. He didn't do much but wriggle around Tom and ask if he could eat Sir Owl, to which Tom promptly responded by kicking him out. Tom thought of possibly asking Sly about the fairy lady, but realized that for now, he was meant to be by Sir Owl.

The Koi Masters never came, even though Tom wasn't really sure how they could, since they only swam. However, Tom knew how much Sir Owl valued the Koi Masters. One fish that surely had to visit was Kat, who came in clutching her cane and holding her tears back.

Kat sat down by Sir Owl, "Oh, my dear friend, Owley. Heal up, and we shall fish together soon."

Tom heard her sweet words and almost came to tears himself. Kat stayed for a while but then began to struggle to breathe and needed to return to the water.

Before she left, she faced Tom and said, "I have learned more about you, Tom. While digging around your ship's wreckage, I discovered some vital details about you. First, you must forgive me. I mislabeled you. Your real name isn't Tom. It does start with a T though, so I wasn't far off. Would you like to know what your real name is?"

Tom carefully thought about the nature of names and what was more prominent on his mind. "No, thank you. I'm truly grateful, but I'm happy being Tom, at least for right now."

Kat respected Tom's wishes and didn't share any more about Tom's mysterious origins. She reminded him to visit the Koi. Tom still resisted and remained with Sir Owl. The whole world and all its matters could wait for when Sir Owl was well.

The day went by, and it mostly just became Tom and Sir Owl. Occasionally, Tom would pace about the room and urgently turn his attention to Sir Owl when he thought he heard him move. However, it was nothing. No new sounds or movements. Tom's mind played tricks on him. The room remained the same, with the only new thing being Tom's growing fears every day. Yet, Tom tried his hardest to hold onto the hope that Sir Owl would recover.

One day, the new visitors surprised him. It was the group of performers: two catfish and a cricket. They had quietly whispered a greeting to Tom and bowed their heads to Sir Owl. Tom couldn't help but recall the song Sir Owl and he had hummed climbing the mountain, the rather infectious and encouraging melody.

Tom thought to himself a crazy idea and said to the performers, "Would you please play something for him?"

The performers awkwardly exchanged glances with each other. Then the young boy said, "We're sorry, we only play for fun."

The girl added, "And right now, there is no fun."

The cricket chirped, and Tom expressed his understanding, gratitude, and escorted them out. Before they left, Tom realized he needed to apologize to them. He had promised them long ago that he would bring them a special treat from their adventure, and that was a promise he had failed. Tom held his promises so closely to him, but this was one that he had nearly forgotten to even attempt to fulfill.

Tom couldn't be more apologetic, but the performers replied in unison, "It's okay. Your treat can be telling us all about your adventure."

Then there the two companions remained, in the small cave that appeared to shrink more and more every day. Tom had grown so familiar and cramped with that space, spending longer there than anywhere else he could remember. His breathing seemed to suffocate the two of them, making the space much hotter than ordinary. Tom tried to intentionally hold and slow his breath for longer. The tight space and ample carbon dioxide, atop his fears, drove Tom to suffer from the hardest pain in his head. He could hardly think clearly or function. There lurked a fog about his head, and the chain around him strangled his neck. Tapping his foot and trying to keep his head up, Tom sat in the corner and waited.

"Please, Sir Owl. Open your eyes. Please." Tom wished.

Kat and the doctor entered the room. Their demeanors seemed starker than usual. The two stood by the entrance, watching Tom in the corner.

"The Koi Masters demand you—" Kat began.

"Tell them, I'll come later," Tom continued to watch Sir Owl.

"I cannot. You've kept them waiting long. enough"

"They'll understand, I'm sure—"

"No, they will not. It's urgent business—"

"This is urgent—"

"Owley will be okay—"

"Sir Owl!" Tom corrected. "Sir Owl needs me here."

Kat was caught off guard. "He needs rest. The doctor is here to tend to him. If it makes you feel any better, I will stay and keep him company while you speak with the Koi Masters."

"No. I don't know what to do." Tom buried his head between his knees. "I need the fairy. Where is she? She helps others. She can help Sir Owl!"

Kat raised her voice, "Pull yourself together! You'd better go and speak to the Koi, now—"

"She can help, I'm telling you. She's very helpful—" Tom tried to implore.

"Tom—"

"She can heal Sir Owl—"

"Tom—"

"I've seen her help others—"

"Tom!" Kat commanded attention. "Go and see the Koi Masters, now. Please don't keep them waiting any longer. They can address your questions and concerns. I'll wait here."

Can they help? Tom thought, feeling skeptical. He did see them accompanying the girl. Maybe they would have some answers. However, what convinced Tom was how utterly helpless he felt. He felt he had failed Sir Owl. What more could be gained from eating away at Sir Owl's air?

"Fine," Tom gave in. Before he left, he stepped to Sir Owl. "I'll be back, Sir Owl. I'm sorry I failed you. I'm sorry."

Tom then braced himself and turned to walk away. He had failed in every way. When he approached the entrance, Tom let his head hang.

Then he heard, "Tom… Foolery." Sir Owl awoke and whispered.

The tears in Tom's eyes could not be quelled as he repeatedly apologized and thanked Sir Owl. A few more seconds, Tom spent by Sir Owl's side as they looked at each other with the most caring eyes.

In the pond, Tom stood feeling the moss and algae under his feet. It was a solitary conference between the Koi and Tom. With Sir Owl having awakened, Tom felt a pressure off his shoulders. On his back, however, he felt the same pain and marker of doom from the day he fell from atop the mountain. The outside temperature was far warmer, the skies grayer, and all the golden flowers had wilted and floated lifelessly amongst the murky pond. The wise Koi Masters still circled each other at the heart of the pond, but even their colors and spirits appeared weathered down. They also moved more slowly, and Tom could discern where Ko ended and Oi began.

"I'm sorry to keep you waiting," Tom apologized, but did not express regret.

Koi did not respond.

"We have learned—" Ko began.

"Much about you—" Oi finished.

"Within the depths—"

"Of the sea."

"Your name—"

"Is not Tom."

"You were brought—"

"To us—"

"By the sea—"

"As an agent of chaos—"

"To conquer the mountain—"

"To disturb the peace—"

"To remove our protector—"

"To banish our spirit—"

"Of the silver lining," Koi gathered. "We were foolish to trust you. You must leave, now. You gave us your word. You have completed your dream. Leave our island."

Tom hesitated, but spoke, "Wise Koi Masters, please forgive me for any mistakes I've made. I don't know what you're talking about. I am Tom, and I've tried to help every chance I've been given—"

"We gave you an order. Do not help us. You broke your word."

"They needed help! Someone needed to help—"

"We understand their peril—"

"Yet, did you help?"

"Our island used to exist in a perfect harmony with the spirit of the silver lining, who helped and aided us in our endeavors."

Tom realized, "You mean the fairy?"

"You took her from us."

"She was unhappy. All I did was encourage her to follow her dream—"

"And it descended our island into chaos."

"What happened to her?" Tom clenched his fists.

"You know what she wished for."

"Where is she? What did you say to her?"

"We do not answer to you—"

"I promised her I would help you all!" Tom declared.

"Your help is not the help we need. We were founded by her. She raised us from the magical pool by herself and allowed us to roam free on this island." Koi seemed nostalgic and attached to the one who had given them purpose. "Her help was genuine, while yours was a means to an end. Act honorably, now. Fulfill your promise to us and leave our island."

There was no more reason to argue. Tom's fate had been sealed. His dream had proved to be a ruinous one. Somewhere within his dream or being, Tom had been marked to cause chaos and failure.

All he had tried to do was help, he repeatedly thought to himself. The adventure had now ceased, and Tom was left with no clear answers but more questions. He did not know his name nor his dream, and now his memories were tarnished with sadness.

Tom found himself on the beach, staring east. He sat on the flat ground and stared out into the sea. The sea folded in and appeared ashamed of itself for using Tom to gain what it believed to be its mountain. The scheme had unraveled, only for the island to erupt and descend into chaos. Was the prize truly enough? Tom threw a rock toward the sea and questioned. Harmony or disharmony, it seemed everyone had a skewed perspective of it.

As Tom sat, the white fox suddenly appeared and joined him. Silver, the fox, did not sit in his lap, but beside him and looked toward the horizon and—what seemed to be—the shining sun. However, the day was still too bright. The sun could not be in two spots, Tom thought. What was shining above the sea and floating away from them?

Silver had lost her shine. Tom's interest was piqued when he recalled that the girl had sat there and stared out into the sea, wishing to travel. Exploration awaited her, and maybe it was she who traveled and sought to be there, hugging the horizon. The shining spirit of the fox was granted to the girl, as a gift, or maybe it was always her power as the spirit of the silver lining. Perhaps that was how the girl had helped, casting her shine onto the creatures that guided and aided each other in their quests. Tom was unsure, and he didn't know how he would find a true answer. However, he did hold dear what was left behind of the girl: her impact, the fox, and the locket.

Silver whimpered while staring at the sea. Tom turned his attention to the locket he felt pressed against his chest. He heartily opened it, loosening the clasp, and looking into her locket. Where this idea came from, Tom did not understand but trust his intuition. Within the heart was a folded paper. Tom read it.

I shall follow you to the ends of the world.

Then there was a drawing: T + A, encircled within infinity.

8

From the ruins of his old ship, Tom was made a new one. It was just a dinghy. Under the orders of the Koi Masters, Kat and her knot had crafted this for Tom. Kat and Fy made sure it was a sturdy one, and Tom was ever-so-grateful for it.

"The sea will be treacherous to navigate, especially if its will clashes against your will." Kat imparted her wisdom to Tom. "You will learn how to sail it again, as you have learned all the other things you can do now."

"Thank you, Madam Kat," Tom felt deeply indebted to Kat for her help along the way. "I've done nothing to deserve your help and kindness."

"Oh, hush. We're all good friends here. Plus, you brought Owley back to us."

Tom had avoided visiting Sir Owl again. After being given his order to leave, part of him feared seeing Sir Owl and the sadness that would overcome him. So, he kept his head down and continued to make preparations.

His friends helped fill his backpack with supplies, knick-knacks, and the few berries they could find. The time allotted to Tom by the Koi to make his departure was not long. Therefore, atop the supplies, he rushed to gather those precious things called mementos. He kicked around the beach looking for seashells but did not find one. The performer trio saw him and brought him a souvenir: the same clam he had gifted when he first met them. Tom was grateful and truly appreciated hearing the tunes of the band in the background as he continued his search for mementos. Sly, the snake, brought Moorgan with him. They carried together a bundle of forget-me-nots to remind Tom of the time they shared in the meadow. Next, Rattoni and Nastya brought Tom the original bow that was tied around Nastya's baby bottle. The formula on the bow had been memorized and replicated by the frog doctor; Rattoni assured Tom. Plus, Rattoni said he was attempting to learn to read, becoming a truly changed rat. Nastya surprised Tom with a most exquisite scratch: one right across the back of his hand that Tom wished would never properly heal. Then, Shepherd brought Tom a wool sweater! Tom was truly astounded to see Shepherd's craftsmanship, in addition to his leadership skills. Rattoni was a bit annoyed at being overshadowed and so decided he would also commit himself to a craft. What craft that would be, Rattoni had no idea. Harry, the hare, came to visit as well, bringing Tom a baby carrot. Apparently, the carrot had organically grown in their small garden. Sir Hare said something about the fires and ash enriching the land, which Tom, with his limited knowledge, just couldn't quite understand. Sir Curtis, the tortoise, also brought Tom a gift. It was a fake green pear painted by the tortoise himself.

"While it… may be fake… I offer you… this gift of… idealism… and that… even what is fake… may truly… be real." Sir Tortoise held the small pear in his hand and extended it to Tom.

Tom didn't know how to express his gratitude properly. However, he found that the creatures became busier making each other's acquaintances than hearing his thankful speech. That's a relief, Tom thought.

Kat and Fry clapped along to the tunes of the performers. Sly, the snake, playfully swung around Moorgan's neck. Shepherd gave chase to Silver, the fox, as they kicked up dirt and rolled around in mud. Tom thought that Shepherd was due for a break with how much he works. Rattoni argued again with Sir Harry about grievances related to Rattoni's twin brother. Sir Curtis lifted Nastya in his hand and petted her.

"You have… the most… interesting name…" Sir Tortoise spoke as Tom listened. "I finally realized… that your name… is short for… Anastasia."

Nastya purred in Curtis' palm.

Tom thought of that name—Anastasia. It brought warmth to him. Tom opened the locket again and saw the initials, T and A. His name was maybe Tom or something that started with a T, and maybe the girl's name was that—Anastasia. But was this her real name or the name she had chosen to call herself? Tom subdued any assumptions and thought he would help the fairy find her true name.

Then once Tom had finished packing all the things that morning, he turned. On the beach stood Sir Owl, himself, on a crutch and with his torso and wing in bandages. Sir Owl extended his free wing, and lying within it was one of his feathers: Tom's last souvenir.

Tom didn't know what to say upon seeing Sir Owl. He avoided eye contact but remembered politeness. "Thank you, Sir Owl. You should be resting, though."

Sir Owl hobbled a bit with his crutch in the unsteady sand. "I heard you're leaving."

"I'm being kicked out," Tom tried to lighten the tension.

"Finally," Sir Owl looked away. Watching Tom from the corner of his eye, he said, "They told me that you spent days sitting by my side."

"I did."

"Why?"

"Because you're my guardian, and I'm grateful to you for saving my life."

Sir Owl sighed. "It's just my job."

Tom nodded.

The waves came crashing in, muffling Sir Owl's voice, "So this is it, huh?"

"Huh?" Tom couldn't hear him. Then he realized that he asked a question. "I'm sorry."

The two awkwardly faced each other, looking to hear each other properly over the sound of the waves. Tom stood with his hands in his pockets, looking down. Sir Owl, struggling to keep himself up, also stared down.

"Thank you," they both cut each other off. "I'm sorry." They both did it again.

"No need to thank me," Tom said.

"No need to apologize," Sir Owl said.

They looked at each other.

We said we would talk about dreams when we got down," Sir Owl reminded.

"We did," Tom remembered. "I don't know what to say anymore. A lot has happened."

"So, what is your dream now, foolish human? You've climbed the mountain." Sir Owl seemed to puff out his chest. "You told me that you promised someone that you would stay and help us."

"I did." Tom thought of the fairy. "I've learned that not all promises can be kept. I've failed. I've let down the fairy, the performers, the island—"

"No, you have not!"

"No, it's okay. I know I have—"

"You helped them. I saw it with my own eyes, and my senses do not lie. I was right by you. I will speak up for you to the Koi. We can prevent this—"

"Sir Owl, it's okay." Tom had accepted his fate. "I don't know by what means chaos found this island, whether it was because of me, the sea, the spirit of the silver lining leaving, or some other mysterious force. But as the Koi said, I've disturbed the natural harmony and peace of this island. I would've loved to stay, but I think their answer is final."

"We don't know that—"

"Leave it, please. Save us the anguish," Tom requested. "I must also tell you that my heart is still torn. Just like before, when I was torn between dreams, I feel pulled to where this locket leads me." That mysterious sense of isolation and waiting that Tom had experienced had finally made sense.

"But we'll need your help, Tom. The island is in worse shape than ever!"

"My help is overrated," Tom shrugged. "Plus, they have you. You were by my side through the adventure, all of it. You were my guardian. If you can help me with my foolish dream, I have no doubts that you can help all of them. You're the rightful guardian of this island, Sir Owl."

"Who? Me?" Sir Owl did not believe Tom, nor in himself. "I could never live up to that mantle."

"Yes, you can. I know who you are and what you're capable of. You are the bravest, Sir Owl." Tom smiled at Sir Owl as tears began to form in his eyes.

"You're quite something, Tom Foolery," Sir Owl smiled at Tom.

The two companions embraced. Tom assumed his role on the small ship as all his friends lined the shore to say goodbye and wish him well. They cheered on Tom as the tide slowly came in and took him away. There on the shore stood them all: Sly the snake, Moorgan the cow, Kat the old catfish, Fry the youngest of the knot, Shepherd the dog, the little lamb, Sir Curtis the mayor, Sir Harry the second-in-command, the lizard, squirrels, skunk, mole-rate, groundhog, the other tortoise who had fallen over, the moose, Rattoni the rat burglar if that title still applied, Nastya the squealing kitten, the feline family, the performers (two catfish and a cricket), Silver the fox, and ahead of them all was Sir Owl the guardian. Sir

Owl stood with his wing over his heart, vowing to protect the island and ask all the right questions.

Tom waved goodbye, wishing to see them soon, and told them, "I love you!" Then Tom turned to the horizon, dreaming of following the fairy to the ends of the world.

To be continued…

Sweet Dreams

Is the reverie finally over?

The lonesome dance of the feather in the wind exists no longer. Now, the feather merely sits in my hand, idle and timid. I tell the feather that it inspired me to fly, but it just sits there, not even watching me. It simply stares at the sky. This stare feels so familiar. It was the way I had gazed upon the sky and the clouds earlier. Ignoring everything, I had become taken by this feather. A feather had somehow conquered the sky. Realizing the weight of this feather, I keep it enclosed in my hand. Then apologetically, I turn my attention to the sky.

In the past, I had avoided the sky and kept my head down in shame, but now I look up at this constancy. It is there, and it is gentle. The sky simply floats. And far away, it houses the shining lights of hope. All the stars act as small windows into the world of master artists and philosophers sitting for hours at their desks and committing themselves to their crafts. The romantic in me watches them from afar with fascination for how they create. They are an inspiration. From that firmament, great works have been gifted to us so that we may have artistic sustenance and may aspire to be one with them. Transcending into a shining star would be artistic fulfillment, surely. However, I've come to see how far these stars are from me. They are beyond light years away in the loneliness of space. Their distance is growing and fluctuating, relative to my place. They may continue to serve as my guides in the darkness, the mythological figures from another world, and the pretty little lights that are a delight to stare at. I will remain here.

I was once plagued by a melancholy, confronting my inability to take flight. Now, by some miracle, I have found somewhat more peace here. I longed for flight and transcendence. After a while, I found that I had been floating all this time. In full transparency, it was not just a miracle—it was the hooting owl outside my window.

The clock strikes to mark the night. It's time to turn my attention away from the screen and window, and toward my home. It's time to wish those I care deeply about goodnight and sweet dreams. They are the reason I can float and levitate throughout my life. We can spin in circles around each other and chase each other all over the globe. I am here and content, as long as I'm able to float with them. I am just one part, attempting to float in harmony with the rest of the whole. There's a push and a pull. The course of life takes us gently by a hair, and we float through it. We give each other a helpful nudge when one's needed: a hug, kiss, laugh, cry, or even just a moment of our time.

With these wishes, I keep trying to fly. I became afflicted with a love for storytelling as a child, and I am still sick and writing. Part of me truly thought I might never write again when I sank into my melancholic tomb. However, here it is, the culmination of my efforts. A sum that is bigger than its parts, this is the product of my melancholy.

Truly, thank you. You eternally have my gratitude. Sweet dreams, to you, to those sleeping, and to those wishing to take flight.

ABOUT THE AUTHOR

Arashnoor Gill was born in Punjab and now resides in Fresno, California. While working as a full-time therapist, he aspires to continue pursuing his passion for creative writing and storytelling.

www.ingramcontent.com/pod-product-compliance
Lightning Source LLC
Chambersburg PA
CBHW021024310726
48969CB00006B/1533